Ghosts by Gaslight

Stories of Steampunk and Supernatural Suspense

EDITED BY JACK DANN AND NICK GEVERS

HARPER Voyager

An Imprint of HarperCollins*Publishers*

A continuation of this copyright page appears on page 391.

HarperCollins books may be purchased for educational, business, or sales promotional use. For information please write: Special Markets Department, Harper-Collins Publishers, 10 East 53rd Street, New York, NY 10022.

Library of Congress Cataloging-in-Publication Data has been applied for.

ISBN 978-0-06-199971-0

11 12 13 14 15 OV/RRD 10 9 8 7 6 5 4 3 2

In memory of Kage Baker

Contents

Introduction

GHOSTS BY GASLIGHT.
Those three words neatly summarize a great paradox of the Victorian age.

After all, the time of Queen Victoria (1837–1901) was by its own declaration an age of spreading enlightenment—the growth of literacy; the rapid introduction of mass-manufacturing technology; the propagation of humane values; the termination of the slave trade; legislation to curb cruelties inherent in industrial labor; and, on a literal level, the provision of ever more illumination to Britain's (and America's) cities, first by means of gas lighting, then with electricity. Let there be light! And yet even as the darkness of the streets and of some forms of economic deprivation was alleviated, the ghosts imagined by the population multiplied. Old fears, old phantoms and bogeys, old conceptions of bad luck and supernatural revenge combined with new wraiths and monsters born of the torments of social change and ideological awakening; and from the far corners of the British Empire returning soldiers, administrators, traders, travelers, and missionaries imported foreign narratives of yet more apprehension: accounts of Arabian Nights djinns, Transylvanian vampires, accursed rajahs, Chinese phantasms, West Indian duppies, and African totems. Real-life terrors like the depredations of Jack the Ripper mingled in the popular fancy with these improbable but direly potent materials; and in response, even as some Victorian fiction described hopeful or apocalyptic technological advance, many other tales brooded on the fantastic and the ominously irrational. The purposeful light of extrapolation competed with the looming darkness of the horrid.

This anthology pays innovative tribute to both of those streams of Victorian storytelling: the scientific romance and the classic ghost story, as they matured through the Great White Mother's reign and in that of her rotund and jocular son Edward VII, before the outbreak of World War I in 1914 brought shattering disillusionments. After all, a century later, speculative fiction continues to honor the two forms: steampunk novels and stories regularly recapture (and recomplicate) the gadget-encrusted early science fiction of Jules Verne and H. G. Wells, while leading horror and dark fantasy authors (many of them represented in this book) pay recurrent homage to the ghostly tale. So . . .

Why not a feast of fine new stories, filled with the pleasurable disquiet of things that go bump in the night and, at times, the thrills of sinister, arcane machinery as well? Perhaps the paradox of Victorian superstition-amidst-enlightenment can be resolved by way of this mixture; and anyway, the results are bound to be extremely entertaining. Thus *Ghosts by Gaslight,* in which seventeen of the best contemporary writers of supernatural fiction revisit the world of fog and fear that our ancestors knew only too well, on both sides of the Atlantic.

As you'll see reflected in many of the stories in the present volume, the Victorian/Edwardian period's fiction of the fantastic and the ominously irrational sometimes went far beyond instilling simple fright and awe. During the heyday of the classic ghost story in the nineteenth and early twentieth centuries, there were plenty of sensationalistic (and ephemeral) writers whose contributions to the many fiction magazines were all about cheap, garish effects; but their efforts were counterweighed by more profound, psychologically penetrating tales from such major literary names as Edgar Allan Poe, Nathaniel Hawthorne, Charles Dickens, Wilkie Collins, Mrs. Gaskell, Rudyard Kipling, Henry James, Edith Wharton, Robert Louis Stevenson, Walter de la Mare, Mrs. Oliphant, and Ambrose Bierce—and many writing in languages other than English. These authors were not slumming in a superficial popular genre; they had quite serious intent. And they were joined in this by inspired specialists in the supernatural, some of whom remain well known today for their spooky brilliance: J. Sheridan Le Fanu, M. R. James, Bram Stoker, Vernon Lee, Arthur Machen, Algernon Blackwood, William Hope Hodgson. Henry and M. R. James (no relations), in their very different efforts like "The Turn of the Screw" and "Oh, Whistle, and I'll Come to You, My Lad," employed ghosts and other phantoms of the nocturnal hours to cast light on the interior of the human psyche; this was the collective goal. In the hands of all these practitioners, ghosts signified aspects of the mentalities of those still living: a man visiting a haunted house was in a real sense haunting it himself, witnessing apparitions that echoed the proceedings of his own subconscious. Just as the emerging discipline of psychiatry was beginning to probe the subtle, contradictory workings of the human brain, the Victorian and Edwardian canons of the ghostly were projecting upon the printed page flickering specters of our repressed desires and our most terrible impulses. The ghost, in the final analysis, is very often Us. And likewise the vampire, the werewolf, and the many further doppelgängers embodied in literary nightmares.

This approach continues in *Ghosts by Gaslight,* with many a fresh twist. Ghost stories are gothic fictions, in that their objective landscapes— old manor houses, creepy backwoods, art galleries where the portraits stare out more purposefully than usual—are also intensely subjective. When Laird Barron's hunters range the monstrous Washington wilderness in homage to Algernon Blackwood's menacing panoramas of haunted Nature, and when John Langan's Henry-Jamesian protagonist ventures into far more settled but still eerie precincts back east, they are going home to themselves, to self-knowledge. Such knowledge can be utterly horrifying, merely disturbing, subtly discombobulating, quietly domestic, or even somewhat antic. But of whatever color, it is revealing of what we have not been able, or willing, to realize about ourselves. So the part of *Ghosts by Gaslight* that is ghostly is about its afflicted characters staring into the mirror, at their grave reflections, amidst cries of terror and looming shades of night.

But what of the gaslight, which can help to dispel the darkness? The "scientific romances" of Wells, Verne, and others anticipated future times—often very near futures—in which expanding frontiers of knowledge would deliver to humankind, or privileged sections of humankind, enormously increased power over Nature. These were Promethean fictions that expected the prodigious leaps of innovation already being experienced (from horse-drawn carts and carriages to widespread railways in just a generation! from cities of dangerous shadow to modern metropolises with brightly lit streets in just a few years! from crude telegraphy to radio in almost no time!) to continue, to the point where submarines would patrol effortlessly the greatest depths of the sea, airships would wander the skies with serene impunity, and the first spacecraft, propelled by giant cannon or miraculous Cavorite, would allow swift visits to the moon. Human beings would at last ascend beyond their cruel enslavement to the earth's surface, the cycle of the seasons, and the harsh laws of economics. Society would alter radically: utopias were glimpsed in many stories of this kind, whether socialist, anarchist, arcadian, or aristocratic. Grand visions indeed, promising so much . . . And yet Prometheus suffered dreadfully for bestowing the gift of fire upon mankind; and the scientific romancers were only too conscious of the perilous downside of technology run amok. For every victorious adventure there was a waiting catastrophe: the world devastated by novel weapons, political tyranny augmented with new instruments of oppression, aliens invading, *Homo sapiens* speciating into warring tribes of hominids. Early science fiction indeed illuminated the future, but black clouds of war and chaos cast warning shadows across the prospect. Current steampunk writing reflects this balance faithfully: in the stories that follow are to be found such things as death in well-built cities, gear-shifting mummies, ghosts in Faraday cages, the dark matter of balloons, and, of course, machines . . . machines that trap nightmares, machines that trap ghosts, machines that trap and enslave souls.

GASLIGHT AND ITS successor, electrical lighting, lit up immense panoramas for the Victorians and Edwardians, in real life, in reason, and in the imagination. Indeed, the ghost story, as a form of psychological fiction, was a part of the general enlightenment, inasmuch as it shone a torch on the nature of the psyche, permitting expanded understanding of how we ourselves work. Equally, the vast threats unveiled by the scientific romance were necessary, instructive premonitions of the imminent upheavals of world war, revolution, and economic depression. We need light to see our ghosts by, even if it is merely some sort of ectoplasmic refulgence. Ghosts of the past and ghosts from the future unite in the chilling glow of this anthology, extending wisdom as well as fright, fateful comprehension as well as blind terror; and all in highly entertaining form, in some cases as pure fuliginous horror, in others as awestruck observation, or as yearning towards otherworldly radiance, or as cunning satirical fun.

So let there be light . . . and ghosts yet to be revealed.

—JACK DANN AND NICK GEVERS

James Morrow

Shortly after his seventh birthday, James Morrow dictated a loopy fantasy called "The Story of the Dog Family" to his mother, who dutifully typed it up and bound the pages with yarn. Upon reaching adulthood, the author again endeavored to write fiction, eventually winning two Nebula Awards, two World Fantasy Awards, the Theodore Sturgeon Memorial Award, and the Grand Prix de l'Imaginaire. Recent projects include a postmodern historical epic, _The Last Witchfinder,_ praised by the _New York Times_ for fusing "storytelling, showmanship and provocative book-club bait," and a phantasmagoric tragicomedy, _The Philosopher's Apprentice,_ which NPR called "an ingenious riff on _Frankenstein._" Jim's most recent book is a stand-alone novella, _Shambling Towards Hiroshima,_ set in 1945 and dramatizing the US Navy's attempts to leverage a Japanese surrender via a biological weapon that strangely anticipates Godzilla.

James Morrow

The Iron Shroud

Jonathan Hobbwright cannot discourse upon the formic thoughts that flicker through the minds of ants, and he is similarly ignorant concerning the psyches of locusts, toads, moles, apes, and bishops, but he can tell you what it's like to be in hell. The abyss has become his fixed abode. Perdition is now his permanent address.

Although Jonathan's eyes deliver only muddy and monochromatic images, his ears have acquired an uncommon acuity. Encapsulated head to toe in damnation's carapace, he can hear the throbbing heart of a nearby rat, the caw of a proximate raven, the hiss of an immediate snake.

Not only is the abyss acoustically opulent, it is temporally egalitarian. Here every second is commensurate with a minute, every minute with an hour, every hour with an aeon. Has he been immured for a week? A month? A year? Is he reciting to himself the tenth successive account of his incarceration? The hundredth? The thousandth?

Listen carefully, Jonathan Hobbwright. Attend to every word emerging from the gossamer gates of your phantom mouth. Perhaps on this retelling you will discover some reason not to abandon hope. Even in hell stranger things have happened.

It is at the funeral of his mentor and friend, the illustrious Alastair Wohlmeth, that Jonathan meets the woman whose impeccable intentions are to become the paving-stones on his road to perdition. By the terms of Dr. Wohlmeth's last will and testament, the service is churchless and austere: a graveside gathering in Saint Sepulchre's Cemetery, Oxford, not so very far from Wadham College, where Wohlmeth wrought most of his scientific breakthroughs. Per the dead man's prescription, the party is limited to his one true protégé—Jonathan—plus his valet, his beloved but dull-witted sister, his three most promising apprentices, and the Right Reverend Mr. Torrance.

As the vicar mutters the incantation by which an Englishman once again becomes synonymous with ashes and dust, the mourners contemplate the corpse. Dr. Wohlmeth's earthly remains lie within an open coffin suspended above the grave, its oblong form casting a jagged shadow across the cavity like the gnomon on an immense sundial. The inscription on the stone is singularly spare: A. F. WOHLMETH, 1803–1881.

To assert that Alastair Wohlmeth was a latter-day Prometheus would not, in Jonathan's view, distort the truth. Just as the mythic Titan stole fire from the gods, so did Wohlmeth appropriate from nature some of her most obscure principles, transforming them into his own private science, the nascent sphere of knowledge he called vibratology. This new field was for its discoverer a fundamentally esoteric realm, to be explored in a manner reminiscent of the ancient Pythagoreans practicing their cultish geometry. Of course, when the outside world realized that Wohlmeth's quest had yielded a practical invention—a tuning fork capable of cracking the thickest crystal and pulverizing the strongest metal—the British Society of Engineers urged him to patent the device and establish a corporation dedicated to its commercial exploitation. One particularly aggressive B.S.E. member, a demolitions expert named Cardigan, wanted to market the Wohlmeth Resonator as "an earthquake in a satchel-case," a miraculous implement auguring a day when "the dredging of canals, the blasting of mines, the shattering of battlements, and the moving of mountains will be accomplished with the wave of a wand." To Dr. Wohlmeth's eternal credit, or so Jonathan constructed the matter, he resisted all such blandishments. Until the day he died, Wohlmeth forbade his disciples to discuss the resonator in any but the most opaque mathematical terms, confining the conversation to quarterlies concerned solely with theoretical harmonics. The technical periodicals, meanwhile, remained as bereft of articles about the tuning fork as they did of lyric poetry.

Contrary to Wohlmeth's wishes, a ninth mourner has appeared at the service, a parchment-skinned crone in a black-hooded mantle. Her features, Jonathan notes, partake as much of the geological as the anatomical. Her brow is a crag, her nose a promontory, her lower lip a protuberant shelf of rock. With impassive eyes she watches while the sexton, a nimble scarecrow named Foote, leans over the open coffin and, in accordance with the deceased genius's desires, lays a resonator on the frozen bosom, wrapping the stiff fingers around the shank, so that in death Dr. Wohlmeth assumes the demeanor of a sacristan clutching a broom-sized crucifix. An instant later the sexton's assistants—the blockish Garber and the scrawny Osmond—set the lid on the coffin and nail it in place. Foote works the windlass, lowering Wohlmeth to his final resting place. Taking up their spades, Garber and Osmond return the dirt whence it came, the clods striking the coffin lid with percussive thumps, even as the crone approaches Jonathan.

"Dr. Hobbwright, I presume?" she says in a viscous German accent. "Vibratologist extraordinaire?"

"Not nearly so extraordinaire as Alastair Wohlmeth."

Reaching into her canvas sack, the crone produces the January, April, and July issues of *Oscillation Dynamics* for 1879. "But you published articles in all these, *ja?*"

"It was a good year for me," Jonathan replies, nodding. "No fewer than five of my projects came to fruition."

"But 1881 will be even better." The crone's voice suggests a corroded piccolo played by a consumptive. "Before the month is out, you will bring peace and freedom to a myriad unjustly imprisoned souls." From her sack she withdraws a leather-bound volume inscribed with the words *Journal of Baron Gustav Nachtstein.* "I am Countess Helga Nachtstein. Thirty years ago I gave birth to the author of this confession, my beloved Gustav, destined for an untimely end—more untimely, even, than the fate of his father, killed in a duel when Gustav was only ten."

"My heart goes out to you," Jonathan says.

The Countess sighs extravagantly, doubling the furrows of her crenellated brow. "The sins of the sons are visited on the mothers. Please believe me when I say that Gustav Nachtstein was as brilliant a scientist as your Dr. Wohlmeth. Alas, his investigations took him to a dark place, and in consequence many innocent beings have spent the past eleven years locked in an earthly purgatory. Just when I'd begun to despair of their liberation, I happened upon my son's collection of scientific periodicals. The fact that the inventor of the Wohlmeth Resonator is no longer among the living has not dampened my expectations, for I assume you can lay your hands on such a machine and bear it to the site of the tragedy."

"Perhaps."

"As consideration I can offer one thousand English pounds." The Countess presses her son's diary into Jonathan's uncertain grasp. "Open his journal to the entry of August the sixth, 1870, and you will find an initial payment of two hundred pounds, plus the first-class railway tick-

ets that will take you from London to Freiburg to the village of Tübinhausen—and from there to Castle Kralkovnik in the Schwarzwald. May I
assume that a week will suffice for you to put your affairs in order?"

Cracking the spine of the Baron's journal, Jonathan retrieves an envelope containing the promised bank notes and train tickets. "I must confess, Countess, I'm perplexed by your presumption." He glances toward
the grave, noting that the crater is now sealed. The mourners linger beside
the mound, each locked in contemplations doubtless ranging from cherished memories of Dr. Wohlmeth to wonderment over who among them
will next feel the Reaper's scythe to curiosity concerning the location of
the nearest public house. "Does it not occur to you that I may have better
things to do with my time than extirpating your son's transgressions?"

By way of reply, the Countess produces from her sack a tinted daguerreotype of a young woman. "I am not the only one to experience remorse
over Gustav's imprudence. My granddaughter Lotte is also in pain, tormented by her failure to warn her father away from his project. Having
recently extricated herself from an ill-advised engagement, she is pres-
ently in residence at the castle. The thought of meeting the renowned Dr.
Hobbwright has fired her with an anticipation bordering on exhilaration."

JONATHAN SPENDS THE remainder of the afternoon in the Queen's Lane
Coffee-House, perusing the Baron's confession. Shortly after four o'clock,
he finishes reading the last entry, then slams the volume closed. If this
fantastic chronicle can be believed, then the evil that Gustav Nachtstein
perpetrated was of so plenary an intensity as to demand his immediate
intervention.

He will go to the Black Forest, bearing a tuning fork and collateral
voltaic piles. He will redeem the damned souls of Castle Kralkovnik. But
even if their plight had not stirred Jonathan, the case would still entail two
puissant facts: £1,000 is the precise sum by which a competent vibratologist might continue Dr. Wohlmeth's work on a scale befitting its worth,
and never in his life has Jonathan beheld a creature so lovely as Fräulein
Lotte Nachtstein.

15 March 1868

*After many arduous years of research into the dubious science
of spiritualism, I have reached six conclusions concerning so-called
ghosts.*

1. *There is no great beyond—no stable realm where carefree phantoms gambol while awaiting communiqués from turban-topped clairvoyants sitting in candlelit parlors surrounded by the dearly departed's loved ones. Show me a medium, and I'll show you a mountebank. Give me a filament of ectoplasm, and I'll return a strand of taffy.*

2. *There is life after death.*

3. *Once a specter has elected to vacate its fleshly premises, no ordinary barrier of stone or metal will impede its journey. A willful phantom can easily escape a Pharaoh's tomb, a potentate's mausoleum, or a lead casket buried six feet underground.*

4. *With each passing instant, yet another quantum of a specter's incorporeal substance scatters in all directions. Once dissipated, a ghost can never reassemble itself. The post-mortem condition is evanescent in the extreme, not to be envied by anyone possessing an ounce of* joie de vivre.

5. *Despite the radical discontinuity between the two planes, a specter may, under certain rare circumstances, access the material world prior to total dissolution—hence the occasional credible account of a ghost performing a boon for the living. A deceased child places her favorite doll on her mother's dresser. A departed suitor posts a letter declaring eternal devotion to his beloved. A phantom dog barks one last time, warning his master away from a bridge on the point of collapse.*

6. *In theory a competent scientist should be able at the moment of death to encapsulate a person's spectral shade in some spiritually impermeable substance, thus canceling the dissipation process and creating a kind of immortal soul. The question I intend to explore may be framed as follows. Do the laws of nature permit the synthesis of an alloy so dense as to trap an emergent ghost, yet sufficiently pliant that the creature will be free to move about?*

17 May 1868

For the past two months I have not left my laboratory. I am surrounded by the music of science: burbling flasks, bubbling retorts, moaning generators, humming rectifiers. Von Helmholtz, Mendeleyev, and the rest—my alleged peers—will doubtless aver that my quest partakes more of a discredited alchemy than a tenable chemistry. When I go to publish my results, they'll insist with a sneer, I would do better submitting the paper to the Proceedings of the

Paracelsus Society *than to the* Cambridge Journal of Molecularism. *Let the intellectual midgets have their fun with me. Let the ignoramuses scoff. Where angels fear to tread, Baron Nachtstein rushes in—and one day the dead will extol him for it.*

If all goes well, by this time tomorrow I shall be holding in my hand a lump of the vital material. I intend to call it bezalelite, in honor of Judah Löew ben Bezalel, the medieval rabbi from Prague who fashioned a man of clay, giving the creature life by incising on its brow the Hebrew word EMETH—*that is, truth.*

Although Judah Löew's golem was a faithful servant and protector of the ghetto, the rabbi was naturally obliged to prevent it from working on the Sabbath, a simple matter of effacing the first letter of EMETH, *the Aleph, leaving Mem and Taw, characters that spell* METH—*death. But one fateful Friday evening Löew forgot to disable his brainchild. In consequence of this inadvertent sacrilege, the golem ran amok all day Saturday, and so, come Sunday, the heartsick rabbi dutifully ground the thing to dust.*

I shall not lose control of my golems. From the moment they come into the world, they will know who is the puppet and who the puppeteer, who the beast and who the keeper, who the slave and who the master.

9 July 1868

At long last, following a deliriously eventful June, I have found time to again take pen in hand. Not only did I fashion the essential alloy, not only did I learn how to produce it in quantities commensurate with my ambitions, but I have managed to coat living tissue with thin and malleable layers of the stuff. Naturally I first tested the adhesion process on animals. After many false starts and innumerable failures, I managed to electroplate a wasp, a moth, a dragonfly, a frog, a serpent, a tortoise, and a cat, successfully trapping their spirits as the concomitant suffocation deprived them of their lives.

In every case, the challenge was to find an optimum rate at which to replenish the bezalelite anode with fresh quantities of the alloy. If I introduced too many positively charged atoms into the bath, then the cathode—that is, the experimental vertebrate or invertebrate—invariably suffered paralysis. Too few such ions, and the chrysalis became so porous as to allow the soul's egress.

I was pleased and surprised by how quickly a plated specter learns to move. Within hours of its emergence from the electrolyte solution, each subject variously flew, hopped, slithered, crawled, or ran as adeptly as when alive. To the best of my knowledge, a ghost's condition entails only one deficit. Because the olfactory sense is actually heightened by the procedure, the creature will undergo a highly unpleasant interval as its former corporeal host decays within the chrysalis. Once decomposition is complete, however, the encapsulated phantom is free to revel in its immortality.

Finding an experimental subject of the species Homo sapiens *posed no difficulties. Three months ago my manservant Wolfgang was diagnosed with a cancer of the stomach. His anguish soon proved as unimaginable as the physicians' palliatives proved useless. The instant I proposed to sever his tormented soul from his ravaged flesh, he surrendered himself to my science.*

I shall not soon forget the sight of Wolfgang's glazed body rising from the wooden vat—eyeless, noseless, mouthless, hairless: the solution had plated all his features, much as an enormous candle burning atop a bust will, drip by drip, sheath the face in wax. In a single deft gesture I removed the breathing pipe and, taking up a permanent bezalelite plug, stoppered the ventilation hole, so that death by asphyxiation occurred in a matter of minutes. Even as the waters of Wolfgang's rebirth sluiced along his arms and cascaded down his chest, he began teaching his phantom limbs to animate the chrysalis, his phantom eyes to pierce the translucent husk, and so he climbed free of the tar-lined tub without misadventure. The gaslight caught the hardened elixir, causing cold sparks to flash among the bulges and pits. A naïve witness happening upon my golem would have taken him for a knight clad in armor fashioned from phosphorescent brass and polished amber.

"The pain is gone," the ghost reported.

"Naturally," I replied. "I have disembodied you. Henceforth your name is Nonentity 101."

"I can barely see," he moaned.

"A necessary and—as you will soon realize—trivial side effect."

"I feel buried alive. Set me free, Herr Doktor Nachtstein."

"Take heart, Nonentity 101. You are the harbinger of a new and golden race. Welcome to Eden. Before long hundreds of your kind will inhabit this same garden, arrayed in immortal metal, sneering at oblivion."

"Let me out."

"Do not despair. In the present Paradise, the lethal Tree of

Knowledge is nowhere to be found. This time around, my dear
Adam, you will eat only of the Tree of Life."

THE SPARTAN TRAIN that brings Jonathan Hobbwright eastward from the tiny village of Tübinhausen to the outskirts of Castle Kralkovnik comprises a lone passenger carriage hauled by a decrepit switch engine. Shortly after six o'clock post meridiem, he arrives at a forlorn clapboard railway station, terminus of a spur line created solely to service the late Baron Nachtstein's estate.

As Jonathan wanders about the platform, a thunderstorm arises in the Schwarzwald, the harsh winds flogging his weary flesh. The station offers no refuge, being as tightly sealed as Dr. Wohlmeth's grave, its door secured with a padlock as large as a teapot. For a half hour the vibratologist huddles beneath the drizzling eaves and leaky gutters, until at last a humanoid figure comes shambling through the tempest, gripping a kerosene lantern that imparts a coppery glow to its bezalelite skin.

"Good evening, Dr. Hobbwright," the golem says in the voice of a man shouting from within a furnace.

"Actually, it's a deplorable evening."

"I am called Nonentity 157. My race, you will hardly be surprised to learn, regards you as the new Moses, come to set us free." The ghost heaves the vibratologist's steamer trunk onto his massive shoulders. "Judging from its weight, I would surmise that herein lies the mechanism of our deliverance."

"A thousand-ampère Wohlmeth Resonator plus an array of voltaic piles."

Nonentity 157 leads Jonathan down the sodden platform and across the glistening tracks. Peering through the gale, the vibratologist discerns a stout and stationary coach, hitched to a pair of electroplated horses. Nonentity 157 lofts the steamer trunk atop the roof, securing it with ropes, then opens the door and guides Jonathan into the mercifully dry passenger compartment. Climbing into the driver's box, the golem urges his team forward.

By the time the conveyance reaches its destination, the storm has subsided, the curtains of rain parting to reveal a bright gibbous moon. The silver shafts strike Castle Kralkovnik, limning a complex that is less a fortress than a walled hamlet, the whole mass surmounting a hill so bald and craggy as to suggest a skull battered by a mace. The phantom horses trot through a portal flanked by stone gargoyles and began negotiating a labyrinth of cobblestoned streets.

Golems are everywhere on view, skulking along the puddle-pocked alleys, clanking across the bridges, rumbling through the tunnels, huddling beneath the Gothic arches. In this city of the walking dead, every citizen seems to Jonathan a kind of renegade pawn, recently escaped from a tournament whose rules, while ostensibly those of chess, are in fact known only to Lucifer.

The coach halts beside the veranda of the main château. As Jonathan alights, two golems appear, give their names, and set about simplifying his life. While Nonentity 201 takes charge of the steamer trunk, Nonentity 337 leads the vibratologist upward along the graceful curve of the grand staircase to a private bedchamber. A note rests on the pillow. Countess Nachtstein wants him to join her and Lotte for supper at eight o'clock. When the trunk appears, Jonathan changes into dry clothing: a wholly benevolent carapace, he decides, as opposed to the malign husks in which the Baron's progeny are imprisoned.

RETURNING TO THE first floor, Jonathan employs his olfactory sense—his nose is almost as keen as a golem's—in finding the dining hall. The Countess and her granddaughter are seated at a ponderous banquet table, drinking Rhenish.

"Welcome, Dr. Hobbwright," the Countess says. "Do you prefer white wine or red?"

"Red, please."

"Will burgundy suffice?"

"Yes, thank you."

Owing to the tinted daguerreotype, Lotte Nachtstein seems to Jonathan a familiar presence. Like the reputation of a famous personage, her high cheekbones, supple mouth, and flashing green eyes have preceded her. Jonathan soon learns, however, that her nature is as harsh as her features are fair. While a cadre of golems serves the dinner—a veritable feast predicated on an entire roast boar—it becomes apparent that gentle words rarely fall from this fräulein's generous lips.

"Evidently I've become something of a legend among your father's experimental subjects," Jonathan says, savoring his wine. "They see me as the source of their salvation."

"My father never regarded the golems as mere experimental subjects," Lotte says in an acerbic tone. "If you'd read his journal more carefully, you would have grasped that fact."

)

"Nevertheless, his project went beyond the pale."

"For a man of Gustav Nachtstein's genius there are no pales," Lotte says haughtily. "You are not the first prospective savior to visit us, Dr. Hobbwright. In recent months my grandmother and I have consulted with experts from all over England and the Continent. Every imaginable remedy has been tried and found wanting: acids, chisels, hacksaws, steam drills, welding torches, explosives."

"But Dr. Hobbwright is our first vibratologist," the Countess reminds Lotte, then turns to Jonathan and says, "My granddaughter and I believe that the right sort of specialist has finally come to Castle Kralkovnik."

"Speak for yourself, Mother," Lotte says. "You were convinced that Dr. Pollifax's silver bullets would free the golems, likewise Dr. Edelman's caustic butter, not to mention your misplaced faith in Dr. Callistratus, who wasted six days attempting to deplate the cat."

Jonathan helps himself to a second glass of burgundy. "Might I presume to ask how Baron Nachtstein met his end?"

"Violently," Lotte says.

"His creatures assassinated him," the Countess says with equal candor. "The details are unpleasant."

"My father died even more horribly than my mother, who suffered a fatal hemorrhage giving birth to me," Lotte says. "Just as the Baroness Nachtstein's fertility destroyed her, so did Baron Nachtstein's brilliance occasion his downfall."

"Your father was extraordinarily gifted, but his journal also reveals a man obsessed," Jonathan says.

Lotte sips her rhenish and glowers at the vibratologist. "It's the *golems* who are obsessed, incapable of seeing beyond their idée fixe about damnation. I ask you, Dr. Hobbwright, does not the fact that they declined to plate my father argue for the fundamental benevolence of the procedure? If their condition is as intolerable as they maintain, they would have logically inflicted it on their creator instead of simply murdering him."

"In that case, perhaps I should return to Oxford," Jonathan says, sensing that in defending the Baron so vociferously, Lotte has overstepped the bounds of her actual beliefs. "Given that your father's creatures are such incurable dissemblers, I see no point in helping them."

"No, please—you must stay," Lotte insists. "Perhaps my father was mistaken. If the golems say their situation is unendurable, it behooves us to give them the benefit of the doubt."

*   *   *

13 January 1869

Nonentity 157 and his bezalelite brethren are adamant on one point. They insist that a wandering soul's burning need is to venture forth from its cadaverous habitat and dissipate, occasionally favoring its survivors with a benevolent gesture en passant. By tampering with this process, I have plunged the golems into an irreparable despair. Indeed, I have dispatched them to hell.

My instincts tell me to ignore these complaints. Creatures in such a metaphysically unprecedented state are wont to indulge in hyperbole. Like the vast majority of sentient beings, my golems are unreliable narrators of their own lives.

As it happens, their illusion of damnation is useful to my purposes. By promising to return them to the electrolyte bath any day now, subsequently reversing the plating process and dissolving their husks, I retain a remarkable measure of control over their minds. I cannot speak for the whole of creation, but here in the Schwarzwald law and order enjoy a proper degree of hegemony over anarchy and chaos.

Judging from my latest series of animal experiments, I would have to say that, alas, bezalelite plating can occur in one direction only. I would do well to sequester that unhappy fact in the pages of this journal. Were the golems to comprehend the immutability of their situation, they would suffer unnecessary distress.

To date I have brought forth one hundred and thirteen electroplated souls, most of them terminal consumptives and cancer patients from Freiburg, Pforzheim, Reutlingen, and Stuttgart. With each such parturition I come closer to perfecting my methods. To help maintain a constant ion level, I have learned to add potassium cyanide to the bath, along with salts of the bezalelite itself. Conductivity can be further enhanced with carbonates and phosphates. As it happens, if the golem-maker first deposits a layer of pure silver on the subject's epidermis, no more than one-tenth of a micrometer thick, total adhesion of the alloy to the protein substrate is virtually guaranteed. Finally, if the experimenter wishes to hasten the process by means of high current densities, he should employ pulse plating to prevent erratic deposition rates. In the case of human subjects, the ideal cycle is fifteen seconds on followed by three seconds off. To ensure a wholly homogeneous chrysalis, the golem-maker will want to vary the direction of the electricity flowing from *the rectifier. In density the reverse should exceed the forward pulse by a factor of four, while the width of the forward pulse must be three times that of the reverse.*

6 August 1870

I must confess, though with a certain understandable reluctance, that I have found in the Franco-Prussian War a catastrophe of enormous convenience. Approach a man who has just been blown apart by an artillery shell, his viscera spilling forth like turnips from a torn sack, and propose to translate him into a domain where his agony will vanish and his soul endure forever, and he will invariably assent. If you kneel beside a soldier recently trampled during a cavalry charge and offer to sign him up for an eternity of painless existence, he will forthwith beg for a contract and a pen.

This afternoon my creatures and I landed in the Alsatian town of Fröschwiller, where earlier in the day Marshal Patrice de Mac-Mahon's French brigades had clashed with a combined force of Prussians, Bavarians, Badeners, Württembergens, and Saxons. Perhaps historians will ultimately frame the Battle of Fröschwiller as the cradle of a unified German state, but what I beheld on that ghastly field was not so much a cradle as a mass grave. Each side, I would estimate, lost at least 10,000 men to instant death or irremediable wounds.

Crossing the bloody terrain with a large convoy of tumbrels, the golems collected over five hundred candidates for bezalelite immortality. Thanks to humankind's affection for mayhem, I shall soon have an army of my own.

3 October 1870

Immediately after the necessary plans and diagrams arrived from Prague, along with a team of master builders, I embarked on a colossal endeavor. Here in the heart of the Schwarzwald we have razed my ancestral manor and begun to assemble in its stead a structure of stupefying splendor. My new abode will replicate the Bohemian castle of Kralkovnik wall for wall, gate for gate, lane for lane, arch for arch, and vault for vault.

Among their many virtues, my golems are extraordinarily diligent laborers. Already the first, second, and third courtyards have been paved. Tomorrow a crew of three hundred and fifty will start erecting

*Poelsig Tower, even as the remaining seven hundred and twenty-five
lay the foundations of the principal château.*

*A man's home, it has been remarked, is his castle. By analogy, a
man's castle is his kingdom and his kingdom his empire. I intend to
administer my dominion in a manner befitting the first scientist to
weld the carnal plane to its spectral counterpart—that is, with a firm
but enlightened hand. As Lotte told me this morning, "When the
golems undertake to compose their epics, they will sing their creator's
praises in rapturous words, borne by the most sublime music ever
heard in heaven or on earth."*

AT FIRST LIGHT Jonathan Hobbwright rises from his canopied bed and,
venturing beyond the castle walls, begins his quest for a suitable site on
which to stage the golems' salvation. From seven o'clock until noon he
roams the fields and woods, eventually happening upon a clearing so wide
it could accommodate a circus act featuring a troupe of elephants. The
vibratologist returns to the castle, seeks out Nonentity 157, and enlists its
aid in transporting the apparatus to the place where, God willing, he will
redeem the Baron's creatures.

After Nonentity 157 departs, Jonathan bears the Wohlmeth Resonator
to the center of the circle. Coils of fog sinuate across the ground like phantom serpents. Meticulously he deploys the tuning fork, prongs pointed upwards in a configuration evoking the Devil's own trident bursting through
the crust of the earth. Next he places the voltaic piles a full hundred yards
from the resonator, fearing that without this margin the vibrations will
shatter not only the bezalelite husks but the battery array itself, thus ter-
minating the golems' deliverance in medias res.

At this juncture Countess Nachtstein's icily beautiful granddaughter
appears, dressed in a bright scarlet cloak, so that her emergence from
the fog suggests the Red Death exiting a white tent. In the moist but
congenial glow of morning, Lotte seems a rather different person from
the high-minded moralist who dominated the previous night's dinner
conversation, and she addresses Jonathan in tones that betray genuine
contrition.

"Please accept this lunch along with my apology for scolding you last
night," she says, handing over a sack containing, Jonathan is gratified to
see, cold meat, warm bread, two apples, and a flask of burgundy. "My
father did monstrous things. I would deny that fact only at my peril."

"In most contexts, honoring one's parents is a laudable endeavor. I cannot blame you for defending Baron Nachtstein, injudicious as his project might have been."

"The man who would expiate my father's sins is not only a great scientist but a paragon of graciousness."

When Lotte squeezes Jonathan's arm and suggests that she help him finish installing the resonator, he can discern no ulterior motive. During the subsequent hour they connect a long rubber-sheathed wire to the positive terminals of the voltaic piles, then attach a second such strand to the negative terminals, subsequently running the insulated copper filaments to the fork and wrapping them around the outer prongs. Returning to the piles, Jonathan fastens the wires to a pair of chronometers, the first enabling him to determine how many minutes will elapse before the blade of the concomitant knife-switch descends, the second allowing him to fix the interval between the initial vibrations and the termination of the circuit.

"I see no reason not to move quickly," Lotte says. Suddenly her imperious aspect is ascendant. It seems she has taken command of the experiment, a situation to which Jonathan is expected to acquiesce. "We shall switch on the resonator at three o'clock. Is that acceptable to you?"

"What if it were unacceptable?"

Lotte makes no reply but instead points to the rheostat. "I assume that, given bezalelite's extreme density, we should run the apparatus for at least an hour—and at full power."

"I would advise against it. To drive a Wohlmeth Resonator beyond eight hundred amperes would be to create an acoustic cyclone. My preferred parameters would be four hundred amperes for twenty minutes."

"We shall compromise," Lotte informs Jonathan. "Six hundred amperes for forty minutes. After setting the chronometers, we shall retreat to the safety of the castle. We needn't worry about the golems' welfare. After all, they're already dead."

3 November 1877

When I embarked on this project, I fully anticipated the delight I would derive from observing the golems prepare our meals, make our beds, brew our beer, plow our fields, and harvest our crops. But I had no inkling of the satisfactions to be had in commanding them to engage in meaningless tasks.

Come to Castle Kralkovnik, ladies and gentlemen. Behold the

*living dead playing polo in the moonlight using pumpkins instead
of balls. Watch the tethered spirits build a tower to heaven on an
inviolable order from Yahweh, then tear it down in response to an
equally sacrosanct command. Bear witness to my metal phantoms
as they plan and rehearse nine separate productions of* Macbeth,
*each to unfold five seconds out of phase with both its antecedent and
its successor, then stage multiple command performances for their
favorite baron.*

*On the whole, it is wrong for a person to spawn a race of artificial
beings and demand their unquestioning obedience. Godhead too
easily goes to one's head. From time to time, however, the world is
blessed with an individual so wise that he may play the part of locally
situated deity without any attendant corruption to his character.*

12 *February* 1878

*Last month I made a momentous discovery. No matter how much
he may be adored, worshiped, and feared, a man in my position will
not be satisfied until his progeny come to blows over how best to
interpret their creator's will. We demiurges cannot rest until a great
quantity of violence has occurred on our behalf. If I am to enjoy
genuine peace of mind, my adherents must go to war.*

*In keeping with the scenario I wrote for them, the orthodox
golems—the Singularists, led by Nonentity 741—believe in a unitary
deity. The Quadripartists, under Nonentity 899, insist that I am of a
piece with a pantheon that includes my mother, Helga, my daughter,
Lotte, and my alter ego, Rabbi Judah Löew ben Bezalel. Both
sides employ incineration as their principal method for punishing
incorrect understandings of my unknowable essence. Once a heretic
has been tried and convicted, he is chained to a stake, engulfed by
mounds of kindling, and put to the torch. Of course, unlike most
victims of religious persecution, Singularists and Quadripartists
actually wish to be treated in this brutal fashion, for they imagine
that the flames might prove hot enough to melt their shells: a
physical impossibility, but desperate specters will not be reconciled
to the laws of nature.*

*This same expectation of deliverance undergirds the theological
wars that periodically ravage the Schwarzwald. The sight of a
thousand golems falling upon one another with claymores, cudgels,
and battle-axes is as exhilarating a spectacle as a deity could ever*

hope to witness. Needless to say, the carapaces always remain intact.
Like the golems themselves, my bezalelite is essentially a supernatural
phenomenon, impervious to the ambitions of the quick and the
desires of the dead.

12 August 1879

Today I endured one of the most distressing events of my life.
Shortly after Nonentity 316 and Nonentity 214 appeared at the
breakfast table, the former serving my morning eggs and sausage,
the latter bringing me my newspaper, Nonentity 667 strode into the
dining hall, looming over me while I attempted to read an article
detailing how the spiritualism fad has come to Vienna.

"You are blocking my light," I told the golem.

"Rather the way you have occluded our enlightenment,"
Nonentity 667 replied. "We have read your journal, Herr Doktor
Nachtstein. You have deceived us. The procedure cannot be undone."

"Nonsense. You have misinterpreted the entry in question. I now
have in hand the knowledge by which you will transcend the alloy.
Allow me two more experiments, three at the most, and I shall bless
you all with oblivion."

"Perhaps we shall exact our retribution tomorrow, perhaps the
next day, perhaps a year from now. But know that our vengeance is
coming."

"You cannot frighten me," I said, though in truth I was terrified.
"For Singularists and Quadripartists alike, I am the only possible
source of salvation."

"Fiat justitia, ruat caelum," Nonentity 667 said. "Let justice be
done though the heavens may fall."

HEAVY OF HEART, unquiet of mind, Jonathan paces Castle Kralkovnik's
highest point, the roof of Poelsig Tower. His path is an ellipse, its eastern
focus marked by Countess Nachtstein, the western by Lotte, the center by
a telescope pointing toward the clearing. He wishes he had not assented to
Lotte's insistence on running the resonator at six hundred amperes. Con-
ceivably her directive sprang from some intuitive insight into her father's
intractable alloy, but more likely it bespoke only a mania to cleanse his
legacy.

Pausing before the telescope, Jonathan presses his right orb to the eyepiece. He adjusts the tubes, making the image crisp. The golems stand in three concentric circles around the tuning fork, a tableau suggesting a tossed pebble raising rings in a pond. A palpable serenity has descended upon the creatures. They are patience personified. Having waited so many years for their freedom, they can endure whatever interval remains before the chronometer blade drops.

"One month after they stole my father's journal and learned that the plating is seemingly permanent," Lotte says, "a mob of golems, two dozen at least, appropriated every dagger, hatchet, and sword in the castle."

"With military precision—most of them were soldiers—they disassembled my son," the Countess says. "Each bore away a different piece of him and buried it in the forest."

"It speaks well of your Christian generosity that you would seek to liberate the Baron's murderers," Jonathan says, stepping away from the telescope.

"Our project has less to do with compassion than with self-preservation," the Countess replies. "Upon consummating their plot against Gustav, the golems gave Lotte and myself to know that their next victims would be we ourselves. Only after it became clear that we were taking every conceivable step to free them, hiring one metallurgist, galvanicist, and molecularist after another, did they become as compliant as when my son first brought them into being."

A white-hot bead of anger burns through Jonathan's breast. If the present experiment fails, he will surely become entangled in whatever lethal designs the golems draw against Lotte and the Countess. How dare these women presume to put him in such jeopardy? But before he can articulate his fury, he hears the sharp electric report of the chronometer blade snapping into place.

Jonathan again avails himself of the telescope. Already the trident had become a humming, wailing, incandescent blur, each prong oscillating like the pendulum of some demonic inverted clock. At the edge of the circle, poplars and beeches shiver in the aural storm. The trunks fracture, and the trees crash to the forest floor, even as scores of owls, rooks, larks, foxes, hares, hedgehogs, and deer flee the cataclysm. On all sides of the resonator, jagged crevasses open in the earth.

So great is the pain in Jonathan's head that he abandons the telescope, shuts his eyes, and massages his throbbing temples. His tendons tremble like harp strings plucked by invisible hands. Were the tower nearer to the fork by as few as ten yards, he calculates, his eardrums would rip, his heart burst, and his skeleton turn to powder.

Fighting his way through the crashing waves of sound, Jonathan returns to the telescope. Everywhere he looks, fault lines zigzag across the golems' metal flesh. Their faceless heads resemble ancient vases, cracked and battered by history's vicissitudes. Like an ancient mosaic shedding its tiles, the creatures molt bit by bit. Bezalelite fragments drop from their phantom arms, legs, and torsos, revealing the moldering bones beneath. Momentarily mastering his fear and transcending his astonishment, Jonathan takes satisfaction in knowing that—given the intensity of the tremors—the fork is probably freeing not only the human golems but also the Baron's experimental insects, reptiles, and mammals.

"Mirabile dictu!" the Countess cries.

"The specters are hatching!" Lotte shouts.

"It's not safe here!" Jonathan screams, urging the women toward the stairwell. "Run!"

Despite her advanced age, the Countess manages to negotiate the steps two at a time, as do Jonathan and Lotte, so that everyone reaches the ground floor within three minutes. No sooner does Jonathan start charging down the corridor than the ceiling disintegrates, squalls of plaster cascading into his path. Frantically he sidles and weaves amidst the plummeting timbers and errant chunks of masonry, but his athleticism proves useless before the force he has unleashed. As he reaches the door to the conservatory, a wayward chandelier, luminous with gas, lands squarely atop his skull. The bright bludgeon plunges him into darkness, but not before he notices that the hall now swarms with a thousand phantoms, each a disquieting shade of red and all wearing strangely despondent expressions, utterly unbefitting of persons recently released from the bottomless pit.

AT FIRST JONATHAN assumes that he has fallen prey to a nightmare. How else might he explain the scene now stretching before him? Heaped with kindling, two wooden obelisks rise from the central courtyard, each holding a Nachtstein woman—bound, gagged, and blindfolded. The plaque above Lotte's head reads *Singularist*. Countess Nachtstein's stake is labeled *Quadripartist*.

The phantoms have immobilized Jonathan as well, cuffing his wrists with manacles, hobbling his feet with fetters, and they have additionally stripped away his clothing. The vibratologist shivers in the Schwarzwald wind, goose bumps erupting on his bare skin like rivets, even as his cranium aches with the aftermath of his encounter with the chandelier. Vapor-faced phantoms throng across the plaza, their visages twisted by an inscrutable sadness. As if ignorant of the laws of actuality, the former golems attempt to prolong their purchase on the world. They flex their nonmuscles, tense their nonligaments, curl their nonfingers.

"Surely you don't mean to burn these women," Jonathan says. "They rescued you. You owe them everything."

"We mean to burn them—as surely as we mean to electroplate you," says a crimson specter in a fluttering voice.

"That makes no sense."

"True," says a scarlet specter. "We understand your frustration. You want your ghosts to be outré but not perverse, weird but not recondite, occasionally sublime though never ridiculous. So sorry, Herr Doktor. We are avatars of the abyss. Coherence is not our business."

Jonathan watches helplessly as a vermilion ghost applies a firebrand to the fagots encircling the Countess's stake. As the flames climb the fleshly ladder of the victim's form, a carmine specter flourishes a Wohlmeth Resonator—the very fork, Jonathan realizes, that gave the golems their freedom—and hurls it into the burgeoning conflagration.

"The dead don't lack for foresight," a maroon ghost avers. "In a matter of minutes the fork will become a charred ruin, thus canceling any hopes you might entertain of liberation by a passing Samaritan."

Now a ruby specter sets Lotte's pyre aflame, but not before jamming the Baron's journal into the fagots.

"Set her free!" Jonathan screams.

A BAND OF phantoms drags the vibratologist out of the plaza and down a maze of stairways to the Baron's subterranean laboratory, a cavernous space dominated by the electrolyte vat. Although they've never done this before, his captors act with great efficiency, ramming a respiration tube down his throat, dumping him into the solution, chaining his naked body to the cathode column.

Ignoring his pleas for mercy, a magenta specter connects the rectifier to the anode, agleam with the Baron's alloy. Countless positively charged bezalelite atoms drift through the bath and accumulate on Jonathan's flesh. Atom by atom, molecule by molecule, the metal embraces the helpless vibratologist, each instance of adherence like the sting of a microscopic hornet.

Within one hour the process is complete, leaving him encapsulated, immobile, and half blind. A gurgling reaches his ears. The phantoms are draining the vat. A searing pain rips though his chest as a ghost yanks the respiration tube from his trachea. An instant later another specter seals the air-hole with an immortal bezalelite plug.

Mummified by the exotic alloy, the prisoner is soon deprived of oxygen, and then of life itself. He is also deprived of death. Now and forever he will be the ghost of Jonathan Hobbwright—vibratologist extraordinaire become solitary golem—affixed to the cathode of Baron Nachtstein's infernal machine. Someday, perhaps, when entropy has dismantled the universe, he will be a free man, but for now he must reconcile himself to the unendurable, the interminable, and the endlessly absurd.

JONATHAN HOBBWRIGHT CANNOT discourse upon the formic thoughts that flicker through the minds of ants, and he is similarly ignorant concerning the psyches of locusts, toads, moles, apes, and bishops, but he can tell you what it's like to be in hell. His imagination affords him only fleeting respite. Each time he dreams himself free of his bezalelite coffin—passing through the portals of the abyss, striking out for terra incognita—Satan's angels give chase, and they inevitably track him down.

Come back, Dr. Hobbwright. Return to perdition. Tell your story for the tenth time, the hundredth, the thousandth. The more frequently you give voice to the wretched chronicle of your life, death, and damnation, the more likely you are to stumble upon hope's hidden wellspring.

And until that improbable miracle occurs, you might take heart in recalling that the progenitor of your race is dead and gone. In the aeons to come, you will not be made to laud Gustav Nachtstein in song or build an altar to his glory. Cold comfort, to be sure, but in the bottomless pit one seizes upon whatever consolations lie to hand.

AGAINST THE ODDS and in defiance of his circumstances, Jonathan Hobbwright's most recent recitation yields the very fount of hope he seeks. According to the Baron's confession, on certain rare occasions, despite the essential incompatibility between the human plane and the spectral, a disintegrating ghost will perform a philanthropic act. And so it happens that, when a fresh barrage of vibrations assaults Castle Kralkovnik—roaring through the Baron's laboratory like a tornado, reducing the walls to rubble as it cracks the prisoner's chrysalis—Jonathan is not entirely surprised.

Sloughing off his husk, abandoning his corpse, the vibratologist floats free of the cathode, then fixes on Lotte's crimson ghost. "How long was I entombed?" he asks.

"Ten days," she replies.

"It felt like forever."

"Hell knows nothing of clocks."

"Where did you obtain the fork?" Jonathan asks.

"From Alastair Wohlmeth," Countess Nachtstein's scarlet specter replies. "The task we set ourselves was grueling. In our given tenure Lotte and I had to reach Oxford, unseal the grave, open the coffin, steal the resonator, and return to the castle."

"I am deeply grateful."

"We have no need of your gratitude," the Countess says. "Nor do you have need of ours."

"And now we must take eternal leave of you," Lotte says as her misty form dissolves. "Oblivion beckons."

"Farewell, Dr. Hobbwright." The Countess has become as transparent as the surrounding air. "Please know that it was never my intention to occasion your death."

It suddenly occurs to Jonathan that he desperately wants to enlighten humanity concerning the destiny of the dead. So tenuous is the spectral plane, so ultimately meaningless, he must share this knowledge with his former fleshly confederates. The Baron's journal having been reduced to specks of carbon, Jonathan alone can tell the world about the appalling insipidity of ghosts.

"I wish to perform a philanthropic act of my own," he declares.

"What do you have in mind?" the invisible Lotte asks.

Even as the answer forms on Jonathan's airy lips, he realizes that his aspiration is futile. There is no time to find a pen, an ink pot, a sheet of paper. Already he is less than ashes. Already he is a brother to dust.

Wrenching sobs burst from the vibratologist's ethereal throat. Briny droplets roll down his ephemeral cheeks. For an infinitesimal instant Jonathan Hobbwright is seized by an infinite remorse, but then his sorrow evaporates—like rain, like dew, like sweat, like the last and least of his tears.

Afterword to "The Iron Shroud"

Equipped with uni-ball pens and legal pads, I composed "The Iron Shroud" in longhand during a protracted trip to Eastern Europe. I'd been invited to give a talk at the 2010 International Tolstoy Conference at Yasnaya Polyana, and my wife and I decided to return home in slow motion, stopping off in Poland and the Czech Republic. If the reader detects a whiff of Kafka about my tale, this may be because much of it was written in cafés not far from the mesmerizing Franz Kafka Museum in Prague. And, of course, the story features considerably more than a soupçon of that city's legendary Golem.

—JAMES MORROW

Peter S. Beagle

Peter S. Beagle is one of America's leading fantasists. His books include the novels *A Fine and Private Place, The Last Unicorn* (which has sold more than six million copies worldwide and was made into a popular animated film), *The Folk of the Air, The Innkeeper's Song,* and *Tamsin;* the short story collections *Giant Bones, The Rhinoceros Who Quoted Nietzsche, The Line Between, We Never Talk About My Brother, Mirror Kingdoms,* and *Sleight of Hand;* and the nonfiction books *The California Feeling, The Lady and Her Tiger, In the Presence of Elephants,* and *The Garden of Earthly Delights.* After a career pause, in 2002 he came roaring back on the scene with an extraordinary run of short fiction—over sixty stories, novelettes, and novellas—including a sequel to *The Last Unicorn* called "Two Hearts," which won both the Hugo and Nebula Awards.

Now seventy-two, Peter continues to write steadily and has more than a dozen books in the publishing pipeline, including new novels (*Summerlong* and *I'm Afraid You've Got Dragons*); new collections (*The First Last Unicorn & Other Beginnings, Green-Eyed Boy, 6 Unicorns,* and *Four Years, Five Seasons*); revised and updated editions of older works (*The Innkeeper's Song, The Magician of Karakosk, Avicenna*); new nonfiction books (*Sméagol, Déagol, and Beagle: Essays from the Headwaters of My Voice* and *Me Is Us*); and his first two children's books. Since late 2001 he has made his home in Oakland, California. For more information on Peter Beagle and his works, go to www.conlanpress.com.

PETER S. BEAGLE

Music, When Soft Voices Die

T HERE WERE FOUR of them living in the gabled rooming house with two chimneys on Geraldine Row, on the east side of Russell Square. This would have been perhaps six years after the Ottoman War, and quite shortly following the wedding of Queen Victoria's youngest daughter, Princess Maude Charlotte Mary, to Prince Selim Ali, who eventually became Sultan Selim IV. The marriage was not a happy one.

The four men's names were Vordran, Scheuch, Griffith, and Angelos. They were not friends.

Scheuch and Vordran might have been thought to have something in common, since Scheuch was a bank clerk, while Vordran, eldest of the four, worked in a Bishopsgate law firm. But Vordran was not a clerk, nor ever would be, no more than he would ever be a barrister or a solicitor. He was merely a copyist and, since he took shorthand, an occasional secretary. Once, when jolly young Scheuch had the bad form to invite him to join him for tea, Vordran ticked him off sharply before the other two, saying coldly, in his slight, unplaceable accent, "I am a jumped-up office boy, and I will be treated so or left in peace. Do not ever dare to condescend to me again." Scheuch kept his distance from then on.

Angelos was a second-year medical student at Christ's Hospital, himself quite sensible of the fact that names such as his—further, his mother was Jewish—were rarely admitted to study at the ancient institution. Even younger than Scheuch, he appeared a much more serious soul, but on fur-

ther acquaintance one discovered that his interests and fancies ranged from
pigeon-racing to hot-air ballooning (very much in vogue since the Turkish
bombing of London) to the newly recognized science of galvanic phrenol-
ogy, by means of which one could unfailingly identify a future Mozart or
a mass murderer-to-be through analyzing the electrical resistance in different portions of the skull, neck bones, and clavicles. He played the banjo,
but never past eight o'clock, or before ten.

Griffith had been at Balliol. That was very nearly all one was allowed
to know about Griffith, besides the fact that he was a waiter at Simpson's-
in-the-Strand. His term at university had apparently been interrupted by
his enlistment in the war, of which he was justifiably very proud; but why
he never returned to Oxford after the Pact of Trieste remained a mystery.
What was *not* mysterious about him was the fact that, where Vordran was
undeniably brittle and prickly, Griffith was, quite simply, arrogant to the
point of being unbearable. Everything in his life—and, consequently, every
person as well—was viewed through the prism of his lost world, and found
wanting. He seemed less a proper snob than a kind of wretched exile, but
this understanding made him no more likable, or even tolerable; the others
came to speak to him as little as they could, except when encountered entering or leaving the house, or meeting on the stair. Griffith appeared more
than satisfied with this arrangement.

The rooming house was managed by a smiling, swarthy man named
Emanetoglu, whose brother actually owned it, as well as two other buildings across the river. Mr. Emanetoglu manifested himself promptly at
8 A.M. on the fifteenth of every month, to collect the rent, and to drift into
corners and corridors like smoke, commenting diffidently on the condition
of paint, wallpaper, and bathroom floorboards. Impossible to dislike—
except by Griffith, who referred to him as "Glue Pot," when he was not
calling him "The Wog"—he had, nevertheless, the rainy air of an apologetic ghost, as much trapped in the house by fate as they by finances. On
the rare occasion that any roomer was briefly late with a rent payment, he
was patient but oddly sorrowful, as though the lapse were somehow his
own fault.

"You shouldn't call him that, you know," Scheuch chided Griffith once.
"He's a decent enough chap, Turk or no."

"I hate seeing them strutting around so, that's all." Griffith bit down
hard on the stem of the briar pipe he had lately taken to affecting. "Never
used to see a one of them west of Greek Street. Now they're all over
London, got themselves the Ritz, got themselves Lord's, got themselves
Marks and Sparks, got themselves a bloody princess, they'll shove a white

man off the sidewalk if he don't look slippy about it. You'd think they'd won the bloody war—and by God, I think that's what *they* think. But they *didn't* win the bloody war!"

Vordran spoke up then, in the way he had that always made him sound as though he were talking to himself. "Didn't they, then? They fought us to a standstill. We bled ourselves dry, for no reason that I could ever see, and now they own half the Empire. We were fools."

"Feel that way, you ought to go and enlist for a Turk," Griffith mumbled as he stalked away.

It was during the late summer and early fall of 18__ that Angelos became obsessed with the study of what he called "etheric telegraphy." His top-floor room—inconvenient to reach, but immensely practical for his pigeons—quickly became a hotbed of strange small sounds, and he began increasingly to ask Scheuch for assistance in dealing with certain mathematical issues. "There's this chap named Faraday, and another one named Maxwell, and there's a Yank *dentist,* if you'll believe it, with some outlandish name like Mahlon Loomis, and all of them rattling on about electromagnetism, etheric force, amperes, communal fields . . . I don't half know what three-quarters of that gibberish means, but I have to know. Can't say why, I just *do*." Scheuch, who was by nature an amiable, accommodating man, did his best to oblige.

Knowing Angelos better than either Griffith or Vordran ever bothered to know anyone, Scheuch expected this new passion to burn itself out by Boxing Day, at the very latest. But time passed, and snow fell; and, if anything, Angelos's fervor grew only more intense. He spoke to Scheuch of partial differential equations, of spark-gap transmission and a thing called a coherer, apparently as indescribable as a state of grace. He returned late from work with packages from shops Scheuch had never heard of, crammed with wire coils, hand-cranks and strangely shaped glass bottles, along with magnets—endless magnets of every form and size. He went frequently without sleep; and Scheuch, who left for work at the same time as he, often saw him stumbling downstairs, his eyes plainly fogged and his step unsteady. He would not have been at all surprised to see Angelos brusquely dismissed from Christ's for habitual drunkenness, but somehow he continued to be well regarded by his instructors, and to keep his marks at least at a respectable level. The tattered oilcloth leftovers from the last experimental balloon gathered dust in a far corner, in company with the banjo. The pigeons disappeared.

"I cannot even say what it is that he is aiming for," Scheuch told Griffith on one of the days when the latter was in a mood to be comparatively genial with a non-public-school man. "He speaks constantly of ethereal waves of some sort—of induction, *con*duction . . . even of being able to affect physical objects in another room, another *country*. I'd set him down as a pure crackpot, except that he's such a *plausible* chap, if you know what I mean. One could almost believe . . ." He shrugged helplessly and raised his eyebrows.

"We had a fellow like that up at Balliol," Griffith reflected. "Rum cove from the first. Other chaps kept bullpups, ratters—he kept a monkey, called it his *associate*. Never could find a roommate because of that beast. Always experimenting, night and day—chemistry, I suppose, from the smell, or maybe that was the monkey. Killed in the war, poor chap. Him, not the monkey. Can't say what became of the monkey."

"Different sort, Angelos," Scheuch replied. "Not defending him or anything, just saying he's not exactly round the bend. Eccentric, absolutely, but not . . . I don't know—not *potty*, not like that. Eccentric."

Griffith, his interest lost well before Scheuch had finished speaking, raised an eyebrow himself and said, "Jew."

That winter was a hard one, even for London. The Russell Square rooming house, like most such, lacked any form of central heating, and all four men suffered to one degree or another from colds and chilblains. The world-famous London fog, which was not a proper fog at all, settled over the city, leaving a coal-oil film over everything; the Thames froze over, and a few starving wolves invaded from the countryside, as none had been known to do since prewar days. The men trudged to their various occupations through the dirty snow, or—in Vordran's case—waited with hats pulled tightly down for one of the new streetcars, which might, in postwar London, be steam- or battery-driven on one day, then pulled by teams of men or horses the next. Simpson's suffered a notable falling-off in custom, enough that Griffith was on involuntary furlough an extra day out of the week; while the bank where Scheuch was employed frequently went whole days without a single client coming in from the street. The city closed down, as though under a filthy potlid; and—with the same legendary stoicism through which they had endured the Turkish siege—Londoners simply waited for the winter to end.

But in Russell Square, Angelos remained the single cheerful soul. ("Well he might be," Griffith sneered, "as many frozen paupers as he and his grisly crew must be slicing up these days.") The young man still worked a full day at Christ's Hospital, then made his way home to spend half the night making odd, frequently disquieting noises with his homebuilt machines for which Scheuch had no names. Most often he slouched into

Scheuch's rooms to slap down a scribbled-over clutch of foolscap, grumbling, "Bloody Faraday, bloody Hughes, bloody diamagnetism, makes no bloody *sense*!" and appealing for assistance with a new batch of equations. "If you could just cast an eye over these, I swear I'll not trouble you again. *Bloody* Faraday!"

Scheuch aided as best a country day school education and a certain natural bent for mathematics allowed him to do, thus becoming the closest thing Angelos possessed to a colleague, without in the least comprehending exactly what the other could possibly be driving toward. As he commented warily to Vordran, "It's a good bit like playing blindman's buff, where your eyes are covered and you're spun around until you can't tell where you're facing, or which way anything is. I don't know what on earth the man has in mind."

Much to his surprise, the older man answered him slowly and thoughtfully, saying, "Well, many of the people he quotes to you share an interest in wireless communication. Who knows—he may yet have you talking to people in Africa or China, this time next year. If you know anyone there, that is to say," and he made the little half-hiccough sound that qualified as a chuckle with Vordran.

Scheuch gave a weary shrug, spreading his hands, as he found himself doing more and more when asked about Angelos's behavior. "That could be what he's after, for all of me—as much time as I've spent with the fellow, I confess I haven't the least idea." Turning away, he added, "I do sometimes fancy I hear voices in his rooms, you know. Through the door, when I'm passing."

"Voices?" Vordran had a longer attention span than Griffith. "What sort of voices?"

"*Pieces* of voices," Scheuch answered vaguely. "Snatches, phrases . . . probably not voices at all, just Angelos talking to himself, the way he does." Vordran stood looking after him for some while, rubbing his chin.

The winter passed. The snow melted, leaving the city gutters running with soiled water; hawthorn and horse chestnut trees began to bloom in Victoria Park, and bluebells cautiously replaced the snowdrops of Highgate. The women of London began to be seen in the filmy headscarves and baggy iridescent pantaloons that had become the highest style since Princess Maude had worn them to a state dinner in Prince Selim Ali's honor. Griffith was fully employed at Simpson's once more, while the Bishopsgate firm where Vordran would never be a clerk bustled with new clients suing their families. Scheuch spent most days at the bank on his feet, jovial and patient as ever as he handled other people's money and tended the firm's

shining brass calculators. London—at least the London they three knew—
was London again.

And Angelos, one pleasant Sunday afternoon, invited them all to tea
in his rooms.

Scheuch, being the only one who had spent any length of time there,
was far less taken aback than Vordran or Griffith by the cheery chaos
of the sitting room, which—like Angelos's bedroom and the small alcove
which served him as a closet—did double duty as laboratory and storage
space. Tea was brewed over the fireplace, identical to the hearths they all
had, and served at a large round table that had once been a chandler's
cable spool. Vordran sat in the one reasonably sturdy armchair, Scheuch
on the precarious settee. Griffith stood.

Angelos began slowly, uncharacteristically hesitant, plainly feeling for
words. "I believe I have something interesting to tell you. To show you,
rather—and it is entirely likely that you three will be the only chaps I ever
do show it to. It's not something I can exactly take down to the Patent
Office, as you'll see." He started to add something else, but halted, and
only repeated lamely, "As you'll see."

Vordran cleared his throat, "May I make the occasion perhaps a bit
easier for you? I've already suggested to Scheuch here that you are probably attempting to create some form of long-distance communication, such
as others are seeking in France and Germany, and—I believe—America.
Am I correct?"

"Well," Angelos said. "Yes. I mean . . . well, yes and no. *Yes,* that was
how I started out—*yes,* that's what I got caught up in like Faraday and
Maxwell and those fellows. I mean, imagine being able to push a button,
turn a knob, and immediately be speaking to someone on the other side
of the world. Of *course,* I was . . . oh, I'm sorry—more tea, anyone? Bis-
cuit?"

No one wanted either, for excellent reasons. Angelos continued. "But
something else happened . . . yes, something rather else. I can't quite explain it yet, even to myself, so I'll just have to show you. If you'll give me
a moment."

He hurried into his bedroom and returned quickly with an armload of
assorted wires, a fragile-appearing copper disc in a linen wrapper, and a
pair of metal frames. One of these had a spindle that was plainly meant
for the disc, and a hand-crank to turn it; the other featured a small dial
and a needle like that of a compass, mounted on a pivot and surrounded
by a tightly wound copper coil. "In any case," he said, "whatever I was
after, electricity was my main problem from the start—can't do anything

without electricity, can you? Had to produce it myself, since I couldn't afford any sort of voltaic battery, so I did what I could, stealing my betters' ideas. You mount the disc on the generator—so—and connect your galvanometer—that's what this thing is, measures the current, you see—and then you crank the, ah, crank, and there you are. Child's play"—he grinned shyly—"speaking as a child."

He gripped the hand-crank lightly, but did not turn it. "Mind you, it's really not very efficient, for what it does. You get counterflow in certain areas, and there's a lot of energy wasted heating up the disc itself. But I've mounted a couple of magnets on the disc, as you see, and that does seem to settle things down a bit. I'm still tinkering with it—it's all hit or miss, really." He spread his arms in a mock-dramatic attitude. "All my own work, as those screever chaps who draw on the pavement say. And that's how *I* spent my Christmas hols."

Griffith's Oxford drawl cut across the younger man's enthusiasm like a shark's fin in a bathtub. "Perfectly charming, Angelos, utterly captivating, but people are producing electricity left and right everywhere you turn. Can't throw a brick these days, can you, without hitting someone's new toy, someone's *ee*-lectro-whatsit, though what it'll all come to in the end, I'm sure I can't say. What makes *your* toy—ah—unique, distinctive? If I may ask?"

For a moment it seemed to Scheuch that Angelos might actually cry, not so much at Griffith's words as at his tone, which deliberately, precisely and finally implied the insuperable distance between a Balliol College man (if not a graduate) and a Jewish medical student who would never quite lose his East End accent. Then Angelos said quietly, "Right. Quite right. Yes. I'll show you."

He reached into his coat pocket and removed a common stethoscope, of the sort that first-years at Christ's Hospital aspired earnestly toward and wore like a badge of honor after its awarding. "Really a perfect machine, when you think about it," he remarked, fondling it like a cherished pet. "I don't imagine anyone'll ever improve on old Cammann, I really don't. No moving parts—nothing to break down—and no sound made by the human body has the least chance of escaping it. Seemed to me that it might work just as well when it came to . . . voices."

"Voices." Scheuch looked around at the other two men. "There, *told* you I thought I heard voices."

"You have excellent hearing," Angelos said. "Better than mine. It took me some while before I began to make sense of what I thought might even be mice, rustling in the corners late at night. Then I considered whether or not it might be static electricity of some sort, given the nature of my experiments. Finally . . . well. Judge for yourselves."

He fitted the round end of the stethoscope into a clip on the generator frame, settling it carefully. "Had to fix this with soft solder, took me forever. I'm obviously not a dab hand at this type of thing . . . *there*, now the galvanometer . . . *and* off we go." He began, slowly and rhythmically, to turn the crank.

"You don't have to rotate it all that fast, that's the remarkable thing. You just have to keep it going steadily, evenly. It takes a bit of a while— maybe some sort of charge has to build up. Something *like* a charge. I don't really know. You'll see."

Griffith had been whistling thinly and idly as Angelos went on, toying with his watch and paying little attention to the demonstration. Scheuch and Vordran, however, were watching intently, with Vordran appearing especially rapt, as though he were staring at something beyond the rickety generator and its equally flimsy attachments. To Scheuch, the slow whir of the revolving disc became almost hypnotic, somewhat like the pulse of a sewing machine treadle. The air in the room was close and warm, and he felt himself swaying forward on Angelos's old settee.

Vordran said, "What am I hearing?"

Even Griffith looked at him. Angelos said nothing, but only kept on rotating the copper disc. Vordran's voice rose, the terror in it making his accent markedly more pronounced. "What am I hearing? Who is that speaking? *Who is that speaking?*"

The galvanometer needle was jerking on the dial, and Scheuch saw a few small sparks spitting off the edge of the disc, but he heard no voice beyond Vordran's. It seemed to him that Angelos was turning the generator crank slightly faster than before, but the increased speed made no apparent difference to anyone but Vordran. He was out of the armchair, gaping fearfully in every direction. "Don't you hear? Does no one *hear?*" He took a step toward Angelos, raising his arms as though he meant to bring both clenched fists down on the generator. "You *must* be hearing!"

Angelos quickly stopped cranking the generator, holding up his hands with the palms out. "No one's here, it's all right, I promise you. No one's speaking, not now." He reached out to pat Vordran on the arm, a bit timorously. "Really, there's no one."

Vordran stood still, shaking his head heavily, like an exhausted animal. He said, "Not now. But there was. I heard. There *were* voices, more than one. None of you heard?"

Scheuch said, "No, nothing, I'm sorry," and could not have said why he had apologized. Vordran continued to stare at Angelos. "*You*—you yourself—you heard nothing?" Angelos did not respond.

To everyone's astonishment, it was Griffith who suddenly said, "I did." Vordran wheeled to look at him in disbelief, and Scheuch jumped to his feet without realizing that he had done so. Only Angelos's expression remained unchanged.

Griffith had the air of someone who had been shaken out of deep slumber, roughly and without warning. He said dazedly, "How did you do that?"

"What did you hear?" Angelos's voice was clear and without any particular inflection, but it seemed to Scheuch at the time—though he was never sure afterward—that the medical student was smiling faintly. "Tell me exactly what you heard, Griffith."

The Oxford man was plainly struggling to retain control of the tone that mattered most to him. Putting the words one after another, like a blind man finding his way down a strange street, he said hoarsely, "There were two of them. I couldn't understand the woman . . . very faint, you know—rather think she was speaking French, some such." Vordran nodded. Griffith said, "But the man . . . the man was speaking English, no doubt of it." After a moment, he added, somewhat more himself, "His speech had a distinct Midlands accent."

The room was completely silent. All that could be heard was Vordran's breathing, slow as falling blood. Scheuch said finally, "Old chap, Angelos, I really think you ought to clarify things a bit. Elucidate—I believe that's the word. What the *devil* is going on here?"

Angelos sighed. "I don't know."

"Not good enough," Scheuch said, feeling himself flushing in embarrassment. "Really not."

"How are you making those voices?" Vordran demanded. "Where are they coming from?"

"I don't *know*, God's my witness!" Angelos raised his voice for the first time. "I'd tell you if I knew!" He was alternately twisting his fingers together and hugging himself. "I don't bloody *know*!"

Griffith said, surprisingly calmly, "You must have some notion, surely. Are they coming through your electro-thing? Those—what do you call them?—ah, *wave* things?"

Angelos opened his mouth and then shut it again. He stood silent, regarding the three of them with the air, not so much of an animal brought to bay, but that of a lost child in darkening woods. He said, "I think I can bring them in a trifle louder."

Vordran said, "No," but Angelos was already beside the generator, turning the hand-crank notably harder than he had done previously. He used both hands at first; then, as the copper disc picked up speed, he freed his left hand to lift the stethoscope and held the end out toward Scheuch, who took hold of it gingerly. Angelos gestured to him to fit the little rubber earpieces to his head.

At first Scheuch heard nothing beyond the hiss of the disc and an occasional tiny sputter of fluctuating electricity. Then, very slowly, a word, two words, at a time . . . a woman. This one, unlike the woman Griffith had heard, was plainly speaking in English, but Scheuch could make nothing coherent of what she was saying. ". . . *Carrots . . . the minister . . . Martin . . . coal chute . . . Martin . . .*" Her voice dissolved into crackle and buzz, and Scheuch looked up to meet Angelos's inquiring gaze with his own wide eyes. He said, "I heard. Not quite sure *what,* but yes, I did hear . . ." In spite of himself, he let his voice trail away.

"Give it to me," Vordran said. All but snatching the stethoscope from Scheuch's hands, he clamped the earpieces on his head, which being larger than Scheuch's, required angry, hurried readjustment. Angelos kept the generator turning steadily—the galvanometer needle hardly stirred from its near-center point—and Vordran listened with his jaw sagging and his eyes utterly unfocused. Abruptly he tore the stethoscope from his head and hurled it back at Angelos, shouting, "It is a trick, it has to be! This has nothing to do with your electricity, not a thing!" Yet the sound of his words was not so much angry, Scheuch thought, as somehow bereft.

Angelos stopped the generator for a second time. He said softly, "I wish it *were* a trick. Oh, you don't know how much I wish it were." The three others stared at him. Angelos said, "What did you hear?"

Vordran shook his head. "Not important. What is important is how you made me hear it. The rest of this"—he waved a dismissive, if slightly trembling hand—"is nonsense. Tricks, like those American spiritualists. Table-rapping. *Fraudulent,* my good sir!" But his eyes were, astonishingly, bright with tears.

Angelos was a long time responding; or at least it seemed so to Scheuch. When he finally spoke, his rigidly calm voice twanged in a way that Scheuch could not recall ever hearing from him. He said, "Whatever it is, Vordran, it's not fraudulent. I think I wish it were."

He glanced around the room at them all, his eyes squirrel-quick, squirrel-anxious, never quite meeting anyone else's eyes fully. "You're right about one thing. I did start out rather larking about with wireless telegraphy, just out of curiosity, wanting to see if an ordinary chap like me could do it. It's been pretty well established since the Maxwell equations that electromagnetism travels in waves, and I started by seeing whether I could tap into those waves some way and use them to conduct voices, actual human voices, you know. No experience, no training, no proper equipment—and, of course, no laboratory assistants, except for good old Scheuch there." He patted Scheuch's arm, adding, "Eternally obliged, old man."

"Don't mention it," Scheuch mumbled. "Glad to be of service." Then, louder, "But if you aren't making them, those voices—"

"Tricks," Vordran said again, louder than before.

"—and if they aren't here, some way, in your rooms—"

"They aren't—" Angelos started to reply, but he caught himself noticeably, and Scheuch pressed on.

"Then, as Griffith just asked, are they speaking through your generator, through your stethoscope, or . . . or *what?* Whose voices *are* they? Where are they coming from? And stop saying you don't know—you must have *some* notion!" He turned to Vordran on his right, then to Griffith. "I think I speak for all of us when I say we're not leaving until you tell us a bit more."

Vordran nodded. Griffith said grimly, "Quite a bit more." He coughed, longer than he needed to, and then asked, "What about—ah—ghosts? We had a ghost up at Balliol. Old scout, don't you know—spent his whole life cleaning after students, didn't have anywhere else to go after he died. Quite true. Saw him myself."

Angelos did not answer. He began disassembling the generator and its attachments, putting the copper disc carefully back in its linen pocket, folding the stethoscope away. Scheuch put a hand on his wrist. "That can wait, don't you think, Angelos? Talk to us."

Angelos clasped his hands together behind his back, rocking slightly from foot to foot as he spoke. "All I can tell you with any degree of certainty is that they are real voices of real persons. That I do believe, however absurd it may seem to anyone else. I also suspect—I'm not sure of this, mind you—that they are somehow being carried to us on electromagnetic radio waves, as Maxwell calls them." He wet his dry lips, took a long, slow breath. "But what I have also come to believe"—a very small chuckle, nearly inaudible—"which might very well get me stuck away in Northampton, is that *all* voices, every word ever spoken or sung or shouted, everything screamed or whispered . . . it's all still here, all around us, whether we can hear it or not. The ghosts of voices, if you like, Griffith. The radio waves pick them up—they attach themselves in some way I don't understand. I can't say what the range is, or how far back in time the voices go—"

"Oh, by all means, go all the way with it," Griffith jeered. "Do let us know when you listen in on Adam and Eve."

Angelos shrugged. "You've heard what you've heard. Myself, I've caught medieval church Latin, I'd swear to that, and a few bits and scraps of English that didn't sound as though they'd been spoken in this century—or the last one, either. I've heard a woman who seemed to be scolding a child, and a man crying and cursing some faithless friend as though his heart would break. German, that last." He rubbed the back of his bent neck, wincing wearily. "There's no pattern to it, there doesn't seem to be any predominance of language or nationality—it's a wilderness of voices, that's all I can tell you. If any of you can explain it to me any better, I should certainly appreciate it."

The room was silent. Angelos began to gather up the teacups and un-eaten biscuits. Griffith left without speaking. Scheuch said, "Well, then, cheery-bye," and followed him out. Vordran, however, stood in the doorway for a long moment before he turned and said, "This is a bad idea, Angelos."

Angelos blinked in apparent puzzlement. "Idea? It's not an *idea* at all, Vordran, it's barely an experiment. I'm only listening, as best I can—listening to people talking as I might overhear them in the street, at the next table in a restaurant. Eavesdropping, if you like. Nothing more structured or scientific than that."

"Eavesdropping," Vordran repeated. "Yes. And you do remember what they say about eavesdroppers, Angelos?"

Angelos's long sigh was dramatically elaborate. "Why, no, Vordran, I *don't* remember what they say about eavesdroppers. Do enlighten me."

"That sooner or later they hear something they don't like at all. Sooner or later." Vordran was gone.

Ramadan came early that year, the moon giving its blessing on the eleventh of August. For all the country's postwar fascination with everything Turkish, the monthlong holiday had not yet made its way onto the calendar of the United Kingdom; but Griffith groused daily about the fact that Simpson's-in-the-Strand, fabled home of good English roast beef and saddle of mutton, always carved at your table, was now offering kebabs and hummus, along with *kofte, doner, kokorec, borek* and *gozleme.* "Not to mention their bloody sweets—rot your teeth just *looking* at them. I promise you, I'd quit the damnation job in two shakes, if there were something else going fit for a white man." But Mr. Emanetoglu, coming for the month's rent, also brought delicacies from his family's celebration, and at least three of his four roomers consumed all their share, without ever learning the dishes' names.

When he climbed, panting slightly, to Angelos's top-floor rooms, he shook his head in wonder, as he always did, saying, "My goodness, how do you ever find what things you need?" And Angelos, as always, made his usual joking response. "Oh, I never do, Mr. E. Instead, I find wonderful things I didn't know I needed. Remarkable, the way that happens."

"Well and good," Mr. Emanetoglu customarily replied, "so long as you can pretend you are not looking for the rent, so that you can find it for me." And they laughed together, loudly enough to annoy Vordran, who lived on the floor below.

But on this occasion, Mr. Emanetoglu felt himself curiously oppressed by the air of Angelos's rooms. Or perhaps neither *oppressed* nor *air* was the correct word: the effect on him, rather, was of being somehow over-crowded, pushed in upon, whether by clutter, which had never particularly disturbed him before, or by Angelos's obvious distraction and poorly concealed disquiet. He was not even offered a cup of tea, a drink which Mr. Emanetoglu was determined to like, however long it took him. He asked hesitantly, "Is all well with you, Mr. Angelos? You are not perhaps troubled in some way?"

Angelos, fishing hastily in his purse for the monthly payment, reassured him that all could not be better, calling him "old man" in the process, not once but twice. Mr. Emanetoglu pondered this development as he pattered down the stair. *Old man* . . . there was an expression that meant something to the English: an admission to a certain closeness, if any dark-skinned foreigner could ever be said to be close to an Englishman. Mr. Emanetoglu knew himself to be a naïve soul, quite often feeling out of place in this bewildering country, but he was not a fool.

"I know how many of them see every Turk as that dog Griffith does," he said that night at dinner in Haringey, where he lived with his elder brother Ismail, his sister-in-law Ceylan, and their three young sons. "I hear them on the street when they think I do not understand—I know very well what they say, how bitter and spiteful they still are about the war, how many of them would wish us all drowned in the Strait of Marmora, if they did not more and more need our money. But there are some, like Mr. Angelos . . ." He sighed, his smile more than half mocking his own words. "I don't know—what should I say? *Old man* . . . I am sure that is more significant than being invited to tea."

"I am ready to believe anything of the English," Ismail said flatly. "They are a mad people, and completely untrustworthy. If they were otherwise, there would not have been a war. It may be *old man* to your face, but it will be *nigger* behind your back. I would put no stock in their words, not ever."

"Perhaps not." Mr. Emanetoglu sighed again. "Perhaps."

But he said nothing of what he had almost felt, almost sensed, in Angelos's rooms, partly because he could find no words in Turkish or English to describe his impression; partly because he knew that his brother regarded him—quite kindly—as a well-intentioned blunderer at the best of times. All the same, hurrying to one or another of Ismail's properties, he often found himself going out of his way to pass the tall old house in Russell Square, often lingering in the street for no purpose that he could have explained either to Ismail or to Angelos—or, for that matter, to the helmeted policemen who came along more than once to stare and sniff and harry him elsewhere.

He did talk about it, a little, to his youngest nephew, Ekrem, who was five years old, because he talked to Ekrem a good deal, as he had done almost since the boy's birth. Being a practical child for his age, Ekrem asked him, "Why don't you ask the *hodja*?," meaning the venerable healer who lived two streets over from the Emanetoglus' home. The *hodja* always kept sweets for children in the pouches at his waist, and Ekrem had great faith in him.

"What could I ask him?" Mr. Emanetoglu demanded. "What could I tell him? That I think something is wrong in that house, when I don't even know whether that really is what I think? The *hodja* would laugh at me, as he should."

"Well, he would give you candy, anyway," Ekrem insisted stubbornly. "The *hodja* is nice."

Angelos was becoming increasingly withdrawn, seeing less and less of his housemates, who, by and large, appeared plainly relieved to have a polite excuse to avoid him. Griffith, of all people, occasionally came seeking him at Christ's, stepping as haughtily as a cat between hurrying lecturers, prankish students, and charity patients moaning in their own filth, waiting to be seen. Inconvenienced and irritated, Angelos would nevertheless give him a brief account of his latest experiments, and Griffith would stalk away again, apparently unwilling to be seen by social equals asking for information. Griffith was a notably catlike person in a number of ways.

Dispensing early with the stethoscope, Angelos had managed to set granules of common charcoal between two metal plates to create what he called "a carbon button," serving as an improvised amplifier when connected to his hand-cranked generator. The fragmented whispers, mumbles and cries came crowding in, the vast majority of them in languages that Angelos could barely distinguish from each other, let alone translate or even guess at. The rare English voices were hardly any easier to understand: very few came in university accents, but rather from all points and ancestors of the empire. On the occasions when he actually sought Angelos out in his rooms, Griffith himself sometimes became as intrigued by a recognizable Lancashire or Cornish inflection as though he were coming home at last to Balliol. To Angelos he commented, "D'you know, even the wog—old Glue Pot—even he's starting to sound human after a bit of this gabble. Remarkable, rather."

Only Scheuch continued to spend any considerable time in Angelos's rooms, frequently—as Angelos was forced to admit—to the project's benefit. He proved to have the most discerning hearing of all four men, often catching phrases completely opaque to Angelos himself, and learning to react to tones rather than guessing at literal meaning. Crouching as close to the "carbon button" as he could, he would mutter, "Couldn't make out a bloody word, but there's a sweet voice she's got . . ." and, later, "What're *they* all on about, then? Sounds like my mum's whole family on Christmas morning . . . That chap's an idiot. You don't have to understand an idiot to know he's an idiot . . . Oh, *that* poor bugger's in trouble—that one's in awful trouble, poor soul—you can hear it. I wish . . ."

He always made his comments in the present tense, without exception. When Angelos pointed out to him that if his theory was correct, the chances were that almost every voice he was hearing—if not, indeed, every single one—was of someone long dead, Scheuch answered simply, "I know that, old fellow. But I *can't* know that, if you follow me. Just can't, that's all." Angelos never raised the matter again.

Vordran did come once, quite late at night, to ask directly when Angelos opened the door, "Do you ever hear the same voice twice? Do you ever recognize a voice you might have heard before?"

Angelos frowned. "What could the odds be? It would be like recognizing the same fish in a school that swam past you—lord, even an hour ago. Vordran, it's as I told you, we could be sweeping up the remains of every word that's ever been uttered—perhaps only in England, only in London, perhaps only within a few square miles of this house. And even so . . ."

"And even so . . ." Vordran nodded. "I understand. London is very old. I was only wondering." He stood looking down at Angelos for a moment. "I am impressed, Angelos. You have taught yourself a great deal in a short time." He paused, frowning. "Do you find the voices louder than they were?"

"Louder?" Angelos shook his head. "I don't think so. A bit more intelligible, yes—that's the carbon button—but louder? I only wish they were."

"Perhaps you do not. Remember what I told you about eavesdroppers." Vordran paused, seemingly waiting for an answer or a further question. He got neither and left.

Yet as spring aged into a patchy, dusty London summer, one at least, of all the numberless voices, was indeed growing clearer in Angelos's rooms, and steadily more familiar as well, if no louder. It was a woman's voice, though low enough in timbre that Angelos at first took it for the sobs of a man in soul-strangling anguish. He could never determine its language or nationality, no matter how carefully he listened, nor how piercingly pleading the voice became. Never swelling in volume, it did not pass on like the others, but only continued to wail in soft desperation: a cry like wind over stone at first, though later it took on the sound of a torture victim long beyond screaming for mercy, broken and barely whining with each turn of the rack. At other times, it—*she*—sounded as though she were making love with a demon, which terrified Angelos and made him squeeze his eyes shut until they hurt. There were words in it then, but none he knew.

No one heard it beyond his rooms, at first. There were times when he was certain that the little homemade amplifier could not possibly contain the terrible crying; that it existed only in his riven head. He shut down the generator altogether, sometimes for days, but the voice continued whimpering in the walls of his rooms when he tried forlornly to sleep, and followed him pitilessly when he dragged himself to lectures at Christ's Hospital. It came to grieve, finally, through his entire life, and he wept nightly for the horror it witnessed at the same time that he cursed it and prayed for it to leave him alone. He grew to believe beyond question that he was going mad and had a lawyer draw up papers to make certain that he was to be delivered to Bensham Asylum, and not to Devon Pauper. He made copies for each of his housemates and slipped them under their doors.

When they in their turn at last began, one at a time, to hear the lone voice in its own context—whether or not Angelos had the generator running—each reacted as differently as might have been expected. Griffith denied fiercely that anything unusual was happening at all, while Vordran admitted to the voice, but blamed Angelos's foolhardy experiments for waking some ghost or spirit long resident in the old rooming house. Only Scheuch considered the situation more or less as it was: the four of them bound, whether as victims, prey, or helpless bystanders, to the endless imploring sorrow of a single human being from another time and—in all likelihood—another country. No less frightened than the others, he determined consciously to drown himself in the voice, to listen to it to the point of numb boredom, inoculating himself against its eternal misery. The technique had proven remarkably effective against the mean arrogance of his bank's manager; he saw no reason why it should not aid him in this situation. Scheuch was not a highly imaginative man, but he paid attention to what worked.

With his keen hearing, he was the one who first noticed that the voice was beginning to be audible in Russell Square. He thought at first that he might be imagining it; but when Vordran commented on it, and Angelos's increased pallor and sleeplessness gave silent assent, Scheuch conducted his own research, carefully pacing out the exact range of the voice—which increased, block by block, every week or thereabouts—and also making note of the local residents' awareness of the sound, or lack of it. Some seemed as yet unaffected, but many were beginning to look as though, like himself, they had taken to spending their nights with their heads buried under several pillows. Scheuch found it cheaper than gin and laudanum, though no more effective.

It was at this point, on the fifteenth of August—a Saturday morning— that Mr. Emanetoglu came to collect the rent.

The small, dark man turned, as always, at the northeast corner of the square, passed the Cabmen's Shelter, walked another block—and then abruptly froze where he stood, raising his head and cocking it sideways, like an attentive bird or a hound on point. After a moment he began to run, which was not something Mr. Emanetoglu did at all often, and children laughed at his clumsy gait as they scattered out of his way. Reaching the house on Geraldine Row, he first knocked, then rang, as was his invariable custom, no matter his current urgency. When no one responded he waited no longer, but let himself in, thrusting the door open so violently that it rebounded from the wall and banged shut behind him. He took the long stair two steps at a time, like a young man hastening to his beloved. He was talking loudly to himself in Turkish, and his normally serene brown eyes were wide and wild.

Griffith's room being just off the first-floor landing, it was the one that Mr. Emanetoglu burst into without announcing himself, demanding as the door slammed open, "What have you done? What has *happened* here?"

Griffith was not asleep. Griffith did not appear to have ever been asleep. He was sitting on the edge of the bed, with his head in his hands, and he did not immediately look up at Mr. Emanetoglu's furious question. He muttered at last, "Ah, hello there, old Glue Pot—pull up a chair." He raised his head, blinking. "Is it that time already? Half a second, then—"

"Never mind the rental fee!" Mr. Emanetoglu shouted at him. "What have you *done,* you foolish man?" He actually took Griffith by both slumped shoulders, as though to shake him into sense, and then released him and stepped back, making every effort to calm himself.

"Who did this?" he asked. "If it was not you, who then? Answer me!" He realized that he was sweating through his good linen suit, which he always wore on rent-collecting day. "Who is this who is responsible? Which man?" He was vain of his proficiency in English, but knew that when he was hurried or upset, the impossible grammar tended to set gleeful traps for him. "Who? Which?"

Griffith shrugged. "Angelos . . . yes, why not Angelos? Bloody Jew, you know, Angelos . . ." His head lolled forward. Mr. Emanetoglu pushed him back on his bed and went up the stair at a run.

Angelos met him at the top, waiting with his arms folded resignedly across his chest. He looked very nearly skeletal and even nearer to complete collapse than Griffith, but he held himself with a stubborn, painful dignity. He said, "Mr. Emanetoglu, I'm going to have to ask you for one or two days' grace on the rent. No more than two, I assure you."

"Never mind the bloody rent!" Mr. Emanetoglu would go to his grave—he was certain of it—never truly comprehending the significance and usage of that single English word, but he employed it at every sensed opportunity, hoping that if it should fit into the conversation, so perhaps would he. "What has occurred here, Mr. Angelos? Tell me precisely what you and your friends"—for Scheuch and Vordran had come trudging up the stair behind him—"have done to my brother's nice house?" He was outraged to realize that he was close to weeping.

Angelos's voice was wearily conciliatory, without being at all defensive. "Mr. Emanetoglu, this is my fault entirely. I have been experimenting at random to learn whether it might be possible for people, say, in Turkey to speak directly to people here in England—and instead, I began to hear voices right in my rooms—"

"Voices of spirits who haunt my brother's house?" Mr. Emanetoglu broke in furiously. "No, it is you four, you yourselves, who are haunted—whatever ghosts or demons may be in this house, you surely brought them with you! I could feel it, hear it, *smell* it on the street outside!" He checked himself, turning—as he never failed to do in such crises—to the calming words of his personal guru, the great Sufi Muhammad al-Ghazali, who never failed to comfort him by reminding him that it was wisdom always to consider and to doubt. *"Doubt is the scholar's dear friend, and self-doubt the dearest . . ."* Therefore, taking several deep breaths before he spoke again, he said quietly, "It is an old house, this, and I know from my own experience that some old houses can in some way retain the . . . the shadows of those who once lived there. Is that what happened, Mr. Angelos? Did you and your . . . *experiments* awaken Ismail's house?"

Angelos shook his head, which seemed to take an enormous effort from him. "That is not what happened, Mr. Emanetoglu. I dismantled my generator more than two weeks ago"—a crooked half smile at the silent surprise of the others—"without informing these gentlemen, since it was my decision alone to make. Yet we all still keep hearing the voices of people who cannot have lived here, people who can have had nothing to do with this house, this time—perhaps even with London itself. I cannot tell you anything more useful than that. I would if I could. I can only beg your forgiveness, and say that we will do all we can to make things right again."

Mr. Emanetoglu looked slowly around at Scheuch and Vordran, seeing Griffith crossing the landing to join them. Each was obviously as fatigued as Angelos, exhausted down to his bones, and to the soul beyond. He said, "You are all hearing the . . . these voices, then?"

Griffith and Vordran nodded without answering. Scheuch said, "Mine, last night . . . mine was a child, I could tell that much. I think it was being killed. It went on and on." He began to cry, weakly, without making a sound.

Angelos looked at Mr. Emanetoglu, but did not speak. Mr. Emanetoglu said heavily, "I see. Yes, I do see. And I do not know what to do about all this, no more than you do." He paused, lowering his head almost to his chest and then raising it again. He said, "I will not be collecting the rent today. Tomorrow, at two o'clock—will that suit all present?"

Everyone nodded without replying. Mr. Emanetoglu said, as brightly as he could, "Well, then—ta, all?" He could never keep the slang phrase—so jauntily British, so important—from coming out slightly questioning, but he did his best. Then all four men said, as he could not remember them ever saying to him together, "Ta, Mr. Emanetoglu."

He went on home then, to the little courtyard in Haringey, greeted Ceylan—Ismail being in the neighborhood coffee shop with his best friends, as was his custom on Saturday—and waited for Ekrem to come home from playing football in the street with older boys, who always trampled him, but never made him cry. When he could, Mr. Emanetoglu helped Ekrem clean off the worst of the game before his mother noticed the blood and the bruises. Mr. Emanetoglu worried sometimes about the fact that he considered his five-year-old nephew his own best friend; but then he would remind himself that in only a few years the boy would have no time for him. Which would undoubtedly be as it should—Mr. Emanetoglu knew that.

When Ekrem did arrive, Mr. Emanetoglu took him aside as soon as Ceylan had scolded and released him, and asked him earnestly, "Nephew, would you say that the *hodja* would know how to deal with ghosts? Think carefully before you answer."

Superfluous advice: Ekrem always thought things through with great precision. He replied, "How many ghosts, Uncle?"

Mr. Emanetoglu had no idea, and said so. "Maybe a lot—maybe only one. I suppose we had better assume there would be a good many."

Ekrem shook his head decidedly. "Then no. Not for a lot of ghosts, not the *hodja*. I am sorry." He read the disappointment in his uncle's face and brightened suddenly. "But the *hodja* has a *hodja* himself, did you know that? I think the old *hodja* would know all about ghosts."

"The *hodja*'s *hodja*?" Mr. Emanetoglu felt as though he had not laughed in years. Ekrem himself laughed delightedly at his amusement, very proud of himself for causing it. Mr. Emanetoglu said, "Tell me, boy, where does the old *hodja* live, then?"

"I will take you there right away." Ekrem scratched his head solemnly. "You know, Uncle, maybe it would be a good idea for you to bring them both to see the ghosts. Two *hodjas* . . . they could surely fight all the ghosts in London, couldn't they?" He spread his arms as wide as he could. "All the ghosts in *England*!"

"I will be happy if they can help me get rid of all the spirits in your father's house. One or a thousand, however many there may be." Mr. Emanetoglu patted his nephew's shoulder. "Thank you, Ekrem. I knew you would find a way."

So it came about that Mr. Emanetoglu, dressed, not in English clothing but in his finest summer *mintan* and *salvar* trousers, was standing on the doorstep of the Geraldine Row house at two o'clock the next afternoon. Behind him, folded hands hidden in the sleeves of their long robes, stood two bearded old men, one notably older and taller than the other. The second man, on the other hand, was notably plumper, and still had a scattering of black in his chest-long gray beard, while the first man's beard was closer trimmed, and as white as his hair. Both *hodjas* had an air of scholarly command about them, but each wore it lightly, as though they had no reason to parade overweening knowledge or virtue. They were looking, not at the front door, nor at Mr. Emanetoglu, but at each other, their hands already weaving empty cat's cradles in the air, as though they were trying to capture the soft, wild grieving that all three men had heard

all the way up the street. Mr. Emanetoglu wanted badly to cover his ears
with his own hands, but in the presence of the *hodjas* he dared not.

The old men bowed to Griffith, who opened the door at Mr. Emanetoglu's knock, without speaking. Mr. Emanetoglu said politely, "God save
the Queen and Princess Maude. I am honored to present *Hodja* Abbas"—
indicating the older man—"and *Hodja* Cenghiz." He added something
poetically insulting in Turkish and walked calmly past Griffith, followed
by the two old men.

Angelos was coming down the stair to greet him, followed by his two
other housemates, each looking that much more worn than the day before.
Mr. Emanetoglu introduced the *hodjas* to them all.

Angelos bowed himself, as only Scheuch beside him did, saying, "I am
most pleased to meet you both," and, to Mr. Emanetoglu, "Do they speak
any English?"

Mr. Emanetoglu replied, "They understand quite well, but speak
poorly. I shall translate as necessary." He watched the old men moving
in the vestibule, heard them whispering to each other, saw them raising
their heads, just as he had done—only a day ago?—flaring their nostrils to
sample the lightning taste of the air. *Hodja* Abbas turned to look straight
at him, and Mr. Emanetoglu felt himself cringe inside, like a schoolboy
who knows an answer is wrong even as he gives it. *Little Ekrem would
never feel like that, but I do. What is the good of being grown?*

Hodja Abbas spoke in Turkish, and Angelos looked questioningly at
Mr. Emanetoglu. "Was he speaking to me?"

Mr. Emanetoglu nodded. "He wishes to know whether you have had
any training in the philosophy of magic. Magic of any sort—even English."
He could not keep from smiling at the expression on Angelos's face—nor
on the ancient shaman's stern countenance either. "I am of the opinion
that *Hodja* Abbas does not think very much of English magic."

Angelos almost laughed, but looked over at the tall old Turk and muffled the sound into something like a sneeze. "Tell him *no*—tell him I've
no training at all, except in medicine, and not much of that. We English
haven't studied magic since Merlin, tell him. We believe in machinery, just
like the Germans. Tell him that."

Mr. Emanetoglu translated, plainly with a certain trepidation. *Hodja*
Abbas's lean face lost all color; even his dark eyes seemed to pale. He
began to speak very fast, his normally deep voice rising in pitch until the
words clattered and rang against each other like swords. Mr. Emanetoglu
had trouble keeping up with the right English words, but he did his best.

"He says that you are a magician born . . . and the biggest fool he has ever met. He says that he would kill you here and now and bury you under a lime tree, to protect the world from your—forgive me, Mr. Angelos—from your stupidity"—Angelos was not the only one who had noticed the curved dagger in the old man's belt—"if it were not that since he went to Mecca he has sworn never again to take a life."

"Decent of the old boy," Griffith snickered wearily. "Bet he's left a few flourishing lime trees behind him in his time. Along with assorted wives and babas." But the words lacked his usual scornful snap, and he sank down on the stair, leaning his head against the balustrade.

Hodja Abbas appeared to have finished his tirade, but then he burst out again in a further spittle-embroidered rant, which Mr. Emanetoglu did not bother to pretend he was not censoring as he went along. "He says he wants to see your rooms, the place where you do your . . . stupid work. He thinks he knows what you have . . . ah, where you have gone wrong, and there is a chance that he and *Hodja* Cenghiz may be able to help. But he must see where you . . . did it." He looked wretchedly apologetic when he finished, saying, "I am sorry, Mr. Angelos. He is a very old man."

Angelos laughed outright, but it took the remaining strength in his body, and he actually lurched against Mr. Emanetoglu. He said, "Old and tactless he may well be—and downright vulgar, that too—but of course he's absolutely right. But I do wish he'd tell me exactly what it is I'm supposed to have done, so I can apologize for it. Please ask him that, when he calms down a bit."

Mr. Emanetoglu did ask, but *Hodja* Abbas refused to comment further outside of Angelos's rooms. So they climbed the long stair, Englishmen and Turkish sages crowded together, and *Hodja* Abbas strode in the lead. *Hodja* Cenghiz, who had not yet said a word during the entire visit, and who clearly had bellows to mend, toiled in the rear, breathing hard and distinctly wheezing. Scheuch fell back beside him, impulsively offering the small old man his arm. But *Hodja* Cenghiz smiled, showing a full set of brown teeth, and said gently, "I thank you, no. It is good for fat old men to sweat in the middle of children. I shall survive."

"I didn't know you spoke English." Scheuch was frantically going back over his behavior toward both old Turks. "I'm sure I would have—I don't know—paid more attention, if I'd known."

"Yes," said *Hodja* Cenghiz. "I am sure you would have."

The stairway funneled the monstrously suffering voice—as Scheuch had long since come to think of it—making it sound louder than he knew it was. He said as much to *Hodja* Cenghiz, who responded simply, "It is loud enough." Pausing momentarily on the stair to catch his breath, he added, "Loud enough to shake the sun loose in the sky. I sometimes wonder why this has never happened." Scheuch did not know how to respond.

At the top floor, prowling in Angelos's rooms, *Hodja* Abbas moved impatiently from instrument to instrument, device to homemade device, muttering to himself as a curious counterpoint to the haunting, horrible wailing that rose and fell and rose, and never went away. Mr. Emanetoglu, embarrassed but determined, stayed on his heels, translating a jeweled chaplet of Turkish obscenities as *Hodja* Abbas cursed several generations of Angelos's ancestors backwards and forwards for bringing such an imbecile to birth. Angelos himself, not knowing the language, and being more exhausted than even he recognized, only smiled feebly and made sounds that he was certain were words. It was Mr. Emanetoglu who finally plucked up enough courage to demand of the *hodja,* "What has he done, after all? What crime have his experiments committed?"

The two old men looked at each other for a long moment before *Hodja* Abbas spoke again—this time, surprisingly in hoarse, limited, but comprehensible English. "Sorrow . . . Heart of Sorrow . . . he have prowoke— awake—no . . ." He shook his head irritably, groping for the right word. "*Touch.* He have *touch* in deep, deep place, world place. The Sorrowheart. We call." He turned toward *Hodja* Cenghiz for confirmation.

Griffith, having seated himself in the one armchair when Angelos opened his rooms, had promptly fallen asleep, mouth open and his hands futilely covering both ears, since the voice was always more pervasive here, though no stronger. *Hodja* Cenghiz said, "What you are hearing—what Mr. Angelos has reached, roused, by accident—is the grief at the center, the heart of the world. It is just as old as human beings, to the minute, and it is always a woman's voice. We Turks call it *Sorrowheart*—other times, other languages, some other name. But always a woman." He bowed to Angelos, slightly but unmistakably. "How Mr. Angelos reached it, touched it with his little electrical researches, I have no idea—only a very few of our poets have ever done that before. Most of them went mad." He sighed and shrugged. "I sincerely congratulate you, Mr. Angelos."

In the silence, Scheuch's sharp ears heard Angelos's laughter begin, impossibly deep in his belly, well before it ever billowed into daylight. It was not loud laughter, nor did it last very long; but it woke Griffith, and caused even *Hodja* Abbas to take a step backward and regard him with the same anxiety—though less of it—as Mr. Emanetoglu. Angelos said at last, "So. Let me understand. We here, we will all continue to hear these voices?"

The two *hodjas* looked at each other and then back to him without answering. Angelos asked, "Forever?"

Vordran echoed him. "Forever? For the rest of our lives?"

Hodja Cenghiz answered him slowly, "Not all the voices. Only the one. And not all of you: only for him." Angelos stared back at him, not laughing now, his tired eyes as blank as walls. *Hodja* Cenghiz said, "The other voices, they are a different matter—whoever they were, they will pass on ahead, causing no trouble, only showing us the way we will go in our turn. *Hodja* Abbas can make certain that no one living in this house, now or in future, will any longer hear or listen to them. That we can promise in good faith." Angelos nodded.

Scheuch looked away from both Angelos and the *hodjas,* wrapping his arms around his own shoulders. Griffith started to speak and then stopped. Mr. Emanetoglu could not take his eyes from Angelos. To his own considerable surprise, his heart hurt for the Englishman in that moment, as it would have hurt for Ekrem. *Hodja* Cenghiz continued, "But *that* voice— the voice of the Sorrowheart—that voice your friend will never stop hearing. It is not just, for he surely meant no harm. But Allah's justice is not ours." *Hodja* Cenghiz cleared his throat. "For what it is worth, which is nothing, I am sad for you, Mr. Angelos."

Griffith was already dozing off again, and Vordran's eyes had turned as unfocused as when he first listened to Angelos's stethoscope. Scheuch seemed to be the only person reacting to the reality of what Angelos had just been told. He said loudly, "I say, you can't do that! Set that voice trailing him everywhere—haunting him forever! Who do you chaps think you are, anyway?"

Neither *Hodja* Abbas nor *Hodja* Cenghiz even bothered to look at him, so Mr. Emanetoglu plucked up his courage and intervened, saying sternly and earnestly, "Mr. Scheuch, these gentlemen are scholars, healers—even what you would call magistrates, when necessary. Surely you must be at peace with their judgment."

"No, I mustn't be at bloody peace with a damned thing," Scheuch mocked him. "And you're a bloody hypocrite for saying so, Emanetoggle." He had never gotten closer than that to the proper pronunciation. "You heard him say it—it's not *right,* and you all buggering know it! Like Job in the bloody Bible, and I never understood that story either, if you want to know. How you can stand there and say *be at peace . . .*"

He was very tired, and he ran out of words and rage at more or less the same time. Mr. Emanetoglu, looking on heartsick, saw Vordran puzzled and irritated, and Griffith not entirely among those present. Angelos, of them all, remained as strangely calm as though he were opening a letter that promised to be interesting. He said, "Well. Don't exactly see myself staying on in Geraldine Row, I suppose."

Hodja Cenghiz coughed and cleared his throat. "Mr. Angelos, I am afraid that you cannot really stay anywhere, not for long. The Sorrowheart, the deepest pain of the world, has chosen to speak to you, and wherever you go it will follow—wherever you rest, those near you will hear its voice and feel its grief. It will spread like a marsh under a poorly drained road, growing steadily deeper and wider, and sucking everything—everything—down into it on every side." His own voice was very nearly imploring. "Do you understand, Mr. Angelos? Please, do you understand me now?"

"I understand you." Angelos rocked on his heels and ran a hand through his hair. *Such ordinary gestures,* Mr. Emanetoglu marveled dazedly, *for someone who has just had his life shattered, undeservedly. Could I behave so? I wonder.* Angelos said, "Well, if you will excuse me, I'll need, as the phrase has it, to get my affairs in order. I can be gone by tomorrow night." Mr. Emanetoglu saw nothing but affable flatness in his expression.

The *hodjas* consulted, the elder stooping like a hawk to mutter in the younger man's ear. *Hodja* Cenghiz said, "*Hodja* Abbas will speak to the other voices in the house and tell them to be silent. It will take some little while."

"By all means. Fumigate the baseboards to your hearts' content." Angelos bowed formally to the two old men. "I will be at Christ's, seeing whether I can possibly pry some of my fees out of their grasp, since I will clearly not be attending classes this term." He turned to Mr. Emanetoglu, holding out an envelope. "My usual payment."

Mr. Emanetoglu accepted it, shaking his head miserably. "It will be too much by half. You will not have been here the whole month." Their eyes met, and Mr. Emanetoglu whispered, "I am sorry—I am so sorry. I should never have brought them here."

Angelos patted his arm. "You did the best thing for everyone, sir. Even, it may well be, for me. After all, I was never much of a medical student, and I have always wanted to travel. And there will certainly always be company"—he chuckled suddenly—"and voices may be answered, spoken to as well as heard. Imagine . . . *imagine,* if I should actually strike up a conversation with the sorrowing heart of the world." He touched Mr. Emanetoglu's arm a second time. "Perhaps that is what I'm supposed to do, old man. Who knows?"

Behind them, *Hodja* Abbas paced back and forth in what had been

Angelos's rooms, talking to himself—as it seemed—in ponderous, rolling Turkish. *Hodja* Cenghiz followed him, step by step, writing down the words he recited on the strips of gilded paper they had brought with them from Haringey. Folding the strips according to a precise pattern, he then inserted them into various cracks in the floor and in the molding. Mr. Emanetoglu, watching, thought, *Nothing exists for us Turks unless it is written down. Even our magic has to be in writing.* He turned to say this over his shoulder, but Angelos had already left.

The night was cold and still when Angelos finally came back, well after the *hodjas* and Mr. Emanetoglu were gone, and Scheuch, Vordran and Griffith long abed. The only voice he heard was the one he knew, the one that continued and continued: wordlessly, incomprehensibly, pounding itself through his skull like a blazing nail. He stood and listened for a long while, before he finally said aloud, "We will be friends, you and I. There's plenty of time for us to understand one another." He went to bed then, and slept, if not well and deeply, at least without dreams.

Oddly, it was Griffith who was the most help in packing his belongings the next day. Scheuch, being as burly as a navvy, carried most of his bags and boxes to the hired wagon waiting in the street; but Griffith actually quarreled with him for the privilege. He appeared on the edge of telling Angelos the full story behind his failure to return to Oxford after the war, but they were interrupted by Vordran's farewell, which was awkwardly emotional and vaguely accusatory at the same time. Angelos never did learn the truth of Griffith's Balliol days, but he rather suspected that there had been a monkey involved.

Scheuch never said goodbye. He simply shook hands with Angelos, handed him the original envelope Angelos had given Mr. Emanetoglu the day before—it contained the same cheque, as well, and a short message from the Turk—growled, "I believe you know where I live," and walked away. Angelos got up beside the driver, said to someone the driver could not see, "If you don't care for the new digs, we won't be there long," and the cart rumbled away out of Russell Square.

None of his former housemates ever saw Angelos again. Mr. Emanetoglu's brother Ismail quickly found a tenant to replace him, and he jogged along as well with the others as Angelos ever had. Scheuch eventually married and went to work in a Bristol branch of his London bank, while Vordran was eventually and unwillingly pensioned off from the Bishopsgate law firm where he was never a clerk. Griffith moved back to Oxford, went mad so genteelly that no one recognized it for quite some while, and ended his days in Bensham, as Angelos had feared for himself. Russell

Square no longer played host to constant shadowy voices seeping down Geraldine Row—most especially not that *one* which had set children and their cowering parents running futilely indoors with their hands over their ears. There were, over time, legends of similar occurrences in Bayswater, Clerkenwell and Holborn; but each of those faded with the passing months and years of the new century, as happened even with that awful business up in Durham, so there you are.

Afterword to "Music, When Soft Voices Die"

Not having seen him for more than fifty years, I don't know where Ismail Turksen is today. But should he ever chance to read this story I hope he'll understand my gratitude.

We were both freshmen at the University of Pittsburgh in 1955, and my recollection is that, outside of my roommate, Ismail was the first friend I ever made there. He was also the first and only Turk I've ever known at all well, and certainly the first Muslim. I remember him as dark and slim and funny, with a great sudden laugh that contrasted intriguingly with his dry, deadpan sense of humor. Ismail found America a reliably constant source of amusement.

What I know of Turkish history and folklore, I know almost entirely from Ismail. We'd sit in the Student Union cafeteria, or go for long walks along Pittsburgh's Fifth Avenue on mild spring evenings, and he'd recount the rise and fall of the Ottoman Empire, and what Tsar Nicholas I meant by calling Turkey "the sick man of Europe." I remember that we traded our grandmothers' superstitions and household magics, and discussed the similarities and differences between Bronx rabbis and Istanbul hodjas. I could be wrong, but I think he knew at least as much about rabbinical scholarship as I did. Jews have been in Turkey for a very long time.

When I finally sat down to write "Music, When Soft Voices Die," after stalling as much as possible (I knew next to nothing of the steampunk genre and was truly terrified of attempting such a story), those old Pittsburgh chats with Ismail began to come back to me: first by slow degrees, and then with a growing rush. Desperation will do that. Mr. Emanetoglu isn't anything like Ismail as I remember him, but I do hope that Ismail might have recognized him and perhaps approved.

—Peter S. Beagle

Terry Dowling

Terry Dowling is one of Australia's most acclaimed writers of the fantastic. He has been called "Australia's finest writer of horror" by *Locus* magazine and "Australia's premier writer of dark fantasy" by *All Hallows*. His collection *Basic Black: Tales of Appropriate Fear* won the 2007 International Horror Guild Award for Best Collection, earned a starred review in *Publishers Weekly,* and is regarded as "one of the best recent collections of contemporary horror" by the American Library Association. The acclaimed *Year's Best Fantasy and Horror* series featured more horror stories by Terry in its twenty-one-year run than by any other writer.

Dowling's award-winning horror collections are *An Intimate Knowledge of the Night* and *Blackwater Days,* while his most recent titles are *Rynemonn, Amberjack: Tales of Fear & Wonder,* and his debut novel, *Clowns at Midnight,* which London's *Guardian* newspaper called "an exceptional work that bears comparison to John Fowles's *The Magus.*" Major interviews with Terry conducted by *Exotic Gothic* editor Danel Olson can be found in *The New York Review of Science Fiction* and in *Cemetery Dance Magazine.* Terry's home page can be found at www.terrydowling.com.

TERRY DOWLING

The Shaddowwes Box

O N THE FOURTH night the dream remained the same: our train ran along the banks of the Nile, its locomotive fired by the mummies of cats and kings. There was Akhmet, yet again, insisting that it was true, leaning forward, bright-eyed, gesturing wildly in our hard-won compartment. A new tomb-pit, shallow but vast, had been unearthed in the sands south of Cairo, he was telling me as if he never had before, hundreds of mummified cats to one side, dozens of human pauper mummies to the other.

"There had to be kings among them, Mr. Salteri," Akhmet said, eyes flashing with the fine joke of it, exactly as they had on the momentous day itself six years earlier when I had made the fateful journey to the Wadi Hatas. "It's what the reinterment commissions did back in the New Kingdom. They feared looters, professional *tombaroli* such as you, so they moved the royal mummies, hid them. This field had a small precinct to the west. Probably special mummies there, possibly nobles, queens, even kings! But so many mummies. Too many, you understand? What to do? Sell to the Americans? They pay well and take everything, but there is no time. The excavation supervisors search for amulets, jewelry, then dispose of the remains with the railway factors before the authorities arrive. Everything goes into the fireboxes. Whoosh! We ride on the burning dead."

"You can't be serious," I said, those words again, then as now, largely because Akhmet wanted me to, and once again fancying our own late great Queen Victoria, or even the recently crowned King, giving their all like this, blazing away to help complete the run south from Saqqara.

"Very common now, Mr. Salteri. The *moumia* burn like sticks. It's the pitch."

"Akhmet, Mr. Minchin is aboard, you say?"

"Of course, effendi. Even now he will be making his way here. The car-riages are crowded. A few moments more."

And as if the words were indeed a cue, the door opened and Charles Minchin eased into the compartment, short and florid, grandly mousta-chioed, looking impossibly crisp in his suntans and solar topee.

In the dream I stood, now as then, allowing that any archaeologist this well turned out might be a stickler for the niceties. "Mr. Minchin, it's a pleasure." We shook hands.

"Lucas Salteri, the pleasure is mine. I've long admired your work."

I had to control my smile. To what did he refer? My most recent *work* had been looting Etruscan tombs outside Veii and Norschia in western Italy. Before that ten years as a West End stage magician, and eight as an engineer before that. My career echoed the great Giovanni Belzoni's in so many ways. "Our arrangement stands?"

"Of course. We have camels waiting. We will be at the site by early afternoon."

"But between stations—?"

He consulted his timepiece. "The train will stop in a few minutes. It has been arranged."

And indeed the train did begin slowing.

Ten minutes later we stood by the Nile amidst a cluster of date palms, watching swifts and martins darting over the fields of maize and sor-ghum as the train disappeared into the south. Ten more and we were mounted, and Minchin's three fellahin assistants—accomplices they would soon prove to be, Akhmet, Moussa, and Sayeed, nondescript then but made vivid by subsequent events and the dream's repetition—had finished loading the pack camels and we were heading off into the west-ern desert.

And that was where the dream ended, always ended, even in the earli-est hours of this new momentous day, not at the tomb itself, not when Minchin played his hand, not at the betrayal.

HERBERT KRAY ARRIVED almost precisely at three o'clock. The bells of St. Paul's across the Thames had just finished sounding when he knocked at the door, and I heard Mrs. Danvers, my only *human* servant, hurrying to answer.

I sat waiting in the large, elegant drawing room, secretly pleased that the day had turned chill and overcast again beyond the heavy drapes, and watched Ramose. There were fourteen things that he could do really well and tending the fire was one of them. He propped and stilted in his best penny-dreadful/*Boys' Own Paper* mummy fashion over to the grate, poked it several times, then set down the poker and moved to the side, waiting for his next task.

Mrs. Danvers ushered in my guest and left us without saying a word, just as I had instructed. Dr. Kray was very well presented, a tall handsome man in his early to middle forties, with a neatly trimmed beard and wearing a suit of the finest tweed. The golden watch-chain in his waistcoat pocket had a fob in the shape of a Horus falcon, proclaiming something of his trade in antiquities. I had no doubt that the Horus was genuine.

I stood, crossed to him, and shook his hand. But before we could exchange more than a few of the usual pleasantries, I had the distinct if modest pleasure (modest given what was to follow) of seeing his eyes go large at the sight of my favorite manikin.

"Good Lord, Trenton!" Kray said. "Bendeck mentioned that he'd heard one or two odd stories about you, but I would never have thought this! Tell me that you haven't revived one of them!"

"Hardly, Dr. Kray. It's a construct, nothing more, made to resemble one of the partly unwrapped mummies from Maspero's 1881 DB320 cache from Deir el-Bahri."

"It certainly looks authentic to me!"

"You're kind to say so. But listen and you will hear the clockwork. It's all Bryson gears and a rotating oriete of my own design. A fairground diversion, nothing more. Still, if I time it right, you will think it is responding to my commands. But please do be seated."

There were three armchairs arranged before the fire, two in a semicircle facing the cheerful blaze, my own somewhat to the right so I could survey the whole room: the single door, the heavily fastened drapes that deadened most of the street noise, the darkly shrouded shape over by the southern wall.

Even as Kray took the armchair nearest my own, I called, "Ramose, the port, if you please," and the mummiform stirred, moved forward once more, propping and stilting, half toppling along, very much like one of those clever manikins you sometimes saw in the better klatsches and *salons mécaniques* off Fleet Street.

The port had been poured out earlier by Mrs. Danvers, of course, three sets of glasses on three separate trays, all placed carefully out of sight of where Kray now sat. (Ramose was far from having the dexterity to actually pour drinks from a decanter.) This way the bandaged form need only lean forward and bring up the first tray, then do a slow turn, which put it close by Kray's elbow.

With an admiring chuckle at the cleverness of the whole thing, the antiques dealer took a glass, crying, "Bravo! Truly marvelous!"

Ramose straightened, moved behind the semicircle of chairs, and brought the tray and the other glass to me.

Herbert Kray sipped his port, then set his glass on the small occasional table before the chairs. "Dashed clever. I'd love to know the trick of it. But to business, Mr. Trenton. Your message said that you might have a prime antiquity to sell."

I too set aside my glass. "Let us let Ramose do his other party trick first." I made sure Kray saw me take out my timepiece, seem to be consulting and calculating an exact timing. "Ramose, please show our guest the WH38."

Again, as if responding to the spoken command, the mummiform jerked into life. With a whirring of gears and the distinctive *click-shift-lock* of the Bryson armatures, he stiff-legged to the shrouded shape looming behind the curve of the armchairs. Kray craned about to follow the whole thing, showing the same wide-eyed delight as before, watching as the mummy stopped, raised one bandaged, hook-clawed hand and seized the black velvet dust-cloth covering the tall shape beneath. The claw-hand closed, clenched, pulled. Ramose took one, two steps back, tottering slightly as the shroud came fully away.

In my mind I applauded silently. *Exactly as rehearsed.*

"Ah my!" Kray said, and yet again stared in wonder. Before him—behind him more correctly, though by now he was out of his chair and standing once more—was an unadorned wooden Egyptian burial casket propped upright, held at a gentle eight degrees in a gleaming brass frame consisting of rods, brackets, intricate clamps and gears, all fitted close, keeping it secure.

"Wonderful!" Kray said. "But that frame. I see clockwork. What on earth—?"

"Just some new conservation techniques I'm trying, Dr. Kray. Precautions against the local humidity, vibrations caused by traffic, doors closing, that sort of thing. I keep my guest in the drawing room here to offset the effects of damp. Hence the heavy drapes I've had installed. The subdued lighting."

"Of course. Of course. Has it been opened?"

"It never has. Please feel free to examine the seals, if you wish. They are Twentieth Dynasty."

Kray did so, moving in close. His zeal was impossible to hide. He was seeing a lost king, a queen, another of the marvelous reinterred royal mummies of the kind officially discovered by Maspero in 1881, or those from the Loret cache seven years later. "You are prepared to sell this?"

"Dr. Bendeck and yourself are reputable experts in this business. I thought I should come to you first."

"Yes, yes. Capital! But contents unseen? Hm." Kray made as if to be deep in thought, frowning slightly, stroking his neatly bearded chin with one hand.

"Just as I found it, Dr. Kray," I said.

"Which was where, Mr. Trenton, if I may ask?"

"You will understand that this must remain undisclosed for the present."

"Of course. Of course." Kray was examining the casket again, carefully, so carefully, spending long minutes studying the wood, the mixture of pitch and resins keeping it still airtight after so many centuries. He was no doubt imagining a new royal cache, one not yet made known to the Arab Bureau, the Antiquities Service, or the British High Commission, or possibly even more: the barely imaginable wonder of a new *sealed* tomb, possibly that of Herihor or Tutankhamun, for heaven's sake, a continuing stream of artefacts finding their way into the special holds of ships using the Suez Canal or reaching England by way of the old contraband routes out of Morocco and Spain. "I'm sure we can reach an agreement, Mr. Trenton. But please. Why have you invited me here ahead of Dr. Bendeck? We are business associates. He said he was asked to call on you at *four* o'clock, yet your invitation to me specified three and asked for strictest discretion. Surely we might have called on you together. Unless . . . May I assume . . . ?" Kray hesitated a final time, daring not say it.

I spread my hands. *You understand how it is. Make an offer if you wish.* "I know you are a man of discrimination, Dr. Kray. A man of letters. A scholar as well as a collector and a dealer. I merely wanted to give you time to examine this piece in your own time, make an unhurried appraisal, form your own conclusions."

"Yes, yes, I see. I thank you for that."

"And give us a chance to talk. Let me be frank. When Dr. Bendeck arrives, it will be different."

Kray returned to his armchair, seated himself again. He took another sip of port and gave me a shrewd look. "Very well," he said finally, setting down his glass. "May I be equally frank? This is an unadorned casket. It possibly contains the mummy of a nonentity like those unidentified individuals Maspero discovered among the fifty kings of the DB320 cache. The controversial Unknown Man E, for instance, possibly a disgraced royal prince, possibly a murdered royal suitor for Tutankhamun's widow, but, equally possible, nothing more than a favorite servant, even someone the overzealous reinterment officials accidentally included in their haste to stay ahead of the looters." Kray leant forward, well-manicured hands on his knees. "If there were the occasional relic of—not to put too fine a point on it—actual *intrinsic* as well as archaeological value, say, of gold or silver, gemstones, of the finest craftsmanship, I would be happy to reach some mutual accommodation on a more—personal—basis."

I smiled and nodded to indicate that this was exactly what I had had in mind, as if, all going well, there would indeed be such intrinsically valuable pieces on offer.

"Excellent," I said, raising my glass. "This is precisely why I made so bold as to ask you here ahead of your, so I've been told, more officious colleague. As you can appreciate, I prefer not to deal with a consortium."

"Capital." Kray emptied his glass and chuckled with pleasure again as Ramose repeated his earlier performance, stilting and propping across to the decanter, tilting forward to pick up the second tray of the three, and returning with it, setting it down on the occasional table between Kray and me. Fortunately, instinctively, my guest moved his empty glass clear and placed it on the tray when he took a filled one. Ramose could not have managed such a retrieval. The mummy then stiff-legged back to his place to the left of the fire and became still, though, as ever, seeming to be listening, following everything we said.

While Kray's attention was on the construct, I checked the time. A quarter of four. Kray's examination of the WH38 casket had taken longer than expected. Bendeck would be here soon. It was time to give the good doctor his due. Minchin had been their agent in Cairo, the one who did the dirty work, Bendeck the main investor. But Herbert Kray, as several reliable sources had it, had been the mastermind behind all that had happened in the tomb in the rocky defile at Wadi Hatas that day. Minchin and his fellahin may have done the actual deed, Bendeck may have sold the artefacts, but Kray had undoubtedly planned the whole affair. I had simply been an awkwardness, an additional complication to be dealt with, someone to be left behind when they had finished plundering the tomb and sealed it up again. They knew nothing of the two goatherds who had followed us, brothers to the one who had sold me the papyrus. Instead of robbing *me* themselves as they had originally intended, they had become my liberators.

I pretended to sip my port, began directing the small talk that would crown the afternoon's events. "Dr. Kray, do you know what a Shaddowwes Box is?"

"No, Trenton. I can't say that I do."

"The great Elizabethan alchemist John Dee was said to have had one. And Aleister Crowley, our Great Beast. It's a sealed box containing nothing but darkness. A sort of memento mori, really. A reminder of what awaits us all unless we believe in a Creator. Even Shakespeare was said to own one. And it's spelt 'shaddowwe' with the double *d* and *w* after one of the Bard's favoured spellings for shadow."

"I see." Kray didn't see at all, and my rhapsodic tone clearly troubled him.

I gestured at the coffin behind his chair. "I must say that having an unopened casket standing there for the past three weeks has given me a shudder or two. I mean, have you ever wondered about what truly happened to that Unknown Man E in the DB320 cache?"

Kray had to come back from where his own thoughts had taken him. "The Unknown Man? I have to say I know very little about it. He's the chap they found screaming, yes?"

"Indeed. Wrapped in a sheepskin—something ritually unclean to the Ancient Egyptians—bound hand and foot, it seems. Some say it's Pentewere, the conspirator son of Ramesses III who was captured when the Harem Conspiracy against his father failed. Some accounts say he was made to take poison, others that he was buried alive in an unmarked casket."

"Awful business either way."

"Indeed. But it makes you think. *Both* versions may be correct. The poison could have been a sedative and Pentewere awoke in darkness to find himself entombed alive."

"Yes, well." Now Herbert Kray was the one to bring out his timepiece, an impressive gold one, and check the time. "Elleston will be here soon. This mechanical mummy of yours will really take his fancy. He has always loved automata."

Again I pretended to sip my port. "I'm pleased to hear it. And do excuse my rambling on like this. It's having that casket in here. I'm not one to worry about mummies coming back to life, but the *darkness* now, that is another thing. It bothers me. Have you ever wondered what might happen in total darkness, Dr. Kray?"

Irritation showed briefly in Kray's eyes, though it was brought quickly under control. "Presumably nothing, sir. The workings of air and silence, I suppose. Time doing its thing. In windowless rooms the movement of dust particles. In caves the drip of water, I suspect. The formation of stalactites. You tell me."

"But that is *unconsidered* darkness surely. The darkness of nature, chance, and random circumstance. What of the *considered* kind?"

Herbert Kray had no idea how to respond to such a question or, ultimately, even what it meant. Things were taking a definitely queer turn, but if there were treasures, even trinkets, to be gained, he had resolved to be politeness itself. "If you mean to tell me, sir, pray do. I admit that your exact point escapes me."

"If I consider it, I change it."

"Really? How so?"

"By the participating mind, Dr. Kray. Our minds, our very thoughts, galvanise the thing observed at its most basic level. There are religions that turn on this way of thinking. Someday it will be proven beyond doubt as a scientific fact as well."

Kray chuckled. "I'm sure. So I might argue that I could affect this rather fine port by reflecting upon it."

"You may not be able to measure the shift enough for it to matter, but yes. First, you are unconvinced, sceptical. Second, it would take more time than I believe you would care to give it."

Kray chuckled again. "You probably need to do better than that, Mr. Trenton. That's the refrain of mystics and charlatans the world over. You *must* believe! You *must* allow time! Have the correct *discipline*. Oh, and a small donation will help to purchase paraffin for the lamps during such a vigil. Your support will be ever so greatly appreciated."

I made sure that I smiled before pressing my subject again. "I ask my question because the rage and anguish, the despair and agony felt by Unknown Man E waking in his coffin could have been enough to change the imprisoning darkness, if you follow my drift. That darkness would have been the intensely considered kind, I suggest."

"Doubtless true, old fellow. We can only wonder what Maspero and his assistants must have felt when that particular coffin was opened. The pharaoh's curse of the melodramas!"

I turned my glass in my hands. "Or simply sufficiently *changed* darkness. Nothing more."

"Well, let's pray that fellow behind you had a peaceful and easy time of it."

"On the contrary, Dr. Kray. I have it on good authority that the fellow within was *definitely* buried alive. Unlike Pentewere, or whoever Unknown Man E happens to be, this mummy had an accompanying papyrus telling his story."

Kray's eyes widened. "You have this papyrus?"

"I do, and had it translated some years ago. Best of all, it is that rarity amongst Egyptian funerary texts, not the usual fragments of the *Amduat*, not a list of personal accomplishments, but an actual account of a non-royal burial."

"'Nonroyal?"

"And of a desperate reckoning. His name is Panuhe, Dr. Kray, a luck-less courtier who murdered the lesser princess with whom he was smitten when he could not have her for himself. Her slighted husband was high vizier and dealt with him accordingly, had him sealed up in a rough-hewn annexe in her own modest tomb. All very sordid, I know, the very stuff of melodrama in any age!"

Suddenly the clock in the hall began chiming. At the same time, the bells of St. Paul's started sounding across the river. Bendeck's knock came mere moments later.

Kray's relief was palpable, yet quickly replaced by a natural concern. "There were other things in the annexe, did you say?"

I heard Mrs. Danvers answering the door, heard voices in the hall. "You are being mischievous, Dr. Kray. I deliberately did not say."

Kray grinned. "Of course. Of course. Look, old man, about this three o'clock thing. Do you think—?"

I anticipated him. "Best we say that you arrived just a few minutes ago. The keen enthusiast arriving a tad early."

Kray nodded. "Splendid. Greatly appreciated."

Mrs. Danvers showed Elleston Bendeck into the room and left us, clos-ing the door behind her. It was her final duty for me. Her salary was paid; I would never see her again.

Bendeck was a portly man in his late fifties with grey eyes and steel grey hair and as well turned out as Kray was, though wearing one of the new American suits that had become all the fashion lately. Again the pleas-antries were hardly started before he was crying out in astonishment and delight as Ramose repeated his earlier performance, stilting over to fetch the final port tray.

Then, with both men seated before the fire holding their glasses, shar-ing first in the bewildering eccentricity of my toast to the King, then to the success of our negotiations, I prepared to enter our final phase. This time the port contained a strong-enough sedative, though one sufficient to cause mere muscular debilitation rather than unconsciousness. I wanted my guests awake.

"Dr. Bendeck, while awaiting your arrival I was just now showing your colleague that casket behind you and suggesting that it is quite likely the handiwork of the reburial commissions of the Twentieth Dynasty."

"Indeed. Twentieth Dynasty, you say?" Bendeck craned his neck to see, pointedly ignoring any social impropriety in our apparently having commenced proceedings without him. He dealt in antiquities, not always from reputable suppliers. He knew to go with the flow of events if ultimately to his advantage.

"I was also suggesting that it is effectively a Shaddowwes Box, such as Dr. John Dee was said to possess and even William Shakespeare. Not a Shaddowwes Box in intention, mind, more by circumstance, purest chance."

"Right." He turned to his partner. "I see that you have the advantage of me, Kray. Perhaps, Mr. Trenton, you might care to—"

But the door to the drawing room slammed open then and stopped his words. Through that doorway came an old bath chair in which sat slumped none other than Charles Minchin, clearly in a torpor, as if just now roused from an opium sleep. And that wasn't the only cause for amazement. The chair was being pushed by another mummy, stilting and propping as best it could, and the door was now being closed by yet another.

"Minchin!" Bendeck cried, and Kray did too, more in astonishment at the sight of additional clockwork manikins appearing in the room than at seeing their colleague like this, both men rising to their feet, and doing so unsteadily, I noted, as the sedative took effect.

"Our final guest, gentlemen," I announced, watching as Ahmose wheeled Minchin in alongside Bendeck's armchair. Senawe had closed the door and now came prop-stilting over to join Ramose and Ahmose. Then, in startling unison, the three mummiforms began hooking away the bandages across their stomachs, each drawing forth a golden dagger concealed there, all three brandishing them in an inevitably comical but clearly menacing fashion.

"Trenton, what's going on?" Bendeck demanded.

"Not Trenton!" Minchin slurred the words. "That's *Salteri*! Lucas Salteri."

"What's that you say?" Kray cried. "Salteri?"

"Left 'im in the tomb," Minchin managed, drooling as he spoke. "Left 'im in the bloody tomb!"

"You did, Minchin," I said. "Took everything and sealed it up again. But the fellah I'd bought the papyrus from had sent his brothers to follow us. They meant to loot the place themselves, you see, but wanted to have this document translated first before attempting it. That's why they sold it to me. They were being cautious. I mean, gentlemen, how many tombs have a papyrus in a sealed canopic-style vessel deliberately left at their main entrance, right beneath the traditional seal of the nine bound captives? Our vengeful vizier *wanted* posterity, possibly the great gods, to *know* Panuhe's story. Anyway, the brothers released me, and we found *this* casket in its hidden annexe."

"The brothers—" Kray could barely manage the words. "Not these?"

"My three friends here? Hardly. Well, parts of them at least."

I was now moving to the doorway, about to close and lock it behind me. Mrs. Danvers had long since departed the premises. The mummies stood with their gilded daggers between the three men in the chairs and the room's only exit.

"You surely do not hope to scare us with a few sideshow gimmicks, Salteri?" Bendeck called, his words slurred.

"No, Dr. Bendeck. They are mere diversions, window dressing to distract you from the sound of additional clockwork now operating at the casket behind you. If you turn your heads, if you can manage it, you will notice that a special mechanism has already been activated, is even now preparing to apply pressure to the casket."

"What, an' set 'nother mummy on us?" Bendeck said. The words were still recognizable.

"Hardly. Just as the papyrus says, the body in that coffin was never mummified."

"I don't follow," Kray said, slumped heavily in his chair.

"Unlike Unknown Man E, this sorry fellow truly was interred alive in that casket, bound and helpless. He *filled* that darkness, gentlemen. Surely *changed* it in more than a casual way. I now give you that darkness. It is my gift to you."

And with that I extinguished the remaining lights, closed and locked the heavy mahogany door, and arranged the special bolster at the bottom to shut out all hope of illumination.

All timed. All of it. The pressure edges would be touching the wood by now, relentless. A true full minute to the splintering point, so far as I could judge. But now it was ten seconds to step through the front door, eight more to turn the key behind me. Five seconds for the front steps. Twelve paces along the pavement, fifteen, possibly twenty.

Then darkness in darkness.
And the screaming.

Afterword to "The Shaddowwes Box"

As so often happens, "The Shaddowwes Box" came from a blending of things. First there was a lifelong interest in Egyptology, and more specifically in the circumstances surrounding the fate of Unknown Man E in the 1881 Maspero cache and how it must have been for the poor wretch whose burial it was.

I already had the opening line from earlier in 2010 and fancied doing a mummy story at last, but where to take it? The invitation from the editors brought the Maspero connection to mind and some even earlier reading on the mind's effects on the material world. If we can allow that the properties of water and ice crystals can be changed by the human observer, why not other things?

Completing the inspiration package were Shakespeare's spelling of shadow as "shaddowwe" and the Italian word for tomb robbers: *tombaroli*.

—TERRY DOWLING

Garth Nix

Garth Nix was born in 1963 in Melbourne, Australia. A full-time writer since 2001, he has previously worked as a literary agent, marketing consultant, book editor, book publicist, book sales representative, bookseller, and part-time soldier in the Australian Army Reserve. Garth's novels include the award-winning fantasies *Sabriel, Lirael,* and *Abhorsen* and the YA SF novel *Shade's Children.* His fantasy books for children include *The Ragwitch;* the six books of *The Seventh Tower* sequence; and the seven books of *The Keys to the Kingdom* series. His books have appeared on the bestseller lists of the *New York Times, Publishers Weekly,* the *Guardian,* the *Sunday Times,* and the *Australian,* and his work has been translated into thirty-eight languages. He lives in a Sydney beach suburb with his wife and two children.

GARTH NIX

The Curious Case of the Moondawn Daffodils Murder

As Experienced by Sir Magnus Holmes and
Almost-Doctor Susan Shrike

"HOLMES IS HERE, Inspector," announced the sergeant, peering around the door of Inspector Lestrade's office, which was currently occupied by the newly promoted Inspector McIntyre, as Lestrade was on his holiday. "In a manner of speaking, that is."

McIntyre, aware of the susceptibility of those risen from the ranks to pranks from those less fortunate, chose to play a straight bat.

"What do you mean, in a manner of speaking?" he asked calmly, placing the file he had been reading slowly down upon Lestrade's desk. "Is he or is he not present in the antechamber?"

"Well, he is present," said the sergeant. His name was Cumber and his intellect was not particularly finely honed. "Only it isn't Mr. *Sherlock* Holmes, as you invited."

McIntyre set both his hands flat on the table, as they trembled with visible tension.

"You don't mean to say that Mr. Mycroft Holmes has come to see me!"

McIntyre was well aware of Mr. Mycroft Holmes's importance within the government, and the range and power of his influence. He also knew that the elder Holmes never left his club, and he could not even begin to consider just how much more serious the case before him must be if My-croft Holmes himself had come to consult upon it. Why, it was more than the mountain going to Mahomet, it was unprecedented, it was—

The sergeant broke into McIntyre's slightly panicked thoughts.

"No, it isn't Mr. Mycroft Holmes. It's a Sir Magnus Holmes."

"Sir Magnus Holmes . . ." muttered the inspector. "I don't believe I've even heard of the fellow."

"He has a woman with him," said the sergeant darkly. "One of them modern women."

"What!?" exploded McIntyre. "If this is all some sort of joke, Cumber, it's gone too far."

"Not a joke," said Cumber. He paused for a moment to reflect, then added, "Least, not that I know of. Shall I send them in?"

"No!" roared McIntyre. He thumped his fist on the desk, making the file jump and his half-empty teacup rattle on its saucer, the tea inside almost slopping over the edge.

"Very good, sir," replied Sergeant Cumber. He started to close the door, but just before it snapped shut, he added, " 'E did say Mr. Sherlock sent him over, sir."

The door shut before McIntyre could answer. He sat there with his mouth open for an instant; then with an explosion that this time did send his tea slopping over the saucer and on to the desk, he erupted from behind the chair and stalked to the door. A big man, who had fought heavyweight for his uniformed division before joining Scotland Yard, he flung the door open with a weighty fist and was all set to bellow again when he saw that he was being stared at by a lady and a gentleman, and by Cumber, who clearly had not quite gathered the intellectual power to tell them to go away in a nice fashion suitable to their obviously superior social standing.

McIntyre saw a relatively young man, perhaps twenty-eight or thirty, with a not very memorable face, short pale hair, and something on his upper lip and chin that could charitably be viewed as a Vandyke beard. He was only of medium height, had a slight build, and was wearing a very well-cut grey morning suit, made somewhat eccentric by a curiously shaped and very heavy gold watch-chain visible on his waistcoat, which was surmounted by a pearly white stiff-necked shirt with a dark red ascot tie, again made odd by the large and peculiar tiepin that was thrust through it, which had the appearance of being made of a bundle of small golden sticks and so looked rather raffish.

The woman next to him was a very different matter. She was of a simi-lar age, but where he was very much of average appearance, she was striking, dark-haired, and blue-eyed. Her charms were subdued under her not very flattering black-and-white dress that was somewhat reminiscent of a uniform, though it was drawn in tightly at the waist and had an elegant ruffled neck of obviously very expensive lace. She carried a small leather Gladstone bag, which was not at all a normal item of apparel for a lady of quality. McIntyre automatically noted she wasn't wearing a wedding ring.

"Inspector McIntyre!" called out the man. "We were just trying to impress on the good sergeant here that we had come to call upon you, at the express request of my cousin Sherlock."

"Mr. Sherlock Holmes?" asked McIntyre warily. "He is your cousin?"

"Second cousin, actually," said the man. "Something to do with our grandfathers. I can't quite recall, but my father grew up with Sherlock, and when my grandfather gambled away the old place and my father had to turn to trade, Sherlock was one of the few who stood by him, or so Father always said, though I don't—"

"And you are?" asked McIntyre, cutting short what otherwise seemed likely to be a long discourse on Holmes family history.

"Oh, I'm Sir Magnus Holmes," said the man happily. "Just plain Magnus Holmes till Father dropped off the perch last year. He was made a baronet in '87, services to the Worshipful Company of Tallow Chandlers . . . Lucky for me, if they'd left it any later I'd have missed out inheriting. Makes it easier to get a decent table, don't you know, and theatre tickets—"

"Indeed," said McIntyre. He looked at the door to the corridor, which had a glass window and thus might show the shadows of any observers, as he was beginning to wonder whether Mr. Sherlock Holmes himself was playing a trick upon him. Seeing nothing untoward, he glanced at the lady, who had maintained her station a pace or two away from Sir Magnus and was looking with detached interest at both the inspector and the baronet.

"And Miss . . ."

"Allow me to introduce Almost-Doctor Susan Shrike," declared Sir Magnus. "My . . . um . . . keeper."

McIntyre's brow lowered, a frown compressing his rather bull-like features, a likeness now accentuated by the narrowing of his mighty nostrils.

"I don't appreciate having a May-game made of me—" he began.

"I beg your pardon, Inspector," interrupted Susan Shrike. Her voice was cool and commanding and both soothed and dominated all the menfolk in the room. "Sir Magnus sometimes gets carried away. My name is Miss Susan Shrike, and I *am* almost a doctor, in that I am in the final year of my medical studies at the London School of Medicine for Women. I also am upon occasion employed to care for certain patients who are allowed excursions from Bethlem Royal Hosp—"

It was the inspector's turn to interrupt. He raised a finger to point at Magnus.

"You mean . . . you mean to say he's a lunatic from Bedlam!"

"Well, I am getting better," said Magnus reasonably. "I wouldn't be allowed out otherwise, even with Almost-Doctor Susan."

"Sir Magnus is not at all dangerous," said Susan. "He has been at the hospital for a few months recovering himself after an unfortunate accident. He is now well enough to begin to resume everyday activities. My presence is merely a precaution insisted upon by his aunt."

Magnus grimaced.

"Lady Meredith Foxton," he said in a stage whisper. "Ghastly woman. Specialises in making people miserable."

"Now then, Inspector," said Susan. "As I must have Sir Magnus back at the hospital before nightfall, perhaps you would be kind enough to tell us exactly what your problem is and we shall see if Sir Magnus can assist you."

"Sir Magnus assist me?" asked McIntyre. He was having difficulty comprehending what was going on and was wondering if perhaps he wasn't better suited to a more lowly rank after all. If only Lestrade hadn't gone on holiday!

"I like to help," said Sir Magnus brightly. "Sherlock said you had a case that was right up my alley and that . . . let me see . . ."

He strode to the fireplace and leant one elbow on the mantelpiece, then turned his head back to look at the inspector. Somehow his face had assumed an entirely different aspect, and he now looked far more hawklike and acute, with a hint of suppressed arrogance.

"Magnus, my boy," he drawled, in a voice that McIntyre recognised as a very good imitation of Sherlock's. "When you have eliminated the impossible, whatever remains, however improbable, must be the truth—and the very highly improbable is I suspect exactly what Mr. McIntyre is facing. As this is very much more your area of expertise, I suggest that you answer the inspector's clarion call and leave me to my practice."

Magnus dropped his elbow, and the likeness with it.

"Revolver practice, that was, not violin," he added in his own voice. "Shooting initials in the wall. And they say I'm mad."

"What is your area of expertise, Sir Magnus?" asked McIntyre. He felt that this was perhaps a foolish question, but the truth of the matter was that he needed help, and if Sherlock Holmes really had said those words, which after seeing that impression he was inclined to believe, then perhaps this unlikely lunatic might be of some assistance.

"I am a s . . . s . . . s . . ." Magnus started to say, stopping suddenly as Susan looked at him intently. "That is, I have made a study of the unusual, the arcane, and the occult. Also I make things. I am an inventor and have a supple and surprising mind. Sherlock said that, too, by the way. Mycroft says that I am a throwback to another era and should be burned at the stake, but he doesn't mean it, not after that business with the . . . the . . . things that I'm not supposed to mention. Let's go into your office, shall we, Inspector?"

McIntyre surprised himself again by swaying back to allow Magnus to slide past him, and he held the door open for Susan Shrike, before letting it swing shut on Cumber's inquisitive face.

"Go and get my guests some tea," ordered McIntyre through the door.

"Yes, sir," came the muffled response.

"I trust he won't have to wait for the tea," said Sir Magnus.

"No, I shouldn't think so," replied McIntyre, rather baffled by this new conversational sally. He returned behind his desk and indicated the chairs on the other side. "Please, do sit down."

"If he had to wait in a line, then he would be a queue cumber," said Magnus.

"What?" asked McIntyre, who had opened the file again and allowed his thoughts to wander. "What?"

"Hush," said Susan Shrike to Magnus. "Why don't we let the inspector tell us about the matter in question."

"Queue," muttered Sir Magnus. "If Cumber grew his hair long at the back, then it could—"

"Magnus," said Susan Shrike softly.

Magnus nodded.

"Yes, yes, awfully sorry. Please do explicate the matter, Inspector."

McIntyre picked up the top paper from the file, gripping it as if he might hurl it to the ground and throw himself upon it in a wrestling check.

"These are the salient points," he said. Clearing his throat, he began to read.

"On the morning of the ninth instant, that is to say yesterday, at twenty-one minutes past five o'clock in the morning, P.C. Whitstable was proceeding upon his usual beat and had reached the corner of Clarges Street and Piccadilly when he heard a shout on the other side of the road, at the point where a path exits from the Green Park. Dawn was approaching, the gas lamps were still lit, and there was no fog. He clearly saw a man in a long coat and unusual wide-brimmed hat run out of the park and start to cross the road. But on seeing P.C. Whitstable approaching, he turned to the left and increased his speed. P.C. Whitstable, blowing his whistle, set off in pursuit, and was joined by Park Keeper Moulincourt—"

"Moulincourt?" asked Sir Magnus. "I knew a fellow called Moulincourt. He wasn't a park keeper, though—"

McIntyre shook his paper and resumed reading. " . . . and was joined by Park Keeper Moulincourt, who was shouting 'Stop! Stop the murderer!' Moulincourt, who had already pursued the suspect for some distance, fell back as P.C. Whitstable took over the chase. Whitstable, a champion runner and keen footballer, soon caught the fellow. However—"

"There's always a however," said Sir Magnus. "Had to be. I was expecting it to come in before this. However."

"However!" blasted McIntyre, shaking his paper in barely suppressed fury. "When Whitstable gripped the fellow's arm, the coat and hat came off, and there was no one inside, only a great shower of daffodils that fell onto the road."

Sir Magnus tilted his head until it was completely sideways and peered at McIntyre.

"Daffodils," he repeated. "Stolen from the park?"

"Yes," said McIntyre, through gritted teeth. "Stolen from the park, and a park keeper murdered in the process."

"It wasn't Moulincourt who got murdered, obviously," added Sir Magnus, whose head was slowly righting itself again. "Were they the first daffodils of the spring?"

"I don't know!" protested McIntyre. "No one's ever tried to steal flowers from the park before. There are daffodils all over the place. Why bother with those ones? And anyway, how did the bloke escape—"

"First flowers of spring from a royal park, cut with a silver blade between dawn and moonset," mused Sir Magnus, almost to himself. "Your park keeper had his throat cut?"

"Yes, how on earth . . ."

A look of suspicion crossed the inspector's face. Perhaps Sherlock Holmes was not playing a game with him, but sending him a suspect.

"Where were you yesterday morning between five and six o'clock?"

"Locked up," replied Sir Magnus. He looked across at Susan Shrike and gave her a cheery smile.

"Yes, that's true, Inspector," said Susan. "Sir Magnus is locked inside his rooms at the hospital from dusk to dawn. It is part of his treatment."

"Then how did you know about the throat cutting?" asked McIntyre.

"None of this has been in the papers. Did Sherlock tell you? He has his ways of finding out."

"No, Sherlock didn't tell me," complained Sir Magnus. "Why does everyone always think Sherlock does my thinking for me? No, I deduced it, from my knowledge of folklore and ritual."

"What are you talking about?" demanded the inspector.

"It's quite simple, really," drawled Sir Magnus. He slid his chair away and leaned backwards for a moment, precipitating a mad grab at the edge of the desk as he almost tipped over. "There is a . . . belief . . . among certain quarters that if flowers from a royal park are cut with a silver knife at a particular time, it will enormously enhance their natural poison. Lycorine, as Sherlock would tell you. Nasty stuff in general, but a moondawn daffodil's poison is far, far more dangerous."

"That can't be true," protested McIntyre. "How could it make any difference?"

Sir Magnus shrugged.

"Clearly someone believes they need moondawn daffodils to make a terrible poison. I wonder what they intend to use it for?"

"And what about the empty coat?" asked McIntyre. "The running man who was . . . was just daffodils?"

"Oh, that's easy," said Magnus. "The adept would have cut the keeper's throat, and when the blood spilled on the earth he quickly fashioned a kind of simple golem from the resulting mud, using cut daffodils for the arms and legs. He threw his own coat and hat over it and sent it away to create a diversion."

"Magnus . . ." warned Susan Shrike. "Remember?"

"Or, far more likely," Magnus continued after a moment's pause, "in the relative darkness—he was between two gaslights, I expect—as the constable took his arm, the murderer spun about, at the same time turning himself out of the coat and throwing the daffodils at the policeman's face, blinding him for the few seconds required to drop to the ground and then crawl away along in the darker shadows next to the park railings."

"I prefer the second explanation," said McIntyre. He stared at Magnus for a few seconds, then stood up, casting an air of finality over the proceedings.

"Thank you very much for your time and thought, Sir Magnus," he said, shaking hands over the desk. "You have given me something to think on, to be sure. A pleasure to meet you, likewise, Miss Shrike. Sergeant Cumber will show you out. Please pay my respects to Mr. Sherlock Holmes when next you see him."

"But the adept . . . the murderer . . . you'll need my help to find him and bring him to justice," protested Sir Magnus.

"We'll get our man," said McIntyre. "Thank you again, but this is pure police business now. Good day."

"Sherlock said that apart from Lestrade and . . . and Gudgeon or someone . . . you were—"

"Sir Magnus! We really must be going," said Susan forcefully. "Thank you, Inspector."

Outside the inspector's office, Sir Magnus turned to Susan. "We didn't even get our tea," he grumbled.

"I expect there was a queue, after all," said Susan. She took Magnus by the arm and led him out into the corridor, hustling him along past the startled Sergeant Cumber and the department's best silver tea tray loaded with the good china.

"You know we can't let you out if you will insist on telling people the truth," she admonished him as they climbed into their hackney cab, which was not, despite its very ordinary appearance, one for hire by the general public.

"I can't help it," said Sir Magnus. "Krongeitz really knew what he was doing with that curse. It's all I can do not to babble out all sorts of esoteric stuff."

"It is fading, though," remarked Susan. "You'll be right as rain in a few months."

"The forced veracity is fading," said Magnus. "But the transformations continue."

"My, you are cheerful today. Magister Dadd says it will go in time, with the treatment, and he should know."

"He also said it will get worse before it gets better," said Sir Magnus. He leaned over and took Susan's hand. "Promise me that you'll act at once if it seems to be . . . spreading into the daylight hours of its own accord. I mean, without the use of the blue pill to bring it on."

Susan gently withdrew her hand and rested it on her Gladstone bag.

"You know I will do whatever is necessary, Magnus," she said. "But I am sure it won't be necessary. Now tell me, do you have any thoughts about who might be behind this moondawn daffodil business?"

"An adept who can make a golem from blood, mud, and flowers on the fly? And who wants moondawn daffodils to reap their poison? I'm not sure we should try to find whoever it is. Could be very dangerous."

"Magnus. We can't leave it to the police. Tell me about this moondawn poison business. Does it really make the flowers that much worse?"

Magnus chuckled grimly.

"I didn't even tell the inspector the best part. If you distil the poison properly, you don't even have to deliver it physically to the target. You can use the poison on something sympathetically attuned to a similar object the victim will use. A comb is quite popular."

"A comb?" asked Susan. "I don't understand."

"It's quite straightforward sympathetic magic," said Magnus. "In essence, the adept makes an identical copy of the target's favorite comb, using some of their hair. Then, some distance away, they drip moondawn daffodil poison on the copy and by magical transference, the poison soaks into the real comb. The next time it is used, the poison enters the victim through their scalp and kills them instantly, with the perpetrator nowhere to be seen. Even better, someone else may have been plying the comb, so they get the blame."

"I see," mused Susan. "And is this process of distillation difficult to manage? Does it require any particular apparatus?"

"Yes it does," said Magnus. "And I see what you're thinking. Interestingly, and I never realized it before, it also ties in with a comb being the typical sympathetic object of moondawn daffodil poisoning."

"Why?"

"Because the ritual involves the daffodils being cut up with a silver blade and placed in a retort with a scented oil. A silver razor, or scissors, would work a treat, and for the scented oil you could use the barber's favorite—"

"Macassar oil!" interrupted Susan.

"Indeed," said Magnus. "So the adept works with hair, silver razor or scissors, and hair oil."

"What else?"

"It needs to take place underground, with the usual harmonization requirement," mused Magnus. "An old Mithraeum, or something like that. An Anglo-Saxon crypt would work, maybe a Norman one at a pinch. It all points to one of those below-street barbers—"

"How long does the ritual take? How much time do we have?"

"I'm not entirely sure, never having undertaken the dastardly deed myself. But I seem to recall the daffs have to fester for several days in the oil, with lots of highly repetitive incantation . . ."

"So we need to look for an underground barbershop on the site of an old temple or church."

"Yes . . . it will also be relatively close to Green Park, as the daffodils have to be in oil before the sun is fully up. Even so, it could take a while to find out somewhere that matches all that. There are a lot of barbers about. Damned tedious to sort through them all, looking for old temples or whatnot."

"You could ask your cousin."

"Sherlock? He hates this kind of . . . oh . . . Mycroft. I suppose I could think about that."

"It might even be in his bailiwick, as it were," said Susan. "After all, who would our adept want to poison in this way? Someone difficult to reach by other means."

"Yes," said Magnus. "The Queen is one possible target, though perhaps the prime minister is more likely. Easier to get his hair, anyway. I suppose if I put it like that, Mycroft might even be polite."

He tapped the ceiling twice, and the small hatch beneath the driver's seat slid back.

"Carstairs! The Diogenes Club, thank you."

FOLLOWING HIS VISIT, Sir Magnus returned to the hackney in a bad mood and handed Susan a note on which an address was written in Mycroft's distinctive copperplate.

"It really is the most boorish place," complained the baronet. "All I said was 'Good morning, Mycroft.' I whispered, but you would have thought I was bellowing out 'Hello, ladies, I'm just looking in' from the way they carried on. Mycroft wouldn't even talk to me, I had to write everything down for him."

"You know their rules," said Susan. "I believe you talk just to annoy him. Anyway, you got an address."

"Gregory Cornet's in Curzon Street is the only barbershop that fits all the criteria," said Sir Magnus. "Its lower cellar was a temple to Bast, once upon a time."

"The Egyptian goddess?"

"Yes, the fiscal procurator for several successive Roman governors was Egyptian and had a thing for the old cat . . . I get my hair cut at Cornet's by Radziwill. I do hope he's not involved. A good barber is hard to find."

"Really?" asked Susan, pointedly staring at the not very successful Vandyke which was a fairly recent addition to Magnus's upper lip and chin.

"Yes. It makes the whole thing so much more difficult. Maybe we should hand this over to Dadd and the Peep O'Day Boys."

"Because of your barber?"

"No. Yes. I don't know. I suppose I've lost confidence after the whole Krongeitz business."

"I think we should go to Cornet's and you should get your beard shaved off," said Susan. "I will wait and observe, making caustic comments, in the role of your fiancée."

"I wish you would be my fiancée."

"You know we're not going to talk about that until you're completely recovered," said Susan. "As I was saying, this will allow us to get a feel for the place, and we may well sense any unusual vibrations that would confirm the location."

"So we walk into what is probably an enemy lair and I sit down and ask to have a razor put to my throat," said Magnus. "Besides, what do we do if it is the place?"

"I doubt the barbershop, or your Radziwill, is actually involved," said Susan. "Think about it. They've been there too long, and it's too public. I expect we'll find they've a new odd-jobs man who lurks in the cellar, or something like that."

"Maybe," replied Magnus. "But it could be they're all in it, a secret society of barber-illuminati."

"Yes, it could," admitted Susan. "In which case, I will give you the blue pill."

Magnus looked at her very seriously. "I really would prefer it didn't come to that."

"Dadd is sure that occasional use of the blue pill will actually advance your cure," said Susan gently.

"Dadd is sure of more things than he should be," said Magnus. "But it's you I'm worried about. You know I can't control—"

"I have the necklace, and the antagonist. I'll be fine."

"Are you sure we shouldn't hand this over to Dadd?"

"Yes," replied Susan, with considerable certainty. "Here we are. Do we go in?"

"I suppose we do," said Magnus.

"YOU WISH ME to shave the beard?" asked Radziwill. "It has barely had a chance to begin."

"Cut off in its youth," sighed Sir Magnus. He rolled his eyes to where Susan was sitting primly on a chair, apparently reading the copy of the *Englishwoman's Domestic Magazine* that she had taken from her bag. "But it has to go."

"Interesting place you have here, Mr. Radzorwell," said Susan over the top of the magazine. "I've never seen anywhere like this."

"Ladies do not usually come inside," said Radziwill in a very dampening manner. He began to strop his razor, which both Magnus and Susan noted was silver handled, and possibly the blade was silver too. "It is a gentlemen's establishment."

"Where does that charming little stair go?" asked Susan. She pointed past the row of curtained booths to the far end of the room, where a brass-railed stair curled down beside a wall of massive, ancient stones.

"The cellar, ma'am, where we store our scents and oils," said Radziwill.

"Oh, I should like to see that!" exclaimed Susan. She got up and started to walk towards the stair. But she had hardly taken a step when the curtains of every booth on either side slid back, to reveal twelve other barbers, each holding a silver razor. Radziwill made the thirteenth, and there were no customers in sight.

"Damn," exclaimed Magnus, delivering a savage kick to Radziwill's groin at the same time he leapt out of the chair. The barber grimaced and swung back with the razor, which Magnus countered with a swirl of the sheet that had been around his shoulders a moment before.

Susan sat back down and opened her bag with a click. Reaching quickly inside, she pulled out a large blue pill.

"Magnus!"

Magnus turned his head and opened his mouth. Susan threw the blue pill unerringly down his gullet and immediately reached into the bag to withdraw a necklace of shimmering blue stones, which she dropped over her head.

"I really wish you weren't involved in this, Radziwill," said Magnus, parrying another swipe. "You're an excellent barber . . . argh!"

Radziwill looked at his razor in puzzlement. He had swung, but as far as he could tell had cut only the sheet which Magnus had been employing as something between a baffle and a main-gauche.

Magnus screamed and raised his arm. Only it wasn't an arm anymore, but a loathsome tentacle, lined with huge suckers that were ringed with glistening fangs.

Radziwill was clearly the adept, for he immediately recognized what Magnus was becoming. He shouted a word of power that had no effect whatsoever and ran for the door, only to be shot in the head by Susan. She stood on the chair with her back pressed to the wall, the glowing necklace on her breast and a lady's purse revolver in her hand, the barrel smoking.

Magnus's screams quickly became no longer human, many more tentacles manifested out of what had once been his body, and within a minute at the most, there were no more living barber-illuminati.

The thing that Magnus had become slid across the floor of the shop, squelching through blood and torn flesh towards the front door and the street.

Susan put her revolver away, took a twisted paper packet from her bag, and stepped off the chair. The monster paid her no attention. One long tentacle began to caress the door, feeling for how it might be opened.

Susan lifted off the necklace with her left hand. Instantly the creature swung about. Two tentacles shot towards her, sucker-rings protruding, all the teeth out. She calmly ducked aside and threw the contents of the paper across the tentacles, creating a cloud of blue dust that very slowly twisted and danced about on its slow way to the floor.

It took a few minutes for Magnus to become human again. Susan spent the time preparing a slow match to the store of hair oil in the cellar, being careful not to disturb the daffodil brew that was bubbling on the iron stove in one corner, though she did pocket the comb that was on a worn marble plinth next to the stove. It was a very fine ivory comb engraved with a crest that she recognized at once, though it was not a royal one.

When she came back up, Magnus had managed to get most of the blood and matter off himself and was wearing a clean robe with a towel wrapped around his head. He had not managed to completely clean the vomit from the corners of his mouth, and his eyes were wild.

"He . . . the adept . . . put a s-s-s-ilence charm and interrupt-me-not on the d-d-door," he said, teeth chattering. "It will break when you pull it open. N-n-n-ice of them, don't you think?"

"Very handy," agreed Susan. She took him by the arm and pulled the door open, putting two fingers in her mouth to whistle for Carstairs. The cab was just down the street and it came smartly up, so that Susan and Magnus could jump inside and be away at least thirty seconds before smoke began to billow from the underparts of the barbershop.

"What was I this time?" asked Magnus, as they sped away.

"I don't know," replied Susan. "Something with tentacles. A lot of tentacles."

Magnus was silent for a while. He looked out the window at the city and all the people and the life beyond. Susan watched him. Finally he turned to her and spoke.

"Sometimes I think you are too ready to employ the blue pill."

"No!" protested Susan. "I really didn't expect to need you to transform. I never thought they'd all be in it, or that they would suspect us and be ready. I mean, how could they know we were coming . . . oh, I see."

"Yes," agreed Magnus. "Much more convenient for Mycroft if all the barbers were eliminated. He, too, finds feeding me blue pills useful. Especially when I can be directed against enemies of the state. Sometimes I wonder if he has told Dadd to tell me they are helpful, when I fear that in fact they prolong my condition."

Susan nodded and reached out to pull him down, so that his head was on her lap. Magnus resisted for a moment, then relented. Susan took off the towel and lightly scratched his head through his hair.

"I'll get better," whispered Magnus. "No blue pill then, and my nights will be my own."

"Yes," said Susan. "You will get better."

She did not look at her bag, and its box of Krongeitz pills, the blue . . . and the yellow. Magnus did not know about the yellow pills.

Susan hoped he never would.

Afterword to "The Curious Case of the Moondawn Daffodils Murder"

The genesis for this story came from a recent visit to London. I had just flown in from Australia, and one of the first things I did was to have my hair cut at an old barbershop in Mayfair, at least in part just to stay awake and stave off jet lag. While my hair was being cut I wondered who else might have sat in that same chair over the years. As the barbershop has been in business since 1875, my thoughts naturally turned to the late Victorian era, and of course, Sir Arthur Conan Doyle and his most famous creation, Sherlock Holmes. Following my tonsorial shortening, I walked through the Green Park. It was the wrong time of the year for daffodils, and there were no sinister wielders of silver razors, but from that haircut and a short walk in the park, a story idea was sown.

— GARTH NIX

Gene Wolfe

Gene Wolfe was born in 1931 and served as a GI in the Korean War. After many years working as an engineer—both a practicing one and an engineering journalist—he turned in 1984 to full-time fiction writing, having already laid the basis for an acclaimed creative career with his early masterpieces, *The Fifth Head of Cerberus, Peace,* and four-volume *The Book of the New Sun.*

Subsequent works, always extremely ambitious and highly praised, have included *The Urth of the New Sun, There Are Doors, The Book of the Long Sun, The Book of the Short Sun, The Wizard Knight,* and three linked novels set in Ancient Greece and Egypt: *Soldier of the Mist, Soldier of Arete,* and *Soldier of Sidon.* Wolfe's major story collections are *The Island of Doctor Death and Other Stories and Other Stories, Endangered Species, Storeys from the Old Hotel, Castle of Days, Strange Travelers, Innocents Aboard, Starwater Strains,* and *The Best of Gene Wolfe.* His most recent novels are *The Sorcerer's House* and *Home Fires.*

Gene Wolfe has lived in Barrington, Illinois, for many years, with his wife, Rosemary, and a dog called Bobby.

GENE WOLFE

Why I Was Hanged

[The following account was supplied by a man who owns a great many books but searches fearfully for another, a yellowing pamphlet he may already own. In looking for a quite different title, he stumbled upon this remarkable narrative, which he had never read and could not recall buying. He read it, and says he remembers it almost word for word.]

MY NAME IS James Brooks. I was brought up in service and trained by my father, himself a valet of some distinction. At the age of eighteen I had the good fortune of obtaining a position with an elderly gentleman, of a good Yorkshire family, whose valet had died. I served him faithfully, and as I believe skillfully, for upwards of three years, at which time he himself closed his eyes for the final time, much mourned by his relations. Young as I was and knowing far less than I then believed of the ways of the world, I hoped for a substantial legacy. He would, I thought, have inserted into his final testament some clause bequeathing a considerable sum to one styled by him *my faithful valet*. Conceive then, of my disappointment when the will was read. The clause I had so hopefully envisioned was indeed to be found there; but its wording cast all my hopes into that darkling pit from which they have never emerged. My master had accorded the not inconsequential sum of one hundred guineas to *my faithful servant Samuel Satterfield,* this Samuel Satterfield aforesaid having been, as may be supposed, the one whose passing had, as I thought, so greatly benefited me. My master's testament had been written, it transpired, some ten years before his demise and had lain untouched in his solicitor's box until the soil had been heaped upon his grave. Samuel Satterfield having predeceased his master, it was ruled that the sum vouchsafed him should go to his widow, an ill-favoured and ill-tempered hag who had begun life, as I have been reliably informed, as a scullery maid. In short, I received not a whit more than the stable boy, which was nothing.

Greatly embittered, I left domestic service and went to sea. My misadventures there I shall pass over in silence; but four years later, having suffered more than a sufficiency of horrid weather, bad food, and kicks from the mates, I resolved to return to my profession, registering with an agency that offered to supply domestic servants of good character to employers for a fee.

Months passed. My savings, never large, dwindled to nothing. I did whatever work I could find, and rough and dirty work it was for the most part. At last, when I had resolved to return to sea, which I must do or starve, the agency informed me that I was to appear for an interview with a prospective employer. It was only by the generosity of an acquaintance of my late father's that I acquired decent clothing for the occasion, he having grown overstout for the trousers, shirt, and waistcoat that hung so slack upon my wasted frame. A jacket was, providentially, provided by the agency.

My employer-to-be was a young gentleman of fashion, high coloured and good humoured, and so clearly wealthy and well tailored that my gaze fixed upon him as a starving cur's upon a beefsteak. After several prosaic questions regarding a manservant's duties as I understood them, questions easy to anticipate, he inquired, "What do you know of foxhunting, Brooks?" The intensity apparent in his voice and the narrowing of his eyes showed me plainly that this question was of greatest importance: that the entire affair hinged upon my answer. I would gladly have proclaimed myself an expert if I could, but I knew that the most trifling enquiry would at once reveal any such imposture. "Nothing, sir," I replied. "I fear that I know nothing at all of it."

"Thank Heaven for that!" was my future employer's rejoinder. "After discovering me ignorant of it, my last man would speak of nothing else. If I hadn't discharged him, I should have been forced to throw him under a train."

My joy was complete and perfectly unbounded, so that the latter part of his remarkable statement made but small impression on my mind at the time, though it was to return with great force.

He had commodious rooms in the West End, and in them I discovered items of apparel well suited to my duties, items abandoned, as it seemed, by my predecessor in his service. These I examined with delight and at once made my own. As soon as I could, I repaired my scant wardrobe from my wages and from the gifts, sometimes generous, accorded me by my master's friends. I should mention that I was our entire staff, save for a fat and rather pleasant woman, styled the housekeeper but in fact a cook, whose services we enjoyed but three days per week.

Parliament adjourned, the season ended, and the heat and dirt of the city, which had been most mercifully swept aside, resumed. Wealthy families and single men of fashion alike retired to the country or the seaside, and we with them. My new master's parents resided in Westmoreland, not far from this antiquated town of Windermere in which my life must end. The house is large and old, and in part ruinous. It is said to have been occupied for a time by Cromwell's Roundheads, and boasts what is called a priest's hole, this though in my judgment it looks more like a Necessary Closet. Here there was a large staff, at first distrustful but quickly welcoming when it was seen that I was adept at my duties and disinclined to shirk.

In London, I had gloried in my return to service, in light work I well understood and the entire absence of hectoring officers. Here my life was indeed delightful. I would, I resolved, hold to my post at all costs. My new master and I would grow old together; and should death come first for me I should bless him as I breathed my last. Little did I know what was to come!

There is not one of the visitations I endured that is not burned forever in my memory, but none is seared more clearly or more deeply than the first. I lay abed, having slept soundly, I believe, for some hours. Waking, I saw bending over me a maiden of mist whose hair was night and whose eyes were stars. Her hand moved toward my face—it stroked my brow, and I was conscious of no touch but only of a sensation of cold, as though I slept before an open window through which snow had blown.

I sat up, and she was gone. I rose and lit the gas, opened the door and looked out at the empty hallway, and in short did every foolish thing that may be imagined, all of them achieving every success that might be expected. That is to say, they availed nothing at all.

It may have been a week or a fortnight before she returned; I recall only that I had nearly been persuaded—this by my own arguments, for I had confided in no one—that the apparition had been a dream, the waking fantasy of an ill-ordered mind.

My master was in the habit of bathing before he retired each Saturday evening. Upon that occasion, his bath had not been ready at the accustomed time, this due to a mechanical difficulty with the apparatus employed to heat the water. He, being still rather in his cups, had berated me soundly for it, and had at last struck me a good, solid blow with his fist. I had suffered worse aboard the *Jack Robinson*, yet the injustice rankled. Thus I, who most frequently welcomed the embrace of Morpheus while the wick still smouldered, as the expression has it, lay awake that night staring at the ceiling, foolishly tormented. How might I have repaired the geyser, as the apparatus is styled? How might I have heated water upon the kitchen stove in more timely fashion than I had? Might I have lit the bedroom fire and employed that? And many more such questions, equally futile.

After lying sleepless for an hour or so, I chanced to glance to my left and beheld her melting through the door. Although dressed in nothing more substantial than an old linen nightshirt, I sprang from my bed. Indeed, I do not remember it, yet surely I did so, for I found myself standing and trembling before her. Should I have shouted? To this day I do not know; I know only that I was so unmanned by astonishment, and, aye, by terror, that I could not speak. My mouth opened, I believe. And closed, too, more than once. But not a sound did I utter.

I saw her as one sees moonlight, thin and lacking all substance, yet undeniably present. Did I think I dreamt? you ask. No, not that or any other thing; write, rather, that my mind was emptied of all thought, every thought having been driven out by fear.

She smiled, and my fear would have grown greater if it could. She gestured; at first I knew not at what, but when she repeated the gesture I saw it was at the stocking I had been darning while the light lasted. I had hurried the work, I confess, in the hope of completing it ere darkness fell; in that I had failed, and thus had left it, still incomplete, by the window, upon the only chair my room in that house afforded. When at last I understood what it was she indicated, I picked up the stocking and offered it to her. Let me say here, sir, and say now that there was no odour as of brimstone nor any such thing about her. Nor did she smell of grave-soil, decay, or the like. No, it was as though in that soft July I had winded a winter's night, cold and silent.

She refused my stocking with a humble little gesture. Once, in Calcutta, I saw a child offer a beggar a stone; the beggar's gesture was the same. "What is it you wish?" I asked. She seemed to endeavour to speak. No sound issued from her lips, not so much as a sigh.

"I shall do whatever you wish," I told her, "but I must first know what it is." By that time I was, I believe, regaining some shreds of self-possession. Fearfully, she indicated the darning needle, which was at that time still thrust through the worsted. I removed it and offered it to her.

She backed away, clearly frightened, and I recalled that the fairies were said, by those who feigned to credit them, to fear cold iron. I made as if to throw it out the window, but she hastened to prevent it. "What would you have me do?" I enquired, at which she mimed for me the thrusting of the needle into a forefinger.

I did. She bent and kissed my finger. The sensation was far beyond my meagre powers of description. At length she straightened up, licked her lips, and smiled. She had been moonlight before, as I have said. She was candlelight now, or rather, like the light of a candelabrum; she might almost have been a true woman, a living woman. You may think when you read this that you comprehend all that I have said, yet I beg leave to doubt it.

I offered my one poor chair, saying, "Will you not sit?"

"Thank you for speaking." She smiled again. "Won't you take it yourself? You must feel weak after giving so much strength to me." The golden bells of an elfin steeple beyond Land's End—should such a thing exist—could not have spoken more sweetly.

"I will sit on my bed if you seat yourself, madam," I replied. "I could not possibly sit in the presence of a lady who was standing."

"Then sit I shall!" She suited her actions to these words; and the old chair, which always creaked abominably when supporting my weight, uttered not a sound.

I asked whether she did not wish some service of me, for it appeared to me, my initial awe having passed, that she would scarcely have mounted two pairs of stairs to a garret save she desired my assistance.

"You are a gentleman," she said, "which makes it all the better; but let me first say that I could not have entered this chamber at all had you not invited me in your dreams. Nor could I have spoken had you not addressed me."

"You are welcome here at any time," I told her.

"Thank you, Brooks. It is an honour, one of which I am truly appreciative." This was said with no hint of levity. "However, I must inform you that I can now enter whenever I wish. From those who invite us once, no second invitation is required. I can never speak, however, unless you invite it. That is the law."

I well understood; our own situation is, as a moment's reflection will show, quite similar. When the matter is urgent, we must clear our throats or cough in the hope that we will be addressed.

"You may have heard my name, or so I flatter myself. I am called Alice Landon. It is not unfamiliar to you?"

"Always with praise," I replied, "though that praise has done little to prepare me for the perfection I observe at the present moment. But if you will allow it, Miss Landon?"

"Speak."

"You were so kind as to style me a gentleman, this although I am, as you surely know, only what is called a gentleman's gentleman."

She laughed again—that thrilling sound. "Why, a gentleman's gentleman is a gentleman twice over, surely. Our dear Queen is waited upon by women who are styled ladies-in-waiting. Do you imagine they are not ladies-in-actuality? They would be dismissed at once. No, you are a gentleman, and I am a ghost. Does that surprise you?"

"It horrifies me," I confessed, "although I guessed it long before. Even though I have heard your name more than once, you were always named as a living lady. Many must bitterly regret your passing, and I count myself among them."

"Allow me to relieve your grief. I am at the present moment still alive, though I shan't live out this pleasant weather."

"If you are not yet gone . . . ?"

"The explanation is easily given, yet difficult to comprehend." She rose sighing and went to the open window. "Indeed, Brooks, I must confess that I myself comprehend it only imperfectly. It will assist us, perhaps, if you are familiar with a tale much read at Christmas. Dickens is the author's name." She turned to face me, smiling. "He is the man who composed *The Pickwick Papers,* unless I am greatly mistaken."

I had risen when she rose. "I have never read those, I fear. Do you intend the tale of Ebenezer Scrooge and Marley's ghost?"

"Yes. Precisely that. I'm happy to find you familiar with it."

"I heard it read," I explained. "My master was asked to spend the holiday at the home of Sir Edward Darby. The tale was read while Sir Edward's guests were seated around the table, and we were permitted to stand behind and listen if we wished. I did, having no work to do just then and thinking it possible my master might require some service."

She smiled; it is a strange woman who is not made more beautiful by a smile. "You are familiar with it at least. You must recall that there were several ghosts."

"I do," I replied. "I was struck most particularly by that of Mr. Scrooge's

former partner. Mr. Marley's ghost seemed to me a most unpleasant—
ah . . ."

"Apparition?"

"Yes, a fearful apparition if I may say it. You . . ." I was seized by a
cough.

"Marley was a most unpleasing person," Miss Landon confided. "I am
somewhat different, or so I hope. Three spectres visited Mr. Scrooge subsequently. Can you name them?"

"Not precisely, perhaps. There was the Ghost of the current Christmas,
by which I mean that of the Christmas we were then celebrating."

"And the others?"

"One who returned, if I may so phrase it, Mr. Scrooge to Christmases
he had celebrated many years ago. After him, I believe there came a third
ghost who vouchsafed him a view of a Christmas that had not yet been."

"Excellent!" Her smile warmed me. "We ghosts are constrained by certain laws; you know of that, for I have already explained a pair of those
to you. We are freed, however, from the domination of certain others. You
living are permitted only one specific time: the present. You can act in the
present, or you cannot act. To plan to act in the future is not to act but only
to intend it. As for the past, it is beyond your reach."

I nodded. "There is much there that I would change if I could."

"You have only the present," she repeated. "This moment, and nothing
more; for us there is Eternity."

I said, "I don't believe I understand that, Miss Landon."

"Understand Eternity, Brooks? Why, neither do I! No one understands
it, nor ever will. It is the place outside all time, and the place that sur-
rounds all time. Because we are there, we can observe all time, and even
visit any time we wish."

"Can you tell me whether I shall ever marry? And to whom, if I shall?"

"I could learn these things, but I will not. They are kept from you for
good reasons—"

The great clock downstairs had begun to toll the hour of twelve, and
so silent was the house at that hour, and so silent the night itself, that the
measured strokes of its steel hammer upon its sounding gong were distinctly audible in my garret.

"I must go." Miss Landon hastened to my window. "You need not
throw up the sash for me, Brooks. You are a most estimable man. I shall
see you anon, and you shall have your reward."

After that, as may well be believed, I did all that I could conceive of to
learn all that I could regarding Miss Landon. She was, it transpired, the

only daughter of a physician who had in addition three stalwart sons, her older brothers. Dr. Landon practiced in Windermere and owned a town house there; he had also, by inheritance, a country house built by his father at the edge of the fells and by him styled Cauldwell Grange. I never learned the reason, assuming that one existed, for this appellation; nor did I make any great effort to do so.

Several descriptions I had of Miss Landon, all more or less accurate. There would be little point in giving them here, since I was soon to see her for myself. She was at that time of marriageable age but not greatly sought after; such suitors as she had were said to be tradesmen's sons and the like. This last I had from my master's father's man, Peter Hugh, who added that Sir Walter thought Miss Landon rather too forward. "As for me," Hugh added with a shrug, "I think her daft."

Naturally I endeavoured to learn the basis for this opinion, but he would say no more upon the topic.

It was the very next day, I believe, that my master consulted me regarding a gift for his mother. "The old girl's birthday," he told me, "will be upon us before we know it, and I must not neglect my duty towards her. The old chap means to invite all manner of guests. How would it look if everyone showers her with silks and laces and all manner of nonsense, while I give her nothing?"

I acknowledged that it would look very bad indeed, thinking furiously all the while.

"Can't you suggest something, Brooks? I gave her a picnic hamper last year, and she liked it or said she did; but I can scarcely give her another."

By that time I had hit upon an idea. "Allow me a day or two, sir," I told him, "and I shall be able to advise you to some purpose."

That very evening I contrived to sit beside Lady Margaret's maid at our supper in the kitchen. It was far from difficult to steer our conversation toward the great dinner planned for The Day, all the extra work that would be involved, Lady Margaret's ever more frequent shopping trips, and the visits of her dressmaker.

"There was the prettiest little book in Cobbler & Bowen's," the maid confided. "All white it was, and gold everywhere. She wanted it ever so much, only then she said what would the master say to paying so much for a little book and put it back."

Thus I was able to tell my own master that a certain collection of the works of the celebrated poetess Elizabeth Browning, a volume in bleached calf with gilt edges, would make an eminently satisfactory gift. Together we journeyed to Windermere; it was still in the shop, and he purchased it forthwith.

He was in so fine a mood thereafter that I made bold to broach the matter of Miss Landon, asking whether she would be at Lady Margaret's dinner. He pretended to know nothing of her; the pinchbeck falsity of his disclaimer shone like brass, and so it was that I ventured a statement of the same kidney, saying that it was alleged among the servants that he and Miss Landon were soon to wed.

"Oh," said he, "you intended Miss Alice Landon? I had supposed you spoke of an older sister. I have met her, but as for intending her, there is little enough to recommend her to any man."

"Then she will not be at the dinner, sir?"

"Well now," he replied with a feigned indifference, "I've no way of knowing. The mater has seen the lady's pater regarding some complaint or other, faintness from tight lacing if I were to guess; so the Landons may have been invited. I really wouldn't know."

Recollecting the ghost, I remarked that Miss Landon possessed good features, and he shrugged. "If you care for blotches, she'll do well enough, I suppose. Yellow hair and blue eyes give her some charm from a distance. That much I'll allow."

I scratched my head.

"What puzzles you so, Brooks?"

I said, "Why, I had heard that you and she were to be united next summer, sir, and now I cannot imagine what gave rise to so absurd a report."

"Nor can I. She's a bit daft, they say, and hasn't a farthing. Oh, I've spoken to her and danced, and all that. One must have a partner for the waltzes, and most of these country misses outweigh the white heifer."

"She has no prospects then?"

He laughed. He had a most hearty and most engaging laugh, sir; I feel that I can hear it even as we speak. "From a medico?" he asked. "And there are four brothers."

I ventured a few further questions, but learned little of substance. Needless to say, I awaited the dinner, and the dancing which was to follow it, styled by some a ball, with the highest interest. For reasons I cannot explain, I felt confident that Miss Landon's ghost should not trouble me until I had seen Miss Landon in the flesh. In that, I was wholly mistaken, for I woke to find her bending over my bed.

"The time grows short," she said. "I've tried to come to you before, Brooks, but was prevented."

"N-n-not b-by me, I hope, madam," I ventured, and at once discovered that my teeth chattered.

She gave my question no heed. "I must soon die, save you prevent it. Will you not save me?"

I nodded, though fumbling for the matches I had placed next to my lamp.

"You are not going to light that, I hope. I'd thought better of you."

"I fear I dream. I wish to see if it be so." Even as I spoke, I struck a match on the floorboard; she weakened and backed away from its flare of light and hellish smoke.

"And will you light the gas, beast?"

That was my purpose; rising from my bed, I turned the valve and applied the flame.

"Do you dream, or no?"

Though I could no longer see her, I had heard her voice. "I do not dream," I conceded. "Where are you?"

"Not in hell, the place to which you would consign me if you could." Her tone was despairing.

"I would consign no soul to hell," I said.

"In that, you differ from God, Brooks. Would you save a soul from hell if you could?"

"Who would not?"

"Millions. Extinguish the light and I shall show you how it may be done."

"No, madam." I shook my head.

"Then I must tell you, and that only. First, I must tell you that I seek to save my own life. You saw me in this very chamber not so long ago. Did you think me young and fair?"

"Very much so, Miss Landon."

"So I will die, Brooks, save you prevent it."

"And go to hell? Surely not!"

"Not I, but my murderer." Her voice was fainter, yet still distinct. "Would you be blessed, Brooks? Blessed as the saints were? Would you join those who sit at the right hand of the Lord? Prevent my murder, and you shall. I swear it! Although I do not decide these things, I know how they are decided."

"But, madam," I began.

"Have you a knife? You need but—"

"Oh, Miss Landon! Do not speak of that, I beg you." I wept then, and turning back to my bed buried my face in the sheet, but wept still.

"You bear the mark of Cain." Her whisper was an icy caress. "I did not know it, but am cognizant of it now. I shall tell you how that mark may be expunged anon."

I wept on until at length I felt the touch of a female hand; at it, my tears ceased, and I sat bolt upright, for it had not been the chill digits of the ghost I had felt upon my shoulder but the warm fingers of a living woman. One of the housemaids, hearing my sobs, had come in to enquire as to their cause.

"I am weeping for my sins," I told her. "At times I wake in the night and am oppressed by them."

"Are they many?" You may laugh at the naïveté of the question, but the sympathy it held touched me deeply.

"I hope not," I said, "but there is one . . ." I could not complete the thought.

"You have repented of it."

I nodded. "A hundred times over."

"In that case, God has forgiven you, Mr. Brooks. You must come to forgive yourself."

We talked longer, but I need not give it all. When we parted, I said, "There are spirits of evil abroad, Kate. Tonight I have learned that the angels of Heaven move among them." I do not believe she grasped my meaning.

The great day arrived, and brought so many guests that every servant who could be made presentable was needed to wait upon them all; and, indeed, we might have made good use of a round dozen more. Eleven courses made the meal; and though I had scarcely a moment to take breath between serving and clearing, I had also many occasions to steal a glimpse at the living Miss Alice Landon. Her golden hair and wide blue eyes were her best features, and I verily believe that those alone might have made her fortune on the stage. If her complexion were blotched, as my master had alleged, its disfigurements were well concealed by powder. She was, possibly, some trifle too slim for fashionable beauty; but that was a fault the mere passage of time would likely mend.

I tried not to stare at her, yet ere long I realized that she was staring at me, and I thought her expression both wondering and puzzled. When I was clearing off the game, I saw her whisper to the young gentleman to her right; it seemed clear that she was enquiring about me, and had received a satisfactory answer, too, for she nodded at it. Her satisfaction, however, did not put an end to her stares.

Her ghost came again that night, not a moment after I had stretched my weary frame upon my bed. "This is the night," she told me; her voice held a breathless urgency I had not heard before. "I will not speak of the mark you bear upon your immortal soul, nor seek to learn whom it was you killed—"

I sat up. "I must tell someone," I exclaimed, "or else go mad. It was I who slew Mr. Bolter, third mate of the *Jack Robinson*."

"We have not time—"

"You need me," I whispered, "thus you shall listen as I speak, and for as long as it takes me to tell my tale. For if you do not listen, you shall surely die this night."

She nodded a reluctant acquiescence.

"I had been in a fight in a low dive in Shanghai. It has never been my custom to frequent such places, but no others were available to common sailors. The better places, though they were very bad, were not so bad as to admit us. I had been knocked down and kicked. Yes, I who had been so often kicked on board had been kicked worse ashore. Kicked and spat upon. I lay doggo then, playing dead until the fight was over and all those who still lived had left. Then I opened my eyes again and found very near my right hand a long dagger, double-edged, with an ivory grip. I picked it up."

I paused and found I had already stood, although I had not been conscious of it; I looked at my right hand, recalling that carved grip, and how it had felt to grasp it. "I took it, and was glad to have it. My first thought was that I might meet some of my previous foes outside, *Kestrel* men who would attack me again. Then that such a finely made weapon might be sold for a good sum to one of the many shops in that city. I had not gone more than a street or two before I saw walking before me my tormentor of a year's time and more; his swagger, and the tilt of his cap, identified him at once. I had no need to see his face, and if I had seen that face I think I might have thrust the dagger into both his eyes before I had done."

"You killed him." The ghost's sigh held no question. "Because you did, I, who can but rarely converse with the living, have been able to converse with you."

"I did. I stabbed him from behind and saw him turn and goggle at me, and watched him fall. There had been no mistake. I had killed John Frederick Bolter, third mate of the *Jack Robinson*. I had been avenged, but the price was the blood-guilt I bear to this hour."

"You can expunge that guilt by preventing my murder, Brooks. You can expunge it by killing the man who will kill me." By all that is holy those words should have been delivered in an invidious whisper. So we are taught, and so temptation speaks upon the stage. It was not so for me that night. I heard only the faint voice of the spectre of a desperate young woman, a desperate woman pleading for my help; and I asked who he was, and where he might be found.

"He is in a room of this house, and it is a room that you may enter at any time without arousing suspicion."

I knew then, and felt as though a bucket of icy seawater had been flung into my face. "You intend my master," I said. "I will never raise my hand against him."

"Then I must die tonight!"

My answer was to strike a match and light the gas. By the time its lambent light had filled the room, the ghost was gone.

She came again, an hour before dawn, and woke me with her icy touch. "Sit up, I beg you. You refused the great service I asked of you. I ask a small one now. I perished by violence and died a virgin. You have not earned my blessing, but you may yet escape my curse."

I sat up, rubbing my eyes.

"My body lies unprotected upon the hill, Brooks. Listen!"

I did, and heard far off the lonely howling of some cur.

"Wild dogs rove the fells, and are the curse of the shepherds. Doubtless you have heard of it. They will savage my body when they find it. I ask that you bear it to some place where it will be discovered quickly. No more than that, and it is the last service I shall ever ask of anyone. Won't you come to my assistance? I implore you!"

I rose, dressed, and followed her. It was two miles, perhaps, to the place where her body lay. By the light of the dimming stars I stood and looked down upon it. No living woman, the thought was inescapable, sir, had ever looked so fair as Miss Alice Landon did then, recumbent upon the rocky soil, her eyes closed and her skirt above her knees.

Kneeling, I felt her wrist. There was no pulse. I swear that there was none. Her flesh was not yet cold, though not as warm as that of a living person.

"He struck my neck, and all his hatred and disdain were in the blow. It was sufficient, for girls such as I was are not so difficult to kill as rabbits."

There was yet no stench of decay, only a faint perfume as of lilies of the valley.

"You would not save me, and I know that you will not avenge me. Take me now, if you wish. It will be release for you; and I, who never knew love in life, shall know it in death."

I hesitated, and she said, "Do you imagine that you will be the first man to ravish a corpse? You go where tens of thousands have gone before you, and you will leave in your wake no bitter tears."

God help me, sir, I did as she had suggested. When I rose, she was gone. I called out to her, but received no response.

I had promised to carry her to a place where she would soon be found; I did so and set out to avenge her. Of my desperate struggle with my master I shall say nothing. The court has recorded it, and posterity may read of it if it chooses. Suffice it to say that his shouts and the sounds of my blows roused the whole house. Those who would have rescued him arrived too late, but subdued me without the least struggle.

A fettered prisoner in a cell has no news save what his visitors bring him, and I had no visitors until my trial had begun. Conceive, then, of my amazement when I saw Miss Landon in the courtroom, seated primly beside her father. She sobbed quite audibly when the condition of my master's body was described, and I could do nothing and say nothing.

Her father came alone the next day to hear the jury's verdict, and to my astonishment visited me in my cell not long after I was returned to it.

"You live wretchedly here," he said.

To which I nodded. "Wretchedly, and not long."

"Do you smoke? I will give you a cigar."

Shaking my head, I thanked him.

"A tot of brandy then." He unscrewed the top of his walking stick and passed it to me. I took a good long swallow, thanked him, and returned it to him. You are not to believe from my drinking so that the thought of poison had not crossed my mind. He was a physician, after all, and might readily have introduced some devilish compound; but I had sooner died in my cell than wait there to be hanged.

He wiped the rim and drank himself, and truly drank, for I saw the movement of his throat. A handkerchief served to blot his lips. "It is my understanding," he told me, "that prisoners in possession of funds may buy certain comforts here, things sold by the warders. Shillings might be best, I suppose. I will give you twenty if you desire them, and a one-pound note to wrap them in."

I thanked him and accepted the money. "You wish my friendship, plainly," I declared. "You have it. How can such a wretch as I be of service to you?"

"First, I am indebted to you. The man you slew broke my daughter's heart. Were you aware of it?"

I confessed that it had been hinted in my hearing.

"She mourns his passing. I do not."

"Sir, I understand."

"She came out last season. It was thought then, by her mother, by her brothers, and by Alice herself, that she would be married in a matter of months. She rejected other suitors, thinking it cruel to encourage them."

Waiting, I nodded.

"His ardour waned. As I speak of your master, I assume you were to some degree aware of it."

"I asked him once," I said, "about a report that he was to marry your daughter. He disparaged it, saying he enjoyed dancing with her, and that alone had given rise to the gossip."

"They were quite close, not long ago. I had begun to think of him as another son." Dr. Landon sighed. "Would you defame my daughter, Brooks, were I to put it in your power?"

"Certainly not, sir."

He nodded, mostly, I would say, to himself. "You are a good and a decent man, though you sleep here upon straw. I would save you if I could."

I thanked him.

"Perhaps I can do something. I doubt it, but I shall make the attempt. If ever in your life you have been honest, answer me honestly now. My daughter is ruined, Brooks. You take my meaning, I feel certain."

"Yes, sir. I do."

"Her child will be my grandchild. I will not neglect my duty to that child, nor to her. Tell me plainly. Was your late master my grandchild's father?"

"I cannot answer," I replied. "I can say only that he confided nothing of the sort to me."

"It is not unknown for a young gentleman to pursue a young woman and, when he has had his way with her, treat her with detestation."

"No, sir," I said. "It is not."

"You killed him."

"Sir, I did."

He shook my hand and turned to go, but did not shout for the warder, turning back to me instead. "My daughter suffers fainting spells, a disorder by no means uncommon among young women. It is part and parcel with the green sickness."

I waited.

"She lies, sometimes for hours, quite insensible, and seems scarcely to breathe. At such times, she dreams that her soul departs her body and ventures abroad, committing mischief. It is no more than a fancy, you understand."

"I do, sir."

"And yet . . ." He shrugged. "There is a doctor in Vienna who holds that there is a second mind below the one we inhabit. If that seems less than clear, I can but say it is by no means clear to me. That mind, he alleges, has fears and desires unconstrained by morality. His theories interest me because Alice's dreams often seem the products of such a mind. I do not allege that he is correct, and in fact I think it more probable that he is mistaken."

"I agree," I said. "It seems quite impossible. Would not such a mind require a separate soul?"

"I should think so. I tell you this because you may have heard that she is mad. She is not, and upon the point I give you my word as a physician. She is only a girl who dreams, and gives her dreams much more credence than they deserve. You have done her a kindness, intended or not. Someday she may be sensible of it."

I said, "Thank you, sir."

He smiled. "I shall send my solicitor to you, Brooks. He is a good man, kind, and not much older than yourself. He may be able to do something for you. I hope so."

There is no more to tell. I have recounted my story to that solicitor, Mr. Josiah Willis, who has inscribed this record as I spoke. He promises me it will never be made public but that he will exhibit it to the child Alice Landon bears when that child is of age. Thus the child, whom I believe my own, shall know who I was and why I was hanged. There is a God in Heaven, I know, and He must know how sincerely I have repented. I pray that He will make this record known not only to Miss Landon's child but to all my descendants, unto the seventh generation and beyond.

[So many years have passed since James Brooks told his story to Mr. Josiah Willis that no harm can come of making his account public. In no other way can his dying wish be granted, or so the matter appears to us. No doubt the same thought motivated the publisher of the pamphlet.]

Afterword to "Why I Was Hanged"

"Why I Was Hanged" owes as much to Nigel Price as it does to me. Nigel, who is intimately familiar with the culture of Victorian England, spent much time and effort in meticulously checking facts and practices. I owe him much more than this brief mention.

—GENE WOLFE

Margo Lanagan

Margo Lanagan has won four World Fantasy Awards in four different categories, including Best Short Story, and her short stories have won and been short-listed for many other awards. Her fourth collection, *Yellowcake,* was published in Australia by Allen & Unwin in March 2011, and her next novel, based on her WFA-winning novella "Sea-Hearts" (from *X6: a novellanthology,* ed. Keith Stevenson, coeur de lion publishing, 2008), will be published in 2012. Margo lives in Sydney and is currently working as a technical writer and an arts bureaucrat. She has never seen a ghost (sigh).

MARGO LANAGAN

The Proving of Smollett Standforth

ALWAYS SHE SPRANG from the same dark corner. Smoll could never anticipate the moment she would appear, though night after night she came in the same way and performed the same actions in the same order. He fixed his attention on the place, all terrified expectation, but each night her appearance startled him as greatly as it had the first time. She seemed to wait, indeed, before she leapt forth, for approaching sleep to lower his guard by a fraction, to loosen his joints and sinews, to slow his heartbeat to a pace no more urgent than would be expected of an organ going to its rest upon a day's gainful industry.

The corner from which she rushed was not the corner with the door. Or at least not the door Smoll used himself—and Mrs. Gallon used it too, he supposed, for she swept and grumbled everywhere about the house, so it was likely she swept and grumbled here too—and which a casual observer would maintain was the only door to the attic room. No, there had once been a door in the other corner. By day, seams in the wall showed where boards had been used to seal it, and in Pinkney's room below, short, staggered lines in the wallboards showed where steps so steep as to be almost a ladder had once angled up. Not only was the night-lady a phantom herself, she also emerged from a phantom house. Eyeing the rectangle of the no-longer-existent doorway, Smoll wondered about the person—a grown man, stronger and more practical and authoritative than Smoll was—who had tried to shut her out, the tilting woman, her beads, her voice. And when all the sawing and hammering and painting over had failed, the man, sensibly, had gathered up his household and left. Smoll wished heartily that he could pursue them. *Please, oh please!* he wished he could say. *Let me come with you, to whatever safe place you found!*

It was not that Mr. Beecham's house was not perfectly safe in the daytime, and full of distractions—even, on occasion, amusements, even for a boy so timid and easily mortified as Smoll. But nighttime always loomed again. Always the glad morning (the darkness easing, the clop of the passing milk-horse giving him heart) was followed—no, rushed upon, hurried out of mind, pounced on and briskly swept aside as of no account—by oncoming evening. However much Smoll lingered over the boots in the evening (*See your face in 'em yet?* Ridley would say, passing behind him with the last slop pail from the kitchen), there would come a point where they were done, when they were placed each pair outside the doors: Mister's and Missus's, Miss Edwina's, Miss Pargeter's, Miss Annabelle's, Master Howard's, Mr. Pinkney's—and sometimes Mr. Rossiter the coachman's as well, those wonderful long boots with all their mud that Smoll was always so grateful for. And Smoll having placed them must proceed up his flight of tiny stairs, through the hole in his floor, through the door not much larger than a coalhole cover. He must shut himself away behind that door, shake off his clothes and shrug on his chilled nightshirt and leap abed, blow out the candle and wrap himself tightly in the clean patched sheet and the blanket—as if tonight of all nights that wrapping, that tightness, might be effective against her, when every previous night, since first Smoll had been elevated from country scamp to Beecham's boot boy, it had utterly failed to protect him.

"Smoll, are you well?"

"Quite well, thank you, Mr. Pinkney."

"It is only that you have . . . well, rather a *burdened* look about you."

Smoll felt it and unrounded his shoulders. "Oh no, sir. I am nothing like so burdened as I was at home, carrying water and wood."

"That is better, Smoll. It behooves a young man to maintain a good posture, whether he be in the public gaze or no, do you not think?"

"Yes, sir."

She was neither old nor young, the dream-lady; she was neither beautiful nor monstrous to look upon. She was *difficult* to look upon; though her presence was so sudden and so strong in the sensations it produced, her actual shape was indistinct against the surrounding darkness, except in the middle, where it resembled an hourglass. Above and below the narrow waist, she was corseted into a shape that even Smoll, whose eyes were so often cast down in the presence of ladies, or indeed of anyone taller or more important than himself, recognized as old-fashioned. Below this shape she gave to skirts that faded to nothingness, although their rustlings pressed most forcefully upon his ear. Above it, her flat-bound bosom and hunched shoulders supported a head all the more terrible for being entirely without features, except for the impression of a wealth of hair, pulled and piled and pinned into place with the same energy of compression that had been exerted on the body below. Tightness, tightness was all, about this body and about the personage that was borne about in it—tightness and a little madness, which the tightness held in check.

She carried her faceless head with an intent tilt, and it was in this tiltedness that Smoll's fear formed, for she was intent on *him;* she tilted her head at *him.* He would scramble upright in the bed, his back pressed to the wall, the back of his head hard against the frame of the little uncurtained window, which, admitting as it might the fullest moonlight or the strongest effusions of a clear night's stars, never showed him what he needed to see of the woman, never illuminated her brightly enough to convince him that he had seen all the evil there was to see of her, that he now knew what she was, that he could begin to bring some measure of rationality to his encounters with her. Instead he only underwent yet again this deep abjection, this wholesale shrinking of body and being from whatever she was, whatever she wanted.

For she did want something; she made the same demand of him night after night. She rattled the beads in her hands and pushed them at Smoll, pushed them *into* him sometimes. Did her touch itself, her thrusting at his middle, produce those pond ripples of horror up and down him, or was only the *idea* of her touch, in his appalled mind, sufficient to generate them?

The beads themselves were grotesque, bulbous; her handfuls of them reminded him of Arthur Cleal at Hobson's farm, gathering up innards after the butchering, the slippery tubes and organs overflowing the bowl of his hands.

Take it, she hissed, and shook the thing and pushed it at him again. *Take it; I don't want it.* Her voice was muddied—from having crossed time to reach him, perhaps, or from the invisibility of her mouth. She was hurried and guilty; she crouched at him. *'Tis not as if I can ever wear it. Take it!*

He might say *No*. He might say *I don't want it either*. He might ask her who she was and why she plagued him. Whatever he said, fear crawled and shook in his voice. And she always answered the same, angrily: *Take it!*, bobbing at him, bobbing into him a little, bobbing back. There might be the flash of an eye, fixing on him with horrible inexactitude, as if she were blind; there might be something of a mouth, a ghost of teeth, momentarily, against the hollow attic room behind her, which resounded with the muddied sounds of ghost steps. *What would I do with it, for heaven's sake? Take it! Take it, before Mistress comes!*

AT FIRST HE felt only faint pains, here and there about his neck, a slight heat in the skin of his chest where the locket lay. Sometimes these were itches and no more, and if he lifted the neck of his shirt to search for signs of them, he saw no mark—the first few times, the pains themselves eased utterly, he was so reassured by the sight of his clear skin.

Then a redness began to grow and to glow in the flesh there, visible in the light of a bright day outdoors but not by candlelight or lamp. The reddened skin was sensitive to the touch of a finger or the rubbing of shirt cloth; if he scratched it absentmindedly it would sting and burn, and the pain of that would linger.

There rose blisters, then, pepperings of them where each bead had lain in the night, and a flowering on his breast from the locket's weight. They burst and itched and wept, and the skin stayed raw; sometimes by nightfall it had healed dry, but the dream-lady's visit would inflame it again, when she forced the unnatural burden of the ghost beads on him.

The wounds never quite bled; at worst they leaked a watery fluid that stained Smoll's shirt and nightshirt yellow. "What have you spilt on yourself?" Cook might scold him, but it was less a question than a lament at the general carelessness of boys, and she did not pursue him for an explanation.

THE DREAM-LADY WOULD thrust the beads one last nervous time at Smoll, her shining, rattling handfuls of them. His own hands would turn palm up to take them. He was an obedient boy, and before he had left to live here his mother had kissed him and instructed him to do exactly as he was told by all at Mr. Beecham's house. Also, he was afraid that the beads, if he did not catch them, would slither and crash to the floor. The noise they would make terrified him enough; the consequences of such a concussion, he could not begin to imagine.

And once she had poured the beads into his hands, their weight and coldness compelled him; he understood himself to have made some kind of pledge in accepting them. There was no handing the necklace back, however much it pained him to hold it, the weight like a load of polished river stones. They chilled his hands, and the dragging of the overspilt ones made his whole arms shake. She had pushed them out of her time into his, and by taking them he had taken them *on,* somehow; he had become responsible for them. *That's right—you have it!* she now exulted, and she had an eye again, a jagged gleam on the darkness as she nodded. *It's beautiful, isn't it?*

He might say *Yes.* He might creak out the truth: *It is the ugliest thing I have ever seen.* He might gather the spills of beads or leave them depending from the fat gold locket for which the whole embarrassment of ivory, amber, and jet had been assembled. No matter what he chose to do—if choice, indeed, played any part in it—she would nod and gleam in the same way; the same impression of her tight smile would hang there in the night before him. *Put it on,* she now said; they were only partway through whatever bewitchment she was working. Her voice issued not from her tensed lips but from the fearful air all around; it rose at Smoll from inside him, from the marrow of his own small bones.

Always he put the necklace on, although it was cold, and painfully heavy. The sooner he put it on, the sooner this trial would end.

You see? The woman melted into relief. Her head tilted more. Her smile flickered, then became more distinct; for an appalling moment it was too large for her face, the next instant it shrank too small, then the mouth was extinguished altogether. *It suits you,* she said unctuously, mouthlessly. Then she leaned forward and hissed, *Hide it under your clothes, before Mistress comes and sees.*

He did as she bid him, covering the noose of beads and locket with his nightshirt. Each time they made him gasp, the cold striking through his breastbone, the sudden weight straining at his neck.

Yes, that's right, the lady would say—she was not a lady, of course; she was a servant like himself. She leaned at him; she had eyes and teeth. Her words caught up with her mouth, and some nights he would feel not only the ice-burden of the beads but also feathers of her historical breath against his face and front. By now he was fixed and imprisoned, by the beads and by his fear, by her face tilted forward, her forehead white and broad, the eyes wide and drinking up the sight of the hidden necklace.

Then she would be gone. But the necklace would stay, coldly burning. And the horror of her presence stayed too, the boxed-in attic air crawling with it as a street-dog's coat crawls with vermin. All Smoll's skin crawled too, and his ears still heard her hisses, and his spine still jolted with the ghost noises behind her, the ghost steps climbing the nonexistent stairs.

When the steps ceased, and the fear loosened its hold on him sufficiently, he lay back down, crushed to his little bed by the beads and locket, collared and chained down. To breathe, to lift the locket weight on his chest and let in air underneath, he must summon some force and determination. He lay entirely imprisoned, hauling himself from breath to breath, and whether he failed in that effort for want of air, or the task of breathing exhausted him, eventually he would sleep.

"WHY, LOOK HERE! A letter has come for a Master Smollett Standforth."

Smoll looked up from his porridge. Mr. Pinkney placed the note before him. "Posture, boy!" Smoll straightened, and the raw skin of the sores crinkled and burned beneath his shirt.

"That's a nice hand," said Cook, passing behind him with her own bowl.

"The priest will have written it," he said, "for my ma."

Cook sat all bustle across the table corner from him. "Shall I read it to you?"

"Please, if you would." He pushed it towards her. He did not want it near. It promised nothing but complications, and he had not the energy to accommodate them.

"I hope it is not bad news." Cook gave him a kind and serious look through her porridge steam. She examined the glossy seal with approval before breaking it, then she labored through some of the writing within. "She hopes you are well," she said, "and she sends you her love. They are all well there—no bad news, then." Cook patted Smoll's hand before toiling on. "Only Biss has been laid low with a fever. That has broken. All is well. She is coming good. Biss is your sister?"

"She is my cousin. But she lives with us, as good as a sister." And Smoll lost his good posture again, thinking of Biss waving him off in the carriage that day, a little weeping to lose him; of Biss laughing too much sometimes and having to be sat and calmed; of Biss ill and subdued, lying abed (unimaginable!), and how he had not been there to help Ma care for her or to share in the worrying.

"Ah, here is the business. 'Your brother Dravitt has come into the good fortune of being apprenticed to Nape's uncle George Paste down at Caunterbury, and he will be coming through London on the twenty-ninth of January—' " Cook read on, frowning, crouched over the letter. If he had not known her, by her expression right now he would have thought her a most bad-tempered person.

"Your porridge will get cold," said Smoll. His own porridge was all spooned up and eaten, fast and nervously, he had been rendered so self-conscious by the letter, and by his home life being brought out around the breakfast table, here in his new life. It pained him, the thought of Ma relaying to the priest all she wanted Smoll to know, and the way the priest had corrected and embroidered her words with priest language, putting himself and his education between Smoll and his ma.

"She hopes Mr. Beecham will permit young Dravitt to stay here a night on his journey, is the sense of it, boiled down."

They both looked to Mr. Pinkney, at the far end of the table with his tea and thin toast, his braces and his white, white shirtfront on which never a drop was spilt, never a crumb was deposited.

Pinkney tipped his head, sipped his tea. "I am sure Mr. Beecham will have no objection. Dravitt, is it?, should be no trouble to us, sharing your little eyrie for a night." He took another sip and glanced along the table, a glint in his eye. "Unless he is of a much different make from yourself, Smoll. Is he a wild boy, your brother?"

"Oh no, sir. Drav would be timider than me, by far."

"Oh, Smoll." Cook laughed a little at Smoll's earnestness and gave his hand a brisk rub where it lay there on the table.

He barely noticed, he was so occupied with the warring emotions inside him. He felt a stab of missing Dravitt and all the littlies, and Biss and Ma, and the house, and all around it, the village he knew, so humdrum, every stone and weed of it, every codger and kid. This keen distress was cut through by the relief it would be to see Drav again and show his new life to him—yet it would be pain, too, for it would agitate Smoll's homesickness, which until now had been thoroughly obscured by the novelty of his new duties and worries. And all these complexities were in turn flattened by the stark dread, the absolute impossibility of Drav's visiting, the intractable necessity for Mr. Pinkney and Mr. Beecham to forbid it. *Sharing your little eyrie for a night*—that must not happen. Drav must never endure a night with Smoll in the attic room! Clearly Cook and Pinkney knew nothing of what happened up there, once the household slept. Smoll gathered up his posture again, lifted his chin, and the necklace of raw patches stretched and twinged.

"I will ask Mr. Beecham this morning," said Pinkney, "but I dare say he will be entirely happy with the idea."

IT WAS NEAR a fortnight before Dravitt was to come. Smoll proceeded towards the day mazed with terror. Dravitt must not see the dream-lady, he knew that much. He *certainly* must not be forced to take her beads. But even if Smoll took them himself, as usual, how could he save Drav from being terrified by the whole transaction, by the mere sight of the woman, by her voice—now foggy, now sharp and clear—by her urgent attentions?

In a bid to be moved from the attic room he revealed his wounds one morning to Cook. "Gracious!" she cried. "How long have you gone about like this? Look at the boy, Pinkney! What are these? Have you seen anything like them?" And they turned Smoll about and exclaimed some more, the pair of them.

But all they did was smother the lesions with a strong-smelling grease that Cook mixed up, that everyone remarked on and made faces at when Smoll was near—everyone but the dream-lady, who only went at him with her customary combination of impatience and flattery. *It suits you,* she said just the same, as the beads burned on Smoll's slippery chest, and the attic room might have been suspended from a hot air balloon miles above the Beecham house, or might be a wind-whipped hut out on the Arctic ice, for all the help he could expect from beyond its walls.

The night before Dravitt was due, Cook made Smoll bathe, his own small personal bath so that he would not infect anyone with his disease, if infectious he was. He sank back disconsolate in the stinging, soothing water, behind the screen in the kitchen. *Don't rub at them; just soak,* Cook had said, and so he soaked, staring up at the ceiling and listening to Cook come and go, and others who must be explained to, about Smoll and his condition, and his coming brother. *We will bandage you up, the night he's here,* Cook had said, *and put clean sheets on your bed, so's he doesn't catch it. We don't want to send him down Caunterbury covered in bibulous plague, do we? Won't impress his new master.*

Soggy warm from bathing and freshly anointed with the foul salve, Smoll tottered upward through the cold house, carrying his candle and the wrapped hot-brick for his bed. He would meet Dravitt at the coach tomorrow afternoon; Drav would be looking out for him, excited, perhaps a little frightened that Smoll would not be there; when he saw Smoll he would beam, all relief and pleasure at having a companion in his adventure. He would be looking to Smoll for advice, for explanation. He knew nothing of the world, Dravitt, and he was very small (though he would have grown some since Smoll last saw him in the summer); he was easily cowed.

Smoll stood on the steep wooden steps, halfway through the floor into his room, clutching his brick and candle there on the threshold of his exile. The very air felt different here; the top half of him was tainted with its solitude and horror, while his legs stood in a freer, kindlier atmosphere below. He summoned his energies and stepped up wholly into the attic and went to the bed and put down the candle and tucked the hot-brick under the blankets. Then he came back and closed the door in the floor, shutting himself in, untethering himself from the safety of Beecham's household. He climbed into bed, the bed that Dravitt would be sharing tomorrow. He blew out the candle with a frosty breath and hugged the hot-brick to his stomach, and he wept a little for Dravitt, for Dravitt's innocence (which once he himself had shared), and for the distance he was from home and Biss and Ma, and for his own want of courage.

He was dozing when the attic announced the dream-lady's imminence, its cold air curdling, hostile, its space become a little theatre where only unpleasant things might play out. Then she rustled at him out of the darkness, the hourglass waist of her, the cocked featureless head. She thrust at him her handfuls of gleam: *Take it.* Smoll flattened to the wall as always, without deciding to; the fear never lessened, however well he knew her, however often she uttered the same words. There was something distressing, indeed, in their repetition, in the mechanical nature of her performance, the fact that she could be neither paused nor halted.

The necklace shone in the darkness. *What would I do with it, for heaven's sake?* hissed the rustling lady, and Smoll's flesh crept from her touch, and his salved wounds winced and pained. His hands unstuck themselves from the wall as they always did, because he was obedient, and because she would go away if he obeyed, and the most important thing in the world was that she go away.

He had thought he had no room, when the woman was there, for considering or scheming, for outwitting her. She took him over, he had thought, and his whole being underwent her visitation, was ground through it like meat through Cook's great dark mincing machine down in the kitchen.

But tonight he found that he did have an extra thought spare, a small pocket in his mind where ruled, unafraid because unaware, his younger brother—not Dravitt as he would be now, skinny and bright faced and ready to start his new life apprenticing, but Dravitt when he was small and round and red curled, a plaything for Smollett and his sisters; the sleep-sodden Dravitt whom Smollett had carried home after the midsummer bonfire; the Dravitt who had run stout and screaming with laughter, Biss and Clara pursuing him, towards Smollett, whose one hand was tip-fingered on the oak that was Home for this game, whose other reached out to Drav, so that he might reach safety sooner.

The beads began to rattle, from the lady's hands to Smoll's, and to weigh on his palms, fall over his fingers. In the cold light of the winter moon pouring through the attic window each bead was vaguely its own color, the ghostly ivory, the implacable jet, the flecked transparent warmth-that-was-not-warm of the amber. They piled and slid on Smoll's palms; the woman's white hands were emptying; her breath from the other time blew warm, sour and intent on his forehead. He had only these few moments while she poured, while she reached through from her time to his; once the last bead left her grasp, he would be helpless against her returning tomorrow and including his brother in her terrors.

"No." Smoll's voice was small, ineffectual. No matter. The voice it was uttered in did not matter.

He grasped a bead and sprang with it up from his bed. He pushed his arms through from his time into hers, forced his head into the cold syrup of the past. "No," he said to the woman's clear, bright-eyed face, to her alarm, to the smell of the past, to the smell that filled the past house of an old, gone meal, part of it burnt. Against the force of her will and her magic, with all his small strength he pushed the loop of beads back through the thick air and over her head.

He forced it down around her neck. Her face, aghast, almost touched his. "Mistress!" cried Smoll into the syrup, dropping to the bed again, dragging on the necklace, all but swinging from it. "Come quickly! She has your necklace, your lock—"

Her hand stopped his cry. It was not a soft lady's hand; it was worked to leather, cold and strong and real, and smelled of laundry soap. She took him by the mouth and by his nightshirted ribs, and hissing she began to push him out of her time, her eyes wild, her eyes *afraid* as he had never seen them. He saw the enormity of what he was doing, the disgrace and punishment it would entail for her, not a ghost-woman or a dream-woman at all but an ordinary servant like himself, whose good name in her household was the only wealth that she had in the world. Still he fought to stay, to make his voice heard in the house of her time, to make as much noise there as he could, whether words or no. He yammered behind her hand; he threw himself about to loosen her grip on his mouth, and let out more noise.

Slowly her strength succeeded against his—but he had not meant to conquer, only to delay her, only to keep her fighting and in possession of the necklace until the other person, the maker of the dream-footfalls, reached the top of the stairs and entered. He listened for the mistress through the strain and pain and noise of the struggle. His ears were right at the border between the two times now, and all sounds were warped there, the dream-lady's grunts compressed into quacks, her panting concertina'd to weirdly musical whistles. The knocking on the attic door he heard as thunder; the mistress's voice was a god's calling across a breadth of sky.

And then as the doorknob rumbled in its turning, the servant-woman pushed Smoll wholly through the divide, the magicked aperture between the times, back into his rightful night. As she and her era fell away, as she shrank, she tore the necklace off and flung it after him. Soundlessly it splashed against the intervening time as against a window between herself and Smoll. She watched in dismay as it fell, and the door opened behind her no bigger than a playing card now, and the dark opening swallowed up woman and beads and attic and all.

The two times snapped apart to their proper distances; Smoll felt the event of that, in his ears and in the punching of air into his throat and lungs. Somewhere between sprawled and sitting, he stared from his rumpled bed, out into a darkness utterly free of reverberations. No dread sang there, and no historical glee resounded. No weight sat bead by bead around his neck or ached against his breastbone. There was only Smoll in his eyrie, the odor of Cook's salve, warm from his exertions, clouding up from the neck of his nightshirt, the light of the moon pouring down on him from the window.

Afterword to "The Proving of Smollett Standforth"

"The Proving of Smollett Standforth" started out as a more alt-history, regularly steampunkish story about an upper-middle-class boy and his sister. The story was told from her point of view, and the boy was brought near to death by the ghost's visitations, but the sister was the one who vanquished the evil amber-necklace-bearing ghost-chambermaid in the end. That version had an extra romance, a seaside holiday, many tea palaces and decorative floral arrangements throughout, but it always felt to me as if I was playing around with these pretty things slightly to one side of the real story.

Coming back to Smollett, I realized that the engine of the story was my own memories of lying in bed as a child imagining malign beings creeping towards me in the dark, while everyone else in the house slept. The terrible solitude of this haunting and the fact that Smollett can't bring himself to confide in anyone are what works for me. So in the end I stripped away all the interesting interior decoration (and even the gaslight—the poor boy has to use a candle!) *and* the sympathetic sister and made Smollett the hero of his own story.

—Margo Lanagan

Sean Williams

Number one *New York Times*–bestselling author Sean Williams has been called "the premier Australian speculative fiction writer of the age," the "Emperor of Sci-Fi," and the "King of Chameleons" for the diversity of his output, which spans fantasy, science fiction, horror, and even the odd poem. He has published thirty-five novels and seventy-five short stories. These include works for adults (Philip K. Dick Award–nominated *Saturn Returns*, Ditmar and Aurealis Award–winning *The Crooked Letter*), young adults (Locus-recommended *The Storm Weaver & the Sand*) and children (multiple award nominee *The Changeling*, and the *Troubletwister* series cowritten with Garth Nix). He lives with his wife and family in the dry, flat lands of South Australia.

SEAN WILLIAMS

The Jade Woman of the Luminous Star

"YOU MUST GET me out of here, Michaels. I have important work to do."

Those were the first words uttered by Hugh Gordon in my presence. I remember them clearly. On the one hand, I was relieved that he was willing to acknowledge me as a fellow professional, for a man of his standing, even in his dire circumstances, might have been tempted to dismiss me as a physician of no great renown, as in fact I am (and would very much like to return to being, Inspector Berkeley, once you have read this deposition). On the other hand, he seemed genuinely convinced that I could effect his release.

When I declared that this was quite impossible, he became irritable and aggressive. He accused me of gloating, of malpractice, even of spying. The last is outlandish, of course, but might have seemed plausible before his arrest. You are no doubt aware of his reputation—as a scientist, I mean. His advances in aeronautical engineering have been considerable; many have even been adopted by the Ministry of Calculation for employment throughout the Empire. Now that his laboratory has been razed, is it too ghoulish to imagine that someone might want to pick his brains for knowledge the gallows might otherwise claim?

Eventually, he took me at my word. He had no alternative, and I remember thinking that there was no predicament too alien for a keen intellect to confront. I admired the power of his mind, you see, even under such duress. I had not yet glimpsed the depths of his delusion—or of his cunning, depending on your interpretation of subsequent events.

He warned me.

"You will think me certifiable, Michaels, if I tell you the truth. I despaired too, at first, and with good reason: this vile place, with its loathsome inmates and equally loathsome porters, and all that preceded it . . . But then I wondered. Could it possibly be that she sent me here deliberately? You see, I felt something intangible when the door you just came through slammed shut behind me, something profound beyond words. Was this the 'precipice of light' Pattinattar wrote of nine hundred years ago? Had I chanced upon the secret of the ancients, which I must find anew or never see her again?"

His eyes had taken on a remote and urgent look, staring beyond the walls of Exeter Vale Asylum toward vistas unknown. I endeavored to bring him back to more immediate mysteries.

"Margaret, do you mean?"

He sank back onto his cot and put his head in his hands. "No, not Margaret. And no, this was not the right place. I tried, but could not follow in the great poet's footsteps. So here I am, Michaels, at your mercy."

I had been apprised of the statements he had made upon his arrest. I was aware that another woman might be implicated in the affair, although she had neither come forward nor been named. For your part, Inspector, you know that my purpose that day was to ascertain if this woman existed and, if so, whether she was complicit in the murder of Margaret Gordon. I resolved to be resolute in my pursuit of the truth, lest a great man of science be ruined over something of which he might be completely innocent.

I thought, then, that he might be shielding a jealous mistress. I would come to wonder if injured pride and his fall from grace drove him to perpetrate violent acts on all the women around him.

I do not know what I think now.

"You must tell me what happened," I said to him.

"Yes, yes—and if I must tell someone, it might as well be a scholar like me." He raised his head, regarding me with bloodshot but startlingly blue eyes. "I think it was Pattinattar, again, who said: 'I do not mix with idle, useless men. I do not listen to their speech.'"

He was trying to distract me with flattery.

"Tell me who she is, Doctor Gordon. Where did you meet? Where was it she wanted you to go?"

"Such difficult questions! You have no idea what you ask."

I said nothing.

"Very well." He shifted so his shoulders rested against the wall. "Her name is Abiha, and Margaret—poor Margaret—thought she was a ghost."

IT STARTED ON the twenty-fifth (he began, speaking with the clipped precision of one used to addressing the Royal Institution), and I say this, Michaels, with certainty, because it was the night of the lunar eclipse and I had been studying craters by telescope. My thoughts were as full as the face of that distant world. I imagined myself standing upon those jagged, airless mountains, staring up at the darkened globe of the earth. For all the advances we have made in recent decades, our trains, steamers, and airships are no closer to taking us there. We need infinitely more powerful forms of transportation to make these dreams reality, and I, unlike most dreamers, have the means to do just that. I had been working on them that very evening.

It was well past midnight when Margaret came down for me, complaining about the noise. "What noise?" I asked. The household was asleep and the laboratory closed. All of Exeter was hushed. The eclipse had put the town in a somber, premonitory mood.

"Someone has been knocking," she said. "If not you, then who?"

I could tell that she would not be pacified until the matter had received the attention she believed it deserved. Abandoning the telescope, I went inside to prove to her that there had been no knocking, by me or anyone else. With no one to upbraid, I hoped she would let the matter go, return to her bedroom, and leave me to conclude my observations in peace.

We found no one in the house, no windows open, and no note at the front door. The house was empty and silent.

Yet, as I was leading Margaret back to her rest, there came a sound from below—hard and sharp, a sudden clap as of a book falling face-first onto the floor.

Margaret jumped, and I confess I started too. Barely had the echoes faded than I was on my way back down the stairs, convinced that the sound had originated in the laboratory.

Have you seen my laboratory, Michaels? No? Well, it is as big as a barn, and needs to be, for I have tested engines in there and reconstructed whole sections of airship frames at one-to-one scales. These days, it is full of glass bells much larger than a man, dozens of them, connected by copper wires and containing delicate Faraday cages of my own design. If someone were in there, they would find little they understood, but much that they could damage. It is—

Ah, yes, I forget myself. It's all gone—and why not? My research will benefit no one now.

Poor Margaret. The irony that she was the one to draw this phenomenon to my attention is not lost on me.

She waited in the doorway as I searched the vast space, leaving no cupboard or nook untouched. I found nothing, and the sound was not repeated. Yet I had heard it: the evidence of my senses was not to be denied.

All I found was a slight crack in my newest bell, a crack that I was certain had not been there before. The bell was spoiled, but I dismissed it as a simple case of thermal compression in the cooling house, coupled with stored stress in the curved glass, suddenly releasing itself. I ascended with Margaret in tow, confident that I had found enough evidence to put her mind at rest. If it occurred to her to ask how a single crack could have made all the other noises she reported, she said nothing.

I slept soundly. I may have dreamed, but I do not recall. I do have a sense of being plagued by my nightmare all that month, and I suppose this will interest you, Michaels: it is what drives me, day and night, in my quest for the perfect transportation device. It is a dream that has haunted me since childhood, a dream of a world poisoned by the fumes of its industry, where inefficient coal boilers spew smoke and char, interminable lines of vehicles choke the streets, and overloaded airships rain ash upon the sickened races below. For all my successes, all my novel advances, my greatest fear is that I have not done enough to prevent this calamity from coming to pass. I am far less afraid of being forgotten than of leaving no one behind to remember my efforts.

(He chuckled at that, without humor, and I reminded him to adhere to the subject.)

Margaret was the first to talk of haunting. I, of course, wouldn't credit the idea, but it was indisputable that in subsequent days noises were heard in the house that could not be explained away as the servants at work or the walls settling. Strange thumps, scrapes, and sighs came at random intervals, utterly without warning, sometimes seeming near, other times as far away as Selene herself. I told Margaret she was imagining things, but I knew she was not. I could not explain it and would not accept her explanation, and so the phenomenon had to be ignored.

I am embarrassed to admit to the willful disregard of data—data that might have led me much sooner to the understanding I now possess, and might even have prevented the calamity that befell dear Margaret—but there you have it. My mind was fixed on other matters. One week after that first night I was expected to address my peers at the Institution on my latest experiments, and my speech was not yet prepared. Instead of pursuing the matter of our spectral interloper, I worked long hours distilling my thoughts and combing the library for references I might have overlooked. There was no time for Margaret's uneasy superstitions.

On the day of my departure, I descended early to the laboratory, intending to add the final touches to my speech before anyone else awoke— only to find that my notes had been rifled through and scattered across the desk. Several pages had fallen to the floor, there to be trodden on like so much refuse. You can imagine my alarm. I woke the house with Herculean wrath and demanded that every maidservant be questioned. They swore that no one had entered the laboratory during the night. It had in fact been securely locked, by me, before retiring, and the lock had not been tampered with. I had the only key, but I did not believe them. Someone must have entered the laboratory and examined my work. Someone!

My interrogation of the staff might have continued all day had not the urgent need to prepare for my departure intervened. I gathered up the notes in a fury, secured my valise, and rushed out to where my carriage was waiting to whip me to the station. Margaret farewelled me at the steps, in something of a state herself. Unnatural noises in conjunction with physical disturbance added up to a poltergeist in her mind, and she was reluctant to remain in the house without me to protect her.

It would be easy to say that she had been reading too much fabulous fiction—but that would ignore a facet of her character that I had always admired, and which is essential for any wife of mine: an open mind. Some would say that I have said much stranger things, and indeed I proposed a few of them that very day.

I said "peers" earlier, when I referred to my audience at the Royal Institution, but what I mean is my critics. You may not be familiar with my most recent theories—of life on this earth as a river, and an individual, such as you or me, as an eddy in that river, a self-sustaining whirlpool of vital dynamism that endures even though the particles of water comprising it constantly change. This philosophical principle has received a warm welcome in some quarters—but the same cannot be said of the theories of transportation that naturally arise from it. Doesn't it strike you as odd, Michaels, that we lug this ponderous sack of tissues around with us every time we go hither and yon? Wouldn't it be easier to abandon it and adopt an identical one when we arrive—to move the eddy alone and leave the river behind?

Well, you are not alone, and some of my critics dislike my methodology as much as my philosophy. If I am so interested in transportation, they say, why base myself in Exeter, so far from the great steel machines of the north? There, I say, is the answer. Those machines are not in my vision. They crush the landscape and foul the sky. They are the nightmare, not the dream.

Yes, yes, the ghost. I am getting there, have no fear, if by my own slow and tortuous path.

It was well after nightfall by the time I returned home. I was exhausted. My ears rang with the bleating of pedants, and I was in no mood for what greeted me. Who would have been? The house was in an uproar, due to a rash of "manifestations," as Margaret called them, from eerie whispers to strange explosions; even a minor earthquake, I was told, that had upset a row of plates in the kitchen, shattering every one. I was inclined to regard at least the last of these incidents as carelessness, perhaps even willful trickery, but in the face of Margaret's distress I could not dismiss them all. Something was afoot. The question was, what?

Two of the servants had resigned, citing good, Christian horror at such devilish pranks, though not above accepting generous severances if they kept silent in the parish. My presence reassured those who remained, and when they had gone home, leaving me and Margaret alone in the unsettled house, I was able to put my mind to the problem, for that was how I now regarded it—something to be solved and put behind me, rather than dangerously ignored.

Already I knew that the phenomena came at all hours, not just during the night; and that apart from the dishes and the cracked glass bell—both of which might have been coincidence—they consisted solely of sensory impressions. Nothing concrete had been detected. What other data we had were as elusive as the atoms of my imaginary river.

I told Margaret that I was going to make camp in the laboratory that night, in order to study the phenomenon more closely. She told me I was addled even to consider it, but I was adamant. The manifestations were confined to the ground floor, so it made sense to conduct the experiment in situ. I gathered a decanter of sherry and several books from the library to pass the time. Exhausted though I was, I planned to stay awake the entire night and record what I experienced.

Ah, Michaels, if only my notes survived! One sheet would provide you with all the evidence you need, although perhaps you would interpret it as the product of a deranged psyche. You would see in those notes my keenest observations, with each incident dutifully timed and described, accompanied by speculations as to cause, where such was not immediately obvious.

Of the sounds, many were mechanical, such as tiny clicks and whirrs that came at irregular intervals, as though a vast and invisible calculating machine surrounded me. Others were natural: once, for instance, I swear I heard a birdcall, and there were the faintest hints of voices, coming and going at the very fringe of perception.

I monitored several thermometers and recorded numerous wide swings in temperature. Different parts of the room often disagreed by several degrees, and I was forever loosening and tightening my cravat.

At least twice, I swear, something poked me gently, once between the shoulder blades and once in my chest. Nothing at all was to be seen.

I accumulated several pages of notes over the course of the night, but came to no conclusions. My attention wandered back to my work, and to the books I had brought with me for the long vigil. They were translations, mostly, of texts dismissed in these enlightened days, but in which I hoped to find a gleam of inspiration. For thousands of years, you see, alchemists have written of moving in ways that would seem magical to us. Lu Yen's *Chu T'ang Shu* described traversing the tapestry of stars to the edge of day—that is in third-century China, when the most famous Chinese alchemist of all, Ko Hung, believed that he could fly to heaven by mounting the air and treading on light, echoing the Daoist Dance of Yu, where adepts physically trace out the constellations in order to travel to the stars. Such apparently preposterous claims are not confined to China, by any means. Egyptians believed that certain words provided people with the power to travel safely through different worlds after death, while *The Coffin Texts* claim that one can learn how to cross over the sky and explore the entire universe. Thoth boasted of descending to the earth with secrets belonging to the horizon, and that claim was later taken up by the Greeks: in *Corpus Hermeticum*, Hermes Trismegistus instructs students to fly into the heavens without wings. Scholars have often suspected that there was something these venerable philosophers understood that we have forgotten; my intention was not to recover that supposedly lost knowledge, but instead to make it a reality and put it to the salvation of our civilization. If people dreamed thus, once upon an age, then I could make them dream again.

When dawn arrived, the carafe was empty and I was utterly exhausted. The maidservant found me asleep at my drafting table with my head on my arms when she knocked gently at the locked door to see if I required breakfast.

I roused myself and told her that, yes, I would require something even heartier than normal to get the day properly under way. I did not reveal to her that my quest had come to nothing. I was, if anything, more mystified than ever. After a nearly sleepless night, I now faced a long day of research, and questions from Margaret that I was no nearer to answering.

When I returned to the desk, what I saw sent all thoughts of food to the four winds.

Daubed in thick ink across my careful notes was a symbol I had seen before, but which I had not drawn. It was a sign used by alchemists of the fourteenth century to capture the union of the sexes.

Don't scowl at me, Michaels. I'm not being unnecessarily prurient. One must describe what one sees: that is the most important rule of science, particularly if one has broken it already that week!

This crude drawing, this arcane symbol, was the first confirmed, physical manifestation of the creature that was to change my life forever.

You must imagine my wary excitement upon this discovery. I was not frightened by the phenomenon itself, but I very much feared being taken for a fool, and so I conducted a thorough search of the desk and its surroundings, the door and its lock, even the windows, tightly sealed against the night's chill, lest someone had waited until I slept to deliver this cryptic sigil. I found nothing to suggest that it was anything other than an anomaly; and, perhaps, a message from beyond.

Breakfast arrived, with Margaret hard on its heels. I hid the defaced sheet under the rest of my notes and told no one about it. Why? Well, instinct played a part. Margaret was unsettled enough; I didn't want her crying the house down, demanding exorcisms or séances or whatever is the latest fad in London these days. And we had lost enough staff already. Better, I told myself, to keep this development to myself for the time being, until I was absolutely certain of its import.

I know what you must be thinking: I was tired and had been reading alchemical texts all night. The sherry, too, might have played a part. It is only natural for you to assume that I had doodled the symbol myself in some deep hypnagogic state and woken unaware that I was its author. That is in fact the complete reverse of the reality. The symbol appeared *because* I was reading the texts. The hand that so crudely crafted it was drawn to me for this very reason.

Margaret was not persuaded by my assurances that nothing untoward had occurred that night, but the events of the day went some way toward reinforcing the white lie. As though the production of the drawing had calmed our so-called haunting, all further incidents were greatly reduced in magnitude. Nothing happened that could not be attributed to natural causes, and I was careful to ensure that calm prevailed.

That night, to be certain I was not interrupted, I slipped a dose of chlo-

ral into Margaret's evening cocoa. When at last she was breathing peacefully, I returned to the laboratory, intending to open communication with
our provocative ghost.

You see, several things had occurred to me. The ghost knew I was there:
why else would it have placed that symbol directly in front of me, where I
was certain to see it? That it had waited until I was asleep suggested that it
had divined my purpose. Furthermore, it understood what I was reading,
or at least recognized like symbols on the pages before me. All this spoke
strongly of intelligence, so making contact with it was not only possible
but desirable. If replicable, the exchange might dwarf all my other achievements to date.

I had acquired numerous blank sheets of paper, upon which I repro-
duced other alchemical symbols and wrote messages in several different
languages, including Archaic Chinese. I placed them all about the laboratory, and waited. For several hours, nothing happened. I reread *The Writings of the Hidden Chamber* recovered from the tomb of Tuthmosis III in
Luxor, which talks of the gates and ways of the gods, and I revisited the
teachings of the Indian saint Bogar, who boasted that he could travel freely
throughout the three worlds by means of astral projection. I began to grow
sleepy, but drank cup after cup of coffee to ensure I did not succumb. If
my alchemically inclined phantasm was to put in an appearance, I would
be awake to welcome it.

At shortly after four in the morning, I heard footsteps approaching
me across the floor of the laboratory. I sat up, but saw no one. My skin
tingled. The hair on the back of my hands and neck stood to attention. I
smelt something—the faintest hint of another person near me—and felt a
puff of air against my cheek

"You are close," whispered a voice into my ear, "so very close."

I leapt to my feet, filled with excitement and atavistic dread. I was alone
in the laboratory, yet someone was speaking to me. An invisible being, a
spirit—a ghost, why not? We don't have words for such an experience. It
is something that calculating machines could not calculate, that analytical
engines could not analyze—yet I was experiencing it. I alone!

I flailed about, vainly seeking substance in the empty air. The ghost
laughed, as though at the clumsy efforts of a child. One of my hasty pic-
tograms fluttered into the air, and I caught it, crushing it in my fist. I felt
taunted, belittled. Angrily, I demanded that the ghost reveal itself to me
at once.

"I cannot," said that faint whisper in my ear. "You must wait, Doctor
Gordon."

"How long?"

"One more night, and then the congress of our worlds will be complete. Will you be here to greet me?"

"Yes," I said, without hesitation. Who would not? "I will be here."

"Bring no one else," the teasing spirit said, and fell silent. She said nothing more that night, and I felt no further sign of her presence.

Yes, I said "she." The creature haunting my laboratory was plainly a woman, a woman of some intelligence and spirit by the sound of her, although her accent was unfamiliar. There was none of the breathless, echoing death rattles the writers of popular fiction would have us imagine. She clearly was not that kind of ghost.

Naturally, after the encounter, I could not sleep, and I spent the rest of that night and the following day in a fever of anticipation. Margaret was worried. She could sense that something had inflamed my intellectual passion, yet she saw my regular work go ignored. I paced about the laboratory, unwilling to leave, responding only vaguely to her entreaties, barely eating or drinking. I must have seemed like a man possessed; it is a wonder she didn't accuse me of this very thing. A more credulous mind might have wondered if I had somehow fallen under the ghost's spell. Not Margaret. She understood my moods as well as I understood hers. She knew when I had been seized by the power of an idea.

But what, really, did I have? Little that would have impressed the overly critical gentlemen of the Royal Institution, those who had jeered and cat-called at my latest presentation. I needed far more if I was to declare a breakthrough of such magnitude—a breaking through, indeed, between different planes of existence. I didn't for a moment contemplate secreting an observer to witness what might follow that night. If nothing occurred, I would be an instant laughingstock. I needed more evidence before even considering public engagement.

I suppose I am a laughingstock now, Michaels. I expect people whisper terrible things about me and my behavior—that my mind gave way before the derision of my peers and I killed my wife in a moment of mania. If I had braved the possibility of further humiliation, this story might have had a very different conclusion, though I suspect that my visitor would easily have detected an observer and disappeared for good. The truth would have been denied me, and I would forever have wondered what I might have lost.

Again, I dosed poor Margaret so she would not be disturbed. Again, I sealed myself into the laboratory, armed with nothing but my books and my wits. Again, I endured hours of uncertainty before the stillness of the night was broken. Again, I started, but this time not at any mere wisp of air or whispering voice.

I jumped because right in front of me, from absolutely nowhere, appeared the most beautiful woman I have ever seen. Not as a ghost or phantasm. There was nothing ectoplasmic about this visitation. She was as real as you or me.

Describe her? I cannot do her justice. She was Oriental, I thought at first, with full lips and dark eyes, and hair so brown it was almost black. The cut of her tresses was short but finely styled, not like a man's, and her ears were pierced with gold. She was dressed in a way you would find most immodest, I am sure, in some kind of silken uniform, with trousers instead of a dress, a high collar, and gloves; all deep purples and greens, very harsh to my eye. Her smell was rich and tropical, like Amazonian flowers. She looked curiously about her, nodding as though finding her surroundings familiar, before she turned to me.

When she spoke, I knew that she was the being who had visited the night before. I will hear that voice the rest of my days.

"Hello, Doctor Gordon," she said. "My name is Abiha, and I have been looking for you."

AT THIS POINT in his tale, Doctor Gordon became too distraught to speak. He begged my indulgence, and I allowed him a moment or two to gather himself. When it became clear that his distress was mounting, not receding, I offered him a calmative draft, which he accepted.

"Don't knock me out, though, will you?" he asked me. "I must finish what I have begun."

I left the cell and returned some minutes later with a sedative of my own concoction. He drained the vial readily enough. Before long, he grew calm again and his limbs lost some of the restless energy that had made listening to him an exhausting experience. I felt that he was nearing the crisis at the heart of his story, and that he knew, at some level of his being, that to continue would be to confront the true depths of his illness.

I was not disappointed.

"Abiha stayed for one hour," Gordon told me. "She assured me that she was not a spirit from beyond the grave, and that she was no more or less human than I. She said that she had journeyed to our world from another, one called Surobia, although that was not the place of her birth. That was yet another world, Arora, which she had left more than a year ago—to explore, she said, like some female Livingstone. These other worlds she spoke of are not transcendental dimensions or Heaven's empty halls, apparently. They orbit the sun as the earth does, home to animals and plants and civilizations like ours. Sometimes they approach one another, and for periods lasting around a fortnight, which Abiha described as 'congress,' those few individuals who have the trick of it can make the crossing.

"Yes, Michaels, raise your eyebrows. I won't deny I did the same at first. Where are these worlds, exactly? If they were as real as she claimed, would we not see them through our telescopes and feel their effects in our world's stately progression about the sun? But as she talked, I remembered the alchemists of old and their insistence that this world was not the only one of human experience. I thought of the ice ages and the various other cataclysms that have befallen our changeable Earth. What if there truly are such worlds in a reality alongside ours, orbiting a sun that exists in all realities? What if the ancients were right and we moderns so very, very wrong?

"Take Philolaus. He imagined a Central Fire that bright Sol orbited, and about which another Earth, the Antichthon, also circled, forever hidden from us. Then there are the levels and spheres of Cabalism, all reaching out from a central, fiery point. What about the Heart of the Sun in Uthman ibn Suwaid's *Turba Philosophorum*? Or Hermes Trismegistus's Utmost Body, that alchemists could fly to with the Philosopher's Stone?"

I cut across his lecture—almost a sermon, such was the intensity with which he spoke—to convey my surprise that a man of science could place any faith at all in the ravings of lunatics and mystics. Hadn't their theories been proven wrong centuries ago, or exposed as the carefully encoded ceremonies of a depraved cult of sensualists?

"Sir Isaac Newton was an alchemist," Gordon responded. "Did you know that? The man who gave us calculus and the laws of gravitation, perhaps the greatest scientist who ever lived—he would scoff at your skepticism, sir, and with good reason, I think.

"And as for the allegation of copulation, well—all the alchemists I've spoken of believed in the union of the sexes and the power it unleashes, so perhaps there is something to that too. Take *Asclepius,* or *Kulacudamani Tantra* and the Realized Ones of the tantric arts, or *The Yellow Emperor's Canon of the Nine-Vessel Spiritual Elixir*—look them up yourself if you don't believe me!"

Needless to say, Inspector Berkeley, I have not done so. I am no prude, but I have no use for the ravings of charlatans. I was, however, keenly aware of the word *congress* in the context of Doctor Gordon's narration, and the close relation between its appearance and that of the mysterious other woman. His description of her spoke volumes, as did his confusion of intellect with passion, and his willingness to drug his wife in order to conduct an illicit nocturnal rendezvous in his laboratory. It seemed clear to me, then, what dark truth his own mind could not yet bear to look at directly.

I gave him a moment to compose himself, then asked that he tell me all that had transpired between him and the nocturnal, exotic Abiha.

As BEST I can remember (he said) this is it.

"We all of us, Doctor Gordon, have places of significance," she said. "Mine are the workshops of men like you, great thinkers who propel our species out of the darkness of ignorance and into the light of the intellect. I am drawn to such places and to the work performed there. That is why I have come to you. I felt the power of your experiments rippling out across the Helioverse, calling me to you.

"No, do not speak. Listen first. You have evidently mastered the art to some degree, or I would never have found you, congress or no congress, and I see by the books you have assembled that you are treading in the footsteps of great men—and great women, too. Sex is no impediment to inspiration, as your research will have revealed to you, I hope.

"Soon our worlds will diverge once more, and I have therefore only a brief opportunity to examine your progress. I desire to know how far along the path you have come. Will you tell me? Will you hold nothing back? Knowledge shared is knowledge doubled, as we say on my world. Together we will travel much farther than apart."

Thus she set me off into the very same presentation I gave to the Royal Institution, three days earlier. I prefaced it by describing my nightmare of a polluted world and my dream of the perfect means of transportation, at which she nodded most vigorously, her eyes alight with interest. I thought I had found the perfect audience—from whom I expected to learn much more in turn—and I roamed about the laboratory, gesticulating, and demonstrating each piece of equipment as I came to it. She followed me closely and did not interrupt, not even to ask questions about the more esoteric details of my theory.

I mistook her attention for understanding, even approval.

I did not notice her furrowed brow until my demonstration of the prototype flux duplicator, the core component of my dream transport system, concluded.

"What is it?" I asked her. "Where have I erred? The theory is new, I know—I am, perhaps, the only person in this world who could understand it—but I am sure it is as familiar to you as a child's multiplication tables."

"Familiar?" she said. "Hardly, Doctor Gordon. Machines mean nothing to me. I came here to see you, to hear about your work, not theirs. What set you off along this path? What strange occurrence? There must have been some kind of spatial bilocation to prove to you the possibility of this method."

"Bilocation?" I echoed her in turn, and it felt suddenly as though we were speaking different languages.

"Yes, a transference from locus to locus, possibly achieved by accident rather than design. You clearly know nothing of the Helioverse, but that doesn't rule out travel in this world alone. What is your significant location?"

"I don't understand," I said, with utter frankness.

"You don't? So what made you think you could ever enslave this talent to a mere device? Where is the practical principle that guided your research?"

"In all honesty," I said, reminded of my ordeal at the Institute, "I possess nothing other than thought experiments, but I am close to demonstrating a functional circuit—"

"A working execution-machine, you mean. It is guaranteed not to work."

"But my theories—"

"Your eddies in a river are marvellously metaphoric, Doctor Gordon, but you have failed to pursue them to their logical conclusion. What would happen if you froze an eddy long enough to re-create it? On being released from the icebox the eddy would dissolve into ordinary water, and you would be left with nothing. Put yourself through this contraption of yours, and you too would dissolve. Die, if you prefer. Better that these devices remain harmless trinkets, as I originally thought them to be, or you dismantle them and direct your efforts to more accomplishable aims." Abiha flicked the edge of one of my precious glass bells, making it chime a resonant, deep G. "I'm sorry, Doctor Gordon, but I beg you not to eradicate yourself in pursuit of a fundamentally flawed notion."

I stared at her in shock and dawning horror. Could what she said really be true?

"How do you travel, then," I asked her, "if not by machine?"

"By will," she said, "and by art. That is all you need to swim the river of life."

"Will you teach me?"

She didn't answer immediately. On my desk lay a rare edition of the

Picatrix, and she flicked through it as though seeking guidance. I sensed disappointment in her, along with disapproval, and waited anxiously for her response. I am a proud man, but I am not afraid to admit when I am wrong. A rigid mind is not a scientific mind. I would abandon all my research if it meant attaining the reality she had demonstrated to me that evening.

My mind flew with the possibilities. World upon world upon world, all full of human life! She must not be the only traveller of her kind. How many times had voyagers made the crossing during our planets' intimate conjunctions? Magical texts are full of magical visitors who instructed the alchemists of old: you might already know about the giants of Genesis, but what about the companions of Horus who founded the original Egyptian dynasties, or the Fankuang Tzu of the Taoists, the Sons of Reflected Light who came from far across the sea, bringing wisdom and insight with them? Could Abiha's people and these beneficent visitors be one and the same?

In some ancient Chinese traditions you will find reference to the Highest Clarity, a place beyond the sky, where live the Jade Women of the Luminous Star. Was I looking at such a woman right now, in my very own laboratory?

"I am sorry, Doctor Gordon," she said again. "You are not ready."

She closed the book and stepped back from the desk, and in her eyes I saw the certainty of her decision, the futility of all forms of protest I might offer, and a determination to leave.

That was when I made the greatest mistake of my life.

The prospect of losing her was intolerable. She possessed the secret I had pursued for so long; I would not let it slip through my grasp! I lunged for her and took her arm, but she had already begun the charm or spell she used to travel between worlds.

The moment my skin touched hers, I felt a foglike ether envelop me, and all the light and heat was sucked out of the world. She gasped and tried to pull away, but I resisted, gripping so tightly I fear I hurt her—but not out of anger, I swear, or fear of losing her. A terrible sense of emptiness in the ether, of *dissociation,* had me mortally afraid for my life. If I let her go, I thought, I would be lost between worlds and surely die.

We struggled back and forth, she beating at me with her fists, and me imploring her to return with me or take me with her. Whether she heard my cries or not, I do not know. The laboratory faded from sight, and the features of a new world appeared, one with metallic columns and bright lights. The air was dry and smelled of spark-gaps. Shapes rose up around us, and I felt their hands gripping me, pulling us apart. They snarled and spat at me in a foreign tongue. I strained to hang on to her, but could not resist them.

Finally, a stout blow to my forehead tore me loose. I was hurled back into the ether, where I tumbled for an instant, insensate, before landing with a bone-jarring impact on the floor of my laboratory.

I lay there for perhaps a minute, stunned. My skin was cold. I felt frost on my eyelashes. The chill seemed to penetrate right to my bones. But for the hammering of my heart, I might have been frozen solid.

Then the sound of smashing glass stirred me from my delirium.

I sat up, feeling her eyes upon me: Abiha's dark eyes, devoid of pity, demonically invisible. I staggered to my feet and stared wildly about the laboratory.

One of my glass bells chose that moment to shatter. It exploded into a thousand crystalline pieces, struck powerfully by an invisible hand, and I gasped in alarm. What cruel sabotage was this? Denying me her secrets was punishment enough, surely. Why destroy my greatest work as well? If I died in error, wasn't that my own business?

A third bell disintegrated. I picked up a spirit level and went on a rampage of my own, striking at the empty air in an attempt to catch one of my spectral tormentors off-guard—to no avail, of course, although I raged and swore. I begged. My cries went unheard beneath the shattering of the bells. The ground was soon covered in tiny shards, as though an artificial snow had fallen from the roof. My feet crunched at every step.

Soon just one glass bell remained, and I lunged for it, determined to save it at least from the slaughter. When I was barely a hand span away, it shattered in my face, and I thought I heard someone laughing.

I threw the spirit level at the empty air and roared my frustration. And still I could feel her, in the laboratory, all around me, mocking my impotence in silence.

A hand touched my shoulder.

I spun around with fists upraised, ready to do battle with the devil himself.

Margaret fell back, white-faced. "Darling! I heard the noise and came down to see. What in God's name are you doing?"

I dropped my hands and fell back, imagining how this must look to her. To her senses, the laboratory was empty apart from me, and she must surely have witnessed me lunging at that last bell with spirit level in hand. She would of course imagine me the architect of this disaster. But what would she think had occurred in my mind to make such actions possible? What possession, what madness?

In that moment of self-realization, I understood everything.

"My darling," I said to Margaret, striving my utmost to keep my tone level and my expression one of sincerest sanity, "do not be alarmed. I know how this must seem to you. Be assured that the reality is not as it seems. Our visitor—well, as you can see the haunting has got entirely out of hand, and we must leave immediately. It is not too late."

She looked at me without understanding, but with recognition. She knew me and trusted me. She would have left with me—I know it. She was my wife, and I had never before done anything to harm our happiness.

It was then, Michaels, that the most terrible thing of all occurred. Margaret made a soft cry, like a child, and staggered forward. I supported her before she could fall to the ground and cradled her in my arms. Her head lolled backwards, and I felt a vile rush of blood over my hands. Struck a fatal blow from behind, she was dead before I caught her.

Only when I smelled smoke did I begin to fear for my own life.

A SECOND TIME, Doctor Gordon broke down, but this time he forswore all forms of chemical relief. He declared that he would finish or be damned—for damned he already seemed to be. The demons from the other world, he said, had set about demolishing his reputation as well as his work, and in that he acknowledged they had totally succeeded.

The rest of the story differs little from eyewitness testimony. Firemen attending the scene found him lying in the lane at the back of his library, spared by mere inches from flaming debris. He was liberally splashed with blood and in a state of maniacal frenzy. Several witnesses heard him cry out, "Come back to me! Come back!" When asked if he was referring to his wife, he clearly declared that he was not. "The other woman," he said. "And if she can't have me, she means to destroy me!" Upon which, he collapsed unconscious and was borne away for treatment.

Only when investigators found Margaret's charred skeleton in the remains of the house, the back of her head apparently staved in by a hammer, and he was formally accused of murder—only then did Doctor Gordon emerge from the catatonia that had gripped him since his discovery. But he remained stubbornly mute. Even when he was charged, he said nothing. He was transferred from the hospital to Exeter Vale and has remained here ever since, sleepless and to all appearances unrepentant, pending a proper psychological examination.

On the fourth day, he seemed at last ready to talk.

"And here we are," he said when he had finished his sorry tale. "What do you think? Am I deluded? Depraved? Both?"

I refrained from commenting on his condition. It seemed clear to me that the man had suffered a major breakdown. Perhaps he truly believed that someone else had killed Margaret, but the facts of the case are plain. He was alone in the laboratory when Margaret entered. He admits that himself, invisible spirits notwithstanding. She came upon him unexpectedly while he was in the midst of demolishing his recent work. Who knows what he imagined, in the grip of such ungovernable emotions? She intruded; he was discovered. So Margaret Gordon died a violent death in the house she had shared with her husband for twenty years, and only her husband could have killed her.

I believe he understood my conclusions without requiring me to declare them. He was merely deluded, not deprived of his faculties. I knew that, Inspector Berkeley, but I nevertheless allowed him to get the upper hand.

"If you will not release me," he said, "then I would like to see Margaret. Where she lies, anyway. She must have been buried by now. We have adjacent vaults reserved in the Catacombs of the Lower Cemetery, and I hope to lie next to her when this grisly business is over. Do you think that might be arranged? If so, I will go quietly—plead guilty and of sound mind, confess whatever you like. You have heard my story, and if I cannot convince you of the truth of it, then I have no wish to cause further inconvenience to you or anyone else."

The request was not altogether surprising, nor the granting of it wholly unjustified. I will defend that conclusion to the grave. For a dangerous madman, there would have been no question of release. But he, who seemed sane enough, lacking only the honesty and good character to reveal the whole truth about what happened that ghastly night—him I could not deny. It seemed certain to me that, in a deranged state brought on by insomnia, and by romantic circumstances he was naturally wary of revealing, he had murdered the one person he had ever been a danger to, and that I or anyone else was therefore safe in his presence. Granting his request could ease the conclusion of his trial and leave the resources of both judiciary and asylum free for those in greater need.

"Tell me just one thing," I said, before taking my leave to obtain permission from Superintendent Gilfoyle.

"Anything, Michaels."

"You said you felt something when you came here—an intangibility, a profundity, or words to that effect. What do you think that might have been?"

He studied his hands as though looking for bloodstains.

"Perhaps no more than my imagination," he said. "I shouldn't have mentioned it. You will think it the nearness of the Creator, perhaps, or fate's cold hand upon me, some such nonsense."

"Hardly," I rebuffed him. "I am, as you say, a scholar, and I read extensively in the new theories of mind. My speculations on such matters lead me in very different directions—inward, not outward. The feeling came from part of you, I would say, from some unnoticed or suppressed corner of your mind. You felt it when the woman Abiha abandoned you, leaving you trapped in your marriage with Margaret, and you felt it again when locked in this cell. Could your dissociative impulse be nothing more than a method of achieving freedom by the only means available to you—via a fantasy? Could that be why a disturbed mental state accompanied each occurrence of that feeling, and why you seem compelled to expound this unlikely tale to the bitter end?"

He regarded me with a critical eye for a good minute. I felt that he was surprised, and perhaps even slightly amused, by my claims.

"You may be right," he said, finally. "I was wrong to belittle you, Michaels. I'm sorry."

I dismissed his apology as unnecessary, but was secretly pleased to have earned it.

ON THAT ENCOURAGING note, I left him to see about the visit to Margaret's resting place, in the hope that this would put the dreadful affair behind him for good, little knowing how complicit I was about to become in the conclusion of these events.

I wish you to understand and accept, Inspector Berkeley, that I acted unknowingly, and in full faith of Doctor Gordon's good intentions. I will swear before any judge you name, in this world or the next, that I thought him resigned to his fate, that this last concession would see him walk to the dock and ultimately to the gallows. He spoke no more of his work or of the woman he felt had betrayed him. When I returned to his cell with the escorts assigned to him, he was already on his feet, his head bowed and his attire as neat as he could manage, given his circumstances. He seemed a gentleman fallen on hard times, not a villain.

Constables Teale and Collison secured his wrists with handcuffs and led him from the cell. A small steam carriage awaited us at the exit from the administration wing, where the patient's temporary release forms were properly signed and witnessed. I rode with the driver, while my unfortunate companion sat between the two constables in the locked cab. We made our way down the long drive and through the main entrance under a sky as gray and leaden as granite, its featureless expanse broken only by the oval silhouette of an airship rising in stately fashion from the station with propellers deeply droning—one of Gordon's own designs, if I am not mistaken.

The journey to Longbrook Valley and the catacombs of Exeter proceeded uneventfully. We were met, at the steps leading up through the Lower Cemetery to the entrance in the grim hillside, by the priest and, rather disconcertingly, the catacombs' bricklayer, who was of the impression that we required his services. On the discovery that all of our party were living and no vaults needed to be sealed that day, he left muttering under his breath while Doctor Gordon and I ascended.

The arrangement was that the two constables would wait without while I accompanied the patient to the vault. The priest unchained the gate and allowed us through, then secured the entrance behind us. The air was cool and close within the catacombs themselves, and I longed for more light than my meager lantern provided. The walls were made of heavy, dark stone and fashioned to convey a sense of Egyptian antiquity. I was reminded of Gordon's alchemical fantasies and wondered what he made of them now.

"I feel it again," he told me, on that sepulchral threshold. "And I know now that it is fate, after all, brought me here."

He seemed feverish to my quick inspection. "Do you wish to proceed? There would be no dishonor in turning back."

"No," he said. "I must see her. And I know now that I shall."

We walked into the catacombs and followed the priest's directions to the Dissenters' section. There we scoured the sealed vaults, looking for fresh brickwork and a new brass plaque. I found Margaret before he did and stood in silence before telling him, reading the graven message that marked out the record of her days.

"Margaret Josephine Gordon, beloved wife, 1842–18—."

It seemed very little to me then, and still seems so now.

"This is it," said Gordon. He had come up behind me without making a sound. "Do you carry a journal with you, and a pen?"

"Of course," I said—and that is the last thing I remember. Constable Teale found me unconscious on the floor of the catacombs with a large bump protruding from the back of my skull, struck from behind just as Margaret had been—by her husband, Doctor Gordon.

*　*　*

You MIGHT SAY that, if what I tell you is true, I am lucky to be alive. I assure you that I curse the error of my judgment with every breath, and I wish I could explain what happened that day with any more clarity than this.

Certain facts are indisputable. The catacombs were sealed; the only entrance was attended by the two constables and the priest. No one entered or left until sufficient time had passed for them to come in search of us. When they found me unconscious and alone, reinforcements were summoned and the catacombs meticulously searched. Even Margaret's vault, the most recently sealed, was opened, but her body was the only occupant.

Of Doctor Gordon there was no sign. He vanished that day as thoroughly as any ghost, my notepad and pen with him, and I believe you when you assure me, Inspector Berkeley, that no trace of him has been found.

I maintain that I had nothing to do with his disappearance, although I do not blame you for reaching the opposite conclusion. The only material way for the accused murderer to escape from the catacombs was with the assistance of an accomplice, and the constables' solemn oath that they let no one enter or exit is supported by the priest's eyewitness account. If these three are excluded from the list of possible collaborators, that leaves only me. Furthermore, I had the obvious opportunity to concoct this scheme, while supposedly interviewing him in Exeter Vale.

I am, however, sanguine about my confinement, for it has provided me with the opportunity to write this full and frank testimony—and to make one small but possibly critical discovery that escaped my attention in the catacombs.

In the inside pocket of my coat, folded carefully in four, I came upon a note written on one of my own notepapers, but in a hand very unlike my own. I enclose it with this account as evidence of the fugitive's state of mind, and its bearing on the matter of my innocence.

Your conclusions must be your own, Inspector Berkeley. I have nothing left to reveal, and no further speculations to offer. (I presume, however, that you have interviewed the bricklayer, along with the porters of the asylum, and are doing everything in your power to find the woman Abiha, about whom Doctor Gordon speaks so vehemently.)

Yours most sincerely, et cetera,
John Wesley Michaels, M.D.

*   *   *

Michaels—

I am sorry to have used you in this despicable way. On entering the catacombs, I find that hope has returned; for the attainment of another possibility, the one that has thus far eluded me, is now within my grasp.

How much you believe of my story, I may never know. Perhaps none at all—in which case this short missive will provide yet more evidence to support a diagnosis of madness. If, however, you have detected the faintest ring of truth in my account, then you should attend carefully. The import of what I have to tell you has repercussions for not just this great Empire, but all humanity on this world.

Abiha told me that my experiments were flawed, and perhaps they were in application, but not in essence, for what else could possibly have drawn her to me? My machines sent ripples through the ether between worlds, alerting her and her allies to the existence of my work. They came to investigate; they misunderstood what they saw; they approached me, thinking me like them, free to wander the wondrous Helioverse she spoke of. Perhaps they hoped to recruit me. That I do not know—but now I know their cause, I can safely swear that I would never ally myself with such beings.

You see, Michaels, it occurred to me that night to wonder: if so many alchemists in our world had made the same discoveries—how they could possibly have been forgotten. Why, when their conclusions are so openly discussed in their texts, isn't this means of travel available to us all? The answer lies in how you yourself described them: "lunatics and misfits," I believe, were your very words. Someone must have calculatedly driven them into disrepute—but again, why?

It is clear to me now that the one thing Abiha and her people do not desire, under any circumstances, is for someone to build a machine that replicates what they alone can do. Giving such a machine to the masses would open up whole worlds to exploration and exploitation, robbing them of the advantage that they are careful to maintain.

I said that I had made a mistake that night, by resisting her. Had I meekly abandoned my theories, Margaret would not have died, and I would not be as I am now, the center of scandal, my work in disrepute, all that is dear to me in this world dead and demolished—entirely by her hand.

So much for the "light of the intellect"!

What has also become clear to me is the possibility that Abiha too made a mistake. When I grasped her and was pulled into the ether, I did not return unscathed. The ether altered me, as it must alter everyone who touches it. I recognize it now. I feel it when it is near, and I have concluded that I could enter it again, under my own volition, if only given the opportunity.

But how to navigate such formless spaces? How to avoid being lost forever in the void between worlds?

"We all of us have places of significance," Abiha told me. Hers are laboratories like mine, where great men dream of travelling the universe. What if some places resemble the poles of a magnet, except that like attracts like, tuned to an individual's vital experiences? This explains why she came alone to me, not with an army of fiends at her back. Such a navigational mnemonic would enable her to cross the gulf between worlds as easily as stepping from room to room, unfettered by mere matter!

And I could do likewise, if I could manage the trick of it.

Far from egoless acceptance of guilt, dear Doctor Michaels, the dissociation I felt in my cell offers me both the means to escape and an opportunity to gain revenge upon the woman who killed my Margaret. I feel it even more strongly now, here in this place of mourning and loss. The ether presses hard upon the reality of this world—this world I now suspect to be paper-thin and as easy to puncture as water. For the ether is none other than my river of life, the universal fluid we ride like swans, not realizing we can take flight at any time.

In a moment, I will make the attempt. If I succeed, I will follow this fateful catacomb to one in another world—hers, perhaps, if the congress has not ended, or another nearby—leaving you a mystery, this apology, and a further exhortation to read the authors I named during our brief discourse. Don't let the silence subsume their voices, for each is a victim of those who would condemn our world to isolation and ignorance. Take up their dream of the ultimate transportation, and follow, if you can. And when you think of me, remember their words, not mine:

I touched the state when only Truth remains.
I swept away pleasures and pains.
The Highest which is beyond the reach
Of the four ancient Vedas

came
    here
        to me!"

[Author's note: Every reasonable effort has been made to trace the copyright holders of "I left the world" and "The Eightfold Yoga" by Pattinattar, English translation by Kamil V. Zvelebi, and to obtain their permission for the use of this copyright material. The author apologizes for any errors or omissions and would be grateful if notified of any corrections that should be incorporated in future reprints of this story.]

Afterword to "The Jade Woman of the Luminous Star"

After spending a million-plus words and ten novels in one fantasy universe, I've been tinkering recently with something new. My intention is to explore the Helioverse in a novel called *Liminus,* and the opportunity to write this story, a distant prequel, could not be resisted. I'm grateful to John Harwood, for both his assistance and friendship I value beyond words.

—SEAN WILLIAMS

Robert Silverberg

Robert Silverberg has been a professional writer since 1955. Among his many novels are *Lord Valentine's Castle, Dying Inside, Nightwings, A Time of Changes,* and *The Book of Skulls.* He is a many-time winner of the Hugo and Nebula Awards, was Guest of Honor at the 1970 World Science Fiction Convention in Heidelberg, and in 2004 was named a Grand Master by the Science Fiction Writers of America. He and his wife, Karen, live in the San Francisco Bay Area.

ROBERT SILVERBERG

Smithers and the Ghosts of the Thar

W HAT HAPPENED TO Smithers out there in the Great Indian Desert
may seem a trifle hard to believe, but much that happens in Her
Imperial Majesty's subcontinent is a trifle hard to believe, and yet one
disbelieves it at one's peril. Unfortunately, there is nobody to tell the tale
but me, for it all happened many years ago, and Yule has retired from the
Service and is living, so I hear, in Palermo, hard at work on his translation of Marco Polo, and Brewster, the only witness to the tragic events in
the desert, is too far gone in senility now to be of any use to anyone, and
Smithers—ah, poor Smithers—

But let me begin. We start in Calcutta and the year is 1858, with the
memory of the dread and terrible Mutiny still overhanging our dreams,
distant though those bloody events were from our administrative capital
here. That great engineer and brilliant scholar Henry Yule—Lieutenant-
Colonel Yule, as he was then, later to be Sir Henry—having lately returned
from Allahabad, where he was in charge of strengthening and augmenting
our defenses against the rebels, has now been made Secretary of the Public
Works Department, with particular responsibility for designing what one
day will be the vast railroad system that will link every part of India. I hold
the title of Deputy Consulting Engineer for Railways. Our young friend
Brewster is my right-hand man, a splendid draughtsman and planner. And
as my story opens Brewster has come to us, looking oddly flushed, with
the news that Smithers, our intense, romantic, excitable Smithers, whom

we have sent off on a surveying mission to Jodhpur and Bikaner and other sites in the remote West, has returned and is on his way to us at this very moment with an extraordinary tale to tell.

"Is he now?" Yule said, without much sign of animation. Yule is a Scot, stern and outwardly dour and somewhat fierce-looking, though I am in a position to know that behind that grim bearded visage lies a lively mind keenly alert to the romance of exploration. "Did he find a railroad already in place out there, I wonder? Some little project of an enterprising Rajput prince?"

"Here he comes now," said Brewster. "You will hear it all from the man himself." And an instant later Smithers was among us.

Smithers was fair-haired and very pink-skinned, with gleaming blue eyes that blazed out from his face like sapphires. Though he was somewhat below middle height, he was deep-chested and wide-shouldered, and so forceful was his physical presence that he could and did easily dominate a room of much taller men. Certainly he dominated his friend Brewster, who had known him since childhood. They had been to university together and they had entered the service of the East India Company together, taking appointment with the Bengal Engineers and making themselves useful in the Public Works Department, specializing in the building of bridges and canals. I could best describe the lanky, dark-complected Brewster as timid and cautious, one who was designed by Nature as a follower of stronger men, and Smithers, who in his heart of hearts looked upon himself as part of a grand English tradition of adventurous exploration that went back through Burton and Rawlinson and Layard to Walter Raleigh and Francis Drake, was the man to whom he had attached himself.

"Well, Smithers?" Yule asked. "What news from Bikaner?"

"Not from Bikaner, sir," said Smithers, "but from the desert beyond. The Thar, sir! The Thar!" His blazing blue eyes were wilder than ever and his face was rough and reddened from his weeks in the sun.

Yule looked startled. "You went into the Thar?" A reconnaissance of the vast bleak desert that lies beyond the cities of Rajputana had not been part of Smithers's immediate task.

"Only a short way, sir. But what I learned—what I have heard—!"

Yule, who can be impatient and irritable, made a swift circular beckoning gesture, as though to say, "Aye, out with it, man!" But Smithers needed no encouragement. Already a story was tumbling from him: how in the desert city of Bikaner he had fallen in with an itinerant Portuguese merchant newly returned from a venture into the Great Indian Desert— the Thar, as the natives call it, that immense waterless void 150 miles in breadth that stretches northeastward for some 400 miles from the swampy Rann of Cutch. Breathlessly Smithers retold the tale the Portuguese had told him: an unknown valley far out in the Thar, the sound of strange voices floating on the air, sometimes calling alluringly, sometimes wailing or sobbing, voices that could only be the voices of spirits or demons, for there was no one to be seen for miles around; the eerie music of invisible musicians, gongs and drums and bells, echoing against the sands; and above all a distinct sensation as of *summoning*, the awareness of some powerful force pulling one onward, deeper into that valley. The Portuguese had resisted that force, said Smithers, for he was a hard-nosed trader and was able to keep his mind on business; but from villagers at an oasis town the man had picked up fragmentary anecdotes of an entire ancient city hidden away in that valley, a lost civilization, a land of ghosts, in fact, from which that potent summons came, and into whose mysterious realm many a traveler had vanished, never to return.

I saw what I took to be the unmistakable glint of skepticism in Yule's eyes. He has never been a man to suffer foolishness gladly; and from the knotting of his bristling brows I interpreted his response to Smithers's wild fable as annoyance. But I was wrong.

"Singing spirits, eh?" Yule said. "Gongs and drums and bells? Let me read you something, and see if it sounds familiar."

He drew from his desk a sheaf of manuscript pages that were, we already knew, his translation of *The Book of Ser Marco Polo*—the earliest draft of it, rather, for Yule was destined to spend two decades on this magnum opus before giving the world the first edition in 1870, nor did he stop revising and expanding it even then. But even here in 1858 he had done a substantial amount of the work.

"Marco is in the Gobi," said Yule, "in the vicinity of the desert town of Lop, and he writes, 'The length of this desert is so great that 'tis said it would take a year and more to ride from one end of it to the other. Beasts there are none, for there is naught for them to eat. But there is a marvelous thing related of this desert, which is that when travelers are on the move by night, and one of them chances to lag behind or to fall asleep or the like, when he tries to gain his company again he will hear spirits talking, and will suppose them to be his comrades. Sometimes the spirits will call him by name; and thus shall a traveler ofttimes be led astray so that he never finds his party. And in this way many have perished.' "

"It is much like what the Portuguese told me," said Smithers.

Yule nodded. "I will go on. 'Sometimes the stray travelers will hear as it were the tramp and hum of a great cavalcade of people away from the real line of road, and taking this to be their own company they will follow the sound; and when day breaks they find that a cheat has been put upon them and that they are in an ill plight. Even in the daytime one hears those spirits talking. And sometimes you shall hear the sound of a variety of musical instruments, and still more commonly the sound of drums.' "

Smithers said, and his face grew even redder, "How I long to hear those drums!"

"Of course you do," said Yule, and brought out the whisky and soda, and passed around the cigars, and I knew that look in Yule's formidable glittering eyes had not been one of skepticism at all, but of complete and utter captivation.

He went on to tell us that such tales as Marco Polo's were common in medieval travel literature, and, rummaging among his papers, he read us a citation from Pliny of phantoms that appear and vanish in the deserts of Africa, and one from a Chinese named Hiuen Tsang six centuries before Marco that spoke of troops with waving banners marching in the Gobi, vanishing and reappearing and vanishing again, and many another tale of goblins and ghouls and ghostly dancers and musicians in the parched places of the world. "Of course," said Yule, "it is possible to explain some of this music and song merely as the noises made by shifting sands affected by desert winds and extreme heat, and the banners and armies as illusions that the minds of men traveling under such stressful conditions are likely to generate." He stared for a moment into his glass; he took a reflective puff of his cigar. "And then, of course, there is always the possibility that these tales have a rational origin—that somewhere in one of these deserts there does indeed lurk a hidden land that would seem wondrously strange to us, if only we could find it. The great age of discovery, gentlemen, is not yet over."

"I request leave, sir, to look into the Thar beyond Bikaner and see what might be found there," Smithers said.

It was a daring request. Smithers was our best surveyor, and the entire subcontinent needed measuring for the system of railways that we intended to create in its immense expanse, and nobody was planning to run track through the desert beyond Bikaner, for there was nothing there. Plenty of urgent work awaited Smithers between Delhi and Jodhpur, between Calcutta and Bombay, and elsewhere.

But Yule rose with that glitter of excitement in his eyes again and began pulling maps from a portfolio under his desk and spreading them out, the big thirty-two-miles-to-the-inch map and a smaller one of the Frontier, pointing to this place and that one in the Thar and asking if one of them might have been the one of which that Portuguese had spoken, and we knew that Smithers's request had been granted.

WHAT I DID not expect was that Brewster would be allowed to accompany him. Plainly it was a dangerous expedition and Smithers ought not to have been permitted to undertake it alone, but I would have thought that a subaltern or two and half a dozen native trackers would be the appropriate complement. Indeed, Brewster was a strong and healthy young man who would readily be able to handle the rigors of the Thar, but an abundance of work awaited him right here in Calcutta, and it struck me as remarkably extravagant for Yule to be willing to risk not one but two of our best engineers on such a fantastic endeavor at this critical time in the development of the nascent Indian railway system.

But I had failed to reckon with two traits of Yule's character. One was his insatiable scholarly curiosity, which had drawn him to the close study not only of Marco Polo's huge book but of the texts of many another early traveler whose names meant nothing to me: Ibn Batuta, for example, and Friar Jordanus, and Oderic of Pordenone. We were living at a time when the remaining unknown places of the world were opening before us, and the discovery—or rediscovery—of strange and marvelous regions of Asia held great fascination for him. Though he himself could not leave his high responsibilities in Calcutta, Smithers would serve as his surrogate in the far-off Thar.

Then, too, I had overlooked Yule's profound complexity of spirit. As I have already noted, he is not at all the grim, stolid, monolithic administrator that he appears to a casual observer to be. I have spoken of his irritability and impatience; I should mention also his bursts of temper, followed by spells of black depression and almost absolute silence, and also the—well, *eccentricity* that has led him, a man who happens to be color-blind, to dress in the most outlandish garb and think it utterly normal. (I have in mind his brilliant claret-colored trousers, which he always insisted were silver-gray.) He is complicated; he is very much his own man. So if he had taken it into his mind to send our highly valued Smithers off to look for lost cities in the Thar, nothing would stop him.

And when he asked Smithers what sort of complement he thought he would need, Smithers replied, "Why, Brewster and I can probably deal with everything all by ourselves, sir. We don't want a great silly crowd of bearers and trackers, you know, to distract us as we try to cope with those musical specters in the desert."

Quickly I looked at Brewster and saw that he was as amazed as I was to find himself requisitioned for the expedition. But he made a quick recovery and managed a grin of boyish eagerness, as if he could think of nothing more jolly than to go trekking off into a pathless haunted desert with his hero Smithers. And Yule showed no reaction at all to Smithers's request: once again he demonstrated his approval simply through silence.

Of course, getting to the Thar would be no easy matter. It lies at the opposite side of the subcontinent from Calcutta, far off in the northwest, beyond Lucknow, beyond Agra, beyond Delhi. And, as I have said, all of this was taking place at a time before we had built the Indian railway system. Smithers had just made the round trip from Calcutta to Bikaner and back, fifteen hundred miles or more, by an arduous journey down the Grand Trunk Road, India's backbone before the railways existed. I have no idea how he traveled—by horse, by camel, by bullock-cart, by affiliating himself with merchant caravans, by any such means he could. And now he—and Brewster—would have to do it all over again. The journey would take months.

I should mention that Smithers had been engaged for the past year and a half to the Adjutant's daughter, Helena, a young woman as notable for her beauty as for her sweetness of temperament, and the wedding was due to take place in just another dozen weeks or so. I wondered how Smithers would be able to prevail on her for a postponement; but prevail he did, either through his own force of personality or the innately accommodating nature that is so typical of women, and the wedding was postponed. We held a grand farewell party for Smithers and Brewster at Fort William, where nothing was asked and nothing was volunteered about the reason for their departure, and in the small hours of the night we stood by the bank of the river with brandy glasses in hand, singing the grand old songs of our native country so far away, and then in the morning they set out to find whatever it was that they were destined to find in the Great Indian Desert.

The weeks passed, and turned into months.

Helena, the Adjutant's lovely daughter, came to us now and again to ask whether there had been any word from her wandering fiancé. Of course I could see that she was yearning to get him back from the Thar and take him off to England for a lifetime of pink-faced, fair-haired children, tea, cool fresh air, and clean linens. "I love him so," she would say.

The poor girl! The poor girl!

I knew that Smithers was India through and through, and that if she ever did get him back from the Thar there would be another quest after that, and another, and another.

I knew too that there had been an engagement before she had met Smithers, a Major invalided home from Lahore after some sort of dreary scandal involving drinking and gambling, about which I had wanted to hear no details. She was twenty-six, already. The time for making those pink-faced babies was running short.

The months went by, and Smithers and Brewster did not return from the Thar. Yule began to grow furious. His health was not good—the air of India had never been right for him, and Bengal can be a monotonous and depressing place, oppressively dank and humid much of the year—and he could see retirement from the Service not very far in his future; but he desperately wanted to know about that valley in the Thar before he left. And, for all that desperate curiosity of his, work was work and there was a railroad line to build and Smithers and Brewster were needed here, not drifting around in some sandy wasteland far away.

Yule's health gave way quite seriously in the spring of 1859 and he took himself home to Scotland for a rest. His older brother George, who had not been out of India for thirty years, went with him. They were gone three months. Since the voyage out and the voyage back took a month each, that left them only a month at home, but he returned greatly invigorated, only to be much distressed and angered by the news that Smithers and Brewster were still unaccounted for.

From time to time the Adjutant's daughter came to inquire about her fiancé. Of course I had no news for her.

"I love him so!" she cried.

The poor girl.

THEN ONE DAY there was a stir in town, as there often is when a caravan from some distant place arrives, and shortly thereafter Brewster presented himself at my office at the Public Works Department. Not Brewster and Smithers: just Brewster.

I scarcely recognized him. He was decked out not in his usual khakis but in some bizarre native garb, very colorful and strange, flowing robes of rose, magenta, turquoise blue, but that was not the least of the change. The Brewster I had seen off, the year before, had been dark-haired and youthful, perhaps thirty-two years old at most. The man I saw before me now looked forty-five or even fifty. There were prominent streaks of gray in his thick black hair, and the underlying bony structure of his cheeks and chin seemed to have shifted about to some degree, and there was a network of fine lines radiating outward from the corners of his eyes that no man of thirty-two should have had. His posture had changed, too: I remembered him as upright and straight-backed, but he had begun to stoop a little, as tall men sometimes do with the years, and his shoulders seemed rounded and hunched in a way I did not recall. My first thought, which in retrospect shows an amazing lack of insight, was merely that the journey must have been a very taxing one.

"Welcome, old friend," I said. And then I said, carefully, "And Smithers—?"

Brewster gave me a weary stare. "He is still there."

"Ah," I said. And again: "Ah."

Brewster's reply could have meant anything: that Smithers had found something so fascinating that he needed more time for research, that he had fallen under the sway of some native cult and was wandering naked and ash-smeared along the ghats of Benares, or that he had perished on the journey and lay buried somewhere in the desert. But I asked no questions.

"Let me send for Yule," I said. "He will want to hear your story."

There had been a change in Yule's appearance, too, since Brewster's departure. He too had grown bowed and stooped and gray, but in his case that was no surprise, for he was nearly forty and his health had never been strong. But it was impossible not to notice Yule's reaction at the great alteration Brewster had undergone. Indeed, Brewster now looked older than Yule himself.

"Well," said Yule, and waited.

And Brewster began to tell his tale.

THEY HAD SET forth in the grandest of moods, Brewster said. Smithers was almost always exuberant and enthusiastic, and it had ever been Brewster's way, although he was of a different basic temperament, readily to fall in with his friend's customarily jubilant frame of mind. It had been their plan to go with the Spring Caravan heading for Aurangabad, but in India everything happens either after time or before time, and in this case the caravan departed before time, so they were on their own. Smithers found horses for them and off they went, westward along the Grand Trunk Road, that great long river-like highway, going back to the sixteenth century and probably to some prehistoric precursor, that carries all traffic through the heart of India.

It is a comfortable road. I have traveled it myself. It is perfectly straight and capably constructed. Trees planted on both sides of it give welcome shade the whole way. The wide, well-made middle road is for the quick traffic, the sahibs on their horses, and the like. It was on that road that the British armies moved swiftly out of Bengal to conquer the north Indian plain. To the left and right are the rougher roadbeds where the heavy carts with creaking wooden wheels go groaning along, the ones that bear the cotton and grain, the timber, the hides, the produce. And then there is the foot traffic, the hordes and hordes of moneylenders and holy men and native surgeons and pilgrims and peddlers, swarms of them in the thousands going about the daily business of India.

As traveling sahibs, of course, Smithers and Brewster encountered no problems. There are caravanserais at regular intervals to provide food and lodging, and police stations set close together so that order is maintained. When their horses gave out they rented others, and later they hired passage for themselves in bullock-carts until they could find horses once again, and after that they rode on camels for a time. From Durgapur to Benares they went, from Kanpur and Aligarh to Delhi, and there, although the Grand Trunk Road continues on northwestward to Lahore and Peshawar to its terminus, they turned to secondary roads that brought them down via Bikaner to the edge of the desert.

The Thar, then! The vast unwelcoming Thar!

Brewster described it for us: the deep, loose, fine-grained sands, the hillocks that the winds have shaped, running from southwest to northeast, the dunes that rise two hundred feet or more above the dusty plain, the ugly gravel plains. As one might expect, there are no real rivers there, unless you count the Indus, which flows mostly to the west of it, and the Luri, which runs through its southern reaches. The Ghaggar comes down into it from the north but loses itself in the desert sands. There are some salt lakes and a few widely spaced freshwater springs. The vegetation, such as it is, is mostly thorny scrub, and some acacia and tamarisk trees.

Why anyone would plant a city in such a desolate place as the Thar is beyond my comprehension, but men will found cities anywhere, it seems. Most likely they chose sites along the eastern fringe of the desert, which is relatively habitable, because that great forbidding waste just beyond would protect them against invasion from the northwest. So along that fringe one finds the princely states of Rajasthan, and such royal capitals as Jodhpur, Jaipur, and Bikaner; and it was the walled city of Bikaner, famous for its carpets and blankets, that became expedition headquarters for Smithers and Brewster.

Brewster, who was something of a linguist, went among the people to ask about haunted valleys and invisible drum-players and the like. He did not quite use those terms, but his persistent questioning did get some useful answers, after a while. One old fakir thought that the place they sought might lie between Pakpattan and Mubarakpur. Smithers and Brewster bought some camels and laid in provisions and headed out to see. They did not find any lost civilizations between Pakpattan and Mubarakpur. But Smithers was confident that they would find something somewhere, and they went north and then west and then curved south again, tacking to and fro across a pathless sea of sand, making an intricate zigzagging tour through territory so forlorn, Brewster told us, that you felt like weeping when you saw it. And after a week or two, he said, as they plodded on between nowhere and nowhere and were close to thinking themselves altogether and eternally lost, the sound of strange singing came to them on the red-hot wind from the west.

"Do you hear it?" Smithers asked.

"I hear it, yes," said Brewster.

He told us that it was like no singing he had ever heard: delicate, eerie, a high-pitched chant that might have been made up of individual words, but words so slurred and blurred that they carried no meaning at all. Then, too, apart from the chanting they heard spoken words, a low incomprehensible whispering in the air, the urgent chattering conversation of invisible beings, and the tinkling of what might have been camel bells in the distance, and the occasional tapping of drumbeats.

"There are our ghosts," Smithers said. It was a word he liked to use, said Brewster. Like most of us Brewster had read a few ghost stories, and to him the word "ghosts" summoned up the creaking floorboards of a haunted house, shrouded white figures gliding silently through darkness, fluttering robes moving of their own bodiless accord, strangely transparent coaches traveling swiftly down a midnight road, and other such images quite remote from the chanting and drumming of desert folk in gaudy garb, with jingling anklets and necklaces, under a hot fierce sun. But the sounds of the Thar came from some invisible source, and to Smithers they were sounds made by ghosts.

Everything was as the Portuguese merchant had said it would be, even unto the mysterious *summoning* force that emanated from some location to the west. The Portuguese had fought against that pull and had won his struggle, but Smithers and Brewster had no wish to do the same, and they rode onward, wrapping their faces against the burning wind and the scouring gusts of airborne sand. The sounds grew more distinct. It seemed to them both that the voices they heard were those of revelers, laughing and singing in the marketplace of a populous city; but there could be no cities here, in this abysmal trackless wilderness of sand and thin tufts of grass and empty sky. There was nothing here whatever.

And then they entered a narrow canyon that showed a shadowy slit at its farther end. They went toward it—there was scarcely any choice, now, so strong was the pull—and passed through it, and, suddenly, without any sense of transition, they were out of the desert and in some new and altogether unexpected realm. It was more than an oasis; it was like an entire faery kingdom. Before them stretched groves of palms and lemon trees along gently flowing canals, and beyond those gardens were rows of angular, many-windowed buildings rising rank upon rank above a swiftly flowing river that descended out of low, softly rounded green hills in the west. Brewster and Smithers stared at each other in amazement and wonder. When they looked back they no longer could see the desert, for a thick gray film, a kind of solid vapor, stretched like an impenetrable band across the mouth of the canyon.

"A moment later," said Brewster, "we found ourselves surrounded by the inhabitants of this place. They rose up out of nowhere, like phantoms indeed, a great colorful horde of them, and danced a welcome about us in circles, singing and waving their arms aloft and crying out in what we could only interpret as tones of gladness."

THE PEOPLE OF the hidden valley, Brewster told us, were a tall, handsome folk, plainly of the Caucasian race, dark-eyed but light-skinned, with sharp cheekbones and long narrow noses. They seemed rather like Persians in appearance, he thought. They dressed in loose robes of the most vibrant colors, greens, reds, brilliant yellows, the men wearing red or gold pointed skullcaps or beautiful soft-hued turbans striped with bright bands of lemon, pink, yellow, or white, and the women in voluminous mantles, filmy clouds of crepe, shawls shot through with gold brocade, and the like. Below their cascading robes both sexes wore white trousers of a ballooning sort, and an abundance of silver anklets. Their feet were bare. Of course throughout India one sees all manner of flamboyant exotic garb, varying somewhat from region to region but all of it colorful and almost magical in its beauty, and the way these people looked was not fundamentally different from the look of the dwellers in this district of Hindustan or that one, and yet there *was* a difference, a certain quaint touch of antique glamour, an element of the fantastic, that left the two travelers thinking that they had drifted not into some unknown valley but into the thousand-year-old pages of the *Thousand Nights and a Night.*

At no time did they feel as though they were in danger. Perhaps these people might be ghosts of some sort, but goblins, ghouls, demons, no. They were too amiable for that. The welcoming party, never ceasing its prancing and chanting, conducted them into the town, the buildings of which were of wattled mud plastered in white and overpainted with elaborate patterns of the same brilliant hues as the clothing. From there on it was all rather like entering into an unusually vivid dream. They were shown to a kind of caravanserai where they were able to rest and bathe. Their camels, which were the object of great curiosity, were taken away to be given provender and water, and they themselves were supplied with clothing of the native sort to replace the tattered garments in which they had crossed the desert.

"They fed us generously," said Brewster, "with an array of curried meats, and some fruits and vegetables, and a drink much like yoghourt, made of the fermented milk of I know not what creature." The flavor of the food was unfamiliar, rich with spices, particularly black pepper, but wholly lacking in the fiery red capsicums that we associate with the cuisine of the land. Of course the capsicum is not native to India—the Portuguese, I think, brought it here from the New World centuries ago—and perhaps it was impossible to obtain them here in the Thar; but their absence from the food was something that Brewster found especially notable.

He and Smithers were the center of all attention, day after day, as if they were the first to make their way into the valley from the outside world in many years, as most probably they were. Village notables came to them daily, men with flowing white beards and glorious turbans, one of them of particularly majestic bearing who was surely the rajah of the city, and pelted them with an endless flow of questions, none of which, of course, either man could understand. English was unknown here, and when Brewster and Smithers tried Hindustani or Rajasthani or such smatterings of Urdu and Sindhi that they knew, no connection was made. Gradually it dawned on Brewster, who was, as I have said, quite a good linguist, that they were speaking a primitive form of Hindi, something like the Marwari dialect that they speak in and around Bikaner, but as different from it as the English of Chaucer is from that of Queen Victoria's times. He did indeed manage to pick out a few words correctly, and achieved some few moments of successful communication with the valley folk, each time touching off a great gleeful volley of the local kind of applause, which involved stamping of the feet and jingling of the anklets.

In the succeeding weeks Smithers and Brewster became, to some degree, part of the life of the village. They were allowed to wander upriver by themselves, and found garden plots there where spices and vegetables were growing. They saw the workshops where cloth was laboriously woven and cut by women sitting cross-legged. They saw the dyers' tanks, great stone-walled pools of scarlet and mauve and azure and crimson. They saw the fields where livestock grazed.

It was a closed community, utterly self-sufficient, sealed away from the forbidding desert that surrounded it and completely able to meet all its own needs, while outside the valley the world of kings and emperors and railroads and steam engines and guns and newspapers ticked on and on, mattering less than nothing to these oblivious people—these ghosts, as Smithers persisted in calling them.

And yet there was leakage: those sounds of gongs and drums and singing, drifting through that foggy barrier and into the wasteland beyond, and occasionally summoning some outsider to the valley. That was odd. Brewster had no explanation for it. I suppose no one ever shall.

Before long the irrepressible Smithers's innate exuberance came to the fore. He was full of ideas for transforming the lives of these people. He wanted to teach them how to build aqueducts, steam engines, pumps, looms. He urged Brewster, who even now could manage only a few broken sentences in their language, to describe these things to the rajah and his court. Brewster was not convinced that these folk needed aqueducts or pumps or any of the other things Smithers yearned to bestow on them, but he did his best, which was not nearly good enough. Smithers, impatient, began to try to learn their language himself. One of the women of the village—a girl, rather, a striking keen-eyed girl of about twenty, half a head taller than Smithers—seemed to have volunteered to be his tutor. Brewster often saw them together, pantomiming words, acting out little charades, laughing, gesturing. He might perhaps be learning something, Brewster thought.

But Brewster knew that they could not stay there long enough to build aqueducts. Fascinating though the place was, the time had come, he thought, to begin the journey back into the modern world. And so he said, one morning, to Smithers.

At that point in his narrative Brewster fell silent. He seemed entirely played out. "So you would call it truly a lost civilization?" Yule asked when Brewster had said nothing for what might have been several minutes. "Cut off in the desert for hundreds of years or even more from all contact with the rest of India?"

"I would call it that, yes," said Brewster.

"And when the time came for you to leave, Smithers chose to remain?"

"Yes," said Brewster, showing some signs of uneasiness at the question. "That is exactly what happened."

He did not offer details, but merely said that after some weeks he felt that it was incumbent upon them to return to Calcutta and make their report, and, when Smithers insisted on remaining to conduct further studies, of the type that so many venturesome men of our nation have carried out in Africa and Asia and the Americas, Brewster, finding it impossible to shake his resolve, at last reluctantly resolved to leave without him. The valley people seemed distressed at the thought of his departure, and indeed made it so difficult for him to locate the camels that he thought they might intend to restrain him from going; but eventually he found them, and— this part was very difficult too—went back out of the canyon, blundering around in one direction and another in that thick band of vapor before finding the one and only exit into the desert. Getting back to Bikaner from there was another great challenge, and only by some lucky guesswork was he able to retrace his earlier path. And after a lengthy and evidently toilsome journey back across the subcontinent, a journey that he did not choose to describe, but which I thought must have been so exhausting that it had put that strange appearance of premature age upon him, here he was among us once more in Yule's office.

Yule said, when he was done, "And would you be able to find that place again, if you had to? If I were to ask you to go back there now to get Smithers?"

Brewster seemed stunned by the request.

He winced and blinked, like one stepping out of a dark room into Calcutta sunlight. I could see signs of a struggle going on within him. Yule's question had caught him completely by surprise; and plainly he was searching for the strength to refuse any repetition of the ordeal he had just been through. But the indomitable Yule was waiting grimly for a reply, and finally, in a barely audible voice, Brewster said, "Yes, I think that I could. I think so, sir. But is it necessary that I do?"

"It is," said Yule. "We can hardly do without him. It was wrong of you to come away with him still there. You must go back and fetch him."

Brewster considered that. He bowed his head. I think I may have heard a sob. He looked ragged and pale and tired. He was silent a great while, and it seemed to me that he was thinking about something that he did not care to discuss with us.

Yule, waiting once again for a reply, appeared terribly tired himself, as though he wanted nothing more than a year's rest in some gentler clime.

But the great strength of the man was still evident, bearing down on poor Brewster with full force.

After a long, an interminable silence, whatever resistance Brewster had managed to muster seemed to snap. I saw him quiver as it happened. He said quietly, huskily, "Yes, I suppose I must." And planning for the return trip began forthwith.

I was with Brewster the next day when Helena came to inquire about her errant fiancé. Brewster told her that Smithers was making great discoveries, that his discovery of this lost land would assure him eternal fame in the annals of exploration. He has remained behind for a while to complete his notes and sketches, Brewster said. I noticed that he did not meet the Adjutant's daughter's eager gaze as he spoke; in truth, he looked past her shoulder as though she were a creature too bright to behold.

THIS TIME THERE was no grand farewell party. Brewster simply slipped away alone to the Grand Trunk Road. He had insisted that no one should accompany him, and he did so with such un-Brewsterlike firmness that even Yule was taken aback, and yielded, though to me it seemed like madness to let the man make that trip by himself.

And so Brewster departed once more for that valley in the Thar. Soon Yule left us again also—he had another breakdown of his health, and went on recreational leave to Java—and, since we were now in the full throes of planning the Indian railway system and our staff was already undermanned, my own responsibilities multiplied manifold. In 1857 we had had only two hundred miles of track in operation in all of India. Our task was to increase that a hundredfold, not only for greater ease in our own military operations, but also to provide India with a modern system of mass transportation that would further the economic development of that huge and still largely primitive land. As the months went along and my work engulfed me, I confess that I forgot all about Brewster and Smithers.

Yule returned from Java, looking much older. Before long he would resign from the Service to return to England, and then, as his wife's health weakened also, on to the more benevolent clime of Italy, where he would complete and publish his famous translations of Marco Polo and other medieval travelers in Asia. In his remaining time in Calcutta he said nothing about Brewster and Smithers either; I think they had fallen completely out of his mind, which had no room for the irresponsible Smitherses and feckless Brewsters of the world.

One day in 1861 or early 1862 I was hard at work, preparing a report for the Governor-General on the progress of the Bombay-Calcutta line, when an old man in faded robes was shown into my office. He was thin and very tall, with rounded shoulders and a bent, bowed posture, and his long, narrow face was deeply lined, so that his eyes looked out at me from a bewildering webwork of crevices. He was trembling as though palsied, though more likely it was just the tremor of age. Under his arm he carried a rectangular box of some considerable size, fastened with an ornate clasp of native design. Because his skin was so dark and he was wearing those loose robes I mistook him for a native himself at first, but then I began to think he might be a deeply tanned Englishman, and when he spoke his accent left no doubt of that.

"You don't recognize me, do you?" he asked.

I stared. "I'm sorry. I don't think I do." I was annoyed by the interruption. "Are you sure that the business you have is with the Public Works Department?"

"I am, in fact, an employee of the Public Works Department. Or was, at least."

His face was still unrecognizable to me. But the voice—

"Brewster?"

"Brewster, yes. Back at last."

"But this is impossible! You're—what, thirty-five years old? You look to be—"

"Sixty? Seventy?"

"I would have to say so, yes."

He studied me implacably. "I am Brewster," he said. "I will be thirty-seven come January."

"This is impossible," I said, though aware of the foolishness of my words as soon as I spoke them. "For a man to have aged so quickly—"

"Impossible, yes, that's the word. But I am Brewster."

He set that box down on my desk, heedless of the clutter of blueprints and maps on which he was placing it. And he said, "You may recall that Lieutenant-Colonel Yule ordered me to return to a certain valley in the Thar and bring Major Smithers out of it. I have done so. It was not an easy journey, but I have accomplished it, and I have returned. And I have brought Smithers with me."

I peered expectantly at him, thinking that he would wave his age-withered arm and Smithers would come striding in from the hall. But no: instead he worked at the clasp of that big wooden box with those trembling fingers of his for what seemed like half an hour, and opened it at last, and lifted the lid and gestured to me to peer in.

Inside lay a bleached skull, sitting atop a jumble of other bones, looking like relics exhumed from some tumulus of antiquity. They were resting on a bed of sand.

"This is Smithers," he said.

For a moment I could find nothing whatever to say. Then I blurted, "How did he die?"

"He died of extreme age," Brewster said.

And he told me how, after expending many weeks and months crossing India and bashing around in the Thar, he had finally heard the ghostly singers and the distant drums and gongs again, and they had led him to the hidden valley. There he found Smithers, fluent now in the local lingo and busy with all manner of public-works projects in a full-scale attempt to bring the inhabitants of the valley into the nineteenth century overnight.

He was married, Brewster said, to that lovely long-legged native princess who had been teaching him the language.

"Married?" I repeated foolishly, thinking of mournful Helena, the Adjutant's beautiful daughter, faithful to him yet, still waiting hopefully for his return.

"I suppose it was a marriage," said Brewster. "They were man and wife, at any rate, whatever words had been said over them. And seemed very happy together. I spoke to him about returning to his assignment here. As you might suspect, he wasn't eager to do so. I spoke more firmly to him about it." I tried to imagine the diffident Brewster speaking firmly to his strong-willed friend about anything. I couldn't. "I appealed to his sense of duty. I appealed to him as an Englishman. I spoke of the Queen."

"And did he yield?"

"After a while, yes," Brewster said, in a strange tone of voice that made me wonder whether Brewster might have made him yield at gunpoint. I could not bring myself to ask. "But he insisted that we bring his—wife—out of the valley with us. And so we did. And here they are."

He indicated the box, the skull, the bones beneath, the bed of sand.

"Hardly had we passed through the barrier but they began to shrivel and age," he said. "The woman died first. She became a hideous crone in a matter of hours. Then Smithers went."

"But how—how?"

Brewster shrugged. "Time moves at a different rate within the valley. I can't explain it. I don't understand it. The people in there may be living six or eight hundred years ago, or even more. Time is suspended. But when one emerges—well, do you see me? How I look? The suspended years descend on one like an avalanche, once one leaves. I spent a few weeks in that village the first time. I came back here looking ten or twenty years older. This time I was there for some months. Look at me. Smithers had been under the valley's spell for, what, two or three years?"

"And the woman for her entire life."

"Yes. When they came out, he must have been a hundred years old, by the way we reckon time. And she, perhaps a thousand."

How could I believe him? I am an engineer, a builder of railroads and bridges. I give no credence to tales of ghosts and ghouls and invisible specters whose voices are heard on the desert air, nor do I believe that time runs at different rates in different parts of our world. And yet—yet—the skull, the bones, the withered, trembling old man of not quite thirty-seven who stood before me speaking with Brewster's voice—

I understood now that Brewster had been aware of what going back into that terrible valley to fetch Smithers would do to him. It would rob him of most or all of the remaining years of his life. He had known, but Yule had ordered him to go, and yes he had gone. The poor man. The poor doomed man.

To cover my confusion I reached into the box. "And what is this?" I asked, picking up a pinch of something fine and white that I took for desert sand, lying beneath the little heap of bones like a cushion. "A souvenir of the Thar?"

"In a manner of speaking. That's all that remains of her. She crumbled to dust right in front of me. Shriveled and died and went absolutely to dust, all in a moment."

Shuddering, I brushed it free of my fingers, back into the box.

I was silent for a while.

The room was spinning about me. I had spent all my days in a world in which three and three make six, six and six make twelve, but I was not sure that I lived in such a world any longer.

Then I said, "Take what's left of Smithers to the chaplain, and see what he wants to do about a burial."

He nodded, the good obedient Brewster of old. "And what shall I do with this?" he asked, pointing to the sandy deposit in the box.

"Scatter it in the road," I said. "Or spill it into the river, whatever you wish. She was Smithers's undoing. We owe her no courtesies."

And then I thought of Helena, sweet, patient Helena. She had never understood the first thing about him, had she? And yet she had loved him. Poor, sweet Helena.

She must be protected now, I thought. The world is very strange, and sometimes too harsh, and we must protect women like Helena from its mysteries. At least, from such mysteries as this one—not the mystery of that hidden valley, I mean, though that is mysterious enough, but the mysteries of the heart.

I drew a deep breath. "And—with regard to the Adjutant's daughter, Brewster—"

"Yes?

"She will want to know how he died, I suppose. Tell her he died bravely, while in the midst of his greatest adventure in Her Majesty's Service. But you ought not, I think, to tell her very much more than that. Do you understand me? He died bravely. That should suffice, Brewster. That should suffice."

Afterword to "Smithers and the Ghosts of the Thar"

I've long been an admirer of the classic Victorian and Edwardian ghost stories—by M. R. James, Oliver Onions, J. S. Le Fanu, Algernon Blackwood, Arthur Machen, and so on—and had been reading another old favorite, Rudyard Kipling, when news of this new anthology arrived. It seemed a logical thing to write a ghost story in the mode of Kipling for it.

—ROBERT SILVERBERG

John Langan

John Langan is the author of a novel, *House of Windows,* and a collection of stories, *Mr. Gaunt and Other Uneasy Encounters.* His stories have appeared in *The Magazine of Fantasy & Science Fiction, Cthulhu's Reign, By Blood We Live, Poe,* and *The Living Dead.* He has been nominated for the Bram Stoker Award and the International Horror Guild Award. He teaches classes in creative writing and gothic fiction and film at SUNY New Paltz and lives nearby with his wife, son, two cats, and a changing menagerie of insects, amphibians, and reptiles.

JOHN LANGAN

The Unbearable Proximity of Mr. Dunn's Balloons

I

"Come, now," Dunn said. His voice sounded as reasonable as it had at any point these last seven days. "Surely, you must have expected something like this."

On reflection, Coleman supposed the man had a point. That did not stop him from thrusting his rapier into the nearest of the balloons.

II

"I'm sorry?" Coleman said, turning from the train's window. Under the pretense of watching the Hudson slide past, he had been studying his reflection, renewing his debate with himself over shaving the beard he had worn since his midtwenties, the white hairs which he feared added a full decade to his appearance, advancing (distinguished) middle age to premature old age.

"I asked if you are planning to interview Mr. Dunn," the young man seated across the compartment said. "You had said you write, so it occurred to me that you might be at work on an article about him."

"I am not," Coleman said. "I no longer write as much for the magazines as I used to. Of late, I've been concentrating my efforts on my fiction."

"Oh," said the young man, who had introduced himself at Grand Central as Cal Earnshaw. While the suit in which he traveled appeared of reasonable quality, there was a leanness to Cal's face that suggested those of beggars Coleman had passed along the Venetian canals. The even younger woman seated beside Cal, his wife, Isabelle, said, "If I may be forward, Mr. Coleman, why are you on your way to Mr. Dunn's? From what I've read of your novels, it doesn't seem as though the . . . extravagances of Mr. Dunn and his followers would hold much of interest for you."

Despite himself, a little thrill raced up Coleman's spine at Mrs. Earnshaw's admission of familiarity with his work; a similar confession, he felt certain, would not trouble her husband's lips. He said, "You underestimate me, Madame. My father was a Swedenborgian, albeit an idiosyncratic one."

"You don't say," Cal said.

"I do."

"Do you imply that you have inherited your father's beliefs?" Isabelle said.

"I imply nothing of the kind," Coleman said. "My father found Swedenborg sufficient to his needs; my interest, however, has tended towards the manner in which we make our way through this life, rather than any other."

"Yet surely," Isabelle said, "the nature of our beliefs about the life to come may exert a profound influence upon our conduct in the life that is."

"Undoubtedly," Coleman said. "Although, from my observations, that influence is frequently more occult than direct."

"Then why have you joined us?" Cal said. "Not that we regret the company."

"I am on this train," Coleman said, "in hopes of seeing Mr. Dunn's balloons, about which so much has been written."

"You have read Mrs. Barchester's report of them?" Isabelle said.

"It was that which brought them to my attention," Coleman said. "A friend passing through London made me a gift of her book. My thoughts of late have tended in the direction of the place of my birth. I would not call any point along the Hudson my home, but so much of my childhood was spent traveling up and down the shores of what we used to call the North River that something of the word's glamour attaches to the region, as a whole. When my friend's generosity presented me with Mrs. Barchester's record of her tour up the Hudson, I took it as practically an omen that I should revisit the scenes of my boyhood. Her description of Mr. Dunn's rather remarkable paper balloons iced the cake, so to speak. Even before I had turned the last page, I had booked my trip and written to another friend to ask if it were in his powers to arrange a visit to Summerland for me. It was, and"—Coleman spread his hands—"I have the pleasure of your company. I take it your motivations are of a more spiritual character."

"We are going to prepare for my crossing," Cal said.

"I beg your pardon?"

"My husband is ill, Mr. Coleman." Isabelle laid a gloved hand on her husband's. "We have exhausted all of his inheritance and most of mine in search of a cure. There is none. The last physician we consulted—Sir Luke Strett: perhaps you have heard of him? He is very well known on the Continent."

Coleman was unsure. "The name is familiar, yes."

"He advised us that Cal's time is short, and that there are better ways to spend it than chasing false hope."

"I've long had an interest in the writings of Mr. Dunn and his set," Cal said. "Mr. Davis, the Fox sisters . . . the picture of the next life they have advanced seems so much more *reasonable* than that of the traditional faiths. Upon our return to Brooklyn, I threw myself into a study of their work. I read their books; I sat in on their séances; I heard their lectures. Had my health been firmer, I would have attended one of their conventions, although there was no real need of that. What I had learned was enough to justify my previous interest."

Isabelle said, "During one of Mr. Dunn's lectures, he mentioned that, upon occasion, he had aided those approaching this life's end in readying themselves for the next. Afterwards, Cal and I succeeded in speaking to the man, and once he knew our story, he volunteered his services upon the spot."

"Is that so?"

"Yes." Cal nodded. "Not only did Mr. Dunn refuse what little payment we could offer, he provided for our travel from our home to his."

"How very generous of him."

"It was—it is," Isabelle said.

"Perhaps you had rather I defer my visit to Summerland," Coleman said. "Compared to yours, my reasons for this trip are trivial. I would not wish to interfere with Mr. Dunn's plans for you."

"Nonsense," Cal said. "You won't be interfering a bit."

"According to Mr. Dunn's letter to us," Isabelle said, "he will require some time alone with my husband. Although he assures us his house's library is thoroughly stocked, I should be grateful for a companion to help me pass the hours."

"You may consider me at your disposal," Coleman said.

III

Summerland, Poughkeepsie

June 16, 1888

Strange to meet Parrish Dunn today. I wouldn't say I've been brooding on the man, but he has engaged my thoughts for much of the last several months. The successful arms merchant who washes his hands of the blood in which he's steeped them for nigh on twenty years to devote himself to the promulgation of his new Spiritualist beliefs—not to mention, to fashioning his elaborate balloons—how could such a figure not be of interest? I've spent enough time—enough pages in this notebook—supplementing the scant description of him in Mrs. Barchester's North Along the Hudson *that to meet the original to whom my speculations owe their existence gave me a jolt.*

He looks like an arms merchant—strike that, he looks like an arms maker, one of those powers charged by the other gods with forging their spears and shields deep in the bowels of a smoking volcano. Until this point in my life, I have considered my five foot ten inches a more than adequate height, but Dunn must stand somewhere in the vicinity of six foot seven, six foot eight. He rises up to that measurement like a mountain; I've never done well at estimating anyone's weight, so it may be more useful to write that he appears almost as wide as he is tall. Every item he was wearing—black suit, white shirt, black shoes—must have been specially made for him.

Because of his size, Dunn's face, which would otherwise fall somewhere in the broad middle of the human spectrum, has something of the grotesque to it. He is bald, and the expanse of his great skull somehow contributes to this impression. His heavy lips frame a mouth whose thick teeth seem formed for tearing the meat from a leg of venison. His nose is flat, wide, crossed by a white scar that continues across the right cheek. His eyes protrude from their sockets, so that he appears to watch you intensely.

His appearance aside, Dunn has been the model host. His carriage was waiting for us at the train station, and he was waiting for us at the front gate to Summerland. (Note: Must check details of house. I'm fairly sure it's the style known as Second Empire—tall and narrow, like a collection of rectangles stood on their short ends.

Roof—Mansard roof?—like a cap. White with black trim, freshly
painted, so the white blinding in the afternoon, the black shining.
Extensive gardens in the English fashion. Situated on a hilltop
overlooking the Hudson and the step hills on the other shore.) The
room in which I have been housed is easily four times as large as the
cabin in which I crossed the Atlantic, and extravagantly furnished.

The single most interesting feature of my room, though, is the
balloon floating in the center of it, at the foot of the bed. I've read
Mrs. Barchester's description of Dunn's balloons over and over again;
it's one of the few passages in her book in which my fascination
with the subject matter blinds me to the dreadfulness of her prose.
Not surprisingly, she has not done the things justice. The size, for
example: no doubt she's measured the diameter correctly as three
feet, but she has failed utterly in conveying a sense of the balloon's
volume, of the manner in which it fills the space in which it hangs
like a globe set loose from its moorings. The things are apparently
composed of brown paper, which appears heavy, coarse grained,
and which still bears the folds and creases necessary to achieve the
balloon's shape. Its seams are dark with whatever Dunn used to seal
them. Perhaps the most serious defect in Mrs. Barchester's account
of the balloons, however, lies in her remarks upon the designs that
cover their surfaces. She writes of the "quaint, Oriental patterns with
which Mr. Dunn has decorated his inventions." Yet the arrangement
of the figures in latitudinal lines, their irregular repetition, give more
the impression of communication than ornamentation. The script is
none I can read or even recognize: its characters appear drawn from
the loops and twists woven into the room's Turkey carpet; nor am I
certain of the medium in which Dunn has applied them, which shines
as if fresh, and in whose depths I catch traces of crimson, viridian,
and purple.

And there is more to note. A distinct odor clouds the air around
the balloon. It mixes the wood-pulp smell of the paper with another,
faintly medicinal scent, possibly that of ether. (Is this due to the
manner in which Dunn suspends his creations?) Underneath the
combined smells, I perceive a third—damp, earthy. The balloon's
surface produces a low and constant crackling as it shifts in the
currents of air wafting into the room through its windows. I went to
touch the thing, to add its texture to my catalogue of impressions,
only to hesitate with the tips of my fingers a hairsbreadth from its

paper. I was seized by the most overpowering repugnance, such that the hairs from the back of my hand right up my forearm stood rigid. I swear, my flesh actually shrank from the thing. For the briefest of instants, I wanted nothing more than to see the balloon destroyed— torn apart, set alight. It was the kind and intensity of response I would have expected at confronting an especially loathsome insect, not an eccentric's amusement. I dropped my hand and decided my investigations had proceeded far enough for the moment.

Such a curious reaction—a consequence of the day's travel?

IV

Given his response to the balloon in his chamber, Coleman did not expect that he would be able to sleep in its presence, and he intended to ask Dunn to have it removed after dinner. At the conclusion of the meal, however, Dunn retreated to the library with Cal, whose preparations for their imminent work together the man declared must be seen to, posthaste. Not to mention, removed from close quarters with the thing, Coleman's initial antipathy towards it seemed vague, ridiculous. He could wait, he decided, for morning.

Once he was outside the door to his room, though, the self-assurance of minutes before felt cavalier, reckless. So he was relieved when he found the balloon had drifted to the window, where its presence was, if not pleasant, not as repellent.

V

"Do you believe Mr. Dunn?" Isabelle asked.

"Heavens, no." Coleman laughed. "A meeting with old Ahasuerus, the Wandering Jew himself, on the eve of the battle at Gettysburg? Tutelage in the secret arts of Simon Magus? A saving intercession in his later life by the spirits of his mother, Paracelsus, and Swedenborg? It's like a distillation of every melodrama produced these last fifty years. No, I suspect Mr. Dunn's narrative is no more than a way for him to align his past acts with his present practices."

Isabelle frowned, but did not reply. She inclined towards a bush whose name Coleman didn't know but on whose branches a large orange-and-black butterfly moved its wings.

"I am much more interested," Coleman said, "in our host's reluctance to describe the means by which he fashions his balloons."

VI

"You are preoccupied today," Isabelle said.

"Am I?" Coleman turned his gaze from the blue sheet of the Hudson. She nodded. "Since Mr. Dunn's recitation of his years as an arms merchant last night, your thoughts have been elsewhere, I believe."

Coleman smiled. "I fear I am not as cryptic as I would like."

"Or I am becoming more adept at deciphering you."

One of Dunn's balloons had drifted near. Coleman raised his hand to push it away, only to find himself once more hesitating before his fingers touched its papery surface, his skin literally crawling at the thing's proximity. Instead, he stood from the bench upon which he and Mrs. Earnshaw had admired the view from Dunn's garden and set off at a slow pace along its paths. Isabelle hurried after him. He preempted her question about his response to the balloon by saying, "You are correct. I have been distracted, and our host's words were the cause of it—specifically, his account of the bargain he struck for the rifles taken from the so-called Paris Commune. I was in Paris during the Commune. I'd come in with the second or third shipment of food Great Britain sent after the Prussians lifted their siege of the city. I'd thought I might write a series of articles about the state of the capital, which during the siege had become a focus of international attention and sympathy. It was a project for which I was well suited. Not only was I fluent in the language, but I had visited Paris several times during my youth, and I had maintained my correspondence with several of the friends I had made during those trips. One of these friends helped me secure lodgings in the Vaugirard district, and I settled down to work.

"I was staying at the edge of the city, so each morning, I set out to walk into it. While I was cautious at first, I soon became more confident and was ranging far and wide. Some parts of the city seemed hardly to have been affected at all, others—I can recall my shock at seeing the Ministry of Finances, which had been pounded almost entirely into rubble by the Prussian guns, so that what remained resembled an antique ruin. Towards the end of the day, I would return home and record my experiences. Once a week, I would write a short essay detailing my impressions, which I sent off to Rupert Cook at *Howell's*. He liked the pieces well enough, although he paid the bare minimum for them. To be frank, I did not expect Cook would continue to purchase my essays for very long, once their novelty wore off. For the moment, however, I was in Paris, gathering details for my next novel, which (I hoped) would meet with more success than either of my previous attempts had. If I harbored my resources, I judged I might be able to extend my stay by as much as another year.

"In the wake of the French defeat, the city—the country—was in tumult. Indeed, the new government chose to convene in Versailles, for fear of the Parisian crowds. One of President Thiers's first moves was to pass the Law of Maturities, whose ostensible purpose was to refill the coffers depleted by the war, but whose not-so-secret intent was to bring Paris, which was to provide an undue share of the revenue, to heel. The Commune arose as an attempt by the residents of the city to administer their own affairs more justly. For the two months of the Commune's rule, Paris was—it was no less turbulent, but the daily chaos was shot through with optimism, with excitement. There was a significant population of foreigners living in the city, exiles, many of them, from more repressive states—and perhaps because of this, what was taking place felt as if its implications went far beyond the city's borders. I filled all of one notebook and most of a second.

"There had been some skirmishes between the forces defending Paris and those loyal to the national government, but nothing of consequence, or so I judged. How naïve do I sound if I say that I did not believe the dispute between the city and the country would be settled through force of arms? Yet the morning of May twenty-first, I awakened to the sound of the first of the national government's forces marching through the streets. I had not appreciated the unhappiness the residents of the city's western districts felt towards the Commune. This included one of my oldest correspondents, a former professor of the classics who I later learned had been passing information along to the president's agents. In fact, he was among those to suggest the route by which the French army might gain access to the city, and to offer reassurance that the soldiers would receive a warm welcome when they arrived.

"Which they did: the avenue outside my window was lined with men, women, children, there to greet the troops as liberators. I stared down at the ranks of men in their blue jackets and red trousers, their kepi caps perched on their heads, their rifles shouldered, and it was as if I were witnessing a performance, some new variety of theater performed in the open air. I could not accept its reality. I kept thinking, *Surely not, surely not.*

"The seven days that followed have come to be known as La Semaine Sanglante, the Bloody Week. In short order, Thiers's forces took the western districts; the east, however, was the seat of the Commune, and the fighting there was fierce. Travel through the streets was difficult, sometimes impossible, but it wasn't necessary to go very far to know what was happening. All you had to do was walk to your window to hear the crack of the rifles, the boom of the cannons. The sharp smells of gunpowder and burning wood stained the air. Later, I read that, at the president's request, the Prussians had expedited the release of thousands of the French soldiers they had captured, in order to swell the ranks of the national army. The Commune had no centralized plan for defense; rather, each district was charged with its own security. This allowed the army to divide and conquer the Commune. I, who had missed the civil war in the land of my birth, found myself at the heart of another.

"Nor was the Bloody Week the worst of it. Following the army's conquest of the city, the members of the Commune were subject to extended reprisals. Having been associated with the city's government to the slightest degree might lead to trial and execution. The cemetery at Père Lachaise, the Luxembourg Gardens, were taken over by firing squads. I might have fallen under suspicion, myself, were it not for my old friend the professor of the classics, who testified to my character.

"I could have stayed, I suppose, but the prospect of remaining in the ruin of the Commune was too bleak. Rupert Cook had lost interest in my reports, so I judged the time right to depart Paris. I stopped at Geneva for a few months, spent the winter in Florence, and settled in Venice. There I remained for the next fifteen years, for the first five of which Paris remained under martial law. Needless to say, the novel I had hoped would emerge from my time in the city remained unwritten. It has only been the past few years that I have been able to return to Paris. I had thought I might live there again, but it was impossible. The ghosts of seventeen years past would not allow it.

"So to hear that Mr. Dunn had built his early fortune by trading in the Commune's weapons was . . . unsettling. To say the least." His smile was humorless.

Another balloon had drawn close to them. "I believe your husband's afternoon session should be drawing to a close," Coleman said. He walked away from the balloon, towards the house.

VII

"Were you of age during the War Between the States?" Dunn asked.

"I was," Coleman said without turning his gaze from the swords

racked between two of the library's considerable bookcases. He touched
the pommel of a rapier. "May I?"

"Of course."

The sword was heavier than Coleman anticipated. It took him a
moment to find its balance, after which, he slashed right to left, left to
right, theatrically.

"You were an officer," Dunn said.

"I was not," Coleman said, replacing the sword. "I suffered an . . .
injury a few years before the outbreak of hostilities. I was visiting family
friends, and there was a fire in their barn, which I joined the effort to extinguish. I was standing too close to one of the walls when it collapsed and
showered me with debris. The quick response of my fellows saved me, but
I was left unfit for service. Both my older brothers, Will and Bob, distinguished themselves in the war; in fact, Bob became one of Grant's aides."
He spared a glance at Dunn, who was studying him intently. Coleman
went on, "Since moving to London I've taken up fencing as a way to hold
the effects of aging at bay."

"The effects of your injury have lessened with the years," Dunn said.

"They have not hindered my exercise, no."

"Perhaps they would have allowed you to join your brothers."

"Perhaps," Coleman said. "I was in England when Sumter was shelled,
and my father insisted I remain there."

"Due to your wound."

Coleman felt his face redden. "If there is an inference you would like
to make clear—"

"Nothing of the kind," Dunn said, waving one of his massive hands.
"You should be grateful—you should fall on your knees and give thanks to
whatever God you venerate for that injury. Whatever discomfort, whatever
pain it has brought to you has preserved you from an experience vastly
more terrible, from wading knee-deep in a tide of blood and gore. It was
something of a witticism among my fellow soldiers that should any of us
fall in battle, he need have no fear of the Christian hell, because next to
the sights we had witnessed, its famous torments would count as naught."
Dunn paused. "I beg your pardon: I don't mean to bore you with an old
soldier's platitudes. Lunch should be ready on the patio."

Coleman followed Dunn out of the library with the enormous oak table
at its center, the handful of balloons floating amidst its bookcases. He was
thinking that Dunn had uttered his description of the war in a tone not of
horror, but nostalgia.

VIII

"I wonder, sir, what you regret," Cal Earnshaw said.

"I beg your pardon?" Coleman looked up from his book.

Cal pushed himself slightly higher in his Adirondack chair. "You may imagine," he said, panting from the effort, "a man in my position finds a great deal he wishes he could do or undo. Some of it is fairly obvious: Isabelle and I will never have a family. Some of it is more idiosyncratic: I will not see the pyramids, which has been an ambition of mine since I read about them as a boy. I've tried to reconcile myself to these facts, for really, what else can I do? Yet I am so far unable to rise above my frustration—my anger, if I am to speak candidly—at everything I am to lose. I keep hoping that the peace which is supposed to descend on those nearing death's precincts will find me, but it has not.

"All of which," he continued, "is preamble to my asking what regrets a man like you might harbor. You have lived longer than have I; you have traveled far, resided in places that are only names on a map to me. You have authored several novels, many more stories; you have written extensively for an assortment of periodicals. In short, you have had a life whose fullness, if not its exact details, I should have liked for mine. I know that you must have had your disappointments, but weighed against that fullness, I find it difficult to believe that any mistake or missed opportunity could matter that much."

Coleman set his book on the arm of his chair. A quartet of balloons hovered in the near distance; he fought the urge to depart the porch with all due speed. He had promised Isabelle that he would sit with her husband while he recovered from his morning session with Dunn (which appeared to be hastening the end they were supposed to be preparing him for: in the last five days, Cal had gone from gaunt to skeletal, his skin stretched taut over his bones—his skin had become gray and papery, and a sour odor clung to him). Doing his best not to listen to the balloons' soft, incessant rustling, Coleman let his gaze drift to the Hudson, full of craft large and small this sunny day. "When I was a young man," he began, "not very much older than you . . ." His voice trailed off.

After a moment, Cal said, "Mr. Coleman?"

With a shake of his head, Coleman said, "Forgive me, Mr. Earnshaw. In many ways, you're right: my life has been much as I wished it to be. What part of it I could control, at least. And what has lain outside my control, I have tried to cultivate a philosophical attitude towards. Often, I've been able to console myself with the thought that whatever reversal of fortune I was experiencing would serve as the germ of a future story. In fact, what I'm about to tell you made it to a rather lengthy opening.

"That scene was from the point of view of a young Venetian gondolier. I can't remember the name I gave him. What was important was that he was a poet whose verses had not found success—thus his employment in the gondola—and his youth. This was contrasted with that of his passenger, whose middle age seemed to the gondolier just this side of the grave." Coleman caught himself. "I apologize—"

Cal waved his words away. "Go on. Please."

"Very well. The young man stares at his passenger openly, but the older man is too preoccupied either to notice or to mind. He is dressed for mourning, which may explain his distraction. Heaped on the passenger's lap are a dozen dresses—well made, as far as the gondolier can tell, though a bit threadbare.

"It is early morning. The sky is light, but the sun has yet to rise into it. In his heavily accented Italian, the passenger has requested that he be rowed out of the city and into the lagoon that borders it. The deepest point in the lagoon, he has said—he has insisted. The gondolier is not certain where the water is deepest. He waits until they are a suitable distance from the city, slows the gondola, and announces to the man that they have reached their destination.

"The passenger does not question him. Instead, he shifts to his right, raises the dress on top of the pile, and places it into the dark water. He does the same with the next dress, and the dress below that, laying each in the water with remarkable tenderness, so that the gondolier is reminded of a groom bringing his new bride to the wedding bed.

"However, when the man has only a handful of dresses in his lap, something happens that causes him to start back from the water. The dresses he has submerged have returned, buoyed to the surface by the air trapped in their folds. On his knees, the passenger rushes to the side of the gondola with such violence that the gondolier has to shift his stance to keep the craft from tilting into the lagoon. Without removing his jacket, the passenger thrusts his arms into the water up to the elbow, pushing down on the risen dresses. It does no good. Pressing one part of the dress causes the rest of it to rise even higher. The man shoves the dresses down frantically, as if he's trying to drown them. He's soaked, but he doesn't care. The gondolier thinks that he should speak to his passenger, but he cannot decide what to say.

"At last the man slumps against the side of the gondola, exhausted, drenched, his face a mask of sorrow. That was where the scene ended, with him contracted in grief, the gondola surrounded by floating dresses, each moving slightly in the green water, the gondolier watching everything and contemplating a new poem he might write."

"The man," Cal said, "the passenger—"

"Yes," Coleman said.

"But the dresses—"

"Belonged to a woman named Philippa Irving Ventner. She was a writer, an American—in fact, she was born in Phoenicia, up in the Catskills. I met her in Geneva. She was touring the continent along with her younger sister, Grace. She was supposed to be educating Grace in the finer points of European civilization, but her knowledge of the subject was less than complete. Not that this stopped her: if there was one thing she had perfected, it was in moving ahead, regardless of the circumstances. To be fair, it had led to her producing a novel, *The Naturalist's Lament,* which had done extremely well. If I'm to be completely frank with you, none of my books has sold anywhere close to what hers did. The profits had funded her trip with Grace, which in turn led to another novel, *Joanna's Secret,* which allowed her to remain abroad after she had returned her sister home.

"No picture does her justice. There are many of them. She was happy to sit for any artist who cared to paint her, and she loved to be photographed. Look at the better portraits in either medium, and you will see her high cheekbones, her pointed nose, her brown hair. You will not see the watchfulness, the attentiveness that was her habitual expression. You will not see the wit that animated her eyes, her lips—the tilt of her head ever so slightly forward—when she was engaged in conversation. She had a keen sense of humor, though her response to most humorous stories and remarks was to hide her laughter behind her hands."

"You were—were you—"

"I met her several times over the next half a dozen years," Coleman said, "most often in Venice after I had settled there. She tried life in London, then Berlin, then Vienna, before finally taking up my suggestion that Venice might prove more agreeable to her. For a time, it was. We saw a great deal of each other, and the circles we frequented soon grew used to the pair of us attending their functions together. We had our routines, our rituals, our walks to St. Mark's, our meals at Caffè Florian, our trips to the opera. She was the most agreeable person I have ever known; in her company, time ran more quickly, so that our excursions were over much too soon.

"When she approached me about renting rooms in a palace together, the idea struck me as inspired." At the expression of shock on Cal's face, Coleman hurried on: "The palace was the property of Constance Aspern, a very old woman who in her youth was supposed to have been one of Lord Byron's lovers. The fortune that had sustained her decades in Venice was drying up, the consequence of a series of bad investments, and she thought that by taking in lodgers, she might at least slow its loss. She offered a suite of rooms on the top floor, and another on the ground floor, but really, whichever floor you chose, you had the run of it, since Miss Aspern did not stray often or far from her rooms on the middle floor. The entire palace had seen better days, but there was a kind of shabby glory to it—not to mention, the rent was ridiculously low. I took the top floor, Philippa the ground floor, and we settled into what seemed a particularly fortuitous arrangement.

"For one winter and part of the following spring, it was. Philippa and I passed our mornings working, then joined Miss Aspern for lunch, then ventured out into Venice. So might we have continued to this very day, I daresay."

"What happened?" Cal asked.

"Our friendship changed," Coleman said after a moment. "It . . . deepened. I was—Philippa was a good ten years my junior. Children were . . . I . . . a long time ago, I had decided that, in order for me to achieve the art it was my ambition to produce, I would have to lead a certain kind of life. Until this point, I had remained true to my original plan. I suppose my resolve had borne fruit, albeit in books that were more praised than read. At private moments over the years, I had wondered whether the course I'd chosen was the best one, but I'd never had so clear an alternative presented to me. For a week in early, spring, I—we. . .

"The end of that time found me on a train to Paris. I was not—I had been contacted by an editor about the possibility of writing a piece for his magazine about the French capital ten years after its emergence from martial law. I decided that the ten days such a trip would require would allow me to evaluate the path onto which my life had swerved. I feared—I knew how my departure would appear to Philippa, and I did my best to reassure her that I was not fleeing her. She wasn't pleased, but neither was she overwrought. I would be back soon, and we would talk when I was.

"That was the last I saw of her. The night I left, the railing on which she was leaning as she stood at the window gave way, plummeting her to the courtyard thirty feet below. She was not killed instantly; she survived another three days in the hospital. No one knew how to reach me. Philippa departed this life without regaining consciousness, with only Miss Aspern for company. By the time I returned, a day later than I'd planned, she had been buried for several days."

"You had decided . . ."

"Does it matter?" Coleman said.

Cal did not answer.

"I left Venice not long after," Coleman said. "Miss Aspern had no objection to my maintaining my rooms; I believe she had some notion of congruence between us. I had neither the inclination nor the desire to figure in her tableau. I did see Grace—Philippa's younger sister, now married with four children. I met her at her sister's grave. I hadn't remembered Grace as especially remarkable, and in the years since I had seen her last, she had grown into one of those Americans who make you embarrassed for the country: vain, provincial, willfully ignorant. I had expected, had steeled myself for, an outpouring of sorrow at the sudden extinguishing of so bright a light. Instead, I was subject to a torrent of scorn for such an 'odd duck.' I did my best to defend Philippa, but I was so astonished, I fumbled the effort. I grew angry, furious, so much so that I had no choice but to leave the cemetery immediately or risk doing violence to the woman."

Coleman slumped back in his chair. The quartet of balloons had settled into close orbit around him and Cal. He picked up his book and said, "In no way do I wish to minimize what you face losing. But there are times I have thought that, the longer I've lived, the more elaborate have grown the disasters in which I have enmeshed myself."

IX

"And how is your work proceeding, Mr. Coleman?" Dunn asked. Isabelle and Cal had retired to their room for an hour before a late dinner. Coleman was seated in the lounge, his notebook open in his lap, when Dunn walked into the room. Closing the notebook, Coleman said, "My latest is still in the early stages."

"Would I be presumptuous," Dunn said, seating himself on the chair next to Coleman's, "if I asked its plot?"

"I don't suppose so," Coleman said, "although I should warn you that most of the interest in my fiction arises from its execution, rather than its conception."

"You do yourself a disservice. You must forgive me—I have a terrible memory for the titles of these sorts of things—but your story about the man who is haunted by the ghosts of the family he did not have struck me as very original."

" 'The Undiscovered Country,' " Coleman said, "and thank you. The piece I am working on now is in a similar vein. It concerns a man who, as a result of an injury received in battle, has lost the ability to feel. He is a scientist, and he devotes his efforts to understanding the nature or source of human feeling. This leads to his performing a series of ghastly experiments upon a pair of innocents who seek his aid."

"Fascinating," Dunn said. "You intend the scientist as a villain."

"Not a villain so much as a . . . monomaniac, I would say. Of course, his inability to feel complicates the matter. Can he be held responsible for his actions if he is deficient in so fundamental a way?"

"Yes," Dunn said. "I thought you were going to say that it is the knowledge he pursues that muddies the waters."

"Oh?"

"Surely a great deal may be forgiven if the objective is the advancement of human understanding."

"I'm not sure," Coleman said. "It seems to me more the case that a great number of sins have sought to hide themselves under the fig leaf of knowledge."

"Sin? I am surprised to hear you employ such a useless word. What the world calls sin, Mr. Coleman, is little more than the courage of the uncowed intellect to follow its inclinations."

"A sentiment worthy of Goethe's Faust."

"A character, I remind you, who is rewarded for his ceaseless striving."

"What a consolation to poor Gretchen," Coleman said.

Dunn laughed. "You have an answer to everything, sir."

"So my brothers always complained."

X

"It will not be long, now, will it?" Isabelle said.

Coleman opened his mouth to offer a comforting platitude, but none would come. The sour smell that emanated from Cal had spread throughout the house. He said, "Your husband is in a great deal of pain."

"He is," Isabelle said. "I cannot understand how he bears it. But I might wish he were bearing it with me, rather than Mr. Dunn. I will lose my husband soon enough, Mr. Coleman; I would like to spend what time I have left with him in his company."

"Didn't Dunn inform you—"

"That he would be taking my husband from me for sessions morning, afternoon, and evening? That those sessions would continue for a week, with no end in sight save Cal's? No, Mr. Coleman, he did not. I assumed our stay would last a few days, no more. And I assumed that Mr. Dunn would require a few hours at most to prepare my husband for what is to come. I had read about Mr. Dunn's house—the beauty of its location, its garden—and I fancied that coming here with Cal would be a kind of farewell occasion for us. Instead, it has been a rehearsal for the solitude I am too soon to know."

"Has your husband told you what the sessions consist of?"

"He has. Apparently, Mr. Dunn has him lie on the table in the library. Then he positions several of his balloons around the room."

"The balloons?"

"They are supposed to aid Cal in the process."

"Which consists in what?" Coleman said. "Does Dunn fill his head with pictures of the life to come?"

"No," Isabelle said, "just the opposite. He tells Cal to allow his mind to fill with the agony that afflicts him."

"Whatever for?"

"Mr. Dunn says that since Cal's pain is the route that will lead him out of this world and into the next, it is necessary for him to immerse himself in it, in order for his transition to be a smooth one."

Coleman frowned. "Does your husband at least feel that Dunn's ministrations are helping him?"

"He insists they are when I ask him, but if you could see the look in his eyes . . . I think he cannot stand for his sessions with Mr. Dunn to be anything other than helpful."

XI

Summerland, Poughkeepsie

June 22, 1888

According to Dunn, not just the Hudson but the stretch of the river next to Poughkeepsie is the site of a doorway from this world to the next. Of course it would be, wouldn't it? But (supposedly) all manner of phenomena visible on the surface of the water during the late 1850s, reported in local papers. Must research.

Strange how tired I am—not from any exertion, obviously, but from the stress of Cal Earnshaw's rapidly worsening condition, and its effect on his wife. Tonight, she made her most direct plea yet for Dunn to allow her to take Cal and depart for home. Dunn would have none of it, insisting that he and Cal still have a great deal of preparation to do. He tried to draw me in on his side, but I refused.

Perhaps I should have spoken more forcefully, insisted that Dunn
send the Earnshaws on their way.

Would that I could climb into bed and sink into slumber—but the
combination of the memories the last few days have stirred and the
balloon that floats near my window keeps me awake.

XII

"I intend to take my husband and depart this house immediately," Isabelle
said. "Will you help me?"

"Yes," Coleman said.

XIII

There was a moment's resistance, then the tip of the rapier broke the balloon's skin. Coleman couldn't say what he had expected—for the paper
sphere to burst, or deflate, or shoot across the library on its suddenly released contents—but assuredly, it was not the gout of thick black fluid
over the blade of the sword, across the floor. He drove the rapier in to the
hilt, through the balloon's other side, and withdrew it as his tutor had instructed him, ready for a second thrust.

He need not have bothered. Listing to the right, the balloon was sink-
ing, dark liquid dripping from the cuts Coleman had made to it. The stuff
was thick as treacle and struck the marble tiles with a wet splat. With a
strangled cry, Dunn ran for the sword rack. Coleman stabbed the next balloon, stepped forward, and slashed the balloon after that. By the time he
heard Dunn's shoes slapping the floor behind him, Coleman had opened a
vent in the fourth of the man's inventions. His sword was coated in whatever filled the balloons, which oozed across the floor in growing puddles
that stank of rot. It seemed impossible that such a substance could cause
the balloons to rise, and yet—

Coleman turned, sweeping his sword in a wide arc that caught Dunn's
stab and flung his blade to the side. The man recovered quickly, cutting
an X in front of him. Rather than parry, Coleman retreated several paces.
Dunn was considerably stronger than he and had selected a heavy cavalry
saber for his weapon; Coleman did not rank his chances of defeating the
man especially high. If he could distract him from Isabelle, who had assisted Cal up from the table and was supporting him as he limped toward
the library door, then Coleman would consider his performance a success.

Truth to tell, he was surprised by the fury with which Dunn now attacked him. Without a doubt, the balloons had cost him no small amount of time and effort. But Dunn's face was scarlet, his large eyes protruding with fury. Coleman had little doubt that, were he to allow Dunn the opportunity, his host would put his saber to deadly use. The man's moves were exaggerated, almost parodic, those of someone whose notions of handling a sword were drawn from the stage; should any of his swipes connect, however, its effects would be real enough.

Dunn had backed him to the foot of the table. A pair of balloons floated to Coleman's right, closer to the broad oak expanse (which, he had time to notice, was incised with row after row of the same figures written on the balloons' paper surface). There was no need for him to slash the two of them, yet there was no denying the deep rush of pleasure that accompanied the act. At this latest insult to his inventions, Dunn roared and charged. Coleman ducked the swing at his head and jabbed Dunn's right arm high, near the shoulder. Dunn yelped and retreated a step.

The library door slammed shut behind Isabelle and Cal Earnshaw. Coleman doubted Cal would last out the next hour, let alone the remainder of the night, but at least he would do so in the company of his wife and not splayed on a table surrounded by a charlatan and his paper toys. Coleman lowered the tip of his sword. His breath coming fast, he said, "There. Mrs. Earnshaw's wishes have been fulfilled. Now perhaps you and I can settle matters between us in a more civilized fashion. I apologize for the destruction of your creations. I would be willing to recompense you a fair amount—"

"You fucking idiot," Dunn said. He had pressed his left hand over the wound Coleman had given him; his fingers were scarlet. He had not dropped his saber, which he pointed at the first balloons Coleman had vandalized. "You think these are works of *art*? They're cages."

"More metaphors?" Coleman looked to the other end of the room. The balloons he had stabbed were in a state of half collapse on the floor, surrounded by ever-widening pools of brackish ichor. Those he had sliced open were sagging downwards, raining their contents as they descended. Through the vents he had cut in them, he could distinguish something, a mottled surface his blade had torn and which was the source of the viscous liquid. That layer was pierced by additional holes, lozenge shaped and anywhere in size from that of a small coin to a handbreadth. Each of the holes was moving, opening and closing with a motion that was repellently familiar. Coleman stared at them blankly before understanding rushed in and he recognized the apertures as mouths. For a moment, he felt the room around him tilt crazily. He reached his left hand to his forehead. "My God . . ."

With a sudden burst of speed, Dunn lunged forward and stabbed Coleman in the chest. The blade was a white shock. For a moment, Coleman was propelled out of his body to a lightless place. When he returned, he had fallen to his knees and Dunn was holding forth. "—true," he said. "The veil between the worlds is thinner, here. With the proper preparations, the inhabitants of the other realm may be lured across, captured, and put to work. Their physical capabilities are limited, but what they offer in terms of knowledge . . . Their appetites, however, are considerable, and they require a rather specialized diet. Human sensation sustains them—the more intense, the better the meal. Pain they find particularly satisfying. The agonies of the dying will keep them happy and compliant for days."

"Your . . . services . . ." Coleman panted. With each breath, his chest filled with white fire.

"No doubt some of my clients have taken comfort from their time with me," Dunn said. "They've certainly been more use here than at any other time in their lives. It's a pity," he continued, "I had hoped that you—an artist—might understand the work in which I am engaged here. It was not my intention for your stay to end this way. But since it has, and since you have deprived my friends of their meal . . ." Dunn surveyed the balloons at the head of the table, the pair at its foot. The injuries of the nearer balloons did not appear as grave; indeed, while Dunn had been speaking, they had drifted closer to him. Through the rents in their paper cages, Coleman could see their excess of mouths gulping with a motion that reminded him of hungry fish at the surface of a pool. Dunn said, "Your attempt at gallantry has cost me more than you can conceive."

Coleman's shirt and trousers were warm, sticky, heavy with the blood emptying him. The library paled almost to blank, then returned. "As," he said to Dunn, "as . . . a gentle-gentleman . . . I wonder if . . . if you . . ."

"You must be joking," Dunn said; nonetheless, his bulk inclined towards Coleman.

Gripping its hilt as tightly as he could, Coleman slashed the rapier across Dunn's face. As he did, something broke loose inside him and a tide of blood poured from the wound in his chest. He let go of the sword and fell beside it.

A thin, high-pitched scream rose from Dunn's throat. Coleman's sword had raked his eyes, and his cheeks were wet with blood and fluid. He had dropped the saber and held his hands up on either side of him, as if imploring some supernatural agency to his aid. Still screaming, Dunn crashed into the table with such force it jolted across the floor. He staggered back from the collision, lost his footing, and tumbled down.

The balloons were waiting for him. Their prisons ruptured, the creatures they had contained surged out of them and over Dunn. His vision was failing, but Coleman had the impression of something more liquid than solid, enough like a jellyfish to warrant the comparison. Dunn's voice climbed higher, then failed. He clawed at the things on his chest, but that only allowed them to attach to his hands. With what must have been Herculean effort, Dunn sat up. His lips were forming words Coleman could not hear. Before he had uttered more than a few of them, one of the creatures spread itself over his face. His body shook as if with a seizure, then sagged backwards. In the quiet that followed, Coleman heard the noises of eating. Apparently, the balloons' prisoners were capable of taking their nourishment more directly.

The library faded a second time. When it returned, it was less distinct. Coleman guessed more of his blood was outside his body than remained in it. How odd to die so quickly. How odd to die in a library. In some ways, it was as appropriate a location as any. He hoped that Isabelle had managed to get Cal out of the house. He had waited too long to take her concerns seriously and try to aid her; he hoped it wouldn't be held against him. He wasn't much of a believer in an afterlife, hadn't been for decades. He supposed he'd been mistaken. He wondered what he should expect. Whatever it was, he hoped it wouldn't be hungry.

XIV

From *Benét's Reader's Encyclopedia* (third edition):

Coleman, Mark Stephen (1842–1888). American novelist and short story writer. Born in Kingston, New York, Coleman left for study at Cambridge at the age of eighteen and spent almost the entire rest of his life abroad, living successively in London, Paris, Venice, and then London again before returning to the Hudson Valley in his final months. Like Henry James, with whom he is often compared, Coleman took as his subject the experiences of Americans in Europe; however, Coleman's Americans are plagued by remorse of past sins personal and familial, a preoccupation that links his work to that of Nathaniel Hawthorne. His most famous novel is *Belgrave's Garden* (1879), an account of a wealthy American's attempt to cultivate the land on which his ancestor ordered a brutal massacre during the second Jacobite rebellion in 1745. Coleman's death was notorious: he died as a result of an apparent duel with the spiritualist Parrish Dunn, who also was slain.

For Fiona

Afterword to "The Unbearable Proximity of Mr. Dunn's Balloons"

Almost from the moment I received Nick's invitation to submit to the anthology, I knew that the story would focus on these mysterious, faintly sinister balloons, of whose origins I'm honestly unsure (except that, due to the threat of their flying away should you relax your grip on them, balloons have been a locus of anxiety for me since I was a small child and one escaped up into the sky at the amusement park my parents had taken me to). I could see them clearly in my mind's eye, these large, papery spheres, the creases in whose coverings were clearly visible. The temporal setting of the story suggested a Henry-Jamesian writer as the protagonist, as well as the story's use of spiritualism (it is true that New York's Hudson Valley was a center of spiritualist activity during the 1850s). I originally had it in mind to write a more conventionally structured story, but I stalled on that version not too far into it, and the story remained in a state of partial completion until it occurred to me that I might approach its material in a less conventional way, after which, the story spilled out of me in a couple of weeks. A couple of last-minute edits, and the story was done.

—JOHN LANGAN

John Harwood

John Harwood was born in Hobart, Tasmania, where he grew up in a house full of books, including numerous collections of ghost stories, an interest that would resurface many years later in his first novel, *The Ghost Writer.* He was educated at the Friends' School and the University of Tasmania, where he read English and philosophy, before going on to Cambridge as a graduate student.

The Ghost Writer (first published by Jonathan Cape in 2004) won the International Horror Guild's First Novel Award for Outstanding Achievement in Horror and Dark Fantasy, and the "Children of the Night" Award for Best Gothic Novel of 2004, from the Dracula Society of Great Britain. *The Séance,* a dark mystery set in late Victorian England, was published in 2008; it won the Aurealis Award for Best Horror Novel of 2008. Both novels are published in the United States by Houghton Mifflin Harcourt.

John Harwood

Face to Face

IT WAS, I think, the last Christmas of the old century; at any rate it was certainly at Reginald Carstairs' great barracks of a place down in Surrey that my friend Maurice Trevelyan and I were sitting up late; so late that, excepting the bishop, we had the drawing room fire entirely to ourselves. And since the bishop was, as usual, sound asleep, he made an ideal chaperone. Nobody seemed to know what he was, or had been, bishop of; I very much doubt whether he knew himself, for he was so old and venerable that he woke only long enough to dine, imbibe a glass or two of port, and settle himself back into his favourite armchair. He was invariably asleep in it when the last guest went upstairs, no matter how late; but someone must have put him to bed, for his chair was always empty in the mornings.

Not that we required a chaperone: I was, as everybody knew, simply a married woman whose husband never went out, and Maurice was equally well established in the character of a forty-five-year-old bachelor of quiet habits and modest means. He had remained unmarried, it was rumoured, because of a youthful attachment, prematurely ended by the death of the woman to whose memory he remained devoted. It was not a subject I had ever raised with him, for Maurice hated to be quizzed over his personal life. I had divined this early on, in fact on the very day we were introduced in the office of the review he was then editing. Some acquaintance was chaffing him about a supposed indiscretion; I saw Maurice recoil; he saw my discomfort on his behalf, and a current of sympathy was set flowing between us. The review, to which I contributed a tale or two, lasted less than a year before its patron abandoned it, but our friendship was by then a settled thing.

Some may wonder, if personal matters were excluded, what on earth we had to talk about, to which the answer is: everything under the sun, but more particularly anything and everything that either of us had ever read or written or, in his case, dreamed of writing, for I doubt there was ever a poet with a deeper sense of his vocation than Maurice Trevelyan. Yet he was at the same time so self-effacing as to be almost impossible to describe. Put a pen or a manuscript in his hand, and you could not doubt his force of character: about a passage of writing he could not prevent himself from telling the exact truth, however discomforting to the writer; but on any other subject he would happily yield the floor to men twenty years his junior. Even his physical appearance was not easy to capture; he was unremarkably slender, moderately tall, with dark hair receding at the temples, and fine but regular features, save only that the left side of his face looked strangely seared: I do not mean withered or scarred, but rather marked by a fixed pallor, as though he had come too close to a fire whose flames burned cold instead of hot. At any rate I can put it no better than that, and on the evening in question, as we sat gazing into the flames, our occasional silences filled by the creak and crackle of burning coals and the faint snores of the bishop dreaming peacefully on the far side of the hearth, it remained among the topics that had never been raised between us.

Instead we spoke—or rather Maurice spoke, as he would do only when we were alone—of the unwritten poem that, in various guises, had haunted him all his life. Everything good that he had ever done—and he was the most exacting, indeed ruthless critic of his own writing—seemed to him, at certain moments, only the shadow of this other work whose outlines he constantly glimpsed, but whose substance he could never capture. He believed in the community of all true poets through the ages, and sometimes spoke as if all true poems were but fragments of some great ur-poem, or Platonic quintessence of the art; at other times as if our language, in all its richness and beauty, existed in a fallen state, like some great ruin of antiquity, mere broken remnants of a celestial tongue we had once known, and lost; to this end he was fond of quoting Shelley's remark about the fading coal, or the close of "Kubla Khan": he had an especial sympathy for poets who had left behind great but unfinished works. He agreed, up to a point, with Pater, that all art aspires to the condition of music, but believed that there was a poem, destined for him and him alone to write, that would be the fulfilment of his life and the perfection of his art, and yet be expressible in ordinary English words, however extraordinary the effect of the whole might be. There were moments, he said, in which he could hear the rhythm of its lines falling as clearly as footsteps passing along a hall, and feel certain that if his inner ear were only a little more acute, he could catch the words before their echoes faded.

To some, this fascination with the unattainable might have become a torment, but Maurice seemed content with his lot. I had often wondered what he would make of the remainder of his life if that one perfect poem were ever to swoop down from the heavens and alight upon his outstretched wrist, but I never quite liked to ask, for it seemed an intrusion upon that privacy which, it sometimes struck me, we shared so intimately without ever mentioning.

We sat, then, watching the coals brighten and fade, which put me in mind, as often, of Shelley; almost simultaneously, Maurice began softly to speak the lines from "Adonais":

The One remains, the many change and pass;
Heaven's light forever shines, Earth's shadows fly;
Life, like a dome of many-coloured glass,
Stains the white radiance of Eternity . . .

where he ceased, for which I was grateful, for the trampling of the dome always seems to me wanton and wrong. It may be pagan to think so, but to me the beauty is in the whole: the One *and* the Many, the pure sunlight streaming through stained glass; heaven's light would be poorer without earth's shadows. Though perhaps heaven's light may be as far beyond mere sunlight as the many-coloured dome surpasses a shop window. "For now we see through a glass, darkly; but then face to face."

I did not realise I had spoken the last words aloud until I became aware of a stillness on my right. I looked up from the coals to find Maurice staring at me as if I had become a ghost.

"Laura"—he spoke my name as if suddenly uncertain of its meaning—"how did you know my thought?"

"I did not," I said, "or not knowingly."

As best I could, I retraced my steps for him, but he continued to stare at me with that stricken intensity until I trailed off, at a loss to understand how such a familiar verse could trouble him so profoundly. Gradually he recovered himself and began to look at me in his accustomed way; and then he took my hand, something he did not commonly do except at meeting and parting. His hand was very cold, despite the heat of the fire, and instinctively I sought to cover it with both of mine. But still the prohibition that had nurtured our friendship kept me from speaking.

"Those lines of Shelley's," he resumed, after a long pause, "how often have I read them over or heard them spoken, and yet never until tonight . . . I *saw*"—pointing with his other hand into the heart of the fire—"the dome shatter and re-form into—a thing of darkness. And then you spoke, of all verses, that one. 'Face to Face' is the title of a manuscript I once read—in part. A tale, I must call it, though it was not like any tale I have ever read; indeed it was not like *anything* I have ever read. It was, in its effect upon the reader, the exact reverse, the most sinister inversion"—he shivered slightly, and I noticed that the seared place below his cheekbone looked paler than usual—"of that perfect poem we were discussing just now. And it was written by the woman I once dreamed of marrying."

I had not meant to release his hand, but found that I had done so. In the shadows opposite, the bishop slept on.

"You must first understand," said Maurice, as if answering some objection on my part, "in what extremity she was driven to—manifest it. Her mother and mine were close friends; in a manner of speaking we grew up together. Her letters were extraordinarily vivid. She was nineteen, and I twenty-one, when they came to live in London, and from then on I saw her frequently, until all was changed by the sudden death of her father, whose passing left them in a precarious position. My own father did what he could, but his means were very limited. I felt I could not . . . at any rate I did not . . . suffice to say," he continued somewhat hurriedly, "that my friend came to the notice of Sir Lewis Wainwright, a wealthy man some thirty years older than herself. He had, I think, had some business dealing with her late father; it was certainly within his power to secure not only her future but that of her mother and her two younger sisters. I did not— perhaps could not—believe that she ever loved him. From the first he struck me as cold, indeed evil in the very emanations of his being; I felt in him that capacity to wither and shrivel with a glance, to inspire the shrinking that flesh instinctively feels from sharpened steel, or serpents. To the casual eye, no doubt, he was simply a tall, distinguished gentleman still in the prime of life, immaculately and fastidiously dressed, perfectly courteous in manner; yet how she could have been so deceived . . . it was like watching a sleepwalker moving slowly towards the brink of a precipice and finding oneself unable to move or cry out. My consciousness of my own position kept me silent, and even made me doubt what in my heart of hearts I could not doubt; and besides, what could I have said? A poor student who could barely meet the cost of his own subsistence? Yet I *should* have spoken—"

Though he had kept his voice low, the last words escaped him as a cry of anguish. I glanced uneasily towards the bishop, but our oblivious companion did not stir.

"Maurice," I ventured, when he did not immediately continue, "you have sketched this malignant suitor all too vividly, and yet I have no picture of your—your friend: you have not so much as mentioned her name."

"Her name was Claire," he said slowly, as if struggling with some inhibition on his own side. "She was—dark, and slender—about your own height—quiet, and studious, and yet she—really I cannot, one cannot catch the essence of another. She was gentle, and virtuous, and I watched the jaws of the trap closing upon her, and did nothing. Remember that the fortunes of her mother and sisters were at stake in this; her mother was not, I think, easy about the match, rightly fearing some element of self-sacrifice on Claire's part. The constraint between us grew more tangible once the engagement had been announced. At the wedding—I wish to God I had not been there—she looked serene and calm, but very pale, whilst Sir Lewis gazed upon her with the air of a collector about to lock away some new and greatly coveted acquisition.

"They went immediately abroad, where they remained for some months; and how different her letters, with their dutiful descriptions of scenery and formal professions of happiness, seemed from those I had once received! When we called upon them after their return to London, I knew immediately that she was unhappy, but she contrived, then and afterwards, never to be alone with me. Sir Lewis, furthermore, made it subtly plain to me that I would be a tolerated rather than a welcome visitor. His reptilian eyes seemed to draw out the very feelings I strove most desperately to conceal in his presence, and to flicker distrustfully from her to me.

"Her only child, a daughter, was born before the first anniversary of their wedding, and became the one source of light in the darkness closing upon her; that, and the knowledge that her mother and sisters were now securely provided for, though at a price they would never willingly have paid. We were all of us aware that Claire was deeply unhappy, and yet her manner of bearing it seemed to exact from us a vow of silence, not only in her presence, but between ourselves. We looked at one another and knew that we knew and could not speak of it. Or at least I could not, until the third year of her marriage was drawing to its close, when we began to see even less of her, and that only in the presence of her husband. His manner, formally speaking, remained perfectly polite, yet in his presence all conversation withered and died; you could feel the malevolent force of his personality raying out across the room.

"We had, however, an ally within his house: Claire's maid Rosina, who had been with the family since she was scarcely more than a child. Rosina was quick, observant, and entirely devoted to her mistress, and it was through her eyes that we saw the final scenes of the tragedy unfold.

"Claire had written a great deal before her marriage; though she would always dismiss her work as 'scribbling,' she had shown me some chapters of a novel which I thought very fine. And it seems that in that last autumn, as she became more and more a prisoner, she turned once again to her pen for solace and began secretly to compose—we shall never know what, for despite her precautions he discovered, read, and then destroyed her manuscript. There followed a terrible scene, in which Claire turned at last upon her tormentor and declared her resolution to leave him. He swore that if she did so she would never see her child again, and that her mother and sisters would be turned out into the street. Coldly advising her to reconsider, he left the room.

"That same night, the child was stricken by a raging fever. Doctors were summoned, and every possible remedy tried, but in vain; less than twenty-four hours later, she was dead. Rosina, who had not left her mistress's side throughout the long night and the dreadful day that followed, said that Sir Lewis did not once appear in the sickroom until the poor child's ordeal had ceased. Claire's grief had overwhelmed her, but as he appeared in the doorway, she ceased to weep, and a terrible stillness came over her. She took the dead child in her arms, and though she seemed not even to see her husband looming directly in her path, such was her expression that he fell back and spoke not a word as she bore her daughter's body from the room and slowly descended the stair to her private sitting room, whence came the snap of the key turning in the lock.

"Sir Lewis seemed, for once, at a loss. Slowly recovering his self-possession, he descended the stair in his turn and stood irresolutely at Claire's door. Twice he raised his hand as if to knock, but did not do so; finally, he continued on down and disappeared into his own private domain. Rosina then made haste to rejoin her mistress, expecting Claire to respond when she tapped with their special signal upon the door, and called softly to ask if she could be of help, but there was no reply. The house was very quiet, and as she waited at the door she became aware of a very faint scratching sound from within. She tapped once more, but there was again no response, and the faint scratching or rustling sound continued without pause.

"Several times during the next few hours, as afternoon gave way to evening and darkness fell, Rosina returned to the sitting-room door, with the same result. The rest of the house remained deathly quiet; no one came to give her any orders; no bells were rung. Finally, she went miserably upstairs to her own quarters, where she fell at last into an exhausted sleep.

"Next morning she was awakened by the maidservant with whom she shared the attic with the news that the lock of her mistress's room was about to be forced. Dressing hastily, Rosina was just in time to see this done. A footman broke open the door and stood back to allow Sir Lewis to pass. From her position on the stair, Rosina saw her mistress lying motionless upon a sofa, with her dead child in her arms. Unable to restrain herself, she ran into the room, to be roughly ejected by Sir Lewis's valet, but not before she had taken in the scene in one terrible glimpse: the dead mother and child in their last embrace; the empty vial of laudanum; and on the writing table nearby, a pile of handwritten pages surrounded by several pens, sheets of blotting paper, and an open bottle of ink.

"Rosina was shortly summoned by the housekeeper, given immediate notice, and sent upstairs to pack. Instead, overcome by grief and horror, she threw herself upon her bed and wept until sleep overtook her. By the time she woke, it was late in the evening. She had gathered together her few things and was venturing out upon the landing when a fearful shriek came echoing up the stairwell. There followed a brief silence, then sounds of shouting and of running feet. Afraid to descend, she waited for what seemed like hours until her friend appeared. The cry had been that of Sir Lewis's valet, who had found his master dead on the floor of his dressing room, surrounded by the scattered pages of a manuscript. The corpse's face was frozen into an expression of indescribable terror, and entirely blanched, as if vitriol had been flung across the features."

Maurice paused, staring into the dwindling glow of the coals. A formless dread that had crept upon me was beginning to assume a more definite shape, as if some sinister presence were materialising in the shadows behind the slumbering bishop.

"There was a kind of fatality about the way in which that manuscript came into my possession. It so happened that Sir Lewis's valet was entirely unlettered, but most reluctant to admit as much; and it was he who collected up the scattered pages whilst his master's corpse was being removed under the doctor's direction, and carried them off to the study nearby, where he placed them in one of the pigeonholes in Sir Lewis's desk. And since it was later asserted that Sir Lewis had been looking over some legal document at the time of his death—the cause being given as a stroke, with the curious blanching of the face put down as an unusual complication—I believe the valet mistook one set of papers for another, without any idea

that he had done so. The executors must have been exceptionally scru-
pulous, for they returned all of Claire's personal effects to her mother,
including an envelope labelled "manuscript, in the hand of the late Lady
Wainwright," which her mother, in recognition of the literary ambitions
Claire and I had once shared, passed on to me.

"I was, by then, living in rooms off the Strand, in Essex Court, and I
was quite alone on the evening when I sat down to open the envelope. It
was only a few weeks after Claire's death, and I was still numb with the
shock of it as I began to read, hoping to hear again the voice that . . . no
matter. The hand was hers indeed, but the voice was not.

"It was, or seemed at first to be, simply an account of someone waiting alone, in an upstairs room of an empty house at night. The location
was not specified but you felt the stillness all around, the extremity of the
speaker's isolation; for it was told in the first person, though you could
not tell whether the narrator was male or female, young or old. As I read
on, I felt more and more strongly that the consciousness of the narrative
was in fact my own, until I lost all awareness of my actual surroundings.
In its gradual accumulation of detail it was like the furnishing of a house;
item by item, it crept upon you in a slow and insidious fashion. It seemed
to reach directly into that part of the soul which believes upon instinct,
like a child, but which is normally inaccessible to us except in moments of
absolute terror or utter despair. Something, I know not how it was done,
caused me to recall with intolerable vividness every mean or contemptible
thing I had ever done, from earliest childhood, and worse, every good deed
I had left undone; a great black catalogue of sins and omissions opening
before my eyes. And yet I did not feel this moral terror to be the principal
intent of the narrative upon me, but rather an accompaniment of some still
darker, more ominous purpose.

"The very rhythm of the sentences was like a soft drum, a pulse heard
more and more loudly, until it became the sound of footsteps, still a long
way off, but charged with menace. I was still faintly aware that I was reading, but that awareness only increased my apprehension, for the extraordinary vividness with which the scene had been set seemed now to guarantee
that the face of what was fast approaching would not be left unspecified,
and yet would awaken more, not less, terror than the worst promptings of
my own imagination.

"It was, I think, at that exact moment that I realised that I was hearing the sound of real, actual footfalls in the corridor outside my rooms.
I looked up—or thought I looked up—from the page, and found that my
familiar surroundings had metamorphosed into those of the narrative. I

was alone in a dark and isolated house, far from any other human habitation, with footsteps closing upon me where no footsteps should have been.

"Clutching the manuscript, I rose from my chair and began to back away from the door. The room was lit by a single candelabrum, so placed that I could see the reflection of its flames in the window to which I turned as my one hope of escape. Better to be dashed to pieces on the ground below than endure so much as a glimpse of what was preparing to enter. As I reached for the sash, I saw my own face reflected in the windowpane, caught in the last extremity of terror, its eyes fixed upon a point beyond my shoulder, upon the door opening at my back; upon that visitant whom I saw indeed as in a glass darkly, but whom my reflected self seemed plainly and intolerably to view, in the instant before I covered my eyes with the manuscript and darkness dropped upon me like the hangman's hood.

"I came to myself upon the floor of my room in Essex Court, the unread portion of the narrative pressed against my cheek; you see its mark upon me still. How or why I was spared I know not, but I woke with the conviction that had I reached the end of the manuscript, I should certainly have died. At any rate, I have never yet dared to look upon it again."

He fell silent, staring into the dying embers of the fire.

"Maurice," I said hesitantly, "do you mean to say that this manuscript still exists?"

"Yes; I could not bring myself to destroy it."

Because it was hers, I thought, but did not like to say so.

"You are right, of course," he went on, as if I had spoken. "It is only that—well, supposing I did fall asleep? Or failed some sort of test and turned back when I should have gone on? After all, I did not actually see anything plain; perhaps I was, literally, frightened by my own reflection? Might I not be destroying something that ought to have been preserved?"

"Maurice," I said firmly, "if after twenty years the impression of that experience remains so indelible—and not only the mental impression," I added, glancing at the mark seared across his cheek, "then it would be most unwise to chance a second encounter with it." But then I thought he looked at me a little askance, which made me doubt my own motive, and caused me to add impulsively, "but if you wish, I will sit by you while you look at the manuscript again, or even . . ."

There I pulled up, aware that whilst Maurice was as devoid of egotism as it is possible for a man to be, he might not be well pleased by my offering to assume the risk. But he seemed not to catch the last phrase; he took my hand again, and this time I found that mine was the colder.

"Dear Laura, I could not ask so much of you . . . and yet there is no one else on this earth I *would* ask."

"Then trust me once more. You must not bear this burden any further; at least, not alone."

"Very well. If you are certain, let it be now—"

"Do you mean you have it here?"

"Yes, for I never feel quite easy unless I know that it is safe. But Laura, it is late, and you are cold, I think, and perhaps we should wait for daylight—"

"No," I said, striving to conceal my apprehension, for I could see that he wanted no further delay.

"Very well," he repeated. "You will watch as I read, and unless I was indeed mistaken, you will witness its destruction."

He rose and quietly made up the fire and went softly from the room. The bishop, whom I had quite forgotten, stirred amidst the flickering shadows, but did not wake. I drew my wrap more closely about me, almost overwhelmed by several contrary emotions. The dark spell of his narrative still clung to me, and yet I felt as if a long chapter in the history of my friendship with Maurice had just reached its close, leaving me eager to know what the next might bring. Warmed by the cheerful glow and crackle of the reviving fire, I wondered how mere words on paper could possibly bring about the effect that Maurice had so vividly described. Yet there was the mark upon his cheek and the death of the malignant husband, which led me to thoughts of poor Claire, whom I still could not picture with any distinctness; and so my mind ran on for an indefinite interval, until I became aware that Maurice had been gone far longer than it could reasonably have taken him to ascend to his room and return with the manuscript.

There were, of course, a dozen reasons why he might have been delayed, but as I sat upright, with my heart beginning to race and cold apprehension rushing upon me, they seemed to shrink to one, at least to the only one I dared entertain: Maurice had been taken suddenly ill. Really I ought to ring, or wake someone—but whom?—at two in the morning? And what if it proved to be a false alarm . . . ? But fear already had me on my feet and moving towards the mantelpiece to secure a candle. With a last glance at the unconscious bishop, I hastened towards the door and out into the chill hallway.

Going up the stairs, I had to look to my candle, for the wind had risen outside. The sky was fortunately bright: through the windows above the landing, I could see wisps of cloud scudding past the face of the moon. Save for the faint moaning of the wind, the house was deathly quiet, and as I turned into the corridor which led to Maurice's room, even the sound of the wind dwindled and ceased. My candle flame steadied as I stopped at his door, feeling suddenly conspicuous. No light showed underneath. I tapped as loudly as I dared, glancing over my shoulder. There was no response. Too late to turn back now; I tried the handle, found it unlocked, and entered.

Though I caught the odour of a wick recently extinguished, the room was dark, save for a band of moonlight streaming through the French windows opposite, which were, I realised, open. An icy draught caught at my own candle and, before I could shield it, blew out the flame. But the moonlight falling across the floor had already shown me what I most dreaded finding. Maurice lay sprawled upon the carpet, with his head by the open window and the moon shining full upon his face. For a moment I thought he might be safe, for his eyes were closed and his expression perfectly peaceful; he looked, as sleepers often do, far younger than his years, and in that pure white light the seared mark seemed to have been quite erased. But as I knelt beside him I saw all too plainly that he was not asleep. The freezing wind rose and ruffled his hair, but he did not move. Instead, something stirred and rustled in the darkness on my right, rearing up, as it seemed, from behind a table no more than two feet from where I knelt, something that flapped and swooped above me in a serpentine rush and went howling out upon a sudden gust that flung those terrible pages into the moonlit sky, scattering upon the wind and away into the night.

Afterword to "Face to Face"

"Face to Face" grew out of my fascination with the "fatal book": the anonymous manuscript, hedged with dire warnings, which destroys anyone (usually an aspiring author) foolhardy enough to read it. The story came almost by inner dictation; I didn't know how it would end until I arrived at the closing image. It was partly inspired by Flaubert's remark that when he was composing the final pages of *Madame Bovary,* he could hear the rhythms of the still unwritten sentences approaching like foot-steps before he knew what the actual words would be: I realised as "Face to Face" unfolded that the idea could be given a distinctly sinister twist.

—JOHN HARWOOD

Richard Harland

Richard Harland was born in England but has spent most of his adult life in Australia. He lives in Figtree, south of Sydney, with his wife, Aileen, between golden beaches and green coastal escarpment—and, incongruously, the biggest steelworks in the southern hemisphere.

In 1993, he broke the curse of writer's block and finished his first gothic fantasy. Published by a small press, *The Vicar of Morbing Vyle* became a cult favorite. Richard took up writing full-time in 1997, and since then has had fifteen novels published, ranging from fantasy to science fiction to horror, and from adult to YA to children's. He has won five Aurealis Awards, including the Golden Aurealis for Best Novel in any genre of science fiction, fantasy, or horror.

His recent steampunk fantasy, *Worldshaker,* has been published in the United States, the United Kingdom, Australia, France, Germany, and Brazil. The sequel, *Liberator,* is due to appear in the same countries, starting with Australia and the United Kingdom in May and July 2011. The American edition comes out in April 2012. Richard's websites are www.richardharland.net and www.worldshaker.info.

RICHARD HARLAND

Bad Thoughts and the Mechanism

No, YOU MUST not expect me to describe my nightmares. That I shall
never do. As a respected and respectable gentleman of business, I
have my regular armchair at White's, I sit with my cigar and brandy-and-
soda—and my fellow club members never suspect that, up until the age of
thirteen, I suffered from the most appalling nightmares imaginable. No
one knows there was a time when my heart stopped beating, and I almost
died in my sleep from pure terror.

It was after I almost died that my parents—you need not know our
family name—began to talk about Dr. Kessel. The Harley Street specialist
who examined me must have mentioned the new experimental treatment
to them—at least, I deduce that connection in retrospect. You should understand that large portions of my life in that period took place as if in a
fog. I existed under such oppression of the spirit, such constant weight of
fearful anticipation, that many things were confused and ambiguous to
me. I remember mainly in flashes—luminous moments of clarity shining
out from the general murk.

One luminous moment was our arrival at Dr. Kessel's establishment. I
can hardly tell you how we had travelled up until that point: presumably
by steam locomotive from London to Edinburgh, and thence by horse and
carriage. But I remember vividly the tall surrounding hedges and the sign
on the gatepost:

EXPERIMENTAL INSTITUTE OF ELECTRO-MAGNETIC THERAPY
DR. J. S. KESSEL
BY APPOINTMENT ONLY

When we rolled in through the gate, a number of old brick buildings came into view, half hidden by evergreen yews and firs. Two incongruous chimneys rose up from among the trees, more suited to a factory than a research institute. It was late afternoon, and the sun slanting in low under the clouds threw splashes of honey-coloured light over chimneys and tree-tops.

Attendants came out to meet us. They wore tailcoats and high collars and seemed to comport themselves with more dignity and assurance than ordinary servants. I was aware of the incongruity, but assumed I had been given an explanation, which I had since forgotten. Perhaps that was indeed the case. At any event, they took care of our luggage like ordinary servants and escorted us to our appointment with Dr. Kessel.

Dr. Kessel's study stands out as another vivid memory. We were led through a Gothic arched porch and down a flight of steps—for Dr. Kessel's rooms were below ground level. Or mostly below ground level; a strip of horizontal windows just under the ceiling let in a little daylight. But my overpowering impression was neither the windows nor the leather arm-chairs nor the bookcases lining three of the walls—it was a singular smell, at once sweet and stale. I thought of it then—and think of it now—as Dr. Kessel's own personal odour.

The man himself was not as I had prefigured him. I had heard the tone, rather than the words, when Mother and Father talked about him—a tone of awe and reverence. In my imagination, he had been tall, with burning eyes and a flowing beard; in reality, he was short and balding, with thick pebble glasses. He did have a beard, admittedly, but only a small, neatly trimmed goatee. Even the way he paced up and down on the carpet was fussy and precise.

"So this is the boy." He spoke with a foreign accent, hard and clipped, as though cutting out every word like a piece of metal. "Suffers from nightmares."

"We thought they were ordinary night terrors when he was a child," Father explained. "We expected him to grow out of them. But they've continued and become worse over the last three years. Every second night he wakes up screaming."

"He all but died three weeks ago," said Mother. "His heart stopped in his sleep. If I hadn't been by his bedside . . ."

"Yes, yes, these facts I know," Dr. Kessel interrupted. "This was in your letter. What form of nightmares?"

Mother and Father exchanged glances.

"Shadowy things," said Mother. "Recurring monsters."

"Being trapped," said Father.

"Something about a particular colour," said Mother. "A particular shade of reddish brown."

They looked towards me for assistance, but I had no wish to fill in the details. Even when prostrated by fear, sobbing for deliverance, with my head buried in Mother's lap, still there were some horrors I would never reveal to anyone.

Dr. Kessel looked at me too, indifferently, impersonally. "No matter," he said. "Bad thoughts. My mechanism will draw them off."

"How does it work?" asked Father.

Although Father was a banker by profession, science was his hobby. He must have been reading up on the physics of electricity and the new field of research into the human brain. Dr. Kessel stopped pacing and began an explanation. I tried to pay attention as they discussed experiments with galvanic stimulation . . . individual neurological areas of the brain . . . electrical impulses and electro-magnetic waves . . . the application of Tesla's alternating current . . . the different rhythms of wakefulness and sleep. Names were tossed about that I have since researched myself: Eduard Hitzig, Gustav Fritsch, Sir David Ferrier, Friedrich Goltz, and more. In effect, all of the notable pioneers in the history of electro-therapy.

I could tell from Dr. Kessel's manner that he had scant respect for the pioneers, and even less for Father's amateur knowledge of electro-therapy. By his own estimate, he had already advanced far beyond the discoveries of the 1870s, and he was not modest about it. His responses to Father's queries grew shorter and sharper, while Father grew more and more sceptical. Finally, Mother stepped in, putting a hand on Father's elbow.

"Does it matter, Charles? We don't need to understand how it works, so long as it does. Dr. Kessel knows what he's talking about."

Father frowned and stuck out his lower lip. He wasn't so sure that Dr. Kessel knew what he was talking about.

"Have a little trust," she went on. "What do we have to lose?"

"What indeed?" A small, tight smile appeared on Dr. Kessel's face. Mother's way of putting it didn't much please him either.

Mother overrode his ill humour. "How soon can the treatment start, Doctor?"

"There will be a payment required. A donation to fund further research."

"Of course."

"In that case, we may start tomorrow."

Mother's eyes widened. "But . . . You don't need to do tests first?"

Dr. Kessel uttered a humourless laugh like a dog's bark. "I see he is healthy and young. Only tired by lack of sleep. My mechanism will cure him."

No doubt it had a longer technical name, but he always spoke of it as his *mechanism*. His *mechanism* and my *bad thoughts* . . .

He snapped his fingers and turned to the attendants. "Show them to their rooms, please." That was the end of the interview.

THE ATTENDANTS TOOK us to our rooms in the guest wing. I remember one of them had a strong Yankee accent—the surprise of his American twang was the sole observation that could penetrate the fog now enveloping me. He had a friendly, rough-and-ready sort of face, and his name—as I learned the next day—was Mr. Henry J. Hungerford.

My spirits had sunk with the declining sun. For me, the end of the afternoon meant only one thing: the approach of night and impending nightmares. It was a cycle I went through every twenty-four hours. The foreboding of nightmares was like a dark aura that changed the appearance of ordinary objects in my perception, painting them with deeper shadows and edges of lurid colour. Whether the impression was produced by an actual nightmare brewing in my brain, or merely by my habitual expectations, I cannot say.

You would suppose that such a state of dread would set my pulses racing and keep me from sleep. So it might have been on the first, or second, or fiftieth occasion. But when that same foreboding acquired the inevitability of night after night after night—and stretched ahead with the prospect of endless future nights—then the effect was, on the contrary, soporific. Like a leaden weight, it dragged me down and rendered me dull and insensible.

However, that night was different. I think some gleam of hope had entered my soul. In spite of his lack of personal charisma, Dr. Kessel had been absolutely confident as to the powers of his mechanism. It was just enough to counteract my usual torpor. I lay awake and listened to the rising wind outside, soughing through the trees and shaking the loose frame of my window.

I have said that, in certain random moments, my senses functioned with unusual clarity. Sometimes, I think, my heightened acuity far exceeded any normal sight and hearing. Lying under the sheets in Dr. Kessel's institute, I heard—or seemed to hear—a sound carried on the wind, but not of the wind itself. It was a sound of moving mechanical parts, the faintest rhythm of recurring thuds and clanks.

A fancy came over me then, so wild and odd that I almost laughed aloud. The mechanism awaited my inspection—did I dare visit it *now*? You must know that mine was no bold or hardy temperament; night terrors had extinguished whatever stock of impulsive animal spirits I had been born with. To creep outside in the middle of the night was, for me, almost unthinkable. Yet I thought of it; and the thought grew and grew until I acted upon it.

I pulled on socks and shoes, and an overcoat over the top of my nightshirt. My room was on the first storey, and I had to pass by my parents' room on the way to the stairs. They had left their door a little ajar—as always, since my screams in the night had become a regular occurrence. They were still awake and talking, and the intensity of Mother's voice made me stop and listen.

"It *will* work, Charles, I know it will."

"I didn't say it wouldn't."

"But you don't really believe. If Anthony picks up on your cynicism . . ."

"Not cynicism. Scepticism. I have doubts about the science of it, that's all."

"Oh, science, science! Sometimes, Charles, you could do with a bit less science and a bit more faith."

"Now I hear religion talking."

"Yes, and why not? I was brought up in the Christian faith, and unlike you I haven't lost it."

"But this isn't a matter of faith. Dr. Kessel's mechanism is a machine."

"So?"

"So he's claiming it can locate bad thoughts and draw them off. That's not physics, it's superstition. He talks about brain waves and electrical waves, but there's no science for what he's claiming to do."

"Maybe the world is a more spiritual place than you allow. You didn't always think in this way, Charles."

"I believe in science to explain the physical world. Copper and steel are only copper and steel. There are laws about what they can and can't do."

"Oh, you know all about *laws,* I'm sure. But you don't know what it's like . . ." Mother broke off with a sound like a sob.

When she resumed, her voice was low and muffled. "You don't know what it's like to sit by his bedside in the nights. When he's tormented by those dreams and I can't do a single thing to help. He needs me and I can't reach him. I feel so useless, so utterly, utterly useless. My heart just breaks inside of me."

Father uttered soothing noises, but spoke no words that I could hear.

"There *has* to be a way, Charles. I need you to believe with me. For his sake. Please."

I moved on down the corridor. Father would agree, of course—how could he not? It was a side of Mother's nature I hardly knew. She was normally so very determined and severe. But perhaps severity could come from love . . . I descended the staircase at the end of the corridor, crossed the lobby, and went out into the night.

A strangely agitated night it was—a night to fit my mood. My heart was beating fast as I crossed the lawn. Chill flurries of wind blew this way and that, sending leaves and twigs darting in unpredictable movements around my feet. Overhead, long streamers of cloud raced past in front of the face of the moon. I focused on the mechanical rhythm of thuds and clanks and traced it to the institute's central building—the building with two tall chimneys, where Dr. Kessel had his rooms.

On this side, a screen of yew trees hid the walls of the building. I remember a sudden lull and calm in the space behind the trees, and the louder reverberation of the mechanism. Long, narrow windows were set just a few inches above the ground. It was as though the whole building had sunk down and buried itself in the earth.

That impression was confirmed when I knelt and peered inside the first window. The floor of the gloomy interior was a good seven feet below my own level. I observed steel tanks and boilers; an organlike array of pipes; cylinders shooting out steam; wheels, gears, and rotating shafts. There were furnaces, too, distinguishable only by the lines of fiery orange that marked the rims of their doors. The place was like an industrial workshop.

Following the rotating shafts with my eye, I saw where they passed through a hole in a side wall. Obviously, there had to be an adjoining room with connected machinery. I drew back, looked along to the next low-set window, and resolved to investigate.

In the adjoining room, the shafts fed into a succession of enormous humped machines, curiously rounded, with protruding ribs and ridges. Nothing appeared to move, yet all was throbbing as if alive. The dominant sound was a deep low hum, which I could feel through the ground in vibrations under my feet. There was a further connection to a further room in the form of insulated cables as thick as my arm, which emerged from the machines and passed through the next wall along.

The third room was different again, with rows of metal frames and open cabinets, containing an apparatus of glass, brass, and copper. This room was better lit, not only by overhead lightbulbs, but also by the glowing of the apparatus itself. Tubes, domes, and spirals of glass shimmered with an uncanny yellowish light. Some were half filled with a glutinous-looking jelly; others held coils of silvery metal; others again enclosed tiny plates or leaves of gold foil that fluttered as I watched. Compared to the industrial ugliness of the first room, this was like a laboratory—intriguing and enchanting.

Two men were busy at the back of the room. They wore blue overalls and looked like engineers or workmen. Whatever they were doing, they glanced constantly over their shoulders as if uneasy. Sometimes they glanced towards the next side wall, which drew my attention too. No holes had been knocked through the material of this wall, which was solid wood rather than brick. Evidently, there was no connected machinery on the other side.

Once more I moved along in the space behind the trees, once more I knelt—and found myself looking down into Dr. Kessel's study. In spite of the unfamiliar angle, I recognised the bookshelves, the leather armchairs, and the gleaming bald skull of the doctor himself. Even at this late hour, he was up and about—and he wasn't alone.

The person with him was a third man in blue overalls. While Dr. Kessel paced back and forth on the carpet, the man stood with cap in hand, respectful yet frowning.

"Do I not pay enough?" Dr. Kessel was saying.

"'Tis nae about the money." The man's voice had a thick Scottish burr. "'Tis our safety, sir."

Their words reached my ears only because the window was open half an inch at the bottom. I lowered my head, almost touching the ground, to gain a better hearing.

"Phah!" scoffed Dr. Kessel. "That is a complete nonsense, Norris."

"Nae, sir. The men are with me on this."

"Where is it not safe? Tell me. Which part of the mechanism?"

"'Tis in every room. We canna tell until it happens. I told ye this a week ago, sir."

"You told me nothing about *haunting*."

"Nae, sir. But so the men call it."

"What do you call it?"

Norris avoided a direct answer. "The metal bends and rivets come poppin' out. I've nae seen the like. Good strong rivets, without cause or reason. Last night, boiler number two popped a score of rivets on the main pipe. If we hadna found and fixed it . . ."

"Old machinery. It wears out."

"Aye, because ye keep it workin' day and night. Ye must shut it down and rebuild it."

"I will not shut it down."

"Damp down the boilers, turn off the generators . . ."

"*No,* I'm telling you. I *cannot* shut it down."

"Dr. Kessel, I've worked wi' machines since I was a wee bairn. Ye think I'm only an engineer, but—"

"That's right, only an engineer. Not a scientist. You do not understand the importance of this work. This is the science of the brain, and we advance the science by a hundred years. It will be a great service to humanity when my mechanism is perfected."

Norris thrust out his jaw. "I canna tell about the science of the brain, but I know when there's summat amiss wi' a machine. Ye keep fixin' and fiddlin', but ye willna fix what was wrong from the start. The design was never thought out right."

"The design, is it?" Dr. Kessel sneered. "Or is it ghosts? Or perhaps some of your wee Scottish pixies?"

Norris held his ground. "Mebbe," he said.

Dr. Kessel stopped his pacing. "I shall increase the wages."

" 'Tis nae about the money." Norris chewed at his lower lip. "How much more?"

"One shilling a week." Dr. Kessel studied the other man. "Two shillings." Still no response from Norris. Dr. Kessel flung out his arms. "Four shillings more."

"Aye, ye can find the money when ye need it."

Norris had changed his tone. Seemingly, it *was* about the money after all. Dr. Kessel's relief was obvious.

I had been aware of a few light taps on my shoulders, and a swishing, swooshing sound in the trees. I realised then that it had started to rain— and the drops were rapidly turning into a deluge. My relatively sheltered spot between building and trees was no protection.

I left the window and hastened back to my room in the guest wing.

I WAS PERPLEXED and fearful. The suggestion that the physical components of the mechanism might be unsafe disturbed me; even more so, the talk of ghosts and haunting. Exactly what I had to fear I did not know, but the impressions of my midnight adventure came back to me in a hundred shifting associations. I could hold no one thought still and steady in my mind. I write it out calmly now—you see how measured are my sentences—but all that night a whirlwind blew through my brain.

By morning, I was in an abnormal state even by my own standards. It

was as though countless wheels spun at great speed inside me—yet inef-
fectually, disengaged. I couldn't decide what to do for the best; indeed, I
had lost all power of decision. I felt that a current was sweeping me along
to some inevitable fate. I even felt I had a particular role to play, like an
actor following a script.

Last night's storm had passed, and the new day had a stark, scoured
look. The grass and paths were still wet, and a detritus of leaves and twigs
littered the lawns. Four attendants came to collect us, including Mr. Hungerford with the American accent. I think Mr. Hungerford explained that
I should avoid food before my treatment, so Mother and Father also went
without breakfast.

The next clear scene in my memory was when we trooped again into
Dr. Kessel's study. The room was as it had been on our previous visit and
as I had seen it through the window—with a single significant addition.
Against one wall—the wall *not* lined with bookshelves—there now stood
a curious box, large and shallow and mounted on wheels. It was open at
the top, low to the ground, and upholstered with plush white interior padding. I can't say why, but as soon as I saw that box, I knew I was going to
have to lie down in it.

Dr. Kessel was brisk and business-like this morning. He told Father
that my treatment might require up to five sessions with the mechanism,
but a single donation to the institute would cover all costs. The attendants
brought in the contract for Father to sign, and his eyebrows shot up when
he saw the size of the expected donation. Banker that he was, he read
through all the details of the contract before signing.

Meanwhile, I took the opportunity to wander across to the box. A pair
of leather straps lay loose across the padding, and, although I couldn't
tell their precise purpose, the sight of them made my heart beat faster.
I saw also that the wheels of the box ran on two steel rails embedded
in the carpet, as if half-buried in green grass. The rails continued as far
as the wall behind, then appeared to vanish underneath it. In fact, this
was the same wooden wall I had observed last night from the other side—
and not truly a wall but a partition.

"Anthony!"

Mother called me back. The contract had been signed, and, as one of
the attendants bore it away, another stepped forward with a beaker of
cloudy, milky liquid.

"Dr. Kessel wants you to drink this," she said.

I shook my head. My reluctance was growing stronger by the minute.

Mother's mouth tightened. To my thirteen-year-old eyes, my mother was the most beautiful woman in the world; even now, when I consider her photographs, I can say without a doubt that she was unusually attractive. But her large grey eyes could flash with a steely determination, and I admit I was sometimes a little afraid of her.

"It is only a sleeping draught," said Dr. Kessel, more to my parents than me. "He will sleep and dream, until the bad thoughts come to the surface. Then my mechanism draws them off."

"Only a sleeping draught," Mother repeated. "You want to be cured, don't you, Anthony?"

I stared at the liquid. "I don't like it," I said—meaning the liquid, the box, the straps, everything.

"Do you want to have nightmares for the rest of your life?"

Still I wouldn't take the beaker.

"Let me talk to him," said Mr. Hungerford.

He put an arm over my shoulder and led me aside. One of the other attendants came too. I expected Father or Mother to object—was this the role of a servant? But Mr. Hungerford didn't dress like a servant or behave like a servant, and I soon learned the reason why. Besides, he had such an open, friendly manner, it would have been difficult to take offence. Even his Yankee twang was somehow agreeable.

"You're a lucky fellow," he began. "This is a great opportunity for you."

I remained silent.

"I've been in your position, you know," he went on, unperturbed. "Me and Mr. Jamieson here. We both had doubts about the mechanism. Right, Mr. Jamieson?"

Mr. Jamieson was the other attendant, a tall, thin man with a gingery beard. "That's true indeed," he said.

I began to have an inkling of their real circumstances. "You had the treatment here? I thought you were just . . . I mean, I thought you were . . ."

"Servants?" Mr. Hungerford laughed. "Half right, half right. We serve Dr. Kessel, but only because we choose to. You could call us gentlemen of independent means. Dr. Kessel helped us, so now we help him."

"More than helped us," Mr. Jamieson put in.

"Yes." Mr. Hungerford accepted the correction. "He *saved* us. And he can do the same for you. What he does here is the closest you'll ever come to a miracle in this world."

"Are all the attendants ex-patients?" I asked.

"Sure they are. Though only a few ex-patients become attendants. Most folks go back to their jobs and families. But they've all found peace for themselves, same as us."

"Did you have nightmares too?"

"Not nightmares, no. Mine were waking hallucinations. Terrible bad pictures in my head. I used to see blood running down walls, blood on faces, blood on cups and plates, everywhere. I reckon I'd have gone mad, except I came here for the treatment."

He followed the line of my gaze as I looked towards Mr. Jamieson.

"Ah, Mr. Jamieson," he went on. "Don't ask him about *his* bad thoughts. He was in a seminary training to become a priest, but something went wrong and switched the other way. He used to hear a voice in his head telling him to do ugly, cruel, brutal things. There was a mighty weight of evil on his soul when his family brought him here. Two years ago he had the treatment, and he's been a new man ever since."

Mr. Jamieson merely smiled and nodded, letting the American tell the story on his behalf.

"What do you see when you look at us?" Mr. Hungerford asked suddenly. "How do we seem to you?"

I didn't know how to answer such a personal question. "You seem . . . er, fine."

"We feel fine." Mr. Hungerford grinned broadly. "You should have seen us before the treatment. Now we're happy as a couple of kings."

He did seem happy. There was a twinkle in his eye and the hint of laughter hovering always round his mouth. I envied him.

"Think of it like having a tooth pulled," said Mr. Jamieson. "Have you ever had a tooth pulled?"

"Yes."

"Unpleasant experience?"

I pulled a face.

"But now? Are you glad you had it done?"

I nodded.

Mr. Hungerford snapped his fingers. "All the badness pulled out of you. See, it's exactly the same. Will you give it a try?"

I nodded again.

"You won't regret it, I promise you."

They walked me back to the attendant with the sleeping draught. I suspect that the others had overheard every word; certainly they had begun no conversation among themselves in all the time we'd been talking.

"He'll give it a try," Mr. Hungerford announced.

Dr. Kessel merely nodded, as though he had never expected any other answer.

I drank off the milky liquid, which proved to be quite tasteless. Then, as intuition had foretold, Dr. Kessel instructed me to lie down in the box.

I climbed in and lay on my back, with my head pointing in the direction of the partition. The padding was as soft as eiderdown. The sweet-and-stale odour that pervaded the study at large seemed more concentrated here. Mr. Hungerford and Mr. Jamieson bent over and fastened the straps across my chest. However, the straps were too long and hung loose on me.

"It is no problem," said Dr. Kessel, and turned to signal the other two attendants.

A moment later, they came forward bearing assorted blocks of wood. Triangular blocks of wood, rectangular blocks of wood, blocks in curved shapes and segments—they were like oversize pieces from a child's play set. Under Dr. Kessel's direction, the attendants fitted them around me in the bottom of the box. Two blocks went on either side of my head, two blocks under my armpits, two blocks against my waist, four blocks to keep my legs in place. I was immobilised in a ridiculous outstretched position, legs slightly apart, hands touching the sides of the box.

By now the sleeping draught was beginning to take effect. Sounds and voices came to me loud or soft, sharp or muffled, as if passing in and out of successive tunnels. I heard the noise of the partition being slid back: a slow grinding and grating. Then came the sound of the mechanism itself: rhythmical, pounding, metallic. There was a change in the air as smells of fumes and oil drifted into the study.

Mr. Hungerford and Mr. Jamieson reappeared a moment later, leaning over me, gripping the back of the box. Mr. Hungerford gave me an encouraging wink. They pushed, and the box rolled forward along the rails into the rooms beyond.

Pinned in by the wooden blocks, travelling headfirst and upside-down, I could see only what was straight above me: the bare boards of a ceiling and a network of rubber-coated wires attached to the boards. When we turned gradually to the left, the tops of metal frames entered my field of vision—the same metal frames I had seen last night. Fizzing, crackling noises reminded me of the shimmering glows inside the glass apparatus.

"Our own steam engines and generators supply electricity," Dr. Kessel was saying. "The power supply must never fail . . ."

I entered a muffled tunnel of drowsiness and ceased to pay attention. But *inside* that tunnel, I started to hear something else, a different kind of voice. How to explain it? While all other sounds were muted, this was very distinct, albeit faint. It was a mutter as of somebody talking to himself, preoccupied with his own business. The mutter seemed to move about from place to place, now ahead of the box and now behind it.

I tried to follow the source, but the wooden blocks prevented me from turning my head.

Then the muttering passed across directly above me. Could it be a voice on the other side of the ceiling? I was instantly and absolutely sure that it wasn't. No, it was in one of the rubber-clad wires—actually *inside* the wire. I could even pinpoint the particular wire!

I gasped—and drew Mr. Hungerford's attention.

"He seems agitated," he said.

Mother looked down. "How long does this sleeping draught take to work?" she asked Dr. Kessel.

"It is very fast." The doctor sounded puzzled. "He should be falling asleep by now."

"Just relax, kid," Mr. Hungerford told me. "Don't fight it."

All at once, I was very determined *not* to fall asleep.

The box reached the end of the rails a moment later. There was a click as it came to a halt and locked into place.

Mr. Hungerford and Mr. Jamieson straightened and stood upright. Seven adults loomed above me, tall as trees. Perspective distorted their features, so that their faces were all chin and no eyes. The yellowish light from the apparatus gave them a sallow look.

They were talking among themselves, paying no heed to the strange voice muttering. I realised then that I alone—in my abnormal mental state, under the influence of the sleeping draught—I alone could hear it.

"This is what fits over his head," Dr. Kessel was saying.

"Like a crown," Mother commented.

"Yes, indeed. This is the most important part of the mechanism."

I rolled my eyes back in my head, trying to focus on what the doctor held in his hands. The thing was above and behind me, and I felt giddy, even nauseated, from the vain effort to bring it into view.

"Be calm, Anthony," said Mother.

"He'll be fine," said Mr. Hungerford.

Only when Dr. Kessel stepped a pace forward did the thing become clear to me. It *was* like a crown—a crown of wires—and also like a bird's nest. Strands of copper were woven one over another to an incredible degree of complexity.

And there was another voice inside the strands!

It was a low, sinister whisper that erected the hairs on the back of my neck. Faint and distinct, like the muttering but not the same. I traced its movement as it circled round and round in the woven wires. I could distinguish no individual words, but the tone was insidious, sly and horrible.

An association came instantly to my mind: the voice that Mr. Jamieson had heard in his head, telling him to do things. Ugly, cruel, brutal things!

Was it an arbitrary association? No doubt. But the idea was right.

I tried to call out to the adults towering above. "Listen, listen to them!"

The voice in the crown of wires changed to a revolting laugh, a wet and breathy chuckle.

"What does he mean?" asked Mother.

"Something's going wrong, isn't it?" said Father.

"Not at all." Dr. Kessel sounded snappish. "We shall put this over his head and wait for him to fall asleep."

He meant the crown of wires. But when I saw it coming towards me, I panicked completely. I wrenched my arms free from the blocks, found the buckle, and undid the leather straps. I sat up in the box and gaped at the room around me.

The apparatus was as I had seen last night: tubes, domes, and spirals of glass, contained in rows of frames and cabinets. There was wiring too, more wiring than I had realised. A veritable spider's web connected every item of apparatus to every other item. But that wasn't what I gaped at.

Inside the wiring, inside the frames, inside the metal parts were voices—hundreds and hundreds of them. They scurried this way and that, constantly in motion, whispering, murmuring, gabbling, giggling. I even heard shrill squeals, distant yet close, that came from the silvery coils in a particular set of glass domes.

"Anthony! What are you doing?"

"Lie back down."

"Is he hallucinating?"

Why couldn't they hear what I heard? "Open your ears!" I cried.

Dr. Kessel put a hand on my shoulder. Before he could force me to lie back down, I knocked his hand away, kicked my legs free from the blocks, and jumped right out of the box.

Mother tried to catch hold of me, but I eluded her.

Her eyes flared. "Stay where you are! This is your last chance, Anthony! Don't waste it!"

I continued to back away.

"No!" Dr. Kessel shouted loudest of all. "Keep him away from there!"

Attendants lunged forward—too late. I blundered into the very cabinet that had provoked Dr. Kessel's cry of warning. Even worse, my foot caught in some wiring, and I tumbled over backwards.

There was a tremendous crash, and a sensation like a hammer blow through my bones. I had never experienced an electrical shock before, but I experienced one then.

The cabinet toppled under my weight and I collapsed on top of it. I rolled off sideways, crushing more glass and snapping more wires in the process.

The attendants cried out in dismay. "The control unit!"

"It's wrecked!"

"What'll happen now?"

"Will the whole mechanism stop?"

I looked back and saw a cascade of sparks flying out from the cabinet. There were spitting, explosive sounds and a smell of burning.

I crawled further away, like some criminal from the scene of the crime. The light in the room grew dim as the shimmering glows inside the glass apparatus flickered and died. The mechanism *was* coming to a stop.

Dr. Kessel's reaction went beyond anger or despair. The look on his face conveyed outright terror.

I crawled further and further away. Ahead of me was a brick wall pierced by a jagged archway. No one was watching as I stumbled to my feet and passed through. I found myself in the middle room of massive humped machines—the generators, as I now supposed.

Here too the mechanism was failing. The generators no longer gave off their deep hum, and the silence was eerie, the echoes cavernous. From the next room along I could hear the *click-click-click* of cooling metal and the drip of falling water—but the clanging, pounding rhythm of the engines had stopped.

The only sound was the whispering and muttering of hidden voices. They were in the machinery of this room too. I stood stock-still and clamped my hands over my ears.

I expected someone to come searching for me from the room I had left behind. Instead, a figure entered from the room ahead. I recognised him at once—Norris, the Scottish engineer. He appeared in a further archway, backing away from the engines and boilers. I lowered my hands. He continued backing away for a dozen paces before he caught sight of me.

"What's happenin', lad?" he demanded. His face was white, and he looked shaken.

"The mechanism has stopped," I answered. Guilt or honesty made me add, "I stopped it."

"I can see it's stopped." He hadn't registered my last sentence. "But what's this other thing that's started?"

For a moment, I imagined he was hearing the same voices that I heard. "You hear them too?"

"Them?"

"Voices in the metal."

He shook his head at me as if I were crack-brained. "What I hear is the metal itself. Stress and strain. What's makin' it so?"

Even as he spoke, a bolt that held one of the generators to its mounting snapped off suddenly. The bolthead flew up in the air, then fell back with a clatter.

"It shouldna happen," Norris said, more to himself than to me. "Not when everything's stopped."

A wire that ran across the ceiling broke off and lashed about in front of our faces. It was like someone wielding a whip. Then a cable on the floor started to jump and jerk. Norris took to his heels and fled into the room with the apparatus.

I followed, returning the way I had come. The voices in the metal were no louder, but increasingly urgent and excited. At the same time, I could also hear what Norris heard, a creaking and straining of the metal itself. It was a different sound, but related, surely related.

Mother, Father, and Dr. Kessel still stood beside the box; the attendants surrounded the fallen cabinet; Norris hovered further back, half in and half out of the open partition. They were all motionless yet focused, as in a tableau. At first I couldn't grasp the object of their attention—or objects, for they stared in several directions.

Then, with a sudden movement, a whole mass of apparatus slid from its shelf. Glass tubes smashed on the floor, metallic coils and plates scattered far and wide. I looked again and saw that the frame supporting the shelf had warped away from the vertical—indeed, was *continuing* to warp. And not only that one frame, but every frame in the room. It was as though some tremendous force were twisting and bending the struts from within.

There was another crash as another shelf tilted and discharged its contents. Then an even louder crash as a whole cabinet went over. And at every crash, I heard—with my *other* hearing, attuned to those *other* sounds—I heard a surge of excitement and an evil thrill. Through wires and cables, through struts and rods, those horrible, hidden voices came hurrying towards the wreckage—whispering, muttering, exulting. Like rats they were, converging upon a victim.

On the floor, the metallic fragments continued to twist and bend as if writhing. To my eyes, the process conveyed an impression of indescribable agony.

I broke the spell of horror and shouted at the top of my voice. "I know what it is! It's the bad thoughts! Inside the metal! I can hear them!"

Mr. Jamieson turned. "*What* can he hear?"

"Your bad thoughts!" I shouted again. "The mechanism is having nightmares! It's living your hallucinations!"

Father frowned. "It's only a machine, Anthony."

At that moment, a sound came from the frame I was standing beside: a shriek of tormented metal. The whole structure contorted and buckled slowly sideways. There were similar sounds from other parts of the room, and the machinery in the rooms beyond.

"Out of here!" cried Mr. Hungerford. "Everybody, move!"

I think Mother tugged me by the arm—it was all a blur. We fled through the open partition into Dr. Kessel's study. I looked back and saw Mr. Hungerford and another attendant sliding the wooden wings closed. Dr. Kessel came through just in time before the partition slammed shut. Mr. Hungerford and the other attendant pushed home bolts to lock it at the top and bottom.

The partition was solid, heavy wood, two inches thick. No one stood close, but no one ran out of the study either. We listened to the appalling cacophony building up on the other side. Shrieks and screeches—it might have been the sufferings of the damned, but it was the metal itself. We didn't need to see it to know that in every room the machinery was slowly, inexorably tearing apart.

Then Mr. Jamieson prodded me in the back.

"What did you say just now?" he demanded.

"It's your bad thoughts that got inside the metal," I told him.

"My bad thoughts?"

"And all the other patients."

"Our bad thoughts?" Mr. Jamieson looked incredulous.

"Oh, I feared this," said another voice. It was Dr. Kessel, wide-eyed and teetering on the edge of hysteria. "Bad thoughts infected my mechanism."

"So ye knew all along," Norris chimed in. "Ye knew it was haunted."

"Suspected. Only suspected."

"I told ye the design was wrong."

"No." Dr. Kessel had never been an impressive figure, but now he seemed pathetically cowed and shrunken. "There *was* no other way to build it. As long as the electricity was running . . . I was *saving* people."

"*You* never saved anyone," Mr. Hungerford bluntly. "*It* did."

He nodded towards the machinery on the other side of the partition. The cacophony had now reached a crescendo. I don't think any of us will ever forget those unbearable, piercing sounds of tortured metal.

"It's hurting!" cried Dr. Kessel suddenly. "I have to help . . ."

He ran for the partition and reached for the bolts to unlock it. Norris and Mr. Hungerford were on top of him in an instant. Mr. Hungerford dragged his arms away and pinned them behind his back.

"No one can help anything now," the American said.

When Dr. Kessel tried to struggle, Norris simply cuffed him over the head and knocked him to the ground. Then the two of them hauled him over the floor away from the partition.

He lay there blubbering and snivelling for a while. Then he turned his attention on me. "It is the boy's fault. He caused it to happen."

"Let him be." Mr. Hungerford spoke up on my behalf. "It was bound to happen in the end."

The sounds on the other side of the partition continued unabated for ten minutes, then began to die down. It was another half hour before they ceased altogether.

MY ACCOUNT IS almost finished. Only one last thing remains to tell—and now I know I can tell it calmly. I have maintained my equilibrium, have I not? All these dark experiences suppressed for years in my mind—I *could not* risk reliving them. No one ever had to struggle so hard for their sanity. But finally I have written it out: the nightmares, the box, the crown of wires, the hidden voices, the agony of the metal, and my own guilt.

Oh yes, I accept the guilt. Even if the electricity must have failed eventually, yet I was the one who made it fail *then*. Dr. Kessel and I were both responsible in our different ways. My role was to be the immediate agent and cause. Now that I write it out, the sequence of events seems strangely inevitable—including the one last twist in the story. Make of it what you will.

We waited a long while after the sounds had ceased. Outside, the sun had risen above the buildings of the institute, and Dr. Kessel's study grew bright with morning light. Then Mr. Hungerford and Mr. Jamieson took the lead in unfastening the bolts. They peeped through the partition and opened the wings a little wider. All was silent. I can't explain the impression, but it was a *good* silence.

We trooped through in single file and stared at the wreckage in awe and amazement. It was like some twisted, tangled forest. Fragments of glass littered the floor, and wires hung down from the ceiling. The metal frames were still generally upright, but distorted into the most fantastical shapes . . . shapes of pain, it seemed to me. Many of the cabinets had been ripped open as if disembowelled.

I strained my ears as we moved cautiously forward. Faint creaks accompanied the disturbance of our footsteps, but the whispering and muttering voices had gone.

Mr. Jamieson turned to me. "Is it over?" he asked.

I nodded.

I can't describe the sense of peace, the deep solemnity. I saw tears on Mr. Jamieson's face and realised that I was crying too. Tears of relief or tears of sadness—I don't know which. Daylight entering from the high-set windows filtered through the gaunt, racked metal; motes of dust, the residue of so much violence, drifted in the sunbeams.

"Look!" cried Mother, and flung out an arm.

At first I couldn't see what she was pointing at—though I recognised the spot, where the steel rails terminated. The padded box was there, almost buried under a pile of fallen apparatus.

"Yes!" cried Mr. Jamieson, pointing too.

Then I saw: it was the metal frame behind the box. It had lost most of its struts so that only two remained, warped out of their proper positions in such a way as to form a perfect vertical and a perfect horizontal. In effect, the shape of a cross.

Mr. Jamieson dropped to his knees and put his hands together. He began gabbling a prayer that I'm sure never featured in any prayer book. Norris also knelt and bowed his head; then Mother; then everyone except Father. Mr. Hungerford pushed Dr. Kessel forcibly to his knees.

"Suffered for us," Mr. Jamieson gabbled on. "Pure and innocent . . . bore our sins . . . defiled by human thoughts."

Of course, Mr. Jamieson was an ex-seminarian, so you can understand where his thinking came from. Father remained sceptical and repeated that it was "only a machine" many times on our journey back to London. As for me . . . well, I had panicked before the mechanism ever had the chance to draw off *my* bad thoughts. Yet, from that time on, my nightmares disappeared as if they had never existed. So what does *that* show? I wonder.

Afterword to "Bad Thoughts and the Mechanism"

I know some people have memories that go back to babyhood, but not me. The first memory that I'm sure is my own real memory—and not re-created from what adults told me—comes from a holiday in the seaside town of Fleetwood, in Lancashire, England. I must have been about four or five, and what I remember is Fleetwood pier, which had been recently destroyed by fire. It stuck far out into the sea, a wreckage of tangled, twisted girders, and not just tangled, not just twisted, but racked and contorted like an expression of agony, a frozen shriek of pain. There you have the whole germ and genesis of "Bad Thoughts and the Mechanism."

I'd now count "Bad Thoughts and the Mechanism" as a "steampunk" story. Ten years ago, I'd hardly heard of "steampunk"—I mean, I'd heard of the word, but I'd never thought it had anything to do with me. But I was wrong—I'd been blindly blundering my way towards steampunk from a long time before then. The fascination with nineteenth-century culture and Dickensian atmospheres was already there in *The Black Crusade* and *The Vicar of Morbing Vyle* (the latter my first novel, published in 1993). And the fascination with old-fashioned steam-age machinery was there in the industrial scenery of the Humen Camp in the three *Ferren* books and in the fabulous contraptions of (again) *The Black Crusade*. When I completed *Worldshaker* and it was instantly categorized as "steampunk," I realised I'd discovered my own true home. Or as the poet said, it was like coming home and knowing the place for the first time.

"Bad Thoughts and the Mechanism" was an amazingly difficult story to write, because I couldn't get the voice I needed. I started to write in first person, rewrote in third person, tried again with a different-sounding first person, another go at third person, and finally—phew! gasp!—hit upon a first-person voice that sounded just right. I guess the problem was the contradiction between using formal vocabulary and long sentences, as necessary for a nineteenth-century feel, but also conveying intense emotion and an underlying thrill of horror. My lifeline was Edgar Allan Poe—I confess, I actually read a Poe short story every morning before starting work on "Bad Thoughts and the Mechanism." I've never put myself under an influence in that way before! Yet that too was like coming home, because Poe was the first great love of my adult reading life, which began when a German teacher at school decided to forget about teaching German and instead spent a whole period reading us "The Tell-Tale Heart." But that's another story . . .

—RICHARD HARLAND

Marly Youmans

Marly Youmans is the author of seven books that include novels, a volume of poetry, and two young adult fantasies. Her novel *The Wolf Pit* was short-listed for the Southern Book Award of the Southern Book Critics Circle and won the Michael Shaara Award. Forthcoming are two collections of poetry, *The Throne of Psyche* (Mercer University Press) and *The Foliate Head* (Stanza Press); and three novels, *Glimmerglass* (PS Publishing), *Maze of Blood* (PS Publishing), and *A Death at the White Camellia Orphanage* (winner of the Ferrol Sams Award, Mercer University Press).

MARLY YOUMANS

The Grave Reflection

Some years after my father's decease, I discovered an envelope labeled "Saxton" in his handwriting, tucked inside a chest of papers
left in my possession. On reading the first line on the enclosed sheets,
I guessed what the anecdote enclosed would contain, for its queer,
secret events were long a matter of private wonder and curiosity
to our family. I believe that my father would have liked to publish
the account had it not been for his affection for the "younger Mr.
Saxton," who remained a fast friend and steady correspondent until
my father passed to the next world, wherein all such mysteries as
these will surely be revealed.

This account, released for public inspection now that the principal
parties involved in its uncanny transactions have flown, will, I trust,
be of some interest to my father's many admirers among a new generation of readers.

—R.H.L., 1890

ALTHOUGH I AM by nature a homebody who prefers to immure himself in the nest of family, rejoicing in the little circle of lives that Divine Intelligence has seen fit to bestow upon me, I could not ignore the message that came to me from a village in a remote corner of our district, home to my boyhood friend Theron Saxton. He had been a spirited fellow with always a prank and a jest to enliven the table or hearth, so much so that he earned the enmity of many sagacious, dour souls who could not bear that the often heavy dough of life should be leavened by the yeast and spice of his merriment. The message handed to me at the door was urgent:

> If you love me, come to me at once, my dear Hawthorne, for I am plagued as no man has ever been, and I feel my mind like a mere chip of a boat whirling in a gale, close to capsizing from the storm within and without me.

I knew very well what sort of sorrows had recently accompanied my friend, enveloping him in a sable blackness. Not six months before, a beloved brother, Mr. Edward Saxton, his elder by some twenty minutes and twin to himself in every minute particular, had succumbed to the ravages of consumption. The unfortunate man had borne up under the weight of disease for many months, an example of patience and manly fortitude, before taking to his bed and declining and dying in the space of a fortnight. My wife and I arrived too late for anything but the burial and stood among the other mourners, our cloaks whipping in the autumn gusts. I had not seen my friend since and now regretted my lack of spirit and ambition in correspondence, which might have comforted him and kept me snug at home on a brisk winter's night.

Having tenderly parted from my wife and children, I hurried to town and set out by a clattering mail coach at twilight. The bitterness of the evening seeped into my bones, and I was glad to share some moth-eaten buffalo robes with a stranger. I dozed off and was dreaming an absurd but uneasy dream—struggling with a gigantic warrior in rattling and clanking armor and, as if that were not enough to occupy and challenge my dream self, battling with my Goliath-sized knight in the midst of an earthquake—when I was awakened by a prodigious thumping on the side of the coach. The driver wrenched open the door and informed me that we had gained the foot of the lane leading to Saxton's Folly, as my friend's ancestral house was known to citizens of the nearby town. Although no doubt longing to finish his run, the fellow was good enough to proffer a pull of spirits from his pocket flask and to warn me against the thick pack of ice on the roadway, furnishing me with a sturdy metal-tipped staff that I promised to guard and remit to his care on my homeward journey.

To a man shocked suddenly awake, the gloom and cold of the lane was unwelcome. But the clouds that had recently brought a few pristine feet of snow were scattering from the moon, and patches of mingled moonshine and starlight shone here and there on the uneven surface of ice. The hooves of the horses and the iron-clad wheels of the coach made a racket as the coach proceeded apace without me, and I was left alone with the glitter of the stars.

Wrapping my cloak closely about me, I stepped into the fir-lined lane. Soon I was longing for a wandering 2:00 A.M. dram seller with Jamaica, cognac, strong beer, or a cup of mulled wine. I would have paid a good deal better than the going rate for another small drop of flame to warm my insides. But there was no help for it, so I scudded along with a will in the deep groove of wagon tracks, gazing around me at the black silhouette trees and the dazzle of stars and the faint twisting lights of the aurora borealis, barely visible so far from their native home. Although the shadows of the firs oppressed me with a sense of density—as if they might detach themselves from the ice-fringed trees and pour after me, plucking my sleeve and peering into my face with faces cut from crisp sheets of blackest night—I had a heartening fancy that the bright constellations had shed the snow that crested the tops of my boots and spilled inside, so that the world was knee-deep in tumbled stars.

At the top of the hill I stopped, panting from exertion in the icy air, and looked up at Saxton's Folly. Old Flavel Saxton had spent his fortune on the house, a massive colonial edifice with additions and porches and outbuildings that included a mighty barn for carriages and horses. He died penniless and house proud. The Saxton twins, his great-great-grandsons, had managed to buy the home place back from the descendants of their ancestor's creditors and to restore it to the antique glory of a century before. Further efforts had resulted in the gathering together of much family furniture and some four thousand books belonging to the original Saxton library, an enormous collection in Flavel Saxton's unsettled times. Seen by moonlight, the manse resembled a natural cliff, altogether lifeless, shrouded in snow, and for a moment I lingered, half inclined to turn tail and fly down the lane rather than be taken into such frozen rockiness.

But soon I chided myself for a wayward fancy, long my undoing, and waded forward to cross the lawn. With a deal of care I scaled the treacherous, deep-draped steps to the door and clanged the knocker against its iron plate, sending snowflakes and tiny icicles flying. As if spirited to my summons, someone answered almost immediately, and I glimpsed a candle's flame fluttering within a cupped hand.

"What's this fuss and ruction—"

Blinking, a pink-nosed lady in an old-fashioned mobcap held up the candle to peer at me with cataract-clouded eyes but was soon thrust aside by Saxton, his face flashing with glad humor.

"No problem, Mrs. Molebury, none—it's my boyhood friend, Mr. Hawthorne, who has been good enough to come swiftly when I called—fetch him a hot toddy, will you? He must be as cold as a churchyard stone."

Saxton pulled me inside and ushered me to a bench beside a dying bed of coals. In a trice he had poked the half-extinguished embers into a semblance of life, added kindling and logs, and then helped me to remove my boots.

"It is good of you, Hawthorne, so very agreeable of you to come at such a summons and leave the children and your dear wife. I shall not forget it in a hurry."

When he looked up at me from the ground where he was kneeling, one of my dripping boots still in his hands, I saw that Saxton appeared pallid, as if he had been sitting up many nights—as he had done before Edward Saxton's death. At that instant, nothing of his usual gaiety of manner remained to him. I wondered about his sorrow for his brother: surely grief for a twin was less consolable than most, the two siblings being joined, as it were, metaphysically, one being the enfleshed reflection of the other.

"Indeed, I shall not forget," he said softly. He gave a small shiver, but in another instant he smiled again, and the old joking Theron Saxton I knew peeped out of his face.

"What's the matter, my friend?" I gripped his arm, leaning forward.

"Let's have your cloak," he said; "you must be soaked, scaling that infernal hill in the dark. You're encrusted in snow! You'll be lucky not to take sick, traveling so late."

"It was a fine night for a tramp—the stars out, and wisps of the northern lights." I studied his face as he lifted my ice-sequined cloak and draped it over the back of a Windsor chair that, drawn near the fire, did service as a drying rack.

He turned toward the flames, adjusting a rickety eight-legged fire screen that might have been steady on its wrought-iron lion's feet in the days of Flavel Saxton.

"What is it?" My voice came in a whisper; I felt the quickening pulse of an unreasoning alarm.

"There's time enough to explain in the morning," he said, his eyes going to the grandfather clock. "Surely you are exhausted from travel. Mail coach, was it?"

I nodded, watching him, my sense of something amiss only increasing. Well, I was certainly weary, but I hadn't rushed from home and launched my one-man boat into the teeth of a gale only to take harbor between clean sheets.

"Here's Mrs. Molebury, best of housekeepers," he cried as the old lady appeared in the doorway, balancing candle and toddy on a pewter tray that must have been as old as the fire screen, so crude and massy did it appear. "Doubtless with her famous buttered brandy and cider toddy, doctored with the brown spices and a twist of dried peel, and magically thrown together in a trice."

"Ah, go on with you. There were kitchen coals aplenty to heat a drop for the gentleman." She handed me the drink and stood drowsily looking at the master of the house, the long crimson shawl over her nightgown like a vivid splotch of blood in the dark. "Poor Mr. Theron Saxton, he's had a mort of trouble," she said, "and it's so hard to see him without Mr. Edward Saxton by his side."

"Yes, that *is* a difficulty," Saxton muttered. He met my eyes then, his expression elusive—an element of something like black humor playing in the midst of some unhappiness.

The toddy warmed me as the fire had not; I felt not sleepier but more wakeful and now looked about me. One thing struck me as strange: the mirrors were still covered in black cloth as though his brother had just died. I mentioned this peculiarity, and the housekeeper shook her head.

"It's a queer freak of the younger Mr. Saxton," she said softly. "He can't bear the sight of his own face. Who can blame him? It must be like seeing his elder brother, the two were so alike."

"We were," Saxton said, "but no more. Now we are quite different, the inhabitants of several worlds. Thank you very much for taking pains with the hot drink, Mrs. Molebury. I can depend on your care no matter how wild the hour, it seems."

She gave a bob of pleasure, smiling drowsily, and slipped away through the door. We could see the flare of candlelight wavering down the hall; then it vanished.

"Tell me," I said, nodding at the hangings that shrouded the great mirror above the mantelpiece. "Some dread has captured you, I believe— some secret fear. Why these signs of our mortality that are more than mourning?"

He shook his head as if he would not answer.

"The cloth is no mere token," he whispered, glancing toward the hall where Mrs. Molebury had shuffled away. "It is no outward and visible sign of my grief, though I am well acquainted with that constant article and need no black weavings to remind me. The fading of his life, the hectic fire in his cheeks, the heart's blood on his lips: these things are never far away from my daily meditations. But it is something else."

His hands were clenched in his lap, as if they had seized hold of a secret that they found difficult to disclose.

I waited, letting the drink restore me, gazing at him while my pulse flickered, as if my very blood already knew something fearsome that I did not.

At last he stood and leaned against the mantelpiece, his loose hair falling forward and half hiding the expressive face with its long crooked Saxton nose and the dark blue eyes.

"Can you not tell me?"

He turned his head slightly, staring intently at me as though he wished with all his heart to share a burden that oppressed its inmost chambers.

Then, looking up at the bound mirror, he said, "It's a beautiful glass."

"Shall we take away the pall? Let a little reflective light into the room?"

He gave me another glance freighted with unease. "You don't know what you ask. And yet, we might as well."

I helped him with the cloth, tugging it carefully from the oval mirror, and stood with my head cocked, the black spill in my arms, to examine the gilded and hand-carved souvenir of the Revolution, its massive wooden frame topped with a shrieking eagle, one taloned foot upraised, grasping a sheaf of arrows.

"What a fine piece of work," I said, admiring the boldness of the carving.

Saxton stumbled, stepping back from the mantelpiece. I reached to help him and, as I saw the pallor of his face, swung round to gaze into the looking glass. Then I turned in confusion, not yet comprehending—searching for another mirror, perhaps, or for a portrait of one of the Saxton twins. I have long been prone to mild palpitations of the heart; and as I felt that temperamental organ jump a beat and then race to make up for the lost time, I pressed one hand hard against my chest.

"What do you see?" he said hoarsely.

"I see the two of us." I hesitated to say more, the hair at my nape prickling. Like an animal in blackfly season, I gave a twitch and shivered to cast my biting fears away.

"And is that all? Is that all you see?"

The mug trembled in my hand, and I gripped it harder and with both hands. I drained the rest of the brandy and hard cider before I spoke.

"I see myself. I see you. But there is unmistakably something deeper in the mirror." Coldness swirled around me, as though a key or twist of paper had been plucked from a lock and let in a piercing gust of air. I felt some reluctance to name the vision, as if it would somehow make real what could not be real, but at last I added these words, my voice unsteady: "A face. It resembles the features of Edward. Not as in life, it seems."

Saxton slumped into a wing chair by the fire, shuttering his face in his hands as for some moments his shoulders shook with sobs. Then he recovered himself, wiping his eyes with a handkerchief.

"I fancied for a time that I might be mad," he said. "I was afraid to be among company, fearful what they would detect. I could not bear to risk a confidence—what might have happened to my reputation in this place? You know I was to be married to Miss Mathers, my dear Daphne . . . That blissful date has been postponed indefinitely, perhaps until the end of time. I have told her only that the break from Edward was more grievous than I had foreseen, and that I need some months to recover. More than that her family does not know, and I cannot explain."

His voice gathered power, rushing through the story. "As the days passed, I became demoralized. No longer was I sure which of us was genuine." The fingers of his right hand plucked at the flame-weave fabric of the chair. "I would catch glimpses of his face everywhere, denying reason. I met him in the sides of polished bowls, in pools of water, in every mirror in the house. Even now, all I have to do is gaze into a reflective medium to summon up my dead. Each time, the face comes as a surprise. Sometimes it is the head of a new corpse, sometimes—less than fresh. I can hardly take away my gaze, commanded as it is by the horror of a most beloved brother's dissolution. Some days he seems alive, tubercular roses planted high on his cheeks. Sometimes those crinkled eyelids unstick and flash open, and though they are as mild and blue as summer lakes, such eyes can shock. Who would have thought that I could be afraid, seeing my brother's eyes?"

When Theron Saxton lapsed into silence, I laid a hand upon his shoulder, shuddering inwardly as I peered into the glass.

"Finally," he said, reaching up to clasp my hand, "I bethought myself of our long friendship that no mystery could cloud and nothing break. And so I wrote in haste, and here you are."

"Here I am, and here I shall stay until we penetrate this mystery and banish the ghost of glass." Although I achieved the tone of heartiness for which I strove, my voice wavered.

He blotted his eyes again. "And now I know that others can discern the thing I fear, that I shall be forced to keep myself monastic in dread that others will glimpse this—this grotesquerie that haunts reflection. It harms my brother's memory that elsewise would shine and be a comfort. But more, it means that I cannot be free until they shut my eyes and nail the coffin lid upon my face."

"Come, Saxton," I said gently, seating myself on the footstool by his chair; "you take the thing in true romantic style, desperate, lorn, and without hope. Surely we are beyond such raw panics in these modern days. The world grows quite rational. There may be a path out of this labyrinth." My words were reasonable, but I trembled inwardly, feeling an awe that overmastered confidence.

"This tomb," he murmured, "where lives no love, no bride, no child, nothing. Where I hide from pools and salvers, the least scrap of looking glass, the trough below the pump: I am buried alive, a condemned man!"

"No, you are no longer cut off from sympathy but have confessed your trouble. You have a very constant ghost, and yet not quite a ghost such as is told in tales," I said, "not the sort of creature one can imagine subject to exorcism, or threatened by bell, book, and candle." I bent toward the fire, ignoring the image in the looking glass but feeling the pressure of its face and the eyes under waxen eyelids.

Saxton slumped, head in hands.

"Yet there must be a solution," I said, half to reassure myself.

When he made no reply, I got up and climbed onto the chair, cauling the mirror once more in black cloth.

Rather than sending me to slumber, Mrs. Molebury's hot toddy seemed to have slapped awake my faculties, and I was eager to consider how I might be of assistance. I could not help but be compelled by the image in the mirror as I coaxed the fabric over the eagle's wings. When I allowed my glance to drift to the half-shadowed head, I felt a jolt of raw fright that I credited to the horror of things in the wrong place, the simple source of so much terror.

"Let us survey the books recovered from your great-grandfather's time and investigate. You cannot be singled out for persecution from all of humanity and history, I feel certain."

"Surely you are too far gone for anything but sleep," Saxton protested.

"I embarked on this journey at twilight and spent most of the evening and half the night snoring heartily under buffalo furs, so I am quite able to do a little archaeological digging."

As the twins had taken no small degree of pride in Flavel Saxton's collection of books and added to it considerably, augmenting their forebear's work with volumes written over the past century, I had hope of finding a means of aid. Too, old Flavel Saxton had been alive during the Salem witch trials, when one of my own ancestors played a deadly part in judgment, and so he might have had some passing fascination with things preternatural or in the fate of those poor unfortunates who had caught the visionary eye of Tituba and her witch-haunted girls. Not that I do not believe in witchery and witches, for I believe just as much in the demonic world as I do a world of angelic powers. I have met and wrestled with demons disguised in human form, and I have known angels.

Although Saxton assured me that any delving could wait, he soon fetched a lantern and led me across the hall to a vast comfortable room with library tables and ladders, set about with wing chairs and so many birdcage Windsors that I suspected there must have been an indentured carpenter in the house at some time. Cabinets for books had been built into the walls, but all was higgledy-piggledy and in need of a librarian. *Magnalia Christi Americana* hulked uncomfortably between *The Rape of the Lock* and *The Travels of William Bartram,* and Samuel Johnson was forced to sulk in the shade cast by the preaching Mrs. Augusta Pennyfeather and her *Sermons in Brooks and Stones,* volumes I–IX.

For a long time Saxton and I scanned the shelves, the lantern fastened to a ladder, without finding much to our purpose. The light swung gently back and forth, and I found myself eyeing the polished brass to detect whether I could find a gleam of the third face on its surface. A mirror, mummied in blackness, loomed from the far wall. I felt a wash of ecstatic terror at the thought of Edward Saxton's head locked behind the grid of the loose weave. Perhaps the eyes, the only living element in that face, were awakening.

"I have searched before, you know, without finding anything to help," Saxton said in a low voice.

The first light of dawn had gradually infiltrated the room. I yawned heavily and sat down, overcome by sleepiness.

A young woman with a pan of coals entered the library, gave us a glance, and seemed as if about to retire.

"Come in, it's all right." Saxton waved her inside, and I noticed that she seemed not at all disconcerted by finding a stranger in the house. She dropped a little curtsey but with a roguish air that seemed to say that she knew very well we were equals.

"This is Mr. Hawthorne, Patience. He will be visiting for a few days . . . You must be as gracious to him as you were to my own brother, for he is a great friend of mine and has done me a kindness in attending me so quickly."

Saxton informed me that Patience was Mrs. Molebury's granddaughter, recently graduated from the Beadle Seminary for Young Ladies, where she had won several prizes for her needlework. She had on a loose muslin gown, topped by a short fitted jacket, no doubt a species of her handiwork. I thought privately that Patience must be famous for her beauty as well, for she was light-footed and tall with perfectly proportioned features, although there was a touch of sharpness to her nose and cheekbones that suggested that time might transform her into a bony-faced old woman. No doubt she was a village enchantress now, though, and I wondered whether she had cast the spell of allure on my friend. She wore no cap on her black hair, so that all the glory of its shining cat's cradle of coils and twists was visible, knotted at her neck, a snare to catch a man's gaze.

"Miss Hobbs is no maid but has come to help her grandmother. She was of much assistance to me in the last weeks of Edward's life. Soon she will be away, and then Mrs. Molebury and I shall be as dull as before."

Patience Hobbs was kneeling at the hearth as he spoke, her straight back toward us. In a very few moments, she sat back on her heels as the fire consumed the little palace of splinters she had raised and then caught on the logs. I would not have been surprised to learn that she was as quick at everything she did. When she stood, I thought her even lovelier, cheeks flushed from the fire.

"Are you going to town with your grandmother?" Theron was asking. Evidently the pair of women had the afternoon free.

"If you need me, I will be glad to stay—"

"Do not worry about us," he said. "After a meal, I have no doubt that we shall sleep like a pair of tops, our minds spinning and humming with dreams. By the time you return, we may have crawled from our beds, but don't expect much activity."

Her eye traveled around the room, pausing to take in the tumbled shelves and the scattering of volumes on the table.

"Hawthorne is a man of books," Theron said by way of explanation. "Being that most perilous of creatures, an author, he just couldn't wait to pay homage to my grandfather's collection."

I was surprised by this bit of subterfuge. Although Theron had been a jokester as a boy, he was scrupulously honest.

"I am fond of reading," Patience Hobbs said, "though sad to admit that I do not care much for stories."

"No?" It always surprises me when people utter such sentiments, as though we were not all enmeshed in one great, tangled tale.

"Perhaps I prefer the realm of the possible," she said. "Often stories are merely fanciful pipe dreams without any ground underneath."

I gave a short bow, effectively silenced by the firmness of her assertions.

The dark-haired girl gave me a smile of sheer witchery as she paused in the open door; then she vanished. As if in reproach, Daphne Mathers drifted into my mind: I recalled her standing near the open grave in the wind, her blond hair loosening from its black-ribboned knot and tumbling onto her shoulders. She bent to retrieve a fallen comb, her eyes going to Theron's as she rose up.

Only once previously had I met Daphne, when I found her a laughing, quick-witted girl—a fit wife for Theron. Judging from the little Saxton nieces clinging to her skirts, she seemed the sort of person who attracts children and knows how to amuse them. Daphne had taken to me immediately, no doubt for Theron's sake, and later in the day she walked with me in the park, taking my arm and confiding her love for rambles in the woods, her fondness for animals and for gardening, and the little jokes she and Theron liked to play on each other.

"And now for breaking the fast," Saxton said, "and afterward I wouldn't refuse a tot of Geneva and water with sugar and lemon to send us off for a nap."

The voice startled me, for I had gone far from the room in memory, and my nerves were on edge from travel and lack of sleep. "Yes," I said, "we should nap and rise again when the women leave the house."

Theron cocked his head, staring at me.

"Not that I suspect anything," I added, "but it is always helpful to have a free hand when searching without a clear object."

Although the breakfast was hearty enough to set me nodding and the featherbed proved soft, I woke as the carriage rattled from the yard. My friend Theron slept on; I poked my head in his room and heard the sighing of his breath, as though he grieved even in sleep, and decided not to wake him. I wandered around the house, feeling that I hardly knew what I was about, other than to glance at books and papers. In the kitchen I found a few ancient receipt books, nothing of interest.

The pantry gave up a more exciting result, for there my hand closed on a foxed, leather-bound tome on which I made out the title *On the Nature and Activitie of the Various Spirits*. I cried out in pleasure that was, alas, immediately abated on finding that the chosen volume was a sort of antique cookbook for distillers and brewers.

On peering into the women's chambers, I saw nothing that would not have been at home in my wife's dressing room. A heap of sad-colored cloth and a tumble of scarlet trimmings seemed the makings for a new gown, no doubt chosen to accentuate the dark, flushed complexion of Patience Hobbs. Climbing to the low-ceilinged third storey of the house, seldom used and secret, I felt closer to my quarry, whatever it was. Footsteps in the dust led to a workroom piled with fabric and notions. Methodically I began removing bolts of cloth. A pink light was filtering between the trees before I laid my hand on *Unholy Spirits, Being the Devout Man's Handbooke and Medecine Cabinet for Those Unfortunates Afflikted with Apparitions, Ghosts, and Kindred Spirits.* The book had been shoved to the rear of the shelf, along with several books on the art of millinery, and was obscured by baskets of buttons and scraps of fabric bound with string, saved for some patchwork quilt that might never be.

"'Printed for John Williams,'" I read aloud, "'and Francis Eglesfield, and are to be sold at the Crown and Marygold in Saint Paul Church-yard, 1648.'"

Like many old-fashioned books, this one was luxurious with headings and subheadings and rambling comment.

I carried my prize down the stairs and into Theron's room, where he was yawning as he reached for a pair of carpet slippers left to warm beside a low coal fire. He appeared rumpled and unrested despite his long nap.

"Look what I have found. Ghosts in containers—is a mirror a container? Spirits that linger near staircases. Classification of spirits." I deciphered the odd spellings and typeface; soon Saxton came to sit beside me, peering over my arm at the Gothic-letter pages.

"The matter of haunted objects. The matter of spirits who will not allow a painting to be moved. The matter of chimney ghosts. The matter of the same in wells. The matter of grave reflection. The matter of spirit-enchanted pots. The matter of—"

I stopped, my hand trembling.

The matter of grave reflection.

Quickly I turned the soft, rotting pages, skimming a finger up and down the columns of print. "Here! 'The Matter of Grave Reflection occurs when the image of a Beloved Dead persists in glazed surfaces such as mirrors, metal spoons, glass, perfectly clear ice, butts of water, and such-like materials. Such a seeming-ghost knows no malice or fierceness but the horror of its Presence is highly destructive of daily life. Traditional remedies of the ignorant and afflicted include the withdrawal of the Persecuted to desert places, the abolition of metal from the house, the removal of water barrels to more distant sites, and, among the wealthy, the cessation of bathing in copper tubs.' "

Theron let out a cry.

"That is it," he said, his voice rising in pitch. "I am astounded, Hawthorne, that you could lay your hands on anything that might shed light on my private hell. Yet this gives me no ease. I am already in my 'desert place,' there to be immolated."

"There appear to be instructions," I said, "and we shall try them, no matter how ridiculous. The letters are difficult to make out, and much requires translation to words of today, but we will manage."

We exchanged a long glance, and Saxton nodded.

"And now let me play the proper host. No doubt the ever-prompt Mrs. Molebury is back and ready to dish up a meal." He stood up. "Just don't let the book out of your sight until we know all that is needed."

Over a repast in the dining room, we did not speak of the mirrors. Mrs. Molebury had concocted a meat pie for us, served along with sweet parsnips and yellow carrots yanked from beneath the snow and dusted with cinnamon and sugar, the homely meal ending with bread pudding and a compote of last summer's pears that tasted as though preserved with all the sunshine of their days. Saxton partook liberally of Mrs. Molebury's sweetened boiled drink of cranberries with sherry and offered up many toasts to my ferreting-out skills. He seemed happier than I had seen him heretofore—I supposed that he had been living without hope since his elder brother's death.

An absurd length of table stretched away from our chairs, and I thought again of Daphne, and of how the room begged for children. Patience Hobbs served us, lighting the candles and coming in and out with dishes prepared by her grandmother. She appeared out of sorts, her eyes downcast, and once we heard raised voices from the kitchen.

"Not a good outing, it seems," I whispered.

Saxton shrugged. "I've never known them to quarrel, not in the two years that Patience has been coming to help her grandmother on the weekends."

Afterward, we took the volume into the library, where Miss Hobbs attended us with a tray of brandy. If she had been the one to hide the book, she now knew it had been revealed.

"I wonder if I might ask Mr. Hawthorne a question," she said.

"Certainly," my friend said, staring in surprise as I glanced up, half in pleasure, half in curiosity.

"I only wondered . . . Are you by chance related to the judge John

Hathorne, who was appointed to the Court of Oyer and Terminer so long ago—the witch trial judge?"

The brandy was sweet fire in my mouth. I choked slightly, startled by her words.

"Hobbs, there were Hobbses who were arrested," I murmured. "Is that why—? To my shame, I am the man's descendant and so have set the 'w' in my name to evoke the woods and innocent blossoms and to mark a difference between him and me. Judge Hathorne will always be the shadow and the thorn in our family tree."

"Look here," began Saxton.

"Forgive me," Patience Hobbs said, gripping the now-empty salver against her body like a shield. "It was meddlesome to ask, as my grandmother warned."

So that was the cause of lifted voices in the kitchen!

"Our history follows us—I am not sorry that you asked, only that I had such an answer to give," I told her.

She nodded and busied herself with the fire while we went on transcribing the pages into readable print. As she left the room, Patience Hobbs looked back over one shoulder. Meeting her glance, I thought again how remarkably lovely she was—even when her equanimity was vexed, she somehow reminded me of the dusky beauty of certain dark red roses. Such deep red flowers used to grow by the jailhouse door when I was a boy.

Left to ourselves, we discussed the book in low tones. Instinctively we wished to keep the business quiet. Uncovering one of the mirrors, I examined the face, his and yet subtly estranged from that of Edward Saxton.

"Oh!" Saxton cried, the single note lingering in the air. Once more he looked grief struck, and his hands shook with anxiety.

"Here, have another sip of brandy," I said, handing him the glass, struggling to find cheer that would dissolve his distress. "Shall we try the first method?"

He set the glass on the library table.

"Is it safe, you think? Or could it be evil? Could it be a spell? I fear being involved in mystery." Taking a seat by the flames, he gave a shiver of unrest.

"Laying a ghost is considered a charitable act—surely laying a picture or simulacrum would not be worse or more dangerous," I suggested. "I am no expert, though, and if you wish a priest to attend us—"

"No, no," he said hurriedly.

"Strange how so small a thing makes its presence felt," I murmured.

Soon we drew closer to the mirror, where we tried the oldest of the exhortations: *In the name of all that is holy, go! Get thee gone to heaven or to parts netherward, thou face, thou crookshank remnant, thou unbuttoned picture of the dead!*

"That was no use," Theron Saxton judged; to my surprise, he laughed until his eyes were moist with tears. "I only wish Edward could have heard us shouting such nonsense! Unbuttoned, indeed!"

Swinging around, he stared at the mirror, and the smile on his face lessened until it finally vanished. "What if the book's wrong? What if it's him, a true ghost, or not him but something malevolent?"

"Perhaps we ought to try the words that the author recommended most highly," I said, "as loosening the hold of the living on the reflection. The idea is that you might be keeping his image here out of brotherly love, even though it gives you a fright." I yawned as I rustled through my notes. The deficit in sleep had been catching up to me all day, and I was longing for bed.

I handed Saxton a sheet of foolscap bearing the properly spelled, copied-out words and listened as my friend read:

"Belovéd one, you lost your image in this Looking-glass,
And now I cannot turn and look away from you.
This floating semblance of your face belies the moth-like Peace
That settled on your face the day you left the World.
Bestir yourself to hunt this ghostly Mask of unselved Self
And, if you love me, snatch it in your sleeping hand
And keep it there until we meet in other, better worlds
Where no masks lie and all that's ghostly-lost is found."

"Poulter's measure," Saxton muttered.

"What?"

He didn't answer. Staring into the mirror, I tried to judge whether the face of Edward Saxton wore a softened aspect.

"I don't know." My friend came to stand beside me. "It seems the same, or near enough."

"Forgive me," I said, half dizzy with weariness. "I can't stay awake any longer."

My host exclaimed, reproached himself, and hustled me out the door. In our haste, we left the cloth awry from the glass so that the face of Edward Saxton shone like a moon all night into the chamber where, for all I knew, the Saxton family ghosts trysted and held a confab over these late difficulties. I slept like the dead, except that I awakened sooner.

When a burst of dawn light invaded my room, I sat up, determined to settle Saxton's difficulties before nightfall. Before he rose, I dressed and wandered through the house, meditating what had happened—or had not happened—the day before. I remembered the library mirror and went to check whether anything had changed in its depths.

I paused in the doorway: Patience Hobbs stood in a beam of light, gazing into the glass. She looked radiant, as if the figure of Aurora had stepped from her pedestal in the ancient world into ours. When she smiled, I realized that Edward Saxton's eyes were now open. The floating image looked peaceful and gave the illusion of a living man caught up by day-dream.

"You knew?"

"Yes, I knew," she said, not turning her eyes toward mine. "And I was glad to see Mr. Edward's face. I have never grasped why people thought the two Mr. Saxtons so hard to tell apart."

"Perhaps you should read the words," I said, struck by a sudden idea. "You were here when he died. Of course, we should have your grand-mother do so as well—"

"No, I will not involve my grandmother. And I will not read any words."

"You hid the book."

"Yes." At last she turned toward me, and the decisiveness I had heard in her voice seemed to dissolve. "I am sorry to refuse you, Mr. Hawthorne. But I will not be tied to anything so much like a witch's conjuration."

"I don't believe there is any invocation of dark spirits or reproach to—"

"With my background, you can understand why I might choose to avoid even the appearance of uttering the words of a spell," she said. "Our time is said to be beyond the baking of witch cakes or being swayed by 'spectral evidence' or the hanging of innocent men and women. So we be-lieve. I would not like to test that faith."

She had me: as the great-grandchild of John Hathorne, I wanted noth-ing to do with harming a member of the Hobbs family. The Court of Oyer and Terminer had made too many restless ghosts in New England for me to sanction hurt to a descendant of those who suffered the havoc of my self-righteous ancestor. Yet my unruly imagination instantly conjured up scenes of Patience Hobbs reciting a spell or stirring a potion over the kitchen fire and suggested that she was wrapped in darkness blacker than any shroud upon a mirror. I did my best to suppress these fancies, knowing that story weavers like me are prone to snatch and use our human material as mere material and can blaspheme against the soul in an instant! We are more likely candidates for the Dark Man and damnation than most, I fear . . .

I bowed, unable to divine what I ought to say, and she passed from the room.

The morning was spent in puzzling out more recipes for the banishment of the grave reflection and trying a few, each as absurd as the last, though I was loath to forgo any of them. I had suggested to Theron that he go for a ride, and I was glad to hear his horse clopping up the frozen lane in time for a midday meal. I had just transcribed—without the interesting spelling—the directions for a banishment that the book named "The Scouping; or, the Diminishmente by Poring."

Over a cold collation, we talked indefatigably about where he had ridden, about the cooking of Mrs. Molebury, about turkey hunting and the fine points of setters and a thousand other things—any that did not touch on Mr. Edward Saxton. Outside, sun shattered against the diamonds of snow, lighting up the windowpanes and warming the roof until blazing teardrops plunged from the eaves. The world was beginning to thaw, and so why not this frozen state that had held my friend through a winter of grief and despair?

Afterward we adjourned to the library for a glass of wine. Having taken down the two great mirrors and brought in the eagle-topped looking glass in which I had first glimpsed the reflected death's head of Edward Saxton, I was prepared for our next effort.

"Help me, Saxton—hold one of the mirrors slanted toward me."

Looking first at the directions, I tilted the big eagle mirror, rocking it back and forth. "Begone, grave face of reflection; join your kin," I murmured. The face loosened, flexed, and seemed to float more easily in the depths. When I tried to pour the face into the other mirror, it flew into an unexpected corner.

"What in Heaven's name are we doing?" Theron Saxton stared at the image quivering faintly in the depths.

"The pouring diminishment. A cheerful little activity for two madmen in a library. Don't look so revolted; it's probably as harmless as the rest."

I rocked the mirror back and forth as though panning for gold. Once again the face wobbled and shot off in a surprising direction as I brought the frame close to the other glass. Then suddenly the image darted from one smooth surface to the other with the slipperiness and celerity of yolk and white sliding from one saucer to another, and, when I checked, the face of Edward Saxton had gone from the eagle-crowned mirror.

We bent over the first glass, unsure whether a tiny mask might not swim up from the depths.

"Victory?" The word was a whisper, barely caught.

The mirrors being weighty, I had begun to sweat from exertion. I stripped off my waistcoat and collar and began the whole procedure again.

"We'll have to collect the mirrors in the house and move from large to small," I told him.

"What about dishes? Bowls and porringers and teapots and spoons!" For the first time, excitement seemed to touch Theron's features and make them gleam. "Should I have Mrs. Molebury polish the silver, burnish the old pewter? What about still water and puddles and pools?"

The mirror wobbled in my grasp and spilled its forbidden content. One face vanished into its twin. I smiled at Theron Saxton, elated at this confirmation of success.

"Mirrors are the king and queen of images and govern reflection, or so the book claims—when the household mirrors are emptied, the final glass will fuse duplicate images as one. One can then bury the last looking glass. Or drop it down a deep well—"

"Or grind it into powder," Theron murmured, "for the devil's snuffbox."

For the next hour, we scoured the house from top to bottom, gathering a few shaving mirrors, a pair of lady's hand mirrors, an ancient-looking concave mirror framed in wood that we rummaged from a chest in the attic, and another pair of parlor mirrors.

"You certainly have more of the things than most people," I said to Theron, encountering him on the third floor. He had gone to fetch a tiny bronze mirror that his great-great-grandmother was said to have discovered in a funerary mound somewhere in England.

"I hardly know why," he said. "Flavel Saxton must have liked the cut of his own mug and pigtail."

Abruptly he swung a leg over the stair rail and slid whooping to the next floor and on to the wide center hall. Though I laughed to see him lighthearted as I clattered down the steps after him, my mind still ran on the uncanny. "Perhaps it has something to do with the prevalence of twins in your family line. People feared duplication in the Old Country, but plenty of Saxtons could discover their own looks in a twin."

"People were frightened for good reason. Often enough, the mothers of twins died. Still do," he added, no doubt thinking of his mother's death from childbed fever, three days after the birth of the twins.

We bore our treasures into the library, sorting them by size . . .

"Let me ask Mrs. Molebury to bring us tea," I suggested.

"And a bite to eat," Theron added, picking up one of the mirrors.

Pausing at the kitchen door, I peered in and spied Patience Hobbs seated at a board table. Mrs. Molebury hunkered by the fire, rocking on her stool and humming tunelessly. As I watched, she leaned forward to stir the bubbling kettle hanging on a crane over the fire. Meanwhile her granddaughter was stitching at some piece of millinery—a stiff hat with a wide curved brim. Spying me, she laid the work in her bag and stood up, brushing threads from her lap.

"May I help you, Mr. Hawthorne?"

"Might Theron and I have some refreshment in the library?"

Miss Hobbs drew near, promising to bring us tea and scones on a tray.

"And if you or your grandmother have anything like a mirror in your possession—anything at all that might belong to the house—we would like to borrow it for a little."

She gazed at me for a moment before giving a short nod.

"Does he know that I know? Mr. Theron Saxton, I mean," she said in a low voice. "About the mirror, about the face of—"

"I believe not."

"Though he is a kind, good-humored sort of man, I imagine that he would rather not find out," she said. "The Mr. Saxtons were always very private gentlemen, even secretive about their affairs." She pulled at a chain around her neck, and in an instant a locket lay shining on her palm. "The mirror inside"—she indicated the case—"might be said to belong to the house, though it is graven with my name and was given me by the late Mr. Edward. I have read the book and understand what you are doing and do not object, but I don't want this necklace to go out of my possession because it is a memento of times that hardly were and cannot come again."

I cleared my throat, unsure whether I ought to be embarrassed by her confession. "That looks to be much smaller than any other glass I have found. When the time comes, I will bring the next-to-last mirror to you, if that would be agreeable."

And so, some time later as Theron was exulting in his freedom, his voice echoing in the library, I took the burnished bronze mirror to Miss Hobbs and tipped the blue-eyed image into her locket.

"Perhaps I should take it out into the yard where the melted and re-frozen snow has formed in coarse crystals," she said. "Perhaps I could slip the image into a single crystal, and the sun that is so bright this afternoon could call Edward Saxton's face to ascend to the sky."

"Yes," I said, "you could do that."

I watched from the front parlor as she crossed the buried lawn in a long black cloak and hood and knelt down in the snow with the locket in her hands. Sun flamed, firing the drops that plummeted from the eaves. The world seemed one crystal glory of broken and heaped chandeliers. Amid its sparkling, she glanced toward me but made no sign. Against the white ground, in the unrelieved black that might or might not have been a sign of mourning, she appeared dramatic, bewitching. Had she seemed so to Edward Saxton? She looked at the locket for a time, so long that I turned away, my eyes burning from too much light, feeling that I intruded. Mrs. Molebury rustled past in gray silk, hunched under a moth-eaten fur and mumbling a complaint as she rubbed her arthritic hands.

What might the dark imaginings of John Hathorne have made of these two women? Could it be from him that I had inherited my free-flowing fancy? I will not write all of the thoughts and questions that arose in my mind in my days at Saxton's Folly, for it might make me too much like him. And, as Miss Hobbs asserted, the Saxtons were always reticent about their affairs.

When I swung back to the window, Patience Hobbs had already replaced the locket inside her dress and risen to her feet, so that even now I do not know whether she poured the image into the snow or kept it after gazing into those blue eyes.

In the library, Theron was scribbling a letter to Daphne Mathers, his big loose handwriting sprawled across the fine, hot-pressed sheets of stationery in loops and joyful slashes.

Soon I would be trudging down the cold lane, leaning on the coachman's staff. I felt certain that it would not do to fancy shadow across a human face where there was no shade—to act the part of a darkly meditative man. In dreams of witchery and gloom that veiled their lives, better men than I had been destroyed. Nor was it right to pry and uncover what, if any, silken bonds might have fettered the black-haired young woman to the dying man, Edward Saxton. Consumption has long worn a cloak of romance and horror, and I would not venture to raise its hood and look upon the face within. Some truths should remain secluded in chambers of privacy far beyond the touch of art. Yet the chiaroscuro of a black cloak against the snow would haunt my imaginings forever, I feared, along with that spellbinding rose blossom of a face, and last of all the hands held together but open like a book I was not permitted to read, the curled fingers cupping the locket with its mirror seizing and possessing the blue-eyed face of death.

Afterword to "The Grave Reflection"

The dark, jeweled stories of Nathaniel Hawthorne have long appealed to me. My life is not so very different from his—three children, a house in a village, days spent twisting words into a shape, a childhood lived in the guilt and shadow of the past (in my case, "the giant's dead body" was not Puritan but Southern history).

"The Grave Reflection" borrows my dim image of him, a figure caught in a distant mirror. Hawthorne governs many of the threads in the story as well. Like some magpie of Romanticism, I have plucked and used some of his favorite ideas. The ghostly reflection enforces solitude. It creates a Hawthornean risk that its presence will isolate and transform a human being, barring him from ordinary life and "the magnetic chain of humanity." Opposed to this danger is the character Hawthorne, the family man and friend who knows the necessity of human affections.

As in much of Nathaniel Hawthorne's work, the past dyes the present with shadows from events both recent and faraway in time. If they grow too black, the present and future will be trapped and dark. The setting of Saxton's Folly serves as one of Hawthorne's dream houses that are vessels for both past time and present psychological difficulty.

—MARLY YOUMANS

Theodora Goss

Theodora Goss was born in Hungary and spent her childhood in various European countries before her family moved to the United States. Although she grew up on the classics of English literature, her writing has been influenced by an Eastern European literary tradition in which the boundaries between realism and the fantastic are often ambiguous. Her publications include the short story collection *In the Forest of Forgetting; Interfictions,* a short story anthology coedited with Delia Sherman; and *Voices from Fairyland,* a poetry anthology with critical essays and a selection of her own poems. She has been a finalist for the Nebula, Mythopoeic, and Crawford Awards and has been on the Tiptree Award Honor List. She has won the World Fantasy and Rhysling Awards. Visit her website at www.theodoragoss.com.

THEODORA GOSS

Christopher Raven

WHY HAD I come back to Collingswood? That was what I asked
myself, standing on the path that led to the main school building,
a structure built of gray stone and shadowed by oaks that had stood for
a hundred years. I had ridden the cart from the train station, just as I had
so many years ago at the beginning of each term. Then, I had been accompanied by a trunk almost as large as I was, filled with clothes and books.
Now I carried only a small suitcase. It contained another walking suit, a
dress suitable for dinner, and toiletries. I would be here for only one night.
Why had I come back? Because I had been invited to give a speech. Surely
that was all.

"Lucy!" It was Millicent Tolliver, walking down the path toward me.

"Hello, Tollie!" I called, then wondered if she would mind the schoolgirl nickname. She looked very much like the schoolgirl she had been, with
an untidy blouse and, I could see when she gave me an enthusiastic hug,
an ink stain on one cheek. Only the length of her skirt and the bun of hair
at the back of her head, which threatened to come down at any moment,
marked her as not a schoolgirl any longer, but one of the teachers. I had
wondered how many of the girls I knew would be coming back for Old
Girls' Day, but I knew Tollie would be here. Unlike the rest of us, she had
remained at Collingswood.

"Eleanor Prescott is here, and you won't believe who else—Mary Davenport." She grabbed my suitcase from me and said, "We're upstairs, in
our old room, all four of us."

"Why did they put us up there?" I followed her across the front hall and up the staircase. I remembered it echoing with boots. We used to run down it, almost late for French or geography lessons on the first floor. The school felt so empty, without the noise of girls chattering and whispering, without the smell of cabbage that used to float, like a vague miasma, through the halls. I kept expecting the old sounds, the old smells, but there was only the silence of summer vacation, and beeswax.

But there, at the top of the stairs, was a familiar sight: the portrait of Lord Collingswood in his riding jacket, with a horse and hound at his side, holding a riding whip as though to show who was master. He stared down over his long nose, no doubt shocked by the sight of generations of schoolgirls running through his halls. We had inherited the tradition of calling him Old Nosey.

"Oh, I asked for our old room. When I found out that all of you would be here, I asked Miss Halloway if we could share, and of course she said yes. She was the one who first put us together, remember?"

How well I remembered! The four of us glaring at one another. It was our final year at Collingswood, and we were assigned to room with our mortal enemies. I hated Eleanor Prescott, with her French dresses and stuck-up ways, and despised Mary Davenport for her timidity, her tendency to start every sentence with "Well, I don't really know, but . . ." And I had no use for Millicent Tolliver, who was a scholarship girl like me, but enthusiastically tried to curry favor with Eleanor Prescott and her circle.

Miss Halloway herself had greeted us. She was the new headmistress and was said to have advanced educational ideas. "This will be quite a treat for you, girls," she said. "I've put you in the room Lady Collingswood herself slept in, one hundred years ago. It was used for storage under Miss Temple, but we have so many girls this term that we needed all the available space, and it cleaned up quite beautifully. I even found a portrait of Lady Collingswood while we were inventorying the attic and brought it down for you. You know she was the one who founded Collingswood school. I thought she might inspire you to greater academic achievements." She looked particularly at Eleanor, who preferred outdoor games to studying and cared more about tennis than Latin.

We looked at Lady Collingswood doubtfully. She had clear, pale skin and auburn ringlets cascading over her shoulders. Her eyes were grayish blue, and she wore a dress of the same color with lace at the sleeves. She was smiling at the painter and playing with a small dog in her lap. I would not have called her beautiful, exactly. Her face was too particular, too individual, for that. But she looked intelligent, and much nicer than Old Nosey out in the hall.

"She was a patroness of the arts and painted and wrote poetry herself. Also an excellent gardener—the Lady Collingswood rose is named after her. I found a book on the history of Collingswood in the attic. Perhaps you would like to look at it?"

We murmured politely. We had no interest in the history of Collingswood. Despite our enmity, we all knew what the others were thinking. Wasn't it almost time for tea?

Despite her advanced ideas, Miss Halloway evidently understood schoolgirls and their stomachs. "It will be in my office when you're interested. Tea is in the dining hall in half an hour. Come down when you've finished unpacking. I'll see you there, girls."

"When did you say tea was?" asked Eleanor Prescott. I stepped back, startled. I had been absorbed in memories, but this Eleanor was not the girl I had known. She was Lady Thornton-Smythe, the Terror of the Tories. She looked even more formidable than she had as a schoolgirl, tall and elegant, with elaborate loops of blond hair. I could see a feathered hat on the bed, and I recognized her dress as a model from Worth. It must have cost a small fortune.

"Lucy!" she said now. "How perfectly lovely to see you." She kissed me on both cheeks. "I give copies of *The Modern Diana* to everyone I know. I tell them it's a perfectly scandalous book, all about free love and professions for women."

"Honestly, at first I was afraid to read it," said Mary Davenport, smiling and giving me a hug. "But it really does have an important message. All about using the talents God gave us." She was as short and plump as she had been, although her cheeks were redder from what she had called, in a letter to me, her "country life." There were gray strands in her hair. She had married her father's curate, who was now the Reverend Charles Beaumont, with a living near York. She had come back to visit "dear old Collingswood" while he attended an ecclesiastical conference in London.

Mary had three children living, and one buried. Eleanor had no children, which she did not seem to regret. "Laws to alleviate the oppression of man—and woman—are my children," she had written to me. And Tollie had never married. All this I knew from letters I had received over the years—not many, but we had never entirely lost touch. I suppose what we experienced that last year had bound us together.

I had sent them letters about my own life, my relationship with Louis, his death from tuberculosis, my own efforts to raise little Louie, who had his father's complaint. *The Modern Diana* had sold well enough that I had sent him to a sanatorium in Switzerland, but the money would not last forever. I was grateful that Collingswood had paid for my train ticket and offered me an honorarium for my speech at the Old Girls' Dinner. Would I have come back otherwise?

It was Tollie, of course, who said what the rest of us were thinking but would not say. "I'm so glad we're all here. Now we can talk about Christopher Raven."

TOLLIE DREAMED OF him last, but of course she was the first to say anything.

"Lucy, wake up! I had the strangest dream."

I opened my eyes, then closed them again. "Go away. Can't you see it's still dark?"

"But I dreamed of a man. Have you ever dreamed of a man? With curling black hair and a white blouse—at least it looked like a blouse, like something a woman would wear. Or a pirate. Maybe he was a pirate? Except that he was saying something—like poetry. I was sitting on the parlor sofa, except it was so much nicer than the sofa we have now, and he bowed to me and kissed my hand!"

"You've dreamed about him too!" said Eleanor, sitting up in bed. "Then I'm going to stop dreaming about him. I don't want to share my dreams with Messy Millie."

"Well, I've been dreaming about him for a week," I said. "So you've been sharing your dream with the both of us. How common is that? And what about Mary? Maybe she's been dreaming about him as well."

Mary, who had just opened her eyes, pulled the blanket over her head.

"Have you been dreaming about him too?" asked Eleanor. "Mary, answer me!"

"Yes," came the muffled answer. "For a week."

"Did he kiss your hand?" asked Tollie.

Mary looked out from under the blanket. Her face was bright red. "No. We were in this room, but it had a big bed in it. And he kissed my shoulder."

"He hasn't kissed me," I said. "He just takes me walking around the garden, and he says things—about my hair and eyes. Poetry, like Tollie said."

"Well, he's kissed me," said Eleanor. "We were in the tower, looking out toward Collington, and he told me that I changed like the moon, or something like that, and he kissed me on the *mouth*."

That day, for the first time, we sat together in the front parlor, which was reserved for the older girls, trying to figure it out.

"Maybe he's a ghost, and we're being haunted," said Mary. Her father was a member of the Society for Psychical Research.

"Don't be ridiculous," said Eleanor. "There's no such thing as a ghost."

"Oh yes, there is," said Tollie. "My aunt Harriet was haunted by my uncle, who had lost a leg at sea. She said the ghost went *thump, thump, thump* on its wooden leg, up and down the hallways at night."

"Ugh," said Mary. "You're making me shiver!"

"But even if he is a ghost," I said, "whose ghost is he? And why is he haunting the four of us?"

"We don't know that he is," said Eleanor. "Maybe the other girls have had dreams as well, and they're just not talking about it."

So we went around asking the other girls about what they had dreamed the night before. None of them had dreamed of a man with curling black hair, or brown skin that made him look like a foreigner, or black eyes that looked as though they were laughing at you, although one of them had dreamed of her brother who was in India.

No, it was just us four.

We made a pact. Each morning we would compare notes. We would tell each other what we had dreamed, all the details, no matter how embarrassing. And we would try to remember what the man had said, those poetic words that seemed to slip out of our heads on waking, like water.

"HE TOLD ME that my eyes are like bright stars," said Tollie.

"Oh, for goodness' sake," said Eleanor. "Your eyes are like eyes. He told me that my hair was like a fire burning down a forest, except he used different words. And they rhymed with something, but I don't remember what."

"You have to try to remember," I said. "I wish all of you had Mary's memory."

In my notebook, I had written down what we dreamed each night, and the fragments of what we thought must be poetry:

> Eleanor: tower, dark but moonlight
> "the cascade of your gown"
> something about "sweet surrender" and "sweetly die"

> Mary: in front of fireplace, kissed neck "like a swan's," "proud
> and fair"
> "luxuriance of your hair"

Tollie: passed in hallway and dropped letter
"hide it in your bosom, sweetheart"
"the moon's a secret lover, as am I"

Lucy: kissed several times, passionately
"elements of love" (but hard to hear, could be "dalliance of
love"?)

By this time, we had all been kissed, and we blushed as we told each other.

"It was—soft," said Mary. "This is wrong, isn't it? Even if it's just a dream."

"Forceful," said Eleanor. "I don't think he would have stopped if I'd wanted him to. How can it be wrong if it's only a dream?"

"Is that what it's like, when boys kiss?" asked Tollie.

"No, it's nothing like that," said Eleanor, who had boy cousins. "That's disgusting."

"I don't think we're any closer to working out who he is," I said. "We know he's a poet, because of what he's saying. I mean, neck proud and fair, and all that. So, if he is a ghost, we need to find out if there were any poets who died at Collingswood."

"There's no such thing as a ghost," said Eleanor.

"What about Miss Halloway's book?" asked Tollie.

I was sent to ask Miss Halloway for the book, as the one most likely to, as Eleanor said, "read boring stuff."

"Of course, Lucy," she said. "I'm glad you're interested in the history of the school. Some of the other girls, well, they'll graduate and get married. But I think you are capable of doing something different, some sort of intellectual work. I hope you'll think about that. There are so many opportunities for women nowadays that did not exist when I was your age."

"Yes, Miss Halloway," I said, hoping to escape a lecture. Miss Halloway's advanced educational theories, we had discovered, involved teaching girls the subjects boys were usually taught, and she had a tendency to lecture us about the advancement of women. I did not quite escape one, but it was not as long as I had feared. I closed the door of her office with "and you really should think about a university education, Lucy," in my ears.

"And who's going to read that?" asked Eleanor, when I had brought *The History of Collingswood House, from the Crusades to the Present*

Day to our room. The book had been covered with dust, and now I was covered with it as well.

"How many pages is it?" asked Mary.

I had already looked. "Seven hundred and ninety-two. And there's no index."

By the way they all looked at me, it was obvious who was going to read *The History of Collingswood House.* After all, I was the one who won the prizes in composition, who was at the top of the English class.

I was only on page one 157 the morning Mary woke up gasping. Although we asked and prodded, she would not tell us about her dream.

"I can't," she said. "We were in the bedroom again. He— I just can't."

We were sitting in our nightgowns on Eleanor's bed, as we did every morning for our conferences.

"What was it like?" I asked. I think we all knew, even then, what had happened. Tollie and I had grown up in villages, near farms and animals. And Eleanor had heard the servants gossip.

"I'm sorry. I really don't think I can talk about it."

"Was it so frightening?" asked Tollie, leaning forward.

"Not frightening. Just— I can't, all right?" And we could get nothing else out of her.

Later that day, I looked with dismay at *The History of Collingswood House.* I could not face another list of who had come to visit Collingswood in the Year of Our Lord blankety blank.

"Look, stupid book," I said. "Just tell me what I want to know, all right?" I closed my eyes and opened the book at random. I looked down at the pages I had opened. There it was:

In the autumn of 1817, Lord Collingswood invited the poet Christopher Raven, whom he had met in London, to Collingswood House. Lady Collingswood was taken with the handsome youth, who was supposed to look like an English Adonis, although some critics asserted that he wrote like a second-rate Shelley. The Collingswood library, which was extensive, had fallen into a state of disarray, and Lord Collingswood hoped that Raven would catalogue it. However, the two men quarreled before the work got under way, and the poet left in the middle of the night to join Shelley and Byron in Switzerland. He was overtaken by the snows, and is supposed to have perished in the Alpine passes. Lady Collingswood, who had a tender heart, particularly for poets, artists, and small dogs, was said to have been inconsolable for weeks.

I had found a poet. And he sounded like the right poet. Adonis had been Greek. He would have had curling black hair, the kind they call hyacinthine.

"I think I've found him," I told Eleanor, Mary, and Tollie that afternoon. "His name is Christopher Raven. He was a poet, and I think he was in love with Lady Collingswood. And maybe she was in love with him."

"Why do you think we're dreaming about him?" asked Tollie. "If someone had dreamed about him before, we would have known about it, wouldn't we? I mean, he would be the Collingswood ghost or something. It would have been like calling the picture Old Nosey. Everyone would have known."

"Maybe it's because we're in her room," I said. "The book only says that she was taken with him, but I bet all the things he says to us are the things he said to her. I mean, seriously, none of us has a neck like a swan's, do we? And hair like a forest fire—she had red hair. I bet no one else has slept in her room for a hundred years. That's why we're dreaming about him, when no other girls have."

"The question is, what do we do now?" asked Eleanor. "He doesn't scare me, but that dream Mary had—yes, I know you can't talk about it, but we all know what it was about. If we're dreaming about him and Lady Collingswood, where is this going?"

WHERE INDEED. I'LL give you this, Christopher Raven. I have known love since those days as a schoolgirl at Collingswood, and you loved her as passionately as any poet loves a woman. There is always some selfishness in such a love, always some inclination to turn your love into poetry. But when you walked with her down the garden paths, when you stood beside her on the tower and looked out over the countryside, when you called her the moon and said you were the tide, following her motions, you loved her as passionately as poets love, who are always thinking of the next line. We experienced it, the four of us—experienced that love when we were only schoolgirls and should have been attending to our lessons. We felt the kisses in the darkness, your hand on her shoulder, your fingers running along her collarbone. We felt you slip off her dress of grayish-blue silk and felt what we should not have, a passion we were not ready for.

We changed, in those weeks. We grew languorous, as though we were always walking in a dream. We could not attend to our lessons. Eleanor gave up tennis, and she and Tollie used to sit in our room, talking in whispers about their dreams of the night before. Mary took to praying throughout the day. She told us she was convinced that the dreams were wrong, but like the rest of us, she did not want them to end. She developed dark shadows under her eyes, and sometimes she would jump for no reason, as though she had been frightened by a sound that the rest of us could not hear. And what about me? I was as dreamy as the rest, but my lethargy frightened me, and Mary's condition was a constant source of worry. I felt as though we were all slipping away into some dreamland, losing touch with the prosaic world of school.

Finally, Miss Halloway spoke to me. "Lucy," she said, putting a hand on my shoulder as I leaned over a composition book, tracing the letters CR over and over with my pencil, "what is going on with you girls? Yesterday, Millicent almost fell asleep in Latin, and I'm told that Mary is starting to look, and behave, quite oddly. Is something happening that I should know about?"

I should have told her then, but how could I bear to lose those kisses, the black eyes looking into mine and whispering words sweeter than I had ever heard before, calling me "goddess" and "love"?

"I think we're staying up too late talking," I told her, and looking at me doubtfully, she left it at that.

And so it might have continued, if Eleanor had not woken up one morning screaming.

"Lord Collingswood killed him!" she cried. "He found them together and hit him with his cane! There was blood everywhere!" And then she began to sob into her hands. I had never imagined that Eleanor Prescott could weep, and the sight sent a shiver down my spine.

The next night it was Tollie, and then me. We all dreamed the discovery, the terrifying blow to the back of the head. We all saw blood pooling on the floorboards. And then nothing—that was where the dreams ended. Only Mary was spared. Perhaps the ghost decided that she had seen enough. Certainly she could not take any more.

This time we were all summoned to Miss Halloway's office. "What in the world is going on with you girls?" she asked. "I've heard reports of moans in the night and screams early in the morning. And you all look as though you haven't slept for the past week."

"Miss Halloway," I told her, "we're being haunted. By a ghost." And then I told her everything.

"Good Lord," she said. "That such things should be going on right under my nose! The idea that you're being haunted is ridiculous. There's no such thing as a ghost, Lucy. However, the atmosphere of the room, together with what you read about Collingswood House, may have prompted these dreams. I will move you out of that room immediately."

We were moved into Miss Halloway's own room, for observation. But the dreams did not stop.

"Blood, and then nothing," said Tollie. "I can't see anything after he falls down. Blood on the floor, and then it's as though everything just goes dark."

"But I can still hear something," said Eleanor. "Like Tollie's uncle: *thump, thump, thump.*"

"Miss Halloway," I said, "Lord Collingswood hit him in the front hall, and then there was this sound, as Eleanor said. I think he dragged the body down the stairs. To the cellar."

"I think it's time to summon a brain specialist," said Miss Halloway.

We all stood looking at her silently—Mary looked especially reproachful. "Oh, all right, girls," she said. "The cellar it is."

"THERE'S NOTHING DOWN here," said Tollie.

"Oh, for goodness' sake," said Eleanor. "We haven't even checked for a priest's hole yet. Hillingdon has one, and a secret staircase. Of course some people don't have such things in their houses, but I'm quite familiar with them, I assure you."

For the first time in several weeks, I would have liked to hit Eleanor Prescott, but it was obvious from the shrillness of her voice that she was both excited and afraid. And she was actually doing something useful, walking along each wall and knocking carefully, up and down, listening for anything unusual. These were the foundations of the house, which went back to Norman times. I knew that from having read *The History of Collingswood House,* at least to page 157. They seemed so solid.

But Eleanor said, "Can't you see that the cellar isn't as large as the house?" And she was right.

Of course Tollie had exaggerated in saying that there was nothing in the cellar. In addition to the usual things one finds in cellars, such as the coalbox and stacks of wood, old brooms, a tin bucket, it was filled with the detritus of a girls' school: broken chairs, a pair of crutches, boxes of sports equipment. There were skis stacked against the wall, and an astonishing number of broken tennis rackets.

"There!" said Eleanor. "Can you hear it?"

And we could. Against one wall stood a tall bookshelf that had no doubt once been in the library, but was now water-stained and covered with dust. On the shelves stood boxes containing what looked like onions, but labeled "tulips—early," "tulips—late," "tulips—Rembrandt," pairs of ice skates leaning against one another, and a few books that were too damaged for use even by schoolgirls.

"That's where old Amias keeps his bulbs," said Miss Halloway. "He says this is the perfect place to store them."

"Well, there's a space behind it," said Eleanor. And indeed, we had all heard the echo when she knocked.

"All right, girls," said Miss Halloway. "Let's see what's behind that shelf."

Mary held the lamp while the rest of us helped Miss Halloway stack the books and skates and boxes of tulip bulbs on the floor. "It's going to be heavy," she said. "Should I summon Amias and some of his boys?" We all shook our heads. I think we wanted to see what was behind as quickly—and as privately—as possible. "All right then," she said. "Put your backs into it."

Once, while moving the shelf, as we were taking a momentary rest, we looked at one another—Tollie, Eleanor, and me. When I saw their white faces, I knew mine must be white as well. The lamplight jumped up and down on the walls, no doubt because Mary's hand was trembling. But Miss Halloway looked grim and determined, and I decided then that I rather admired her, despite her boring lectures. All things considered, it would not be a terrible thing to be like Miss Halloway.

When the shelf had been moved, slowly and awkwardly, back from the wall, we could see that it had covered an arched opening—through which we saw only blackness.

I will give us the credit to say that we all, including Mary Davenport, stepped through the archway together. It opened into a smaller room, the other part of the cellar, which must once have held wine. There were still wine racks on the walls.

There, in the circle of light cast by the lamp, was the skeleton of a man. We could still see the shreds of his white shirt, the remains of black boots that had long ago been nibbled away by rats. Around his ankle was an iron cuff, linked by a chain to an iron ring in the wall. Just out of his reach was a bowl that might once have held water.

We stood silent. Then Mary, with a sigh, crumpled to the floor. Miss Halloway caught the lamp just before she fell. The rest of us stood there for what seemed like an interminable moment. Then we followed Miss Halloway, who carried Mary, up the stairs and into the autumn sunshine of the first floor, which seemed so strange to us, after the lamplight and the cellar. She put Mary on the sofa and brought her around with smelling salts, then gave us each a glass of sherry, which made Tollie cough.

Finally, Miss Halloway said, "What a terrible story."

"Do you think she knew?" asked Tollie. "He must have been down there—"

"Dying," I said. "For days."

"She didn't know," said Eleanor. "I think we dreamed exactly what she saw. She didn't know anything after Lord Collingswood hit him with the cane. I think she fainted, like Mary."

"She must have thought he was dead," said Tollie.

"And Lord Collingswood must have told everyone that they'd had a fight, and Raven had left for Switzerland," I said.

"But she must have been here doing all sorts of things—getting dressed and walking in the garden, and eating her dinner—while he was dying below!" said Mary. She started to gasp and sob, and Miss Halloway waved the sal volatile under her nose again.

"Last summer, after I was hired as headmistress here," she said, "I read that book Lucy thought was so dull, *The History of Collingswood House*. If you'd read a little farther, girls, you would have known that Lord Collingswood died in 1818, just a year later. He was said to have died of heart problems, but there was a rumor that he might have been poisoned— digitalis, which comes from foxgloves, is toxic in a high enough dose. Lady Collingswood created this school and specified that Lord Collingswood's portrait was to be hung over the main staircase in perpetuity. I wonder, now, if that was her idea of a joke?"

"What happened to her?" I asked.

"She moved to France. Eventually she became a painter, not a great one but there is a picture of hers in the National Gallery. She particularly liked painting flowers." Miss Halloway was silent for a moment. "We'll have to give him a proper burial," she said. "I think the dreams will stop now."

The dreams did not stop, not as long as we stayed at Collingswood. But they changed character. For the rest of that year, we dreamed that we were with him—sitting by the fire in the parlor, browsing through books in the library and reading lines of poetry to one another, walking through the garden, where the roses were blooming, including the white rose called Lady Collingswood. He still murmured lines of poetry to us, we still felt kisses on our hands, even our shoulders, but the dreams no longer had the passion, the urgency, that we should not have experienced and that changed us, permanently. When we left Collingswood, Eleanor for a London season, Mary for her father's parish, where she would teach Sunday school, Tollie for Newnham Teachers' College, and me for Girton, we were no longer the girls who had glared at one another on the first day of term. We were older, we knew more about the joys and pains of the world, and we were friends.

The remains of Christopher Raven were buried in the garden, and a stone was placed over him with the words "Here lies the poet Christopher Raven, lover of Lady Collingswood, 1797–1817" carved on it, followed by lines of his own poetry:

Let her eyes guide me like bright stars, and bring
Me to the birthing-place of poetry.

I read some of his poetry later—he had published two books, called *Aurora and Other Poems* and *Poems for the Rights of Man*. He was good, and might have become great if he had lived, although he would never have been a Shelley or a Keats. But when I remembered his kisses in the dark, the whispered words, it did not matter. I do not think it mattered to her either. She loved the man, and the poet was part of the man. At least that is what I think now that I have learned something of love—the love one has for a poet, like my Louis.

"WE CHANGED, ALL of us," I said. "Eleanor became less high and mighty, for example."

"Well!" she said, laughing. "I think I'm still both high and mighty. You should see me destroy those pipsqueak MPs on the question of votes for women! They fear my political dinners."

"And Mary became more pious," I added.

"I suppose that's true," said Mary. "I was frightened for a long time. I thought life might be like that, all passion and darkness. My father's faith was reassuring—it made me feel safe. I think I became more judgmental for a while. I went to London once, while Louis was alive, and never visited you, Lucy. I'm sorry about that. But after little Charles died, I think I became more accepting of human frailty. I started to realize that God is there too, in the darkness as well as the light."

We stared at her. "When did you get philosophical?" asked Eleanor.

Mary blushed, the red suffusing her cheeks until she looked like a late apple. "I'm getting older, I suppose. As we all are." She turned to me. "And losing what you love—you must have known how Lady Collingswood felt."

"Perhaps a little," I said. "But I don't think Louis is going to haunt anyone. Our love was an ordinary human love. Oh, he wrote me a poem or two, but I'm no Lady Collingswood. I went to visit his wife once, in France. You would think—insane asylum and all that. But it was perfectly ordinary, kind nurses looking after her. She had no idea who I was. What Christopher Raven and Lady Collingswood had—it was passion and poetry, and it had to end in violence. Could it have ended any other way? Can you imagine them in a cottage in the country, him chopping wood for the fire, her embroidering dish towels?"

"Was he the ghost, or was she?" We looked at Tollie, startled by her question. "I mean, was he the one haunting us? Or was she the one, making us relive her experiences?"

"I've never thought of it like that," I said.

"When I came back to Collingswood, I found something," said Tollie. "It was summer and the school was almost empty. I came in here, and I don't know why exactly, but I looked behind the painting of Lady Collingswood. There was something taped back there."

"What did you find?" I asked. We all leaned forward, curious school-girls once more.

"Probably a letter of some sort," said Eleanor.

"No, not a letter," said Tollie. "I'll show you." She walked over to one of the desks that we had used, so many years ago, and lifted a framed picture that had been lying on it. She held it up so we could see.

Mary gasped, and Eleanor said, "That's him. Exactly."

It was just a watercolor of the head and shoulders, but there was the curling black hair, the brown cheeks, the laughing, mischievous eyes. In the bottom right-hand corner was written, in pen, Adela Collingswood.

"You can see that she loved him," said Tollie. "If she was the ghost, she would have wanted him buried."

"But she didn't know he was in the cellar," I said. "Listen to me! Here I am talking about the habits of ghosts. For all we know, it was both of them together, reliving their lives through us."

"You changed too," said Eleanor. "You'd been so focused on doing well. But after—that was when you started writing stories."

"She did inspire me in the end," I said. "Just as Miss Halloway wanted."

"But Tollie didn't change," continued Eleanor. "Did you, Tollie? You're the same old Tollie as you were back then. The Tollie who would have looked behind the painting. I would never have thought of that."

"I don't know," said Tollie. "I suppose I am the same. Although I think I'm getting lines on my forehead from frowning at students!"

We heard a knock on the door. We had been so immersed in talking about the past that we all jumped.

"Ladies, dinner in half an hour," called Miss Halloway.

"We'd better get dressed," said Mary. "We don't want to be late for dinner."

"Why not?" said Eleanor. "Let them wait for us. After all, we have the guest of honor. They're not going to start the dinner without her. Is that high and mighty enough for you, Lucy?" But she was smiling as she said it.

After that, the conversation turned to dresses. Eleanor lent Tollie the second-best dress she had brought, which must have cost as much as my entire wardrobe, although Tollie insisted that her gray merino was perfectly adequate. So even she looked sufficiently ladylike as we walked down the stairs, under the watchful eyes of Old Nosey, to the dining room.

My speech, "The Necessity for the Rights of Women," went well and was generally applauded, with Eleanor giving a loud "Hear, hear!" The food was better than we had eaten as schoolgirls—no cabbage! But it was strange seeing women, some of whom I remembered, some from other years, sitting around the dining room tables, their faces turned toward me. In some of them, I could see the girls they had once been, like echoes.

It was a relief to be finished, to have fulfilled my duties and be free to go back up the stairs, undress, and lie down on the bed I had slept in so many years ago.

"Maybe you'll all dream of him tonight," said Tollie.

"I certainly hope not," said Eleanor. "Once in a lifetime is enough of Christopher Raven, I think."

THE NEXT MORNING, Mary left early to catch the train, and Eleanor had a meeting with the Fundraising Committee. But I had time before I needed to be at the station, so Tollie and I walked through the garden, smelling the late roses and coming at last to his grave.

"Christopher Raven," I said. "I would not have minded dreaming about him again, just for old times' sake."

"But you didn't?" asked Tollie.

"No, of course not," I said. "But I've been thinking about my next book—my publisher keeps asking whether I'm working on it, and of course I need the money. He wants another *Modern Diana,* but I think I'm going to write about Lady Collingswood. I think I'll call it *Adela; or Free Love.* That ought to shock everyone."

"Lucy, do you think Eleanor's right? Do you think I haven't changed?"

I looked at her carefully. "I think you've changed less than the three of us. Maybe it's because you stayed at Collingswood."

"No, it's not just that. It's something else."

Something in her voice made me say, "Tollie, is everything all right?"

"Yes, of course. It's just that I didn't want to tell the others. I still dream about him."

"What do you mean?" I said.

"I still dream about him, every night. When I found that picture, I had it framed, and then I put it in my room, up on the third floor. And I started dreaming about him again. I thought if the three of you were here, sleeping in her room, under her picture, you would have the dreams too. But it was just me." She paused for a moment, then knelt in front of the grave and traced the letters with her hand. "Maybe because I stayed here. I never married or had a child. I didn't have the sort of life that you and Eleanor and Mary have. And the dreams came back. That's what I have, a new set of students every year—and the dreams. Do you think that's awful?"

"Some of your hair's come down in back. Let me fix it for you." I pinned her bun up again. I looked at her, kneeling there, with both pity and understanding. After a moment of silence, I said, "No, Tollie. I don't think that's awful at all. I think we have to take love where we can find it. That's what I learned with Louis."

"Thank you," she said, standing again and feeling her hair, carefully. "I never can get it to stay up. You know, you always were my best friend."

"You could have fooled me, the way you mooned after Eleanor Prescott!" I said. But I put my arm around her and kissed her cheek.

Later, as the cart bumped over the drive, I turned back to look at Collingswood House and waved to her, knowing that I might never see her again, knowing that I would probably never come back. I had a larger world to live in, a world that included grief and loss and loneliness, but also success and companionship. It included the cafés of London, and seeing my name on red leather in bookshop windows, and the Alps. I thought of Louie in Switzerland, coughing his lungs out and looking at me with the most beautiful eyes in the world, his father's eyes. The world I lived in was more difficult, but I would not have traded it for hers.

Sometimes I would think of Tollie in her world of perpetual girlhood, dreaming of Christopher Raven, of poetry and burning kisses in the dark. And sometimes I would wish for the dreams myself. But I had a life to live, a book to write. I would always remember her this way, standing in front of Collingswood House and waving to me, under the ancient oaks.

Afterword to "Christopher Raven"

The hardest thing about writing "Christopher Raven" was finding the right voice. Finally, I started channeling Daphne du Maurier in *Rebecca*, and it started coming out right.

—THEODORA GOSS

Lucius Shepard

Lucius Shepard's short fiction has won the Hugo, Nebula, and World Fantasy Awards, among others, and has earned him Notable Book of the Year status from the *New York Times*. His acclaimed collections include *The Jaguar Hunter, The Ends of the Earth, Two Trains Running, Trujillo, Dagger Key, The Best of Lucius Shepard,* and *Viator Plus;* upcoming are two new books of novellas and the long-awaited gathering in one volume of all the Dragon Griaule tales, from Subterranean Press. Shepard lives in Portland, Oregon.

LUCIUS SHEPARD

Rose Street Attractors

THOSE WHO KNEW Jeffrey Richmond, if anyone could be truly said
to have known him, viewed him as an acquaintance merely, the sort
of person one tolerates because he belongs to a certain circle, yet avoids
due to his unpleasant character or dubious connections. He was a slight
black-haired chap in his middle thirties, beardless and brown-eyed, sharp-
featured and plain of dress, possessed of a subdued public manner, and
whenever he chanced to visit the Inventors' Club, his fellows hid themselves
behind the pages of a newspaper or pretended to be engrossed in a conversation concerning a cricket match or a minor political issue, or else they
bluntly ignored him. On most such visits he would sit in one of the club's
deep leather chairs and drink a glass or two of port and then take his leave,
both entrance and exit unmarked by the least notice; but infrequently he
would attach himself to a group of men engaged in a discussion concerning
some aspect of science or mechanics, and even more infrequently he would
interject a comment that another member might acknowledge in a distant
tone, saying, "Ah, Richmond," before turning away. Whereupon the group
would close ranks against him and he would drift back to his chair. He
had endured that state of affairs for the past three years, ever since joining
the club, and when I inquired as to the reasons underlying this consistent
display of contempt, I was told that Richmond, holder of a dozen patents
relating to a diverse range of industries, from textile to armaments, and
thus wealthy, had chosen to live in the pernicious slum of Saint Nichol and
was thought to have family in the district—even if untrue, it was apparent
to the discerning eye, so my informant claimed, that his exposure to the
evils endemic to the place had thoroughly corrupted him.

My own status at the club was hardly secure—although I came from a prominent Welsh family with business connections in London, I was but a probationary member and twenty-six years old (all the full members were at the least five years my senior), and otherwise suspect because, despite holding a medical patent, I was an alienist, a discipline not yet accorded the banner of respectability. I had joined the club in order to gain access to the upper classes through its membership, which counted a smattering of dukes and lords among their number, hoping that when one or another of their relations suffered an affliction for which medical science had no obvious remedy, they might call upon me. Indeed, I had already experienced a degree of success, having assisted in the treatment of Sir Thomas Winstone's nephew, whose opium addiction was rooted in a childhood trauma. It was my hope that by attending the ills of parasites like Winstone's nephew, I might garner sufficient wealth to establish clinics that would provide treatment of the mentally afflicted among the lower classes superior to that they received in hospitals such as Bedlam and Broadmoor. And so, while I felt something of an ideological kinship with Richmond, for the sake of my goals I became complicit in shunning him, addressing him with a reserve that verged on rudeness. I would have never done more than tip my hat and nod to the man had he not forced himself upon me.

One foggy autumn evening, a fog so thick that the streetlamps were transformed into inexplicable glowing presences like those said to hover intermittently above the northern marshes, I was returning home from the club, keeping a hand on the clammy bricks to guide me through especially dense eddies, when I heard boot heels behind me. I paid them scant attention until, on rounding a corner onto a poorly lit lane, their pace quickened and, fearing a footpad, I darted ahead and secreted myself in the doorway of an apothecary shop, holding my shooting stick at the ready. Seconds later a man wearing a greatcoat emerged from the billowing fog and passed my hiding place. He stopped several yards farther along and peered about. I recognized Richmond, but did not show myself, hoping he would continue on his way. However, he turned back and, realizing that I would almost certainly be seen, I stepped forth from the doorway and said, "Are you following me, sir?"

He did not seem in the least taken aback by my sudden appearance, but rather smiled and said in a high-pitched, nasal voice, like that of an Irish tenor with a cold, "There you are, Prothero. I thought you had eluded me."

"So you admit it—you were following me. May I ask why?"

"I hoped it might prove less of an embarrassment if I pressed my business with you away from the confines of the club."

This shamed me, since I was a snob by association and not by nature; yet I maintained a cool manner. "I'm unaware of any business between us."

"That remains to be seen. I require the services of an alienist for a day or two. If you come with me to Saint Nichol, I will double your usual fee."

My interest was piqued, but I had concerns. "Tonight? At this hour?"

"If you fear for your safety, let me assure you that at no hour of day or night is Saint Nichol markedly less perilous." A smile touched the corners of his mouth and I had the idea that it was a mocking smile. "While I cannot guarantee with absolute certainty that you will survive the experience," he went on, "I swear that you will be as safe in my company in Saint Nichol as you would be on any other street in London."

I hesitated and, apparently attributing my hesitancy to greed, Richmond said, "Name your price, then. I will gladly pay it."

"Money is not at issue," I told him. "Mental ailments—and I presume this is why you have sought me out, to treat such an ailment—are not easily corrected. I am no carpenter who can repair your steps or patch a hole in your roof in a few hours."

"I do not expect you to effect a cure, simply to give me your counsel."

"On what subject? Is there a patient you wish me to observe?"

"Two. Myself and one other."

I started to speak, but he said, "You have questions for me. That I understand. And I intend to answer them. But my answers, insufficient as they are, will be far more revealing in light of what I have to show you."

Without waiting to learn whether or not I would accept his invitation (I fully intended to accept, seduced by the air of mystery attaching to it), he produced a silver whistle from his coat and sounded a blast. A coach and pair lurched into view at the end of the lane, wheels and hooves raising a clatter. At that distance, rendered featureless and distorted by the fog, it posed an indistinct black mass against the diffuse yellow light, and the coachman's bulky figure, established in vague silhouette, seemed a projection of that blackness, the crude semblance of half a man. I climbed into the coach with no little trepidation, its aspect having brought to mind a Turner seascape I had long admired, not as regards its particulars, but relating to the sinister mood suggested by its depiction of a numinous fiery light smothered beneath lowering grim clouds.

To reach Saint Nichol it was first necessary to cross Bethnal Green, scarcely a fashionable neighborhood itself; but nothing in Bethnal Green prepared me for either the foul stench of Saint Nichol's muddy byways or the view of human dereliction I had through the fluttering curtains of the coach. On the verge of the slum, in the ghastly greenish-yellow light that spilled from the door of a gin shop wherein anonymous figures staggered and shrieked and capered, perhaps dancing to the scrape of a fiddle, a man lurched toward the coach with open arms, as if in welcome, his round face red with drink, almost purplish and so bloated I imagined it would burst and release a spew of fluids. The fog thinned sufficiently to permit closer observation as we drew near Richmond's home in Rose Street. I saw an elderly man on a stoop, his toothless grin expressing lustful anticipation, gutting the flayed carcass of an animal the size of a sheltie. I saw two prodigiously fat whores rolling in the muck, tearing each other's clothing, their pale flesh smeared with ordure. I saw what appeared to be a man's body lying in an alley mouth, a rat sniffing at its bootless feet, and, hard by Richmond's house, I saw a tattered child with limbs like sticks being whipped by a creature with a shaven head, wearing a frock coat that failed to cover its womanly breasts and no trousers to hide hairy, scab-covered legs. All this grotesque misery and more hemmed in by crumbling, soot-blackened brick tenements that towered into the fog, making of the streets a canyon bottom such as might have wound through one of hell's outlying precincts. I had not been long in London and, with the exception of the odd visit to Bedlam and Broadmoor, my experience of the city had been limited to its decorous quarters. Though I had heard tales of the poverty and horrid excess that ruled in Saint Nichol, their harrowing reality affected me more profoundly than had the most shocking of those anecdotes . . . and this, I understood, was merely the surface of the place, the skin beneath which lay greater pathologies yet.

Iron shutters protected the windows of Richmond's house—a tenement no less soot-blackened than the rest, yet in better repair—and iron bands secured the planking of the front door. I heard a rumbling from above, as of the operation of machinery, but was unable to determine the source. Within, a demure young woman, quite fetching, her lustrous brown hair worn in a bun, clad Oriental fashion in a loose-fitting tunic and trousers of plum-colored silk, escorted us into a salon and there served us a restorative. The room had a cloying smell of sandalwood incense and was larger than some lecture halls, furnished with velvet armchairs and sofas, and divans of a Middle Eastern design, all arranged in groupings as if to encourage half a dozen separate conversations, these groups divided one from the other by statuettes and teak tables inlaid by ornate patterns of nacre and standing vases filled with flowering reeds and peacock feathers. It appeared to have been decorated by a sybarite, the walls hung with tapestries and paintings depicting beautiful women in various states of undress, gold candlesticks in the shape of nudes, everywhere bits of gaud and glamour—it seemed at odds with the character of the man who, having removed his greatcoat, sat drab as a beetle in his brown tweed suit, sipping a brandy. Yet I knew many other men who disguised a salacious nature behind a proper façade, and I harkened back to those rumors of Richmond's corruption circulated by the members of the Inventors' Club.

Richmond drained his brandy glass and said, "I'm afraid I have been less than forthcoming as to the reason I require your services. I did not think you would believe me were I to reveal myself prematurely. I hope that now you will forgive the actions of a desperate man and hear me out."

"It appears I have little choice in the matter," I said. "Unless I choose to take a long walk through Saint Nichol."

"On the contrary. I will have my man convey you to your rooms straightaway if that is your desire . . . though it is not mine."

"You have my full attention."

"And you my gratitude." Richmond settled himself more comfortably in his chair. "Following the death of my sister, Christine, three years ago, I moved into her house. This house. But for . . ."

I was incredulous. "Your sister lived in Saint Nichol? Surely not."

"Yes. For seven years, until the moment of her death. May I continue?"

"Of course. Forgive my interruption."

"I intended to gather her effects and sell the place," Richmond said. "But the longer I remained, the more reluctant I was to leave. I felt drawn to the house, and I also became obsessed with the idea of learning what had happened to her. She died alone, unattended, from a blow to the temple, yet it could not be determined whether her injuries were caused by murder or misadventure. I am, as you may know, unmarried. My flat did double duty as my office and workplace, and there were few demands on my time. Eventually I moved into the house and made it my home." He glanced about the room. "Except for some improvements to the exterior and my study, and a renovation of the uppermost floor, little has been changed since she died. This room, for instance, is exactly as she left it."

"It scarcely seems the décor a young lady would have chosen," I said.

"No, I suppose not. But then Christine could not be considered young. She was thirty-four when she died. And though she was gentle and kindly to a fault, I doubt that she would have been thought of as a lady by other than the most generous of souls. The house, you see, was a brothel that catered to the upper classes and my sister, by every account, both owned and served in it."

Attempting to address this revelation with delicacy, I said, "I realize that among the wealthy there are those who derive titillation from visiting squalid locales. Yet I should think even they might find regular visits to Saint Nichol to be something of a risk."

Bitterness invaded his tone. "Who can fathom these people, unless one is to the manor born?" He left a pause. "I suspect it was such a man who financed Christine. She had a modest income from my mother's estate, but not enough to fund an enterprise of this magnitude."

"I meant to ask how your sister became involved in this business," I said. "Am I to take it that you are not privy to that information?"

"I haven't a clue. It came as a shock to me that she was in London. Her letters bore an address on the Continent—in Toulouse, to be precise—and in them she spoke with enthusiasm about her life there. She must have had someone post them for her. When I visited her, and I did so twice a year, we met at the seaside, and whenever she had occasion to visit me, she would arrive by train. She concealed this portion of her life from everyone excepting her clientele. I cannot imagine how she sank to this abysmal state, nor have I encountered anyone who can enlighten me."

A second young woman entered the room and whispered in Richmond's ear. Though taller and more statuesque, more refined of feature, she might have been sister to the first and was clad in the same fashion.

"Very well, Jane," Richmond said. "We will be along directly."

Once she had exited I remarked on the women's resemblance to each other. His response skirted the issue.

"I offered money to the girls who worked here in order that they could start life anew," Richmond said. "Most accepted my offer, but Jane and Dorothea elected to stay with me. They have become my family, assisting me in my work and ministering to my every need."

A touch of defiance in his speech told me all I might wish to know about the extent of their ministrations.

"I will return to the subject of my sister," he went on, "but I must now, for the sake of brevity, tell you something about my work. Six months prior to Christine's death I began construction of a machine that would cleanse the air of London. It was my hope to reduce the incidence of respiratory diseases. After the shock of Christine's death had passed, after I had accepted the fact that she had debased herself, I once again took up my work."

He stood and, beckoning me to join him, crossed to a table whereon lay a leather folio that proved to contain architectural drawings and blue-prints. I did not gain much from the majority of them, save that they were precisely executed and described complex machinery. However, the last drawing made a certain fantastic sense—it was an overview of central London to which had been added eight mountainous conical structures (the cones formed by concentric silver rings, separated by gaps through which one could make out intricate labyrinths of glass and metal) that dwarfed the buildings beneath, standing, I would estimate, five or six times the height of Big Ben.

"Atop the house I have installed four machines like these, only much smaller," said Richmond. "They are each of a variant design—I sought to learn which of them was the most efficient. The basic process is not one of extraction per se, but of attraction. That is, the machines do not wash the air, rather they attract particulates. In effect, they lure the particles into chambers on the sixth floor and these are then vaporized. I call the ma-chines 'attractors.' I'm not altogether happy with that name, but . . ." He made a gesture of helplessness. "As time permits, if you wish, I will explain the process further, although I don't believe an explanation is relevant to your purpose. But to continue, I completed installation of the last machine two and a half months ago and . . ."

"This is astonishing!" I said. "Have you succeeded? If so, my God! Might I see the machines?"

"Not at present. The atmosphere on the roof is poisonous and the visibility poor due to the concentration of coal dust. When I shut the ma-chines down for repairs, I'll take you to the roof. As to my success . . ." He closed the folio. "You may have noticed that the fog in the vicinity of the house is thinner than it was in Bethnal Green. This is due to the op-eration of my machines. So yes, I have succeeded to a degree. However, to contrive a practical application of the process will be the work of de-cades. As things stand now, machines of the requisite size would deafen the population of London. Until I am able to perfect a method of noise reduction, one that does not require buildings several times larger than those in the drawing, installations of an appropriate size will be out of the question. And there are other problems that must be overcome before I can start work on the project, not least among them the problem I wish you to address."

"You may have come to the wrong man," I said. "I know next to noth-ing about this particular branch of science."

He grunted in amusement and said, "Nor, apparently, do I. Come."

* * *

WE ASCENDED TO the sixth and topmost floor in a cramped elevator and, as we inched upward, Richmond informed me that one of the machines had incurred minor damage during its installation—this had altered the settings of certain instruments. To effect repairs would have required several months and thus he had completed the installation, thinking to determine what result the changed settings might achieve, all the while going forward with the fabrication of a machine that would replace it. By the time we reached the sixth floor, scarcely two minutes had elapsed, yet his mood had darkened appreciably. He snapped off his words, as if impatient with me, and would no longer meet my eye.

The sixth floor reeked of machine oil and coal, and—though it had been rendered as silent as possible by doubled walls and other architectural devices designed to muffle sound—the rumbling overhead made it necessary to raise one's voice. A corridor had once run the length of the floor and the rooms along one side had been obliterated to create a dusty space of raw boards and roof beams that was now occupied by wooden benches, each laden with a clutter of tools and schematics. Those on the opposite side had been replaced by chambers with black iron walls, each having an oblong aperture that, when slid open, permitted the sampling of the air within. A gray canvas curtain hid a fourth chamber. Jane, the taller of the women I had earlier seen, waited beside the curtain—she put her mouth to Richmond's ear, imparted a message I could not hear, and walked toward the elevator. After hesitating a moment, Richmond drew back the curtain to reveal a glass wall of surpassing clarity secured by ornamental iron mounts. A brown-haired woman stood within, clad in plum-colored tunic and trousers. I thought this to be Richmond's other assistant, for she greatly resembled the woman who had just left us, but Richmond flattened his palm against the glass and said, "Christine." I realized then that she was not the woman I had seen earlier, being older by a decade or thereabouts, her face and figure less full. Judging by their longing looks (looks, I noticed, that did not quite mesh—her eyes were angled to the right of Richmond), you would have thought they were lovers kept apart by an impenetrable barrier. I felt twice the fool for having submitted to this charade and was about to give voice to my reaction when the woman vanished. No show of any sort preceded this event, no disturbance of the surrounding air, no rush of sound. She simply winked out of existence. I started back from the glass, tripped, and fell heavily on my backside. Once again I made to speak and the woman reappeared in a far corner of the chamber, dressed in a chemise with a lace collar, her head held at a crooked angle, hair loose about her shoulders, except where it was matted against her temple by a welter of blood. She moved haltingly, aimlessly, as though disoriented.

Richmond helped me to regain my feet. "Strange, is it not?" he said. "To think that when one walks about in the London fog, the gauzy stuff of other lives drapes itself over one's coat or cloak, even slips into our eyes and mouth? That all around us drift shades and phantoms, beings who cling to the bonds of the flesh, old friends and enemies who yet wish us well or ill?"

"Are you suggesting that this is your sister's ghost? You have no proof."

"Proof?" He made a derisive noise. "If her presence alone is insufficient proof, watch a while. You will see a veritable host of proofs. Ghosts old and new, the ghosts of men and women, and that of a creature to which I dare not give a name, all unwilling to abandon this plane."

He started to close the curtain.

"Wait!" I said.

"I cannot bear to watch her in torment. Once she reaches this state, she is mostly in whatever world she travels to and cannot or will not see what occurs in this one. She will remain like this a minute more and then vanish. She never stays long and is often absent half the day. But she will return and . . ." He pointed out a grille mounted in the glass. "You may be able to speak with her."

"Ridiculous!"

Richmond shut the curtain.

"Do you believe me so gullible? It's a medium's trick!" I said. "Some type of illusion."

"I invite you to prove your thesis," said Richmond. "Perhaps after you have failed to do so, you can then concentrate on solving my problem."

I sought to hold up logic as a shield against the fact that what I had witnessed overthrew all my notions concerning the composition of reality; but despite my protestations, as I adjusted to this reordering of the world, I was inclined to accept that the woman had been neither flesh nor the projection of a magic lantern. Her body had not been a wavering image on a backlit screen—it had been sharply etched upon the air, a vital presence edged by an almost imperceptible aura, an outline as thin as a knife edge. I knew that I had seen Christine Richmond, her shade, the colored shadow of the person she had been in life.

"Can you define your problem with more precision?" I asked once my nerves had settled. "You wish me observe, to counsel, but I think you have a more complicated task in mind."

"I have devised a machine whose function it is to remove coal dust from air. Instead, for reasons I do not claim to understand, it attracts ghosts, some essence of those who have gone before. One of these is my sister, who manifests regularly within the chamber and is sometimes seen in other rooms, albeit infrequently. I wish to know how she came to own the brothel and who provided the money for her venture. Is that stated precisely enough?"

His tone had been that of a teacher lecturing the dunce of the class, but I ignored this lack of civility and said, "Extracting information from a ghost may prove more difficult than removing coal dust from the air. Should it be possible, well . . . if it were I, my first priority would be to identify her murderer."

"It is not certain that she was murdered. She may have suffered a fall and struck her head. But if it was murder, yes, I should like to know his name as well."

"She can speak, or so you say. Why not ask her yourself?"

"She will not speak to me. Twice she has spoken my name, but no more. Why this is, I can only guess. We were close as children, closer than most brothers and sisters, though we grew apart. Perhaps she feels shame whenever she sees me."

"Shame related to what she became in life?"

"You need not mince words. She was a whore and died a whore's death."

"Shame is a predictable human reaction, not at all what I'd expect of a ghost."

"I told you it was a guess. Whether or not it is correct . . ." He spread his hands. "However, do not think that she is other than human, that she holds some supernatural charge. A ghost is but a human relic, a shred of the soul torn, caught, and left to flutter upon a metaphysical nail. Nor should you hope to communicate with her. You may be able to stimulate a verbal response, but that is a twitch, a reflex, nothing more. It is my hope, a faint one, that your presence here will stimulate a response that will provide me with a clue."

Feeling overtaxed, I sat at one of the benches. I closed my eyes and took a deep breath in order to still my mind; a thought occurred to me. "You joined the Inventors' Club three years ago, did you not? Would I be wrong in assuming that you applied for membership shortly after your sister's demise?"

He glowered at me, but said nothing.

"Might the two events be connected?" I asked. "Did you suspect one of our fellows prior to the appearance of Christine's ghost?"

He withdrew a pocket watch and flicked open the case. "I prefer not to color your opinion with my own."

I objected to this, saying I needed every bit of information he had gathered in order to carry out an exacting investigation, but he deflected my arguments.

"It's late and I am weary," he said. "Let us go down. If you wish, I can offer you a bed and all the amenities. That prospect may have greater appeal than does a lengthy coach ride."

MY ROOM ON the second floor was staid by contrast to the salon, having sensible oak furniture, a bed with a carved headboard and pineapple posts, logs in the fireplace, and only a pair of erotic lithographs on the wall to remind of the house's former occupation. Recalling Richmond's assertion that little had been changed, this led me to hypothesize that while Englishmen might relish an exotic façade, most preferred to take their pleasure in an atmosphere redolent of hearth and home. I had no means of lighting a fire, but just when it seemed I would have to sleep in a cold bed, there came a tapping at the door and Jane entered bearing a small bundle of kindling. Speaking in a northern accent partially scrubbed away by life in London, she said that she had been sent to prepare my room. Once the fire was going, filling the air with the aromatic scent of burning cedar, throwing shadows onto the wall, lending the room the atmosphere of a cozy cave, I sat by the hearth and watched her turn down the sheets, puzzling over the resemblance she and Richmond's other assistant bore to Christine. This likeness, I realized, was not limited to her face, but extended to her body as well—long of limb, lissome yet full-breasted. Once she had finished with the bedding, she began to unbutton her tunic, doing so as though it were the most ordinary and expectable of actions. She had the garment halfway off before I regained my equilibrium and told her forcefully to desist. She covered herself and, with an air of bewilderment, asked if I would prefer that she send up Dorothea to entertain me.

"Entertainment of any sort will not be necessary," I said. "But I should like a few words with you, if you please."

She sat primly in the chair facing mine, hands clasped in her lap.

"My name is Samuel Prothero," I said. "Your employer has asked that I assist him in an inquiry regarding the death of his sister."

"So he told us."

The fire popped and she gave a start.

"Prior to Christine's death, how long were you in the house?"

"Roughly four years. I had my sixteenth birthday shortly after I arrived."

"You knew her well, then?"

"As well as any. She was always lovely to us girls. Honest and kind. She had her peculiar ways, though. And her secrets."

"I'm sure you learned some of them, didn't you?"

"I did."

"Well . . . ?"

"They were private matters. The sorts of things you might confide in a friend, but would never tell your mother."

"And Mister Richmond? Does he also have secrets?"

"Everyone has secrets, Mister Prothero. I'm certain you have yours."

"Why would you say that?"

"You're not the first colleague of Mister Richmond's to visit the house, but you are the first to reject my hospitality." She tipped her head to the side, as if to see me more clearly. "You have a touch of the prude in you, but I believe your rejection was based on something else. Perhaps some tenet of your beliefs was involved . . . though not, I think, a religious principle."

"You're clever, aren't you, Jane?"

"I know men," she said. "Whether or not that demands cleverness is a topic for debate."

"These men Richmond compelled you to sleep with, were . . ."

"I was not compelled. He asked me if I would lie with them. I could have refused."

"Why didn't you?"

"He needed my assistance."

"How so?"

"I'll let Mister Richmond decide whether or not to tell you about that."

Fascinated by her poise and her obvious intelligence, I let a few moments slip past.

"You're very loyal to Richmond," I said. "Why is that?"

"I was loyal to Christine because she saved my life. She used me, it's true, but then every human relationship is founded upon a bargain of some sort, and had she not taken me in, I would surely have come to a bad end. I'm loyal to Jeffrey, Mister Richmond, because I am now in his employ, and because I wish to help with his investigation."

"And so, in order to gain information about them, you slept with men whom he believed might be guilty of the crime?"

She laughed. "You've found me out. Yes, for all the good it did." After a pause, her voice acquired an edge. "I would have preferred to have been brought up in a decent home and lived an exemplary life, but though I regret my past I am not ashamed of it. I've done what I have in order to survive."

I wondered why she bothered to explain herself. "Were these men members of the Inventors' Club?" I asked.

"Some, yes. Perhaps all of them were. I'm not certain."

The idea that the men had availed themselves of illicit pleasure at Richmond's invitation and then reviled him for it—it conformed to my notions of upper-class duplicity.

"And tonight," I said. "Did he ask you to help with me?"

Her lips thinned. "I think you have pried deeply enough into the subject."

I stirred the fire with a poker. "How would you explain the resemblance between you and Christine . . . and Dorothea?"

"Christine was ever on the lookout for girls who took after her. When Dorothea happened along, she was delighted—that was the year before she died. She had a client who favored our type. Sometimes he'd have the two of us together . . . and sometimes he'd pay for Christine to join us, though she came dear."

"Who was this client?"

She shook her head. "I never knew his name. He wore a mask that covered his head from brow to chin, except for his eyes and mouth. Not even Christine knew him. He had money and came highly recommended—that was enough for her."

"Recommended by whom?"

"Another client, I believe. That's all I know."

"Did he bear any marks on his body that might distinguish him?"

"I don't recall anything in particular." She suppressed a smile.

"What is it?" I said. "If you remember a wart, a mole, some aberrant behavior or character trait, anything at all, it could be of immense value."

"Well, he did like tipping the velvet. He never prigged me proper until he was sure I was satisfied."

I may have blushed, for she shot me a mischievous look. Flustered, I told her that I thought it time for me to retire. As she crossed to the door, another question sprang to mind, but I had been unsettled by her boldness.

"I trust you will be available tomorrow?" I said.

"I have errands to accomplish during the day." She put a hand on the doorknob and smiled sweetly. "In the evening, however, I will be here to serve you however I can."

I SLEPT FITFULLY, inflamed by Jane's bold manner and the glimpse I'd had of her breasts, and troubled by dreams of which I could recall mere fragments. When I woke it was half-ten and I realized that I had missed my one scheduled appointment for the day. Folded atop the dresser was a change of clothing and fresh linens. I also found a note from Richmond stating that he would be gone until late that evening and perhaps overnight, doing some work at his factory. Dorothea would serve me breakfast in the kitchen and arrange for transportation whenever I decided to return home. If I chose to begin my researches immediately, and this was his hope, I was to consider the house my own.

Dorothea proved to be a bright, saucy Londoner, born and bred in Saint Nichol, much more indelicate in her speech than Jane and coarser of feature, more like Christine in this regard, though her eyes were cornflower blue, not hazel. She cooked me a sturdy breakfast that I ate at the counter in the drafty, dingy kitchen, a room with a high ceiling, gray walls, an iron stove crouching on clawed feet, and a chimney covered in plaster. While she tidied up I asked her essentially the same questions I had asked of Jane. Her answers shed no new light on Christine's death, but when I pressed her, she disclosed that Christine had tutored her in the art of pleasing a man, with particular attention paid to the pleasing of one man, the mysterious masked client.

"I think she fancied him," Dorothea said. "Which was odd considering she was a bit of a Tom."

"Christine was a lesbian?"

"She had her lady friends, let's say, but now and again a man would catch her eye. And him with the mask—she'd ride him to Bristol and back if given the chance. When he paid for the three of us, often as not Jane and I did nothing more than lie about and coo in his ear for all the attention she paid him. Why, I recall this one—"

"I don't think it necessary to explore specifics," I said. "Why did you choose to remain in the house after her death?"

"Money," she said, leaning on her broom. "What else? Mister Richmond sacked the rest of the girls, but he made Jane and me a most generous offer to stay. The work is easy—a few men and mostly none at all. I feel like a regular toffer and not some dollymop in a bordello. Of course . . ." She winked at me. "Now there's you."

"I doubt I shall be long in residence," I said. "Certainly not long enough to establish the kind of relationship you imagine."

"Oh, la!" She laughed and danced her broom around. "It don't take that long to establish, believe me. And it's not me who's doing the imagining. It's Jane. She fancies you, she does."

"Indeed? Jane?"

"Yes, sir! She told me so herself."

I pooh-poohed the notion.

"You'll see," she said. "Jane will be polishing your trinkets before you know they're out in the air. You've heard what they say about girls from the north?"

"I don't believe I have."

"Give them an inch and they'll take the whole yard."

I felt myself blushing. "What do you know about Jane?"

"Oh, she's nice enough. Very caring, she is. She was always looking out for the other girls."

"I mean before she came to the house."

"She never talks much about her past." Dorothea idly swiped at the floor with her broom. "She did tell me that when she was a child, she and her sisters were the support of her family up in Newcastle. They worked in the theater, playing imps and angels and the like. Her father dosed them regular with gin, hoping to keep them small. So they could still do the job, you understand. But Jane sprouted up and he threw her out of the house when she were but nine. I'd have put a blade in his neck." Dorothea swatted at a spiderweb that spanned between the stove and the wall. "Jane loves the theater. She and Christine would talk about it 'til all hours. I reckon that's why they formed a stronger bond than what I did with her. Me, she trained for the bedroom, but with Jane she went the extra mile. She taught her etiquette, how to dress elegant and speak nice."

"What about you?" I asked. "Was your childhood similar to Jane's?"

"My mother whored, so you might say I was born to the trade. But thieving was my specialty . . . before my bubbies came in, that is. I'd dress as a boy and wander the streets between here and Bethnal Green. There wasn't a pocket watch or a wallet safe from me." She waggled her fingers and grinned. "These very fingers plucked the Duke of Buckingham's watch."

"What in the world was the Duke of Buckingham doing in Saint Nichol?"

"Inspecting his property. He must own half the houses on Boundary Road. Him and Sir Charles Mellor and some other toffs was strolling about, looking at this house and that house."

Charles Mellor was a charter member of the Inventors' Club—I asked Dorothea if she was certain it had been him.

"Oh, it was Charlie, all right. We'd see him down here right frequent. There must have been half a hundred children swarming around with their hands out, begging for pennies. So I sneaked in amongst them and nicked the duke's watch. Didn't get nothing for it, though. My mother took it to a pawnshop and got swindled proper."

"Where is your mother now?" I asked.

"I don't know." She began sweeping in earnest, as if suddenly called to the task.

I left Dorothea to her chores and made my way to the sixth floor and pulled up a chair in front of the glass-walled chamber. Christine was nowhere in evidence, but from time to time a revenant would manifest in the chamber. In the main they were relics of the lower classes, those whose living cousins could be seen in the streets of Saint Nichol, a few dressed in the garments of another era; but there were also richly dressed men and well-appointed ladies. Many were in sharp focus, visible for a span ranging from scant seconds to a minute or two, and others were frayed and tattered like rotten lace, all but worn away—these last brought to mind the phantasmagorias I had delighted in as a boy, yet they exhibited a lifelike quality, a dimensionality, that those illusions had not. They neither spoke nor acknowledged my presence, though they came close enough to touch had there been no glass. Once something dark and whirling, a dervish shadow twice the mass of man that looked to be acquiring human form, materialized in the chamber and I heard above the noise of the machines a faint roaring, as from a distant crowd. This so alarmed me that I scrambled back from the glass, knocking over my chair. The figure was headless and armless, or else its head was tucked close in against its chest, giving the impression that it was surmounted by a massive torso and set of shoulders. It looked rather like a living pencil sketch, a black core encaged within a complexity of slightly less black lines that whirled rapidly about the central darkness, making it appear that the whole of the thing was in motion. Soon this apparition lapsed and I reclaimed my seat.

What most astonished me about the things I saw that day (and other days as well) was my reaction to them . . . or rather the lack thereof. I would not have believed that I could easily adapt to such a drastic shift in the way I perceived the world; yet there I sat, scribbling down observations concerning a subject whose existence I would have decried the day before, and doing so with a reasonable amount of aplomb. I mentioned this to Dorothea once and she replied that human beings were more resilient than most gave them credit for, putting this sentiment in the vernacular. "When a bloke tries to jam tackle the size of a cricket bat up your lolly, you're afraid it's never going to fit," she said. "But once it's in, it's surprising how quickly you adjust to the situation." She went on to say that ghosts no longer troubled her, even when they manifested outside of the chamber, in other portions of the house. I inquired of her about these manifestations and she told me that before Richmond had come to dwell in the house, she and others had encountered presences on the upper floors, notably an elderly woman who dragged her left leg as she walked; but Dorothea had not seen the old woman since Christine had died—it was as though she been evicted and Christine had taken her place.

At quarter past four that first afternoon, Christine appeared within the chamber. I was writing in my notebook and did not witness her entrance, but when I looked up from the page she was standing next to the glass, hands on hips, wearing undergarments obviously intended to arouse: a corset (of Parisian design, I believe) sheathed in emerald-green silk and lace that constricted her waist and exposed the plump upper curves of her breasts; and pantaloons of a filmy material that clung to her hips and thighs. Her hair was a complexity of curls piled high atop her head and framing her face, and her smile had a touch of disdain. She walked away from the glass, displaying her long legs and shapely derriere, glancing over her shoulder—a dram of poison had been added to her smile. I had the thought that she was replaying a scene from her life, showing herself to someone she despised, someone who could no longer afford her charms.

Placing my mouth close to the grille, I called out, not expecting an answer. In truth, I was uncertain whether she had the ability to hear—I had no idea how she perceived the world. After ten or fifteen seconds, as though my outcry had taken an inordinate amount of time to carry across the distance between us, she came toward the glass and pinned me with a stare so fierce and hostile, I had the urge to bolt. Despite Dorothea's acclimation to the company of spirits, I was an interloper and placed no faith in their benevolent disposition. I spoke her name again and laid my palm flat on the glass, as Richmond had done. A confusion of emotions crossed her face. Her eyes grew teary and she became distraught, plucking at her hair, touching her face . . . and suddenly she was gone. I stood beside the chamber awhile, waiting for her to reappear. At last I turned to the bench upon which I had left my notebook and let out a squawk—Christine stood less than an arm's length away. Not the high whore (the toffer, as Dorothea would have said) in her French frillies, but bloody Christine in her chemise, pallid and dead of eye. A distinct emanation of cold proceeded from her. She gave no sign that she saw me, but shuffled off to my right and back again. It seemed she felt some sort of attraction to the spot and yet had not the consciousness to understand it, but muddled about like a chicken habituated to being fed in one particular section of the barnyard. My heart racing, I slipped past her and reclaimed my notebook. She turned, but instead of facing me, she took a step or two toward the end of the corridor. I surmised that in this guise her perceptions might be clouded, her reactions to stimuli uncertain, more so, at any rate, than when appearing in her other aspects. She exhibited a terrible slowness and sluggishness, her fingers knotting in the folds of the chemise. Her irises looked to be revolving a few degrees backward and forward like clockworks, an uncanny thing to see. I wished that I could will her from the world, because while I had no real attachment to her, one could not see her so drained of life, possessed of that eerie glamour, and remain unmoved.

I DREW THE curtain after she had gone and sat at the bench writing until late in the evening, recording a detailed account of what I had seen and felt and thought during the day. On returning to my room I discovered a fire crackling in the hearth and half a roast chicken on a plate covered by a linen cloth, along with bread, cheese, water, and a bottle of Edradour. Apparently Jane had come and gone. I sat by the hearth, sipping the whiskey, made despondent by the dreary prospect that not seeing her presented, not in the least because Dorothea had said that she fancied me, but also because I had been immersed in death and its products for many hours, and I had been anticipating a visit, however perfunctory, from someone alive and vital. As a result I drank more than I should have in an attempt to ameliorate the morbid effects of dealing with Christine. If I felt this way after a day in her company, I wondered how much drink I would need after a week? A month? I had no doubt that the investigation would last at least that long. Truth be told, I thought I could make a career of this single case. Here was a ghost who could be counted upon to appear again and again with regularity—the light that she might shed on the nature of the physical universe, on the nature of life itself, was incalculable. I pictured myself gone gray and creaky, the author of a library of books about Christine Richmond, imprisoned by obsession, incapable of discussing any other topic.

The fire burned low and I lit a lamp. A knock. Unsteadily, I went to the door and flung it open, expecting to find Richmond in the corridor. I was prepared to tell him that I did not have the stomach for this work and would be unable to satisfy his requirements, but it was Jane come to turn down my bed, wearing a crinoline night bonnet and a flannel dressing gown that covered her from neck to ankle. For all her matronly attire, she was no less beautiful than ever and I watched her intently, enlivened by the swell of a breast, the shape of a thigh as she bent to her task. However modestly dressed she was, her every movement was an article of seduction. She asked if there were anything further she might do for me and I bade her sit, saying that I had more questions. Yet I had none. Fuddled by drink, by the idea that I could have her, my mind emptied and, though I racked my brain, I managed to stammer a few phrases by way of preamble, yet nothing more. Once again I had the apprehension that she understood my predicament and was amused. At last I succeeded in dredging up a question that had not occurred to me before that moment . . . or if it had, I had pushed it to the back of my mental shelf.

"Christine's resemblance to both you and Dorothea," I said. "What part do you think it played in Richmond's desire that you remain in the house?"

She seemed to withdraw from me. "He wanted us near to remind him of her."

"I don't doubt that, but there must be more to it. He makes love to you, does he not? To women who remind him of his sister?"

"It's been more than two years since he last touched either of us. He . . . he changed. Our relationship changed. He became more like a cousin, an uncle. He cares for us now, and we for him. That is all."

I was immoderately pleased to learn she had no current involvement with Richmond.

"That begs the issue," I said. "He *did* make love to you. And he kept you here for that purpose. That he has since stopped this practice conjures other questions, but the fact remains that he chose two women who closely resemble his sister to serve as his concubines. Does this not seem a symptom of some tragic family circumstance?"

Jane frowned and spread her fingers on her knees, appearing to examine them for defect. "Dorothea has spoken to you about this?"

"I had a conversation with her earlier."

"I . . ." She sighed and pressed the heel of one hand to her brow. "I will not speak ill of him."

"Jane," I said. "Men and women are often driven to extremes of behavior by emotional distress. In this life we are all at fault. None of us is simon pure, no matter how deeply we may wish it. Society may judge Richmond, but I make no judgments. If I am to determine what is going on, you must be straightforward with me. Anything you tell me will be kept in the strictest confidence."

She searched my face and then lowered her eyes. "On occasion, with me and with Dorothea, he used her name instead of ours."

"In passionate address?"

"Yes." A plaintive quality expressed itself in her face and voice. "But as I said, it's over two years since he last took either of us to bed."

After an interval I asked, "What do you make of his use of Christine's name in these instances?"

"I am not the doctor here," she said firmly. "You will have to draw your own conclusions."

"And I will. But my conclusions will be formed in large part by what you tell me."

"Dorothea believes that . . ." She left the thought unfinished and, after an obvious internal struggle, she stood. "I'm sorry. I have chores to attend before I sleep."

Had I not been drinking, I might have let that end the conversation, but I too stood, blocking her exit, and said, "I would like you to stay, Jane. We need speak no more about Richmond, but please . . . stay awhile with me."

A blank mask aligned with her features and she put a hand to the sash of her dressing gown.

"I want you to stay, not because you feel compelled to do so," I said. "But because it is your choice. Because . . ."

I began to sputter, blurting out the history of my day, the oppressive mood engendered by my encounter with Christine. I suggested that Jane stay until I fell asleep and that nothing more need happen—I did not want to take advantage of her. A lie. I wanted to take complete advantage, but I didn't want her to believe that was my aim . . . and I may have told her as much. So eager was I to have her good opinion that honesty seemed the only course, unprecedented honesty, honesty divested of the slightest hint of subterfuge. Fortunately I do not recall every idiotic thing I said. While I was speaking she went to the bed, removed her dressing gown and bonnet, shook out her hair, and climbed beneath the covers, clad in her chemise. I made no immediate move to join her, immobilized by desire in conflict with an assortment of anxieties, amongst them the fear of looking more the fool than I already had. I might have stood there forever, but she released me from the thrall of my anxieties with the perfect counterspell.

"If you please," she said, turning on her side, facing away from me. "Leave the lamp on when you come to bed."

IN THE MORNING I went to stand in the entranceway of the house to take the air, cold and noxious though it was, perfumed by the ripe scents of Rose Street. A cart passed me by, raising a clatter like an enormous sack of bones and pulled by a moribund horse, its ribs showing through its loose skin, urged along by a driver so muffled in rags that I saw of him nothing apart from steaming breath and reddened cheeks and tufted white eyebrows. Urchins screeched and squealed and whistled to one another, running pell-mell, their flights as erratic as those of birds frightened from their roosts. Ungainly wives lumbered from doorways to empty basins of slops into the gray, gluey mud of the street, disappearing back into the many-eyed oblivions of their black brick homes. Yet all this was given a gloss by the glorious night I had spent with Jane and had for me the quaint charm of a scene from one of Mr. Dickens's gentler tales. I allowed myself to entertain fantasies about a life with Jane, imagining a cottage on the sea, a child or two who would appear only after a ten-year honeymoon, sojourns in the Italian Alps and the like.

Giddy with these delusions, I headed to the kitchen, intending to cut a slab of cheese and some bread to take upstairs with me, and discovered Richmond eating his breakfast. His face was drawn, the lines around his eyes deepened by fatigue. I wished him a good morning—he gave a curt nod, muttered something I could not make out, and attacked his eggs and sausage with ferocity.

"How goes your work?" I asked, dragging up a stool. "Well, I hope."

He swallowed, nodded.

"May I inquire what it is that you are working on?"

He sucked at a particle of food trapped between his teeth—his poor table manners were often made the butt of jokes at the Inventors' Club.

"I am completing a fifth machine," he said. "I intend to install it soon."

I started to speak but he held up a hand to stay me.

"I recognize that your investigation will be of some duration," he said. "I do not plan to replace the machine that summons Christine. Not yet. If I finish before your work is done, I will forbear replacing it or else replace another machine." He wiped his mouth on the back of his hand. "I have left you a check with Dorothea that should suffice for your immediate expenses. Let me know if you need more. I will be busy at the factory for two weeks—I doubt we will see much of each other during that time. If you have business elsewhere, patients to treat, the coach will be at your disposal. And, of course, the house is yours to use as you see fit."

I must admit that this discomfited me—it seemed an abdication of responsibility, implying that he did not actually care about Christine and that whatever concern he felt was perfunctory and had been satisfied by the act of hiring an alienist.

"Would you care to learn what progress I have made?" I asked.

He looked at me, expectant, chewing a mouthful of food.

"Progress may be too optimistic a word," I said. "But I have a theory regarding your sister's . . . promiscuity."

He swallowed. "Yes?"

"I believe she may have been interfered with while still a child."

I had thought he would display some adverse reaction, but he did not. He had a bite of sausage, chewed, and said, "Hmm."

"An incident of the sort I envision often leads the child to have an unhealthy view of sexuality. She might, for instance, be prone to use sex as a means of gaining approval."

He continued eating.

"It might be helpful if I could speak to your father," I said. "He may recall . . ."

"That would be pointless. These days he is like an infant who must be dressed and diapered. His memory is nearly gone, and when frustrated he comes easily to anger. It would be an unnecessary trial for the both of you."

"Is there anyone else with whom I might speak? A nanny or another relative."

"Only myself," said Richmond. "I am occupied today and will be, I anticipate, for the remainder of the week. Next week I can spare a few minutes, though I can't think it will be helpful. Christine and I were brought up more or less separately. Summers I traveled the length and breadth of England and Wales with my father, assisting him with one or another of his engineering projects. The remainder of the year I was away at school. All the while Christine stayed home. We had the occasion to spend time together, of course, but our relationship was based on holidays and a weekend here and there. We were more cousins than brother and sister."

I found this a telling disclaimer and was inclined to press him on the matter; yet I did not think it was the moment to reveal that I suspected him of having had an incestuous encounter with Christine—it would have seemed accusatory and my purpose was to define the problem, not to cast aspersions. I thought to tell him about Christine's masked client, wanting to learn whether or not it would elicit a strong reaction, for I believed that Richmond was capable of such a deception; but I decided that this, too, would have been premature. I made a packet of bread and cheese, wished him good day, and went about my business.

The weeks that followed saw me make little progress. I had a lengthy conversation with Richmond concerning Christine, but it was, as he had promised, unrewarding. My observations of her shade yielded nothing new, though she manifested for longer periods of time, as if she were becoming accustomed to my presence. Isolated with her for up to an hour, sitting for hours more beside the chamber, cataloguing the motley spirits that materialized in her absence, I imagined that I was being watched, studied by a malefic spirit, and I took to carrying a crucifix for protection. Other suspicions plagued me, prominent among them the idea that this practice brought me closer to death each day. Every so often, that dark, dervish creature appeared in the chamber. Although I had become used to it popping in from the afterlife and announcing itself with a distant, many-voiced roar, I came to assign it a demonic value; yet I did not fear it as much as I feared for my mental stability.

Then one morning as I sat at the bench fronting the chamber, searching my pockets for a pen, Christine appeared beside me wearing her plum pajamas (this had been the uniform of the house during its heyday) and asked in a wispy, genteel voice, one rendered nearly inaudible by the rumbling of the machines, if I would care for a glass of wine.

"No, thank you," I said upon recovering my poise. "Your company is more than sufficient stimulation."

A handful of seconds elapsed before she spoke again, looking off to my right and at a point above my shoulder. "Shall I call the ladies in for your inspection?"

"I think not," I said. "I would prefer to spend my time with you."

After another brief delay, she let out a peal of laughter, as though delighted by my response; but she said nothing more, only continued looking above me and to the right. I wondered if she could hear me—judging by her attentive expression, she might have been listening to another voice.

"My name is Samuel," I said. "Samuel Prothero."

The delay again and then she said, "Yes! Of course! I know your father."

My father, as far as I knew, had never been to London and was so conservative in nature that the idea of visiting Saint Nichol would have given him palpitations. I began to doubt that Christine was responding to me. Yet if, as Richmond suggested, a ghost was a scrap of life left behind after death, a fragment caught on a metaphysical nail, and not a faded version of the person entire, these oblique statements might be the only responses of which she was capable and she could be trying to communicate, unable to express herself more fluently than a tourist in a foreign land armed with phrases from a guidebook. I decided to risk a direct approach.

"Christine," I said. "Tell me about the night you were murdered."

Following an interval of twenty or thirty seconds during which she appeared to be frozen, she vanished. Soon thereafter I apprehended a chill presence behind me. I did not want to see her in that bloody guise and kept my head lowered until the feeling of cold dissipated.

That night Jane came to my room with an excellent bottle of pinot noir, and as we sat by the fire, which had gone to embers, I asked her to tell me more about Christine. What had she been like in her unguarded moments? Did she maintain any friendships outside the brothel? Did she spend much time away from it? If so, how did she spend that time?

"I wouldn't know about friends outside the house," said Jane. "She couldn't have had many . . . if any at all. What time she didn't spend here, she was at one music hall or another, or at the theater. She'd tell us about what she saw, all the people and what the ladies wore and such, but she never mentioned anyone specific. And I think she would have. We were her employees, but we were also her confidantes. Like us, she was trapped here, unhappy and on the lookout for something that would make her happy. If she found it, I don't believe she could have kept it to herself."

Light from the hearth ruddied her pale skin. She leaned forward to caress my cheek.

"You'll see again her soon enough," she said. "Stop thinking about her."

"I know. It's just . . ."

"Tell me."

"I'm beginning to feel that my efforts are wasted here."

"But you said you had broken through to her."

"I did, but in retrospect it was the kind of moment that persuades me that what I'm doing here is worthless. I don't believe I will ever be able to communicate with her."

She mulled this over. "Dorothea says that Christine seems to enjoy her singing."

"Dorothea's singing?"

"Yes."

"What does she sing?"

"Popular tunes. 'Pretty Polly Perkins from Paddington Green' and that sort of thing. She says they seem to make her happy. It causes her to hang about longer, she says, but she's not so horrid looking." Jane held up her glass so that the fire added ruby highlights to the wine. "It makes me nervous, her hanging about, so I pretend not to see her and let nature take its course."

"Was 'Pretty Polly Perkins' her favorite song?"

"I don't know as she had a favorite. Oh, wait now! She used to go larking about here singing snatches from 'Champagne Charlie.' If she had a favorite, I reckon that was it."

She had a sip of wine, the voluptuous, vaguely predatory curve of her upper lip kissing the glass. Though she was of Christine's type, her features were so delicate and fine that I no longer thought of Christine when I looked at her, but saw a beauty entirely her own. And it was not just her beauty that moved me. During our time together she had told me of her life, less a life than an escape route, a flight from one brutal circumstance to another. Despite this, some central essence had come through undamaged, a core of strength and sweetness unaffected by this maltreatment. She had a temper, and when something she held dear was threatened, she would defend it with an unladylike ferocity; but these storms passed swiftly.

"You know," I said. "If it were not for you, I would have given up weeks ago."

"I'm glad I can be a comfort for you."

"You're more than a comfort, Jane. Without you to shore me up, I would have been overwhelmed by the morbidity of this enterprise. I can only hope my presence here has meant something to you."

"I think . . ." She bit her lip and fixed her gaze on the hearth.

"Please! Tell me!"

She sighed and, without lifting her eyes from the hearth, said in a small voice, "I think you know my heart. I think you have always known it."

I took her hand and the warmth of the fire, her warmth, went all through me—it was as though our physical contact had created a bubble of time and space apart from the world. I wanted to say more, but was at a loss for words, not knowing what there was to say. Our stations in life were at such a great remove one from the other, it was unlikely we could ever have a lasting connection.

She withdrew her hand from mine and, as though she knew my thoughts, said, "It might be best not to invest too hastily in our relationship . . . or too deeply. I care for you, Samuel, but the situation is difficult. I have divided loyalties, you see. And you, well . . . you have your own difficulties to overcome."

Despite the irresolution of that night, or rather because, irresolute or not, that singular moment had moved our relationship forward, I set about my work with renewed energy. Predicated upon our conversation, I began singing "Champagne Charlie" whenever Christine materialized. As Jane had said, her mood became genial and there were times when she did not revert to her bloody, chemise-clad state prior to vanishing. Initially those were the only changes I observed, but before long I noticed that when I

sang a particular verse, allowing for the apparent delay between my singing and her reaction to the song, she grew more aggressive in her behavior,
coming close to me, staring intently (although her stares were not always
directed toward me), and betraying signs of anxiety. The verse went as
follows:

The way I gained my title is by a hobby which I've got
Of never letting others pay no matter how long the shot.
Whoever drinks with me are treated all the same,
From Dukes and Lords and Cabmen down,
*   I make them drink champagne.*

By the time I finished the chorus ("Oh, Champagne Charlie is my
name . . . etc."), she would have returned to normal, but for the span of
perhaps half a minute her eyes widened, her bosom rose and fell as though
her breathing had quickened, and on one occasion she laid her hand on
my forearm. I was stunned, stricken. Rather than jumping back, I held
perfectly still, imprisoned by that slight weight upon my shirtsleeve. I was
startled to find that her hand had any weight whatsoever, and she too
may have been startled, for she snatched her hand away and disappeared.
I retreated to the elevator and thence to my room and tried to understand
what had happened. Her touch had been light, yet no lighter than the
casual caress of a real woman, and there had been no spectral association, no chill. Upon regaining my composure, I ascended once again to the
sixth floor. Christine was nowhere to be seen and did not return for the
better part of a day, but from that point on she contrived to brush against
me whenever possible—I imagined that these intimacies were reminiscent
of her vital days and gave her pleasure. For my part, I experienced a mild
anxiety, less than I might have when a strange cat unexpectedly rubbed
against my leg, and thus I permitted the touches to continue.

I made an exhaustive report to Richmond on my findings, noting that
of all the spirits who passed through the chamber, Christine was the only
one who appeared in more than one guise. I postulated that because she
was last to die within the confines of the house, her manifestation was cor-
respondingly more complex. I said that her conversation might be random,
yet I half believed that she was attempting to communicate, her capacity
for speech limited by her fragmented state. In support of this, I told him
what Jane had related about "Champagne Charlie" and how Christine
had vanished when asked about her murder. Further, I told him about our
recent physical interactions. This piece of news seemed to anger him.

We were sitting on a bench on the sixth floor and when, at the end of my report, I brought the question of my finances to his attention, he pulled out his wallet, slapped it against the bench, and demanded to know how much I wanted. I replied that he had mentioned twice my usual fee and named a figure. He extracted a sheaf of banknotes in excess of the figure I had named and flung them at me.

"I am nearly two months along in this investigation," I said. "I've reduced my commitment to my other patients and I have bills. I don't think it is unreasonable to ask for payment. But this . . ." I indicated the banknotes. "It's too much."

"When dealing with whores," he said, "it's my habit to pay more than the going rate. It inspires them to perform their duty with a certain brio."

"Listen to me, Richmond," I said evenly. "Christine's case is a remarkable one and if my financial position allowed it, I would work for nothing. But should you address me again in that fashion, I will quit your employ and have nothing more to do with this investigation. Is that understood?"

He snorted, pocketed his wallet, and strode off toward the elevator, leaving me to puzzle over his extreme behavior.

IT WAS SEVERAL weeks later, on a Ladies' Night at the Inventors' Club, that I came to terms with the fact that I had fallen in love with Jane, though I should have reached this conclusion long before—I had found it increasingly difficult to concentrate on my work, thinking of her to the point of distraction. I had tried to convince myself that the subject of that work, Christine, so resembled Jane that the waters had been muddied, and that my feelings were mere sexual infatuation complicated by psychological stress. That evening, however, I was forced to admit that a more base consideration—one of which I was aware but had shunted aside, not wishing to see myself in its light—was to blame.

On Ladies' Night the membership were encouraged to bring their unwed daughters (and their spouses, but this was a secondary consideration) to the club in order that they meet the unwed, younger members, the objective being to spark romance and subsequently create the bloodline that would produce the Great Inventor . . . at least this was my jaundiced view of the proceeding. For probationary members such as myself, attendance was mandatory. I told Jane not to expect me back until the wee hours and that I would likely not see her until the following day. The club's banquet hall had been cleared of its long oak table for the event and was decorated after the fashion of a gala, with floral displays everywhere, a champagne bar, and a string orchestra whose insipid strains had induced several dozen couples in evening dress to dance. Shortly after arriving, I was pinned into a corner by Constance Mellor, the youngest spawn of Sir Charles Mellor, an officer of the club whose work on the London underground and the electric tram had earned him the accolade, and Preshea Liddle, the daughter of Archibald Liddle, whose advances in nonflammable dry-cleaning solvents had made him wealthy. Whether either of these ladies could be considered beautiful was a matter of conjecture—their appearance was artificially enhanced to such an extent, they might have been refugees from the cast of *The Mikado,* and they were both strapped into corsets so cruelly tight, they were forced to speak in gasps. They fluttered and fussed with their gowns, cutting their eyes this way and that, tittering and giggling, exclaiming, as Constance did at one point, "Oh, do look, Presh! Isn't Margaret's gown the absolute be-all and end-all?" She glanced coyly at me and asked what I thought. I replied on cue that no gown, however gilded, could improve on the lilies I had to hand, causing them to blush and quiver and pant breathlessly, gazing at me with painted eyes that seemed as empty as their heads. I was disposed to believe that a pair of enormous parakeets disguised as women were holding me captive. Telling them I would fetch more champagne, I pushed my way through the dancers to the bar, ducked out a side door, hurried along a corridor, and entered the library, a dim, cavernous space in which a mighty crystal chandelier glittered like a far-off galaxy, throwing glints from the gilt-lettered volumes lining its walls, and there I sat in a leather chair, turning things over in my mind, eventually concluding that I had been an ass. Jane was the loveliest, most admirable, most intriguing woman of my acquaintance. I loved her and had denied the fact purely on the basis of social concerns. This revelation did not bring a song to my heart, because those social concerns were far from illusory. If we were to marry, I would have to surrender all thought of a career in London. If she was exposed to the scrutiny of the circles in which I hoped to travel, her past would be ferreted out and we would be disgraced. If I stayed in London and kept her as a mistress, I would have to endure a Constance or a Preshea. It was not a happy choice, but I made it happily and was about to rush home and announce myself to Jane, when the imposing figure of Sir Charles Mellor hove into view.

"Ah, young Prothero!" He eyed me with disfavor. "There you are."

I started to stand, but his hand fell upon my shoulder and I sank back into the chair.

Sir Charles sat down, crossed his legs, and adjusted the hang of his trouser cuff. I have said he was imposing, yet he was not an especially large man; his intimidating effect was produced by a fierce, bearded coun-tenance, a cold, clinical, and composed manner, and a penetrating black stare before which his subordinates were wont to quail. The stare was on full display that evening, more conspicuous than the diamond studs on his starched shirt and the massive gold signet upon his left hand.

"Apparently," he said, "you have made quite the impression on my daughter."

"And she upon me." I racked my brain for a suitable compliment. "She is utterly charming."

"Charming. Yes, I suppose." He made a church and steeple of his fin-gers, tapping the tips together. "Beautiful, I should say as well."

I hastened to agree on this point.

"Witty?" he suggested. "Intelligent?"

"Without a doubt."

"And yet here you are, lost in thought, while Constance waits in the banquet hall, devastated by your abandonment of her."

"I intended no abandonment," I said. "I felt . . ."

"Your intent does not concern me. Or rather it concerns me only as regards your interest or lack thereof in my daughter."

"Sir Charles, I assure you that I meant no insult. I felt ill and came into the library in order to recover."

"Constance is an imbecile," he said. "A shallow, silly young woman. But I will not permit her to be trifled with."

"Sir," I said, summoning all the righteous indignation that a short career in theatricals at Cambridge allowed me to access. "Far be it from me to dictate to you, but I am compelled to say that I thoroughly resent your characterization. I have, I admit, only a passing acquaintance with your daughter, but she seems altogether a splendid girl, a lady of pristine breeding and rare quality."

He studied me a moment longer and then made a noise that I took for a symptom of satisfaction.

"How are you feeling now?" he asked. "Better, I trust."

"Somewhat."

"I will sit with you until you are able to return to the banquet hall."

A silence ensued, alleviated by distant music, after which he said, "I have not seen you at the club lately."

"I have a patient who commands a great deal of attention."

"I see. A troublesome case, is it?"

"Most troublesome."

"I hope you're being paid and that this is not charitable work in Saint Giles . . . or Saint Nichol."

Recalling that Sir Charles was one of Richmond's chief detractors, I attempted to mute my reaction. His statement did not require an answer, so I offered none.

"Charity is an irresponsible act," he said. "So I judge it. No less reprehensible than the act of murder. However profoundly we may regret the pitiable state of the poor, we cannot let their plight distract us from the path of progress, lest we be dragged down to their level."

"You may rest assured that I am being compensated," I said firmly. "As to the larger issue you have raised, I believe true progress to be defined by the resolution of poverty, not its continuance in the service of furthering outmoded concepts of class and empire."

I refused to wilt under his stare.

"The sentiments of an upright young man. An idealist not yet sullied by life's exigencies. I would expect no less." He leaned forward and patted my knee. "Your spirits seem restored. You must be feeling better."

"Immeasurably," I said.

"Then let's go in, shall we? The ladies are waiting."

After several hours passed flirting with Constance under the menace of Sir Charles's unrelenting scrutiny, I returned to Saint Nichol exhausted by the experience, my mind abuzz with trite observances and banalities. Only a few coals remained glowing in the hearth, but I was too weary to kindle another fire and flung myself beneath the covers. I slid down the precipice of sleep, imagining Constance's annoying voice going on and on about some inane topic, but soft hands and a kiss prevented me from completing the descent. Muzzy headed, I made a sound of complaint. Within moments, however, I was enthusiastically engaged with her. I must have fallen asleep directly afterward, for I recall nothing more of the event apart from its intensity.

The next morning I happened upon Jane in the corridor outside Richmond's study, which was situated not far from the kitchen, and made a jocular comment about her early morning visit. Her smile hardened and she pushed past me. I went after her, blocked her path, and asked what I had done to anger her.

"I slept straight through the night!" she said. "Whoever you tupped, it wasn't me!"

She tried to elude me, but I caught her by the wrist.

"Jane," I said. "If this is true . . ."

"Of course it's true! You bastard!"

"I was half asleep and there was no light. I thought it was you."

She struggled against me. "When have you known me not to want the lights on?"

"It was late—I was tired, I didn't think."

"Too right, you didn't!"

"Why would I mention it otherwise? I thought it was you."

She made a halfhearted attempt to break my grip, but her anger had, I thought, diminished.

"It's the God's honest truth, Jane. On my honor."

Her lips thinned. "Let me go."

She seemed calmer—I released her.

"Don't you understand I want only you?" I said. "Haven't I made that clear?"

She darted toward the kitchen.

I stood there bewildered, seeking to consolidate my memories of the previous night. My recollection was hazy and full of gaps, but whoever the woman in my bed had been, she had displayed the full range of Jane's passionate idiosyncrasies. I wondered if she might be a somnambulist.

A shriek, a clangor as of pots and pans falling—I raced for the kitchen and saw Jane swinging a broom at Dorothea, who cowered in a corner beside the stove, crouched down and shielding her head. I managed to interpose my body and ripped the broom from Jane's grasp. Dorothea seized the opportunity to reach across my shoulder and clutch at Jane's hair, snagging it with her fingers, and Jane did the same, yanking Dorothea's hair, provoking a scream of rage and pain. As I separated them, I heard Richmond say behind me, "This is intolerable! Stop it at once!"

Their hair and clothing in disarray, the women fell back. We all looked to Richmond, who came forward into the room and stood with his hands on hips, scowling. "Will someone tell me what is going on? I could hear you in my study."

"She . . ." Dorothea wiped spittle from her lips. "She accused me of lying with him! I told her I had the curse, but she wouldn't hear it."

"Who was it, then?" Jane pushed toward Dorothea, but I held her back.

"Perhaps he brought someone home," said Dorothea. "How should I know who it was? And me curled up with a rag stuffed between my nethers. Why don't you inspect his bedsheets? I was bleeding so profusely, there's bound to be evidence."

"Enough!" An expression of distaste stamped Richmond's features. "Did you bring a woman home with you?" he asked me. "I have given you the run of my house, but my hospitality does not extend to your guests."

"The only woman I was with last night was Constance Mellor," I said. "And she went home in the company of her father."

"Who is this Constance?" Jane asked sharply.

"Jesus, God!" I lifted my eyes to the ceiling.

"An aberration," Richmond said to Jane. "The daughter of an abomination. You need not be jealous of her sort." He turned to me and indicated the door. "A word, if you will." Then to the women: "You will cease your bickering and attend to your duties. If there is an issue between you, and I do not believe there is, we will discuss it later. Is that understood?"

The women muttered their assent, but on exiting the kitchen Jane cast an embittered glance at Dorothea that promised further unpleasantness.

THE PREVAILING ODOR of Richmond's study, a long L-shaped room into which I had never ventured until that morning, put me in mind of my great-aunt's house in Bridgend, the air heavy with a cachet of spice and heather, the perfume of mummified refinement and Georgian depression—but there all similarity stopped. Iron shutters prevented the ingress of natural light and at one end, tucked into the bottom stroke of the L, a reading lamp with a green glass shade, the sole source of illumination, created an island of emerald radiance about a carved oak desk that had the look of an ancient monument, its walls configured by intricate bas-relief. Two chairs sat on opposite sides of the desk. Hundreds of leather-bound books lined the shelves, breathing out musty vibrations. An atmosphere of gloom and hermetic solitude held sway; this was heightened by a wide, unexploited, uncarpeted space upon which pentagrams might be sketched and half-ton entities invoked. Something had once occupied that space, for there were grooves and notches in the wood, marking the passage of a great weight. I suspected the room might have served as Richmond's workplace prior to his renovation of the sixth floor. Considering this room in context of the others, I thought that if the house was in more or less the same condition Christine had left it, then she must have had the sensibilities of a jackdaw, for no decorative theme was carried out—the interior design might have been the work of several women, not one.

I seated myself and apologized for my part in the disturbance, but Richmond, standing by the desk, dismissed my apology and asked which of the women did I think was lying.

"Dorothea," I said. "Yet I would have sworn it was Jane with me last night."

"Do not forget that they were both schooled in the ways of men by Christine," he said. "To distinguish between them in the dark is no easy thing."

I did not like this intimation of his former relationship with Jane. "Jane had no reason to lie," I said.

"Whores need no reason. Lying is second nature to them. They invent reasons that might not appear reasonable to you or me, yet touch upon their innermost secrets."

Bridling at this, I said, "If such is to be the tenor of our conversation, let us end it now. I have no wish to hear you speak crudely of Jane."

"Did you find that statement crude? I thought I was being a realist." Richmond took a seat behind the desk. "Samuel, you're a young man. Younger than your years, I'd say. You are perceptive and, I believe, quite intuitive. But it's obvious that you are in love, and love can blind one to great many painful truths."

"Jane loves me as well."

"Has she said as much?"

"I have made no declaration, nor has she, but I know it to be true."

"Well, though it may be that Jane is in love, I can assure you of one thing. She is not blinded by it. She may be several years your junior, but she has a wide experience of the world. That she has changed since we were involved, I have no doubt—but she has not grown more foolish or less discerning."

"I don't understand how this is relevant. My connection with Jane is my concern, and hers. If you have something to say about Dorothea's lie or upon another subject, I will gladly listen. Otherwise there is no point to continuing."

Richmond cleared his throat and then said, "Is it lost on you that there is a third woman in the house?"

I floundered for a moment. "Are you speaking of Christine?"

"I have watched you with her these last weeks. I've . . ."

"I haven't seen you on the sixth floor since I began my study."

"I drilled a hole that permits observation if one stands in the space between the inner and outer walls. But that is not of moment."

"Oh, no? I find it unbelievably offensive. Are there peepholes elsewhere? In my bedroom, perhaps?"

"Bear with me, I beg you. Hear me out and then I will accept the full brunt of your outrage." Richmond clasped his head in his hands, staring down at the fawn-colored blotter. "I have never spoken of these events to any man, but I believe you have sniffed out a portion of my story. That makes it no easier to disclose, but now . . . now I find disclosure to be necessary."

He sighed and looked up from the desk. "I was sixteen when my mother died. Christine was less than two years younger. My mother fell ill in the spring of the year, and my father brought the family to our country estate near Caerphilly in hopes she might recover there. Within the week he was called away to the Continent on business, leaving my mother to be cared for by servants. He remained absent until a few days prior to her death. Why he did this . . ." He shook his head. "His motives were hidden from me and he has never talked about that summer. At the time I chose to believe he loved her and that his absence was due to an inability to watch her suffer. But now I think he became uninterested in her when she could no longer play the part of wife, and went off to find a new one in Europe. Which, ultimately, he did.

"My mother's decline was swift. After a month in Caerphilly she barely recognized us. The doctor told us she had weeks to live, no more, yet she lingered all that summer. Bedridden, racked by fevers, either in pain and heavily drugged. We did what we could, Christine and I, but the servants kept us from her, fearing the sight of our mother in her delirium and torment would damage our tender souls—they failed to comprehend that seeing her only rarely and then for a few minutes was a torment to us. I wrote my father, pleading with him to return, but he would not respond. And so Christine and I were virtually alone, with no authority to guide us but an elderly nanny whom we no longer heeded. I would read to her and she played the piano for me, but these pursuits soon bored us and we began to wander the estate, taking a picnic lunch and passing entire days in the woods and fields, talking about this and that. Prior to that summer we had been apart so much of the time, and now, thrown together in such a powerful emotional setting, relying upon each other for support, for conversation, for all else . . . it was an unhealthy situation. On occasion I would notice some feature of her beauty, and I would catch her looking at me, instances that caused her to blush and avert her eyes. I repressed these moments—I thrust them aside and refused to acknowledge what they portended."

Richmond gazed at the iron shutters. "There was a pond on the property, large enough to think of as a small lake. We often ate beside it. One afternoon in early June, feeling torpid following lunch, I fell asleep. When I awoke, Christine was gone. I heard a splashing from the direction of the pond and made my way through the bushes that grew alongside the bank. Christine stood in the shallows, completely unclothed, sluicing water over her body. I thought her the most beautiful thing in all of Creation. She saw me as well. Instead of covering herself, she turned full toward me, clasped her hands behind her head, and lifted her face to the sun. I raced back to the house, pierced by shame, but I had remained there long enough to imprint her image on my brain, and shame would not wash it away. That night she came into my bed. I was half asleep, yet I could have resisted her."

He wore such a morose expression, I felt sympathy for him and said, "You are not the first man to have made such an error in judgment."

"Oh, it was hardly that!" He laughed bitterly. "We were in love and love accepts no judgments. Our affair continued for months, even after my father's return, and did not end until I returned to Eaton. Christine was always more aggressive than I. She forced the issue, yet I was equally culpable."

He pressed his hands together, the tips of his fingers touching his chin—a prayerful attitude. "Years later our nanny informed me that Christine had become pregnant and a stable boy let go. She had accused him in order to deflect blame from me. I don't know what became of him . . . or the child."

"Christine never said anything?"

"Not a word. I wrote to her, of course. I asked what had happened. She answered my letters, but not my questions. She had been sent away . . . to school, my father said. In France. I didn't see her again for years. She married a gentleman farmer, or so she claimed. In one of her letters, she enclosed a wedding photograph that showed her with a man with oiled hair and a little mustache. A charade, I suppose. I never had a word from him, neither then nor following her death.

"A year after her purported marriage, she asked me to meet her in Torquay. We spent a few days together and whenever I brought up our personal history, she insisted that we not dwell upon the past. Over the years we met in Margate, Ilfracombe, Ryde, Cardiff, Llandudno . . . in every benighted resort in Britain. Days, we strolled on the esplanade, we laughed and teased each other, we watched the Punch and Judy shows, rode donkeys on the beach, and attended concerts. Only once did she offer affection of the kind I desired. It must have been shortly after she moved to Saint Nichol. She melted into an embrace and kissed me, but apologized immediately and said the kiss was a mistake. I went to sleep that night as I had on all the previous nights, alone and frustrated. You see, I still held in mind the image of her face lit to white gold by the sun, the water beaded on her flesh. I hold it still." His aggrieved expression and slumped posture gave evidence of a defeated attitude. "I hope you understand now why I have been so beastly toward you."

I allowed that, no, I did not.

"Because I'm jealous," he said. "She is returning to us and it is you with whom she speaks, with whom she flirts as she once did with me. She holds me in contempt. She blames me for everything that happened. And now she has come to you exactly as she came to me when we became lovers."

I had been about to suggest that he was reading far too much into the situation, but his last statement left me speechless. My shock must have been discernible, for he said, "Can you not see it? Jane has no reason to lie, as you say, and Dorothea's complaint is easily verified, if you have the stomach for it. Unless Constance Mellor followed you to Saint Nichol, who could it have been but Christine?"

Disordered by this outburst, I took a moment in order to marshal a response. "Firstly, we do not know that Christine is, as you put it, returning. Her behavior and the quality of her materializations reflect a shift in amplitude, but there is nothing to indicate . . ."

"If you were working on a jigsaw puzzle and, having completed it save for two or three pieces, you saw that it constituted the picture of a lion, do you believe that adding those few pieces would transform it into the picture of a giraffe?"

"To use your metaphor, this particular puzzle is missing many more than two or three pieces. We can make no reasonable assumption based on what is known."

"As a scientist you must know that the making of assumptions, the construction of hypotheses, is essential to progress. Take, for example, Christine's reaction to the song 'Champagne Charlie.' Are you aware that Christine had a client who wore a mask and whose identity she claimed not to know?"

"Jane told me. What of it?"

"When you referred to Constance Mellor in the kitchen, I thought instantly of Charles Mellor. When he was young, he had the reputation of being just such a man as the song describes. He enjoyed gadding about the slums, whoring and drinking in the gin shops of Saint Nichol. It's possible that he was the masked client and, further, that he funded Christine's purchase of this house. A sizable portion of his income is derived from the ownership of slum properties. This house may once have belonged to him. I intend to look into the matter. My assumption may be erroneous, but property issues, the change of titles, and so forth . . . it should be easy enough to prove. Now that . . ." He sat up straight, the movement appearing to reflect a sudden and unexpected reinvigoration. "That is merely an assumption. What we have in Christine's case rises to the level of theory, wouldn't you say?"

"No, I would not. The leap one would have to make between an apparition and a revivification, even a temporary one, seems much more extensive than that between your assumption regarding Mellor and his actual guilt. As to that, I trust you will not act precipitately."

"When one takes into account your chosen field of study, you seem a strangely conservative thinker," Richmond said, gazing at me with a ruminative air. "I find it dismaying that you are unable to reach for a height without availing yourself of a stepladder, so to speak."

I had no desire to engage in a running metaphorical battle with him and so I let the comment pass.

"Well," he said pertly. "You have been warned."

"Warned? As to what?"

"Why . . . Christine." He seemed baffled by my failure to grasp the obvious. "It is clear that she has designs on you and that you are in danger. I cannot but think that her ghost is in a perpetual state of torment. How can it be otherwise? Life calls to her and she feels the pull of old desires, yet she cannot answer that call. Now, presented with an opportunity to reinhabit the world of the senses, she must be desperate to taste and touch and feel. Christine was ever prone to abrupt shifts in mood and subject to whims and cravings. As they were when she was in love with me, these tendencies have become exaggerated since she made a connection with you. I foresee a time when those whims evolve into wild and erratic impulse, those cravings into compulsion, and she will let nothing stand in the way of her desires."

ALTHOUGH IT STRAINED credulity, had anyone aside from Richmond warned me against Christine, I might have taken the warning to heart; but I had detected in him an unsound quality, and our conversation had done nothing to ease my mind on that score. Then, too, I had a more enjoyable and distracting business to complete. The following afternoon I had Richmond's coachman, Henry Bladge, a sturdy, balding fellow with pork chop whiskers and a round face as unremarkable as a muffin top, convey Jane and me to a tearoom on the edge of Bethnal Green, an establishment with a small garden at the rear that sought to counterfeit a pleasance, offering an air of relative seclusion amidst shrubbery, several young trees, and a pair of stone benches—yet it lay close enough to a gin shop that we could hear the squabbling of that establishment's poorer patrons who, unable to afford a mug of their poison, stood at the door, holding gin-soaked handkerchiefs to their faces and inhaling the fumes. Snatches of music on occasion drowned out their clamor, testifying to the passage of street musicians. After tea we sat out on a sun-dappled bench, shaded by a thickly leaved elm, and there I told her (more bluntly than I had planned, for I was anxious) that I wished to marry her and make a home with her in Wales. She looked every inch the creature of fashion—under her cashmere shawl, she wore a dress cut from a tartan fabric of brown and green that complemented her eyes and hair, and also matched her sober mien. She did not give me her answer at once, but asked if I intended to complete my investigation.

"I will do my best for Richmond," I said, "if that is your concern."

"My concern is not only for him, but for Christine."

"I have no authority over the spirit world. Were I to promise a satisfactory conclusion in that regard, you would be within your rights to question my veracity."

She maintained her reserve. "I doubt myself, Samuel. I wonder if I can make you a suitable wife. Although Christine taught me how to play the lady, that veneer is thin, as you witnessed the other morning. I understand why you would wish to return to Wales with me. Here in London I would be no asset to your career."

I objected to this, but she took my hand and said, "Please, Samuel! We must be forthright with each other."

"It is true," I said. "I was initially fearful that my career would be damaged by our union, but as my thoughts on the subject evolved, I feared mainly for you. I did not want you to suffer the scorn that would be heaped upon you by the doyennes of polite society should your past be revealed. Now that we have reached this pass, however, I realize your strength is sufficient to withstand such treatment. You have endured far worse. And I must not allow the course of my career to be dependent on the views of people who belong to a world that is fast disappearing. If you wish to remain in London, remain we shall."

"Perhaps that can be a subject for later discussion?"

"Of course."

She glanced up into the elm leaves, as though attracted by some movement there. "Do you think you know me, Samuel? I have been honest with you concerning my past, but I have a great capacity for self-deception. I may have painted myself too much the victim so as to draw you in."

"No one is immune to self-deception," I said. "I doubt the human race would survive without it. As for knowing you, I cannot imagine that any two people at this stage of their lives know each other completely. They can only anticipate learning about the woman or the man they love."

"I have one last question," she said. "I know that your politics predisposes you to have an affection for the underprivileged. Am I to be, then, a kind of political proof, living evidence of that predisposition? A token of your political views, as it were?"

"Were I a creature of the type who populates the rolls of the Inventors' Club, I would never have looked at you as other than an object of lust," I said. "To that extent, politics *has* played a part in this—it has assisted me in perceiving you for the woman you are. But I swear, that is the only part it played."

She drew a breath and released it slowly. "Then I will gladly be your wife, in London or in Wales. That is, if you still want me after all these quibbles and qualifications."

We embraced, albeit not for long—prying eyes peered at us through the rear windows of the tearoom—and then left that place, that bench, and its overshadowing elm. I told Henry Bladge to drive us round Hyde Park. It was a rare lovely day, a high, blue day accented by puffs of cloud, and warm for the first week in March, with flights of swallows banking above Kensington Gardens and people taking their ease on the green lawns; but Jane and I hid ourselves behind the curtains of the coach, kissing and conjuring a future together that, for all its optimism and halcyon vision, had not the slightest chance of coming true.

RICHMOND BEGAN TO install his new machine several days later and, as the two machines that cleansed the air had been shut down (the one that summoned Christine was not, its operation signaled by a throbbing hum, not the louder, steady rumbling of the others), I took the opportunity to climb up to the roof through a trapdoor accessible by means of a ladder and located in the ceiling close to the elevator. From my vantage on the western side of the roof, standing in a thick carpet of black dust, it seemed I was at the center of a choppy sea contrived of roof peaks and chimneys from which darkling smokes trickled upward to commingle with an overcast of much the same color. Four cylindrical sections had been cut out from the eastern side of the roof, and the machines had been set down in the holes thus created, approximately a third of their height hidden from the view of whoever might peer at then from the adjoining houses. The concentric silver rings (I say, silver, but that word refers merely to their color—I never ascertained the name of the metal from which they had been fashioned) that constituted their exterior rose some fifteen feet above the roof and were pitted and discolored; but the new machine was shiny and taller by half. Altogether they resembled Christmas trees of a futuristic design, three stubby and one attenuated, and appeared quite alien in contrast to the blackened bricks and tiles of their surround. I wondered why this bizarre construction atop Richmond's house had not been paid more notice by the residents of Saint Nichol, especially considering the noise it produced; but then I recognized that most had little interest as to what happened in the heavens, their eyes being fixed upon the ground, their ears attuned to baser sounds.

Crouched amidst a clutter of tools (awls, hammers, and so on), Richmond and several workmen were busy bolting down the new machine to an iron plate—I could see the tops of their heads from the edge of the hole. The machine itself differed from the other three not only in height, but also in that various dials and switches occupied the interstices between certain of the concentric rings. I poked around the rooftop for a few minutes more, finding nothing to hold my interest and then, as I prepared to go back down through the trapdoor, I caught sight of an opaque, oblong shape, roughly the size of a man, hovering close by the fourth machine. It trembled, fluttering as would a leaf in a strong wind, and subsequently was drawn out into a thinner, scarflike shape that clung to one of the concentric rings, gliding along it, fitting itself to the ring as though it were a sleeve . . . and then it vanished. I had grown accustomed to ghosts during my stay at Richmond's house, even to the point of being on speaking terms with one, and their formal apparitions, the images, fragmentary and otherwise, of the men and women they had been in life had almost no effect upon me; but this glimpse of the raw stuff of the spirit—that was how I countenanced it—left me petrified, my heart squeezed and stilled for an instant by cold, steely fingers, and made me fully aware of the depths of the pit into which I had lowered myself.

MY WORK WITH Christine had reached an impasse. What I had seen on the roof made me reluctant to engage her, and I spent less time with her than I had, dallying with Jane instead. Richmond remained concentrated on the installation and, though I saw him each and every day, he spoke only in monosyllables and then in passing. He was oblivious to everything but the matter at hand and seemed to have lost interest in talking further about Christine. For once I was happy to accommodate him. However, on the day after the new machine had been activated, he invited me into his study and notified me that he had turned off the fourth machine and from now on, for the duration of my visit the new machine would be the only one functioning.

"You must do as you see fit," I said. "But this is certain to impede my work."

"On the contrary, my dear Samuel," he said with gleeful satisfaction. "It will assist your work no end. Tomorrow or the next day, a window will be installed in the chamber beneath the new machine."

I absorbed this. "So the purpose of this machine is not to purify the atmosphere?"

"It is intended to restore Christine. Not entirely—I don't believe that is possible, though my notion of what is possible changes day by day. But by using the damaged settings on the fourth machine as a starting point, I have devised a means of strengthening her effect. At least that is my hope. This may serve to quicken her perceptions, broaden her range of interactions with our plane of existence, and thus enable her to assist materially in bringing her murderer to justice."

"Materially? Are you suggesting that she may be able to give us conscious, clearly reasoned assistance?"

"That is a distinct possibility."

"Yet when you say 'strengthening her effect,' I have the impression that what you have done is to create an amplification of effect and not a broadening."

"As you yourself have said, you know nothing about this branch of science."

"If you recall, I was speaking at the time about cleansing the air. The creation of the machine that enhanced Christine's presence happened by accident, and I cannot think that you have a complete understanding of the process. Now you are certainly more proficient than I with regard to the technical aspects of your machine, but I have studied your sister for several months and I would hazard that you know less than I about her condition. You are playing a dangerous game, Richmond."

"I'm not playing at anything!" he said. "I am desperate to gain Christine's ear. I must know that she forgives me."

"Is that truly the sum of your desires?" I asked. "At first you told me that you wanted to know who financed the brothel, and then it was a clue to the identity of Christine's murderer. Now it is her forgiveness you want . . . and her restoration to a state of being similar to that she had in life. I infer from this progression that you may never be satisfied and will continue to elevate your expectations."

He gave me an oddly bright look, the sort of look one observes on the faces of certain mental patients, seemingly alert yet too fixed to signal actual alertness.

"I would be remiss if I failed to warn you that you have embarked on a self-destructive course," I said.

He was silent for such a long while that I began to worry.

"Richmond?" I said.

His head twitched. "I still haven't been able to come up with a better name for the machines than 'attractors.' Do you have any thoughts on the subject?"

"Did you hear what I said?"

"About my self-destructive course? Yes, I heard you. And I have moved on." He leafed through some papers that had been lying on his desk. "Having witnessed the machines in operation, perhaps you can suggest a suitable name?"

Unsettled by this abrupt conversational shift, I told him that "attractors" struck me as eminently suitable, but that I would set my mind to the task. He appeared indifferent to my concerns, so I excused myself and went in search of Jane.

In the kitchen I found Dorothea seated at the counter, popping grapes into her mouth and gazing at the wall. I asked if she had encountered Jane that day.

"She was about earlier." She winked at me. "Have you looked under your sheets?"

I sank onto a stool beside her and let my head hang.

"Well, I can tell you're in a fine fettle," Dorothea said.

"I'm worn out."

"Perhaps you need a tonic."

"Perhaps."

She chucked. "I'd rub your shoulders, but I don't care to risk another beating."

I sat mute and discouraged, and at length said, "I'm not physically fatigued. My weakness is purely spiritual."

"I was having you on, referring to Jane taking after me with the broom the other morning."

"Oh . . . right."

She offered me the bunch of grapes and I took one.

"I think Richmond may be mad," I said.

"Wouldn't surprise me. We're all a bit mad 'round here."

"I wasn't speaking in jest."

"Nor was I. Living in Saint Nichol is enough to put a few twists in your noggin, and sharing your home with a ghostie . . ." She gave her head a violent shake. "Our ghostie has been at me all morning."

"Christine?"

"If I've seen her once, I've seen her half a dozen times. She must have important business with someone."

Richmond's newest attractor, I thought. Doing its job.

"She's not in a cheery mood," Dorothea said.

"How do you mean? Was she wearing her chemise, all bloody?"

"No, but she wasn't the least bit happy, even when I sang for her."

I got to my feet, undecided whether or not to notify Richmond of this sudden increase in Christine's manifestations.

"You might want to wait," said Dorothea. "She'll be dropping in again any minute."

"I'm going up to the sixth," I said. "Tell Jane where I'll be, won't you?"

"What about Miss Christine?" Dorothea asked as I went out. "Have you a message for her?"

THE SIXTH FLOOR was deserted, silent except for the oscillating hum of the new attractor. Workmen had not yet come to replace the iron wall of the chamber beneath it with glass. Curious, I opened the sampling aperture and heard from within a far-off roaring like that made by the shadowy creature. I detected movement in the corner of my eye and saw Christine pacing in front of the fourth chamber, wearing her emerald-green corset. I approached her cautiously (Richmond's admonition about her had not gone unheeded) and spoke as I might to a horse that required gentling. This tactic had no good effect, for she vanished before I could reach her. Turning back toward the elevator, I saw something that froze my blood. I had left the sampling aperture open and from it there projected a well-defined beam of black energy or light or some other immateriality I could not name. It was as though a black sun were contained within the chamber and its radiant stuff had shot forth from the aperture to touch the wall opposite . . . and upon that wall an irregular patch of darkness grew, developing into a vaguely anthropomorphic figure that had the shape and size of a small headless child. The roaring had increased in volume and it was this, the implication that somehow a monstrous, whirling shadow was being beamed onto our earthly plane . . . that spurred me to act. I sprang to the aperture and shut it, cutting off the beam. The dark shape on the wall began to dissolve in much the way a puddle of water evaporates under strong sunlight, albeit far more quickly. Once it had gone I sat at one of the benches and sought to analyze what had occurred, but the phenomenon beggared analysis and I was too rattled to think. After ten minutes of fruitless deliberation, it struck me that urgency was called for. Eschewing the elevator, I pelted down the stairs to the second floor, intending to collect my notes and alert the others. Upon entering my bedroom, I found Jane standing by the fireplace, gazing at the dead coals, wearing the tartan dress she wore on the day I asked for her hand. I was eager to tell her all that had happened and caught her by the arm. She looked up at me with Christine's eyes, the hazel irises revolving a fraction of a turn and back again. Seen this close, they no longer reminded me of clockworks, but had the agitated motion of the tiny creatures I had studied under a microscope at university.

I stumbled back and sat down heavily on the bed, staring at her in disbelief. I had no doubt the woman before me was Jane. She had Jane's height and delicacy of feature, yet her stony expression seemed less at home on her face than it had on Christine's. And those eyes . . . I tried to picture the pattern of darks and brights in Jane's hazel irises, but could not bring them to mind. She came toward me, paused a foot away, and uttered a peculiar fluting cry. It seemed that she had difficulty breathing, though in retrospect I believe that the fleshly mechanisms of speech were difficult to master for the spirit who had possessed my fiancée.

She opened her mouth again and this time, with considerable effort and in a voice that fluctuated between Jane's firm contralto and Christine's higher, frailer tones, she said, "Have you come to frolic? It is much too early. We risk being interrupted at our play."

This brief speech so horrified me that I remained half lying on the bed, propped up on my elbows, incapable of answering her.

"Yet risk may add spice to our pleasure. Was that your thought? Naughty Jeffkins!" She turned back and lifted her hair away from the nape of her neck. "Won't you help me with my buttons?"

I came to my feet and turned her to face me. "Jane!" I said, and shook her. "Jane!"

She fought against me, but I shook her again and again, each time more violently, and continued to call her name. Suddenly she went limp and would have fallen to the floor in a swoon had I not supported her. I laid her down on the bed and patted her cheeks until her eyes fluttered open—*her* eyes, devoid of unnatural movement, and not Christine's. She was at first confused, then angry when I told her about Christine, refusing to accept my version of events.

"Do you remember me entering the room?" I asked her. "Or anything that was said?"

"I . . ." She put a hand to her temple. "No, but . . ."

"What is the last thing you recall?"

"I was . . ." A look of consternation cut a line across her brow. "I was in my room. Reading, I think."

"You never wear this dress in the house. Not to my knowledge. Were you wearing it while reading?"

She examined a fold of fabric that she pinched between her thumb and forefinger. "I had not finished dressing. I thought of a quotation—from Jane Austen—and I recall opening my book to search for it."

"Can we assume your lapse of memory encompassed a span of, say, ten minutes or thereabouts?"

"I'm not sure. Everything's cloudy."

She started up from the bed, but I held her down.

"We must tell Jeffrey," she said.

"Do you feel up to it?"

"I'm fine."

"All right. But you must promise that no matter how he reacts, you'll leave with me at once."

"He may need our assistance."

"If you remain in the house, you will be at risk. This may not be the first time that Christine has possessed you."

"What do you mean?"

"I think you may owe Dorothea an apology."

After a moment she said, "Oh, God! Is that possible?"

We went downstairs, collected Dorothea, and bearded Richmond in his study, where I explained things to the best of my ability.

"Well now. That should remove the sting from Samuel's infidelity," he said to Jane, bemused. "It would appear that he was unfaithful to you *with* you."

"I see no humor in this," I said.

"No?" His smile broadened. "Let it be noted that you are a particularly humorless young man."

"I can't speak for Dorothea," I said. "But Jane and I intend to leave before a tragedy occurs."

"Oh, you have my permission to speak for me," Dorothea said. "I'm half out the door."

I leaned down to Richmond, resting my fists on his desk. "If you insist upon staying, a tragedy is inevitable. You are in grave danger."

"Nonsense! Christine is indifferent to me."

"Yet less than an hour ago, in a tone of voice I would describe as playfully seductive, she referred to you as 'Naughty Jeffkins.' Does that strike a chord?"

"Did she say that? But this is wonderful, don't you see?"

"Damn it, Richmond! She's confused me with you. Can you have forgotten what you told me? That she is a mad fraction of her former self with whom true communication was impossible?"

"I may have been in error," he said.

"Jeffrey, please!" Jane laid a hand on his shoulder. "You must leave."

"All you have done is to strengthen that fraction," I said. "And what of that shadowy creature? It seems you have strengthened it as well. Do you have any understanding of its potential?"

"No, I do not," Richmond said. "Nor do you. And because you do not understand, you are afraid."

"It's conceivable that the entity is harmless . . . or inimical in a trifling way, like the ghost of a demonic house pet. But when dealing with something of so menacing an aspect, yes, I deem it wise to practice caution. As would any responsible person."

"Go then!" Enraged, Richmond jumped to his feet and pointed to the door. "Go and practice caution! Be responsible! Leave me to my researches."

"You've done no research! You built your machines and left the research to me. Research, I might add, that would be much further along had you been open with me from the outset."

I held out my hand to Jane, but she looked to Richmond instead. "Do you want us to stay, Jeffrey?"

"I cannot ask it of you," he said. "But yes, of course. A resolution is at hand and I would hope that you see me through it."

"Jane," I said.

"How long will this resolution take?" she asked.

"Perhaps a few hours. A single night. Now that she is stronger, I doubt things will go unresolved for long. Yet I cannot be precise."

"I'll be pushing along," Dorothea said. "I've given you my all, as it were. Mister Richmond. All this talk of possession, though . . . it's not a dance I care to do."

Jane turned to her. "We can spare him one more night, can't we?"

Dorothea said flatly, "I'm sorry."

"I won't leave without you, Jane," I said.

"I swear to you, Samuel." Richmond came out from behind his desk. "I will shut down the machine in the morning, whether or not . . ."

"Why should we believe anything you have to say?" I stepped away as he made to approach me. "You've done nothing but lie and dissemble since the beginning. If a resolution of the problems between you and Christine is what you actually seek, how will our presence assist in that? It will achieve nothing other than placing us in peril."

"You're right," he said. "I'm frightened. I'm afraid of being alone with her. If you feel you must leave, I understand."

Judging by the sympathetic expression on Jane's face, I recognized there was little hope of countering Richmond's self-serving statement; but I tried nevertheless.

"You are afraid, yet you wish us to stay," I said. "And you care so little about our well-being, you expect us to join you in this dangerous folly. How noble!"

Jane shot me a reproving look.

"He's manipulating you," I said.

"He's right," said Richmond with a hangdog expression. "You should leave."

"Good Christ!" I slammed the flat of my hand against the desk, making a loud report. "Now he's feigning weakness to rouse your sympathy. Can't you see?"

Both Jane and Richmond regarded me sadly, as if they were aware of some nuance, some shading of the truth that I had yet to comprehend.

SCIENTIFIC CURIOSITY MAY have played a part in my decision to remain in the house. I was genuinely anxious for Jane, and I wanted to keep an eye on Richmond—I insisted that we wait out the night together, thinking that should Richmond begin to behave erratically or Christine attempt to possess Jane once again, I would take decisive action. But as we sat at a bench on the sixth floor, speaking minimally or not at all, I came to ponder my missed opportunities. Had I not become involved with Jane and focused the bulk of my attention on the ghosts that passed through the chamber, I might have arrived at some firm conclusions about the spirit world. As things stood, I could make only the most general of suppositions. I vowed to devote myself henceforth to uncovering material proofs pertaining to everything I had observed.

Not until that night did I realize how unseemly a perdition the sixth floor was. With its mouse droppings, dusty spaces, and raw boards; its gray canvas curtain, iron walls, and benches laden with machine parts; and its ghosts and the vibration of the attractor, it had an ambiance that was part futuristic charnel house, part wizardly lair. I could not wait to relegate it to memory. My dislike for the place was augmented by Dorothea's absence. Her pragmatism and humor had been necessary to the sustenance of the unusual family we had become during the past months, and I felt a corresponding disunity. Jane leafed through a book of poems, occasionally offering me a nervous smile. Now and then Richmond glanced at the ceiling. He may have been alerted by some aberrance in pitch of the attractor, though I detected none. During the initial hour of our vigil, Christine materialized in her several guises on fourteen separate occasions, never for more than seconds, but made no effort to possess Jane or to do anything other than look morose. After that she appeared no more. I was nonplussed by her withdrawal and Richmond's manner grew funereal, sitting with his hands clasped and eyes downcast. Every so often he would blurt out a question such as "Where do you think she is?" or "Do you think we should move downstairs?" Our response to these and other questions was essentially the same: I don't know. Another two hours passed in this fashion. Finally, during the fourth hour, he told us that he was going up to the roof.

"For what purpose?" I asked.

He drew himself up to his full height, presenting a stern pose. "I will not answer to you in my own house."

I blocked his way to the trapdoor. "In this instance, one in which our safety is at issue, I'm afraid you must."

"Are you threatening me, sir?"

"I am attempting to ensure that you are not going to place us in greater danger than you already have."

"I need to inspect the machine," said Richmond. "Something may be wrong."

"It seems to be running smoothly."

"Idiot! You can't tell by listening to it! I have . . ."

"Yet you were listening to it earlier, were you not?"

Richmond hissed in frustration. "One cannot make such a judgment *merely* by listening. I have to see the instruments."

Jane closed her book. "We should allow him to do what he needs."

"I don't trust him on his own," I said. "And I will not leave you alone down here."

Richmond tried to force his way past me, and I shoved him back.

"I'll go with you," said Jane. "It may well be that something has gone wrong. We'd be foolish not to let him attend to it."

I argued that venturing up onto the roof would be incautious, but with

Richmond attacking me verbally and Jane supporting his basic argument, I relented. I insisted, however, on taking the lead. Nothing out of the ordinary met my eye when I cracked the trapdoor, yet when I threw it open I saw that something had gone very wrong, indeed.

Streamers of fog trailed across the rooftop at eye level, but above the house a bank of thicker fog lowered, though actual fog was not its sole constituent. Its uppermost reaches stretched across half the sky and, depending from its bottom, a funnel had developed, extending downward toward the tip of the new attractor, itself visible above the roof peak, its silver rings glowing with a bilious, yellow-green radiance. At first glance the bank was like a great cloud whose bottom was cobbled with faces, but I saw on its underside a myriad images of not only disembodied faces, but torsos and limbs as well—they roiled up for an instant and were subsumed into the fog, replaced by the other revenants. Rags of filmy, opaque material were disgorged from the mouth of the funnel and these battened onto the attractor, fitted themselves to one or another of the rings, and slid down out of view. Whenever this occurred, and it occurred with increasing frequency, a silent discharge of yellowish-green energy shot upward from the attractor, spreading through the bank like heat lightning, permitting me to see shapes deeper within the fog. I thought that some of the shapes so illuminated were inhuman, yet they passed from sight so quickly that I could not swear to it.

Urged on by Richmond, I clambered up onto the roof, still partly in shock, dismasted by the sight and by the silence as well. Oh, there was the omnipresent humming, loud and variable, but this apocalyptic scene, that of the ghosts of Saint Nichol, the relics of the damaged and the poor lured by the attractor, perhaps to their doom, for God only knew what Richmond's improvements had wrought . . . it should have been accompanied by an explosive music, the final pyrotechnic symphony of a mad Russian who had devoted his life to its creation and then, having awakened to the worthlessness of his work, of all creative labor, had chosen self-slaughter over the ignominy of existence. Jane came up beside me and Richmond scrambled to the roof peak and stood, one hand on the chimney for balance, his hair feathering, superimposed against that insane sky. He let out an agonized shout and pointed—filmy bits were being torn away from the fog, spinning down away from the attractor.

I climbed toward the roof peak, Jane at my heels, and reached it just as Richmond disappeared into the hole into which the new attractor had been set. At the edge of the roof stood the demon, the shadowy, headless thing—I could make out no more of its features or form than I had previously, yet I noticed that its dark substance whirled more slowly, perhaps because it was feeding, absorbing the opaque scraps that were ripped from the underbelly of the bank. That was my interpretation of its actions, that it must also be an attractor, albeit of a vastly different and less potent variety, a living version of Richmond's machine. Some credence was given this viewpoint by Christine, who stood on the slant of the roof fifteen or twenty feet distant, her figure elongating, bending sideways at the waist and seeming to flow partway toward the shadow before snapping back to true, as though she were made of an elastic material and barely able to resist its pull.

We climbed down the slope of the roof toward the hole so as to learn what could be done to help Richmond. I saw him below, his hands busy with the switches on a brass box situated between two of the rings. He shouted and beckoned for me to join him. Whatever hesitancy I felt was erased by the garishly lit fog bank, lowered to within a few feet of the attractor, spewing forth its ghostly issue—the moil of limbs and faces over our heads was supremely grotesque, Dantean in scope, yet the multiplicity of forms also put me in mind of the rococo ornamentation I had seen on the walls of a temple in Udaipur, only in this instance the ornaments were animated by some occult principle. Bursts of yellow-green light now flickered across the breadth of the sky.

I lowered Jane into the hole and jumped down after her. Communicating with shouts and gestures, Richmond demonstrated that the switches no longer functioned—we would have to break the rings in order to stop the machine. There proved to be insufficient room in the hole to swing the long-handled hammers with which he equipped us, and we were forced to climb back onto the roof, leaving Jane to do whatever she could with a smaller hammer.

We stood side by side, Richmond and I, and each blow we delivered against the rings of the attractor sent a huge bloom of radiance into the fog bank. The humming rose in pitch and melded with the roaring of the shadowy creature to create a singing rush. Our blows scarcely dented the metal, however, and so we concentrated our efforts on a single ring. I lost track of Christine, unable to spare her a glance, and swung the hammer until my shoulders and arms ached with strain. I had given up hope that our assault would produce a result, when without warning the attractor crumpled all along its length, as if squeezed by an enormous fist. I cried out in exultation—I had the urge to embrace Richmond and turned to him, but was enveloped in a burst of light and lifted up . . . lifted, I say, and not flung.

If this was an explosion, it was a most peculiar one. There was no concussion, no heat, no sound, and I felt buoyed up in that flickering, yellow-green space. On every side were the fragmentary beings I had formerly seen from beneath. Ghastly, semitranslucent faces bobbled and drifted away from me, some with ragged, immaterial bodies in tow, and it seemed I was passing among them, pushing upward through their closely massed numbers. They did not appear to register my intrusion. A profound calm blanketed my fear and I thought that I had become a ghost and that this calmness must be a natural protection that attended my sudden transition into the afterlife, a kind of emotional shield. Believing that I shared their fate, I studied the spirits nearest me, searching for signs of agony or distress. They were haggard and bore signs of ill-usage and disease, yet their expressions were uniformly neutral, conveying the idea that they had come to terms with death, something that fresher ghosts like Christine had not. I derived little comfort from this, speculating that I might spend decades in a desolate condition before achieving even a negligible measure of peace, and I clutched at the hope that I might still be alive and that my deathly surround was an illusion, a dream I was having as I lay unconscious atop the roof; but all that served was to rouse my discontent, causing me to struggle, to jostle the spirits around me, creating gaps amongst them. Through one such gap I spotted a dark shape that swiftly grew in size and definition—the shadowy creature, heading straight toward me. My capacity for fright had been suppressed and I did not panic, but I did renew my struggles and discovered the yellow-green radiance to have a viscous consistency that hampered movement. Yet the shadow moved through it easily, as if born to that medium . . . though its movement may not have been so facile. I saw that it was spinning ass over teakettle—slowly, mind you, with an ease and grace that caused me to think it had done this many times before. I estimated, judging by its path, that it might miss me, but it did not. As the thing tumbled by, a portion of it grazed my hip, or better said, passed through my hip. It failed to disrupt my course in the least—there was no painful collision—but I felt numbness spread from my hip down my left leg to the knee, and I had an overwhelming sense of joy that may have been the residue of that brief contact. Not a meat joy, not an emotion bred by pleasure or by appetites fulfilled, but a blissful feeling, an ecstasy I would associate with purity, the sort of thing saints claim to experience when communing with God. The joy soon dissipated, however, and with it went my calm. Terrified, I thrashed about, attempting to break free from whatever held me fast. I continued to struggle until the light abruptly dimmed to the ordinary darkness of a London rooftop and I fell.

When I regained consciousness, the fog had thinned to a mist through which I could see a salting of dim stars. Jane kneeled beside me, her face smeared with coal dust, streaked with tears. She could not tell me what had happened, having been down in the hole the entire time, but according to her, everything I had experienced had taken place in a matter of seconds. At length she helped me to stand. My leg was still numb, and I had aches and pain resulting from the fall, though I could not have fallen far, because nothing was broken. All of the attractors were twisted and crumpled, like shriveled silver weeds—since most of them had been shut down, I guessed that a wash of energy from the one we destroyed had resonated with some core element in the machinery of the other three. Richmond lay facedown in the dust a dozen feet away. I hobbled over to him, dropped to my hands and knees, and asked if he was all right. He stirred and made a feeble sound.

"Are you able to stand?" I asked.

He turned his head so that I could see his face—his eyes were closed, blood trickled from his nostrils, but his color was good, his pulse strong. I encouraged him, telling him that we had succeeded, but received no reply.

"Tell me what to do," I said. "Should I fetch Bladge to help me carry you?"

He yielded a throaty squeak and opened his eyes. They were Christine's eyes, hazel irises alive with agitated motion, twitching to the left, then to the right, like the dial of a combination lock that had jammed. All the muscles of his face were taut with strain, the tendons of his neck cabled. He sought to speak once again, making a horrid, guttering noise.

I recoiled, as did Jane, who had been peering over my shoulder. Richmond stared, though not at me—he was looking to my left at something that no longer existed in this world.

"Help him!" Jane reached out a hand to him, but withheld her touch. "Can you not help him as you helped me?"

I was loath to shake him, afraid that whatever injuries he had suffered might be affected; but I felt I had to try, although I knew to my soul that Christine had finally recognized her brother, and now that they were reunited, for better or worse, they would never be parted again.

A WEEK AFTER the events I have related, the body of Sir Charles Mellor was discovered on a mud flat alongside the Thames. The corpse was badly decomposed, and this made it impossible to determine the date of death; but it was obvious that he had been dead for quite some time, and there can be no doubt whatsoever as to the cause: seventeen stab wounds to his neck and torso. His murderer has never been brought to the bar, but I am persuaded to believe that Richmond, half mad and desperate to avenge Christine, acted upon the information I provided, woefully insufficient though it was. I imagine anyone of Mellor's class and character would have suited his purpose and assuaged his guilt.

Shortly before I abandoned the house on Rose Street and returned to Wales, I visited Richmond in Broadmoor, where he was being held preparatory to his transfer to a private facility—the costs of this transfer and all subsequent costs to be assumed by Jane and Dorothea, the chief beneficiaries of his will. An orderly led him into the office where I waited, one belonging to a Dr. Theodore McGuigan, a harried, portly man with a Glaswegian accent, wearing a white smock and braces. When the door opened to admit Richmond, I heard demented laugher and shouts and a scream from off along the corridor. He stood blinking and disheveled, unmindful of my presence . . . of any presence, it appeared. His condition, as far as I could tell, was unchanged, except that his beard was untrimmed and food stains decorated his shirtfront. I asked McGuigan if I might have a moment alone with Richmond, and once the door closed behind him, I perched on the edge of his desk. Richmond stood downcast at the center of the room, his eyes hooded, one hand plucking fitfully at his trouser leg.

"I've had a while to think about things," I said. "Had I been less self-involved, I might have understood what happened long before now. But I believe I've finally pieced it together."

Richmond's mouth worked, making a glutinous noise.

"That first night when you said that you wanted to learn who funded Christine . . . that was all you wanted to know, wasn't it? You knew who had murdered her. You were simply looking for a way to shift the blame for her death onto the shoulders of another guilty soul."

He rubbed the knuckle of his forefinger against his hip.

"You were the masked client. That's why Christine responded to him as she did to no other man. She may have had some instinctual knowledge that you were the client. And then one night the mask slipped, or else you revealed yourself. What happened next? Did she reject you? Did she threaten you? You've told me she was the aggressor, but you've lied about so much, I wonder if that was just another lie."

He shifted his weight from one leg to the other.

"Everything you did, all your attempts to bring her back . . . they were by way of expiation. She did something to infuriate you and you killed her."

He remained unresponsive.

"Isn't that right, Christine?"

With a laborious movement, he lifted his head and stared at me with those strangely animated eyes, eyes alive with dartings and glints of light—it was like looking through a crystal into the depths of an inferno, and I tried to imagine what he felt trapped in that terrible place. I had thought I would have no pity for him, but I was wrong. His facial muscles strained, his lips trembled, and a feeble fluting of indrawn breath issued from his throat. Then his head drooped, and once again he appeared oblivious to his surround.

That, I realized, was likely as close to an answer as I would receive and, seeing no point in prolonging this one-sided dialogue, I called in the orderly, who led him back to his cell, there to continue an internal dialogue with his sister.

As he escorted me to the entrance, a short walk attended by the cries and pleadings of the deranged, Dr. McGuigan said, "I'm told that Richmond was engaged in important work."

"Indeed, he was. But I fear it may never be re-created," I said. "His machines were destroyed and his notes have gone missing."

"What a pity. He was a brilliant man."

We went a few paces in silence and then McGuigan said, "You were there, weren't you? On the night he was stricken. Can you enlighten me as to what happened?"

"I was in another portion of the house."

We approached the door and McGuigan spoke again. "Tell me," he said. "What do you think caused the abnormalities in his eyes?"

"I can be of no assistance to you there," I said. "I know nothing about them."

I DID NOT lie to Dr. McGuigan—I know nothing except that I know nothing. It may be that I am like all men in this, yet it seems they are unaware of their condition and thus act with an authority of which I am no longer capable. Everything in my story is subject to doubt, to words such as "perhaps" and "likely," and since that story is central to my life, I have grown to doubt most of the certainties of my existence.

Jane and I were married in May of the year, and that same summer I opened a clinic in Swansea where I treat the disadvantaged; yet I do so absent the enthusiasm that once I had for the task. I doubt the worth of charity and justice, those values that underscore the work, and find it difficult to reconcile the conviction needed to perform my duties with my loss of faith in the good.

Over the ensuing six years I have taken to writing fiction. Using details gathered during my months on Rose Street, I have gained a wide readership for my ghost stories, which are written with an excess of detachment yet are often praised for their passionate expression. However, the true function of these fictions is self-examination, the same as when I peer into mirrors, looking for shadows in my eyes, afraid that my encounter with that darkness in the cloud of ghosts has infected me and is—despite its apparent state of bliss—responsible for my despairing outlook. Sometimes I remove Richmond's notebooks from the hidden drawer in my desk and go through page after page of equations and technical gibberish, as indecipherable as hieroglyphs, hoping they will magically spark some insight into the essence of that darkness. The feeling of joy it transmitted when I brushed against it, so at odds with its terrible aspect . . . Was joy its natural state? Was that emotion a tool of the divine? Did it signal the opening of a portal into heaven or was it the lure of a devil? Did it offer a sweet oblivion to the revenants of Saint Nichol, a state counterfeited by Richmond's attractors, which instead acted to destroy them? That might explain why they flocked to the rooftop, and it might explain as well why Christine did not hide from it—I may have misinterpreted her presence on the roof. I suspect if I could fathom that mystery, I would understand everything. Perhaps we are all of us either attractors searching for ghosts upon which to feed or ghosts seeking oblivion. And perhaps the salient difference between the spirit world and this one is that here we can be both.

Jane is the single truth in my life, its sole constant. I have no reason to mistrust her affections, yet I often construct scenarios that paint our marriage as the endgame of an elaborate hoax. When I tell her about them (I tell her everything), she is amused and chides me for being so dismal. For instance, the other day, a sunny day with a salt breeze, as we walked in the green hills above the beach at Pwll Du, she responded to my latest fabrication by saying, "I had to labor at it, else you might have escaped my clutches." She glanced at me with mischief in her eyes and said, "Seducing you was no easy task."

"As I remember, it was I who seduced you."

"Oh, please!" She gave me a pitying look. "After you rejected me that first night, we stayed up all hours, Dorothea and I, plotting your downfall."

"You consulted with Dorothea?"

"It was her idea that I dress as I did on the following night. She thought if I wore matronly bedclothes it might put you at ease. And she lent me her robe. You may recall that it fit me rather snugly."

"The crinoline bonnet," I said. "That almost put me off."

"Yes, I suppose that was a bit much. We debated whether or not to employ it."

"Why did you . . . ?" I left the question unstated, but she finished it for me.

"Why did I seduce you?"

I nodded.

"Because you were beautiful," she said. "Because you were sweet . . . and kind."

"Beautiful, perhaps," I said, and smiled. "But these days I don't feel especially kind or sweet."

"You're still the man I fell in love with."

"Not so naïve as that man, perhaps."

She blocked my path, preventing me from walking onward. "You're getting better, Samuel. You may not recognize it, but . . ."

"I don't," I said.

"I wish I'd undergone what you did on the rooftop that night. If I could understand what you went through, I might be able to help you more efficiently."

"I can't understand it myself. It didn't seem like much of anything . . . at least in retrospect. A few seconds of fear, a few seconds when I was unafraid. But it's been six years and everywhere I put my eyes, I see disease, poverty, corruption, things I once wanted to remedy, but now I no longer can . . . I don't know."

"The world is not a happy place. That won't change. But you can. You have! You *are* getting better."

We started walking again.

"You're more vigorous, you're working longer hours." She worried her lower lip. "I think you should give Jeffrey's notebooks to someone. It can't be beneficial to pore over them night after night."

"If I could decipher them and remove the material relating to the attraction of ghosts, I would. That information would surely be exploited."

"Burn them, then. Or give them to me. I'll put them somewhere safe. You need to divest yourself of the past . . . that portion of it, anyway."

We had reached a spot overlooking a strip of white beach guarded at both ends by enormous boulders. The blue sea stretched tranquil and vast to the horizon, and the cloudless sky, a lighter blue, empty of birds, echoed that tranquility. Nothing seemed to move, yet I felt a vibration in the earth and air that signaled the movement of all things, the flux of atoms and the drift of unknown spheres. An emotion swelled in my breast, nourished by that fundamental vista, and I felt, as I had not in years, capable of belief, of hope, of seeing beyond myself. Jane linked her arm through mine and rested her head against my shoulder and whispered something that the wind bore away. And for that moment, for those minutes atop the hill, we were as happy as the unhappiness of the world permits.

Afterword to "Rose Street Attractors"

"Rose Street Attractors" springs from the idea of ghosts as emotionally charged fragments that are left behind at death, and the corresponding thought that these fragments might be somehow isolated or captured and then studied. It also has its roots in my lifelong fascination with the nature of obsession.

—LUCIUS SHEPARD

Laird Barron

Laird Barron is the author of *The Imago Sequence & Other Stories*, winner of the Shirley Jackson Award for best collection, and a second book of stories, *Occultation*. His work has appeared in places such as *The Magazine of Fantasy & Science Fiction, Inferno: New Tales of Terror and the Supernatural, Lovecraft Unbound, Black Wings: New Tales of Lovecraftian Horror, Clockwork Phoenix,* and *The Del Rey Book of Science Fiction and Fantasy*. It has also been reprinted in numerous year's best anthologies and nominated for multiple honors, including the World Fantasy, Sturgeon, and Crawford Awards. Barron resides in Washington State.

LAIRD BARRON

Blackwood's Baby

LATE AFTERNOON SUN baked the clay and plaster buildings of the town. Its dirt streets lay empty, packed as hard as iron. The boardinghouse sweltered. Luke Honey sat in a chair in the shadows across from the window. Nothing stirred except flies buzzing on the window ledge. The window was a gap bracketed by warped shutters, and it opened into a portal view of the blazing white stone wall of the cantina across the alley. Since the fistfight he wasn't welcome in the cantina, although he'd seen the other three men he'd fought there each afternoon, drunk and laughing. The scabs on his knuckles were nearly healed. Every two days, one of the stock boys brought him a bottle.

Today, Luke Honey was drinking good strong Irish whiskey. His hands were clammy and his shirt stuck to his back and armpits. A cockroach scuttled into the long shadow of the bottle and waited. An overhead fan hung motionless. Clerk Galtero leaned on the counter and read a newspaper gone brittle as ancient papyrus, its fiber sucked dry by the heat; a glass of cloudy water pinned the corner. Clerk Galtero's bald skull shone in the gloom, and his mustache drooped, sweat dripping from the tips and onto the paper. The clerk was from Barcelona, and Luke Honey heard the fellow had served in the French Foreign Legion on the Macedonian Front during the Great War, and that he'd been clipped in the arm and that was why it curled tight and useless against his ribs.

A boy entered the house. He was black and covered with the yellow dust that settled upon everything in this place. He wore a uniform of some kind, and a cap with a narrow brim, and no shoes. Luke Honey guessed his age at eleven or twelve, although his face was worn, the flesh creased around his mouth, and his eyes suggested sullen apathy born of wisdom. Here, on the edge of a wasteland, even the children appeared weathered and aged. Perhaps that was how he himself appeared now that he'd lived on the plains and in the jungles for seven years. Perhaps the land had chiseled and filed him down too. He didn't know because he seldom glanced at the mirror anymore. On the other hand, there were some, such as a Boer and another renowned hunter from Canada Luke Honey had accompanied on many safaris, who seemed stronger, more vibrant with each passing season, as if the dust and the heat, the cloying jungle rot and the blood they spilled fed them, bred into them a savage vitality.

The boy handed him a telegram in a stiff white envelope with fingerprints all over it. Luke Honey gave him a fifty-cent piece and the boy left. Luke Honey tossed the envelope on the table. He struck a match with his thumbnail and lighted a cigarette. The light coming through the window began to thicken. Orange shadows tinged black slid across the wall of the cantina. He poured a glass of whiskey and drank it in a gulp. He poured another and set it aside. The cockroach fled under the edge of the table.

Two women descended the stairs. White women, perhaps English, certainly foreign travelers. They wore heavy Victorian dresses, equally staid bonnets, and sheer veils. The younger of the pair inclined her head toward Luke Honey as she passed. Her lips were thinned in disapproval. She and her companion opened the door and walked though its rectangle of shimmering brilliance into the furnace. The door swung shut.

Clerk Galtero folded the newspaper and placed it under the counter. He tipped his glass toward Luke Honey in a sardonic toast. "The ladies complained about you. You make noise in your room at night, the younger one says. You cry out, like a man in delirium. The walls are thin and she cannot sleep, so she complains to me."

"Oh. Is the other one deaf, then?" Luke Honey smoked his cigarette with the corner of his mouth. He sliced open the envelope with a pocketknife and unfolded the telegram and read its contents. The letter was an invitation from one Mr. Liam Welloc Esquire to take part in an annual private hunt in Washington State. The hunt occurred on remote ancestral property, its guests designated by some arcane combination of pedigree and long-standing associations with the host, or by virtue of notoriety in hunting circles. The telegram chilled the sweat trickling down his face. Luke Honey was not a particularly superstitious man; nonetheless, this missive called with an eerie intimacy and struck a chord deep within him, awakened an instinctive dread that fate beckoned across the years, the bloody plains and darkened seas, to claim him.

He stuck the telegram into his shirt pocket, then drank his whiskey. He poured another shot and lighted another cigarette and stared at the window. The light darkened to purple and the wall faded, was almost invisible. "I have nightmares. Give the ladies my apologies." He'd lived in the boardinghouse for three weeks, and this was the second time he and Clerk Galtero had exchanged more than a word in passing. Galtero's brother Enrique managed the place in the evening. Luke Honey hadn't spoken to him much either. After years in the wilderness, he usually talked to himself.

Clerk Galtero spilled the dregs of water on the floor and walked over with his queer, hitching step and poured the glass full of Luke Honey's whiskey. He sat in one of the rickety chairs. His good arm lay atop the table. His hand and arm were thickly muscled. The Legion tattoos had begun to elongate as his flesh loosened. "I know you," he said. "I've heard talk. I've seen your guns. Most of the foreign hunters wear trophies. Your friends, the other Americans, wear teeth and claws from their kills."

"We aren't friends."

"Your associates. I wonder, though, why you have come and why you stay."

"I'm done with the bush. That's all."

"This place is not so good for a man such as yourself. There is only trouble for you here."

Luke Honey smiled wryly. "Oh, you think I've gone native."

"Not at all. I doubt you get along with anyone."

"I'll be leaving soon." Luke Honey touched the paper in his pocket. "For the States. I suppose your customers will finally have some peace."

They finished their drinks and sat in silence. When it became dark, Clerk Galtero rose and went about lighting the lamps. Luke Honey climbed the stairs to his stifling room. He lay sweating on the bed and dreamed of his brother Michael, as he had for six nights running. The next morning, he arranged for transportation to the coast. Three days later he was aboard a cargo plane bound for Morocco. Following Morocco there would be ships and trains until he eventually stood again on American soil after half a lifetime. Meanwhile, he looked out the tiny window. The plains slowly disappeared in the red haze of the rim of the earth.

LUKE HONEY AND his party arrived at the lodge not long before dark. They'd come in two cars, and the staff earned its keep transferring the mountain of bags and steamer trunks indoors before the storm broadsided the valley. Lightning sizzled from the vast snout of fast-approaching

purple-black clouds. Thunder growled. A rising breeze plucked leaves from
the treetops. Luke Honey leaned against a marble colonnade and smoked a
cigarette, personal luggage stacked neatly at his side. He disliked trusting
his rifles and knives to bellhops and porters.

The Black Ram Lodge towered above a lightly wooded hillside overlooking Olde Towne. The lodge and its town lay in the folds of Ransom
Hollow, separated from the lights of Seattle by miles of dirt road and for-
ested hills. "Backward country," one of the men had called it during the
long drive. Luke Honey rode with the Brits Bullard and Wesley. They'd
shared a flask of brandy while the car left the lowlands and climbed
toward the mountains, passing small, quaint townships and ramshackle
farms tenanted by sober yeoman folk. Wesley and Bullard snickered like
a pair of itinerant knights at the potato pickers in filthy motley, bowed
to their labor in dark, muddy fields. Luke Honey didn't share the mirth.
He'd seen enough bloody peasant revolts to know better. He knew also
that fine cars and carriages, horses and guns, the gloss of their own pale
skin, cursed them with a false sense of well-being, of safety. He'd removed
a bullet from his pocket. The bullet was made for a buffalo gun and it was
large. He'd turned it over in his fingers and stared out the window without
speaking again.

After supper, Dr. Landscomb and Mr. Liam Welloc, coproprietors of
the lodge, entertained the small group of far-flung travelers who'd come for
the annual hunt. Servants lighted a fire in the hearth, and the eight gentlemen settled into grand oversized chairs. The parlor was a dramatic landscape of marble statuary and massive bookshelves, stuffed and mounted
heads of ferocious exotic beasts, liquor cabinets, and a pair of billiard
tables. Rain and wind hammered the windows. Lights flickered dangerously, promising a rustic evening of candlelight and kerosene lamps.

The assembly was supremely merry when the tale-telling began.

"We were in Mexico," Lord Bullard said. Lord Bullard hailed from
Essex; he was a decorated former officer in the Queen's Royal Lancers
who'd fought briefly in the Boer War, but had done most of his time paci-
fying the "wogs" in the Punjab. Apparently his family was enormously
wealthy in lands and titles, and these days he traveled to the exclusion of
all else. He puffed on his cigar while a servant held the flame of a long-
handled match steady. "Summer of 1919. Some industrialist friends of
mine were vacationing from Europe. Moaning and sulking about the shut-
downs of their munitions factories and the like. Beastly boring."

"Quite, I'm sure," Dr. Landscomb said. The doctor was tall and thin.
He possessed the ascetic bearing of Eastern European royalty. He had

earned his degree in medicine at Harvard and owned at least a quarter of everything there was to own within two counties.

"Ah, the cessation of hostilities is ever a trying time for the makers of bombs and guns," Mr. Liam Welloc said. He too was tall, but thick and broad with the neck and hands of the ancient Greek statues of Herakles. His hair and beard were bronze and lush for a man his age. His family owned half again what the Landscombs did and reportedly maintained ancestral estates in England and France. "One should think the opportunity to beat swords to plowshares would open whole new realms of entrepreneurial delights."

"Exactly. It's a lack of imagination," Mr. Williams said. A bluff, weather-beaten rancher baron attired in Stetson boots, corduroys and impressive buckle, a starched shirt with ivory buttons, and an immaculate Stetson hat. He drank Jack Daniel's, kept the bottle on a dais at his side. He'd come from Texas with Mr. McEvoy and Mr. Briggs. McEvoy and Briggs were far more buttoned down in Brooks Brothers suits and bowlers; a banker and mine owner, respectively. Williams drained his whiskey and poured another, waving off the ever-hovering servant. "That's what's killing you boys. No diversity, no imagination. Trapped in the 1800s. Can't run an empire without a little imagination."

"Germany is sharpening its knives," Mr. Briggs said. "Your friends will be cranking up the assembly lines inside of five years. Trust me. They've the taste for blood, those Krauts. You can't beat that outta them. My mistress is Bavarian, so I know."

Lord Bullard thumped his cigar in the elegant pot near his foot. He cleared his throat. "Harrumph. Mexico City, 1919. Bloody hot. Miasma, thick and gray from smokestacks and chimneys of all those hovels they heap like ruddy anthills."

"The smog reminded me of home," Mr. Wesley said. Wesley was dressed in a heavy linen coat, and his boots were polished to a high gloss. His hair was slick and parted at the middle, and it shone in the firelight. When Luke Honey looked at him, he thought *Mr. Weasel.*

"A Mexican prince invited us to a hunt on his estate. He was conducting business in the city, so we laid over at his villa. Had a jolly time."

Mr. Wesley said, "Tubs of booze and a veritable harem of randy strumpets. What was not to like? I was sorry when we departed for the countryside."

"Who was it, Wes, you, me, and the chap from York . . . Cantwell? Cotter?"

"Cantwell."

"Yes, right then. The three of us were exhausted and chafed beyond bearing from frantic revels at the good prince's demesne, so we ventured into the streets to seek new pleasures."

"Which, ironically, constituted the pursuit of more liquor and fresh strumpets."

"On the way from one particularly unsavory cantina to another, we were accosted by a ragtag individual who leaped at us from some occulted nook in an alley. This person was of singularly dreadful countenance; wan and emaciated, afflicted by wasting disease and privation. He smelled like the innards of a rotting sheep carcass, and his appearance was most unwelcome. However, he wheedled and beseeched my attention, in passable English, I must add, and clung to my sleeve with such fervor it soon became apparent the only way to rid myself of his attention was to hear him out."

"We were confounded upon learning this wretch was an expatriate American," Mr. Wesley said.

"Thunderstruck!"

"Ye gods," Dr. Landscomb said. "This tale bears the trappings of a penny dreadful. More, more, gentlemen!"

"The man's name was Harris. He'd once done columns for some paper and visited Mexico to conduct research for a story he never got around to writing. The entire tale of his fall from grace is long and sordid. It's enough to say he entered the company of disreputable characters and took to wickedness and vice. The chap was plainly overjoyed to encounter fellow speakers of English, but we soon learned there was much more to this encounter than mere chance. He knew our names, where we intended to hunt, and other details I've put aside."

"It was uncanny," Mr. Wesley said.

"The man was obviously a grifter," Luke Honey said from his spot near the hearth where he'd been lazing with his eyes mostly shut and thinking that the pair of Brits were entirely too smug, especially Lord Bullard with his gold-rimmed monocle and cavalry saber. "A spy. Did he invite you to a séance? To predict your fortune with a handful of runes?"

"In fact, he did inveigle us to join him in a smoky den of cutthroats and thieves where this ancient crone read the entrails of chickens like the pagans read Tarot cards. It was she who sent him into the streets to track us." Lord Bullard fixed Luke Honey with a bloodshot stare. "Mock as you will, it was a rare experience."

Luke Honey chuckled and closed his eyes again. "I wouldn't dream of mocking you. The Romans swore by the custom of gutting pigeons. Who am I to argue?"

"Who indeed? The crone scrabbled in the guts, muttering to herself while Harris crouched at her side and translated. He claimed the hag had dreamed of our arrival in the city for some time and that these visions were driving her to aggravation. She described a 'black cloud' obscuring the future. There was trouble awaiting us, and soon. Something about a cave. We all laughed, of course, just as you did, Mr. Luke Honey." Lord Bullard smiled a wry, wan smile that accentuated the creases of his face, his hangdog mouth. "Eventually, we extricated ourselves and made for the nearest taproom and forgot the whole incident. The prince returned from his business and escorted us in style to a lavish estate deep in the central region of the country. Twelve of us gathered to feast at his table, and in the morning he released boars into the woods."

"Twelve, you say?" Mr. Williams said, brows disappearing under his big hat. "Well, sir, I hope one of you boys got a picture to commemorate the occasion."

"I need another belt to fortify myself in the face of this heckling," Lord Bullard said, snapping his fingers as the servant rushed over to fill his glass. The Englishman drained his glass and wagged his head for another. "To the point then: we shot two boars and wounded another—the largest of them. A prize pig, that one, with tusks like bayonets and the smoothest, blackest hide. Cantwell winged the brute, but the boar escaped and we were forced to spend the better part of two days tracking it through a benighted jungle. The blood trail disappeared into a mountain honeycombed with caves. Naturally, honor dictates pursuing wounded quarry and dispatching it. Alas, a brief discussion with the prince and his guides convinced us of the folly of descending into the caverns. The system extended for many miles and was largely uncharted. No one of any sense attempted to navigate them. We determined to return home, satisfied with the smaller boars."

"Eh, the great white hunters balked at the precipice of the unknown?" Luke Honey said. "Thank God Cabot and Drake couldn't see you fellows quailing in the face of fear."

Lord Bullard spluttered and Mr. Wesley rose quickly, hand on the large ornamented pistol he wore holstered under his coat. He said, "I demand satisfaction!" His smile was sharp and vicious, and Luke Honey had little doubt the man yearned for moments such as these.

Dr. Landscomb smoothly interposed himself, arms spread in a placating manner. "Gentlemen, gentlemen! This isn't the Wild West. There'll be no dueling on these premises. Mr. Wesley, you're among friends. Please, relax and have another drink. Mr. Luke Honey, as for you, perhaps a bit of moderation is in order."

"You may be correct," Luke Honey said, casually sliding his revolver back into his shoulder holster. He looked at Mr. Williams, who nodded approvingly and handed him the rapidly diminishing bottle of Jack Daniel's. Luke Honey took a long pull while staring at Mr. Wesley.

Mr. Wesley sat, folding himself into the chair with lethal grace, but continued to smile through small, crooked teeth. "Go on, Arthur. You were getting to the good part."

Lord Bullard wiped his red face with a handkerchief. His voice scarcely above a mutter, he said, "An American named Henderson had other ideas and he convinced two Austrians to accompany him into the caves while the rest of us made camp for the night. The poor fools slipped away and were gone for at least an hour before the rest of us realized what they'd done. We never saw any of them again. There was a rescue mission. The Mexican Army deployed a squadron of expertly trained and equipped mountaineers to investigate, but hard rains came and the tunnels were treacherous, full of rockslides and floodwater. It would've been suicide to persist, and so our comrades were abandoned to their fates. This became a local legend, and I've reports of peasants who claim to hear men screaming from the caves on certain lonely nights directly before a storm."

The men sat in uncomfortable silence while the windows rattled and wind moaned in the flue. Mr. Liam Welloc eventually stood and went to a bookcase. He retrieved a slim, leather-bound volume and stood before the hearth, book balanced in one hand, a crystal goblet of liquor in the other. "As you may or may not know, Ian's grandfather and mine were among the founders of this town. Most of the early families arrived here from places like New York and Boston, and a few from California when they discovered the golden state not quite to their taste. The Black Ram itself has gone through several incarnations since it was built as a trading post by a merchant named Caldwell Ellis in 1860 on the eve of that nasty business between the Blue and the Gray. My grandfather purchased this property in 1890 and renovated it as the summer home for himself and his new bride, Felicia. Much of this probably isn't of much interest to you, so I'll not blather on about the trials and tribulations of my forebears, nor how this grand house became a lodge. For now, let me welcome you into our most sacred tradition, and we wish each of you good fortune on the morrow."

Dr. Landscomb said, "I concur. As you know, there are plenty of boar and deer on this preserve, but assuredly you've come for the great stag known as Blackwood's Baby—"

"Wot, wot?" Mr. Wesley said in mock surprise. "We're not here for the namesake of this fine establishment? What of the Black Ram?"

Mr. Liam Welloc smiled, and to Luke Honey's mind there was something cold and sinister in the man's expression. Mr. Liam Welloc said, "There was never a black ram. It's a euphemism for . . . well, that's a story for another evening."

Dr. Landscomb cleared his throat politely. "As I said—the stag is a mighty specimen—surely the equal of any beast you've hunted. He is the king of the wood and descended from a venerable line. I will note that while occasionally cornered, none of these beasts has ever been taken. In any event, the man who kills the stag shall claim my great-grandfather's Sharps model 1851 as a prize. The rifle was custom built for Constantine Landscomb III by Christian Sharps himself and is nearly priceless. The victorious fellow shall also perforce earn a place among the hallowed ranks of elite gamesmen the world over."

"And ten thousand dollars, sterling silver," Mr. Wesley said, rubbing his hands together.

"Amen, partner!" Mr. McEvoy said. "Who needs another round?"

It was quite late when the men said their good nights and retired.

THE RAIN SLACKENED to drizzle. Luke Honey lay with his eyes open, listening to it rasp against the window. He'd dreamed of Africa, then of his dead brother Michael toiling in the fields of their home in Ingram, just over the pass through the Cascades. His little brother turned to him and waved. His left eye was a hole. Luke Honey had awakened with sick fear in his heart.

While the sky was still dark he dressed and walked downstairs and outside to the barn. The barn lay across the muddy drive from the lodge. Inside, stable hands drifted through the silty gloom preparing dogs and horses for the day ahead. He breathed in the musk of brutish sweat and green manure, gun oil and oiled leather, the evil stink of dogs swaggering in anticipation of murder. He lighted a cigarette and smoked it leaning against a rail while the air brightened from black to gray.

"There you are, mate." Mr. Wesley stepped into the barn and walked toward Luke Honey. He wore workmanlike breeches, a simple shirt, and a bowler. He briskly rolled his sleeves.

Luke Honey didn't see a gun, although Mr. Wesley had a large knife slung low on his hip. He smiled and tapped the brim of his hat and then tried to put out the Brit's eye with a flick of his flaming cigarette. Mr. Wesley flinched, forearms raised, palms inverted, old London prizefighter style, and Luke Honey made a fist and struck him in the ribs below the heart, and followed that with a clubbing blow to the side of his neck. Mr. Wesley was stouter than he appeared. He shrugged and trapped Luke Honey's lead arm in the crook of his elbow and butted him in the jaw. Luke Honey wrenched his arm loose and swiped his fingers at Mr. Wesley's mouth, hoping to fishhook him, and tried to catch his balance on the rail with his off hand. Rotten wood gave way, and he dropped to his hands and knees. Light began to slide back and forth in the sky as if he'd plunged his head into a water trough. Mr. Wesley slammed his shin across Luke Honey's chest, flipping him onto his back like a turtle. He sprawled in the wet straw, mouth agape, struggling for air, his mind filled with snow.

"Well. That's it, then." Mr. Wesley stood over him for a moment, face shiny, slick hair in disarray. He bent and scooped up his bowler, scuffed it against his pants leg, and smiled at Luke Honey. He clapped the bowler onto his head and limped off.

"Should I call a doctor, kid?" Mr. Williams struck a match on the heel of his boot, momentarily burning away shadows around his perch on a hay bale. A couple of the stable hands had stopped to gawk, and they jolted from their reverie and rushed to quiet the agitated mastiffs that whined and growled and strutted in their pens.

"No, he's okay," Luke Honey said when he could. "Me, I'm going to rest here a bit."

Mr. Williams chuckled. He smoked his cigarette and walked over to Luke Honey and looked down at him with a bemused squint. "Boy, what you got against them limeys anyway?"

The left side of Luke Honey's face was already swollen. Drawing breath caused flames to lick in his chest. "My grandfather chopped cotton. My father picked potatoes."

"Not you, though."

"Nope," Luke Honey said. "Not me."

THE LORD OF the stables was named Scobie, a gaunt and gnarled Welshman whose cunning and guile with dogs and horses, and traps and snares, had elevated him to the status of a peasant prince. He dressed in stained and weathered leather garments from some dim medieval era, and his thin hair bloomed in a white cloud. Dirt ingrained his hands and nails, and when he smiled, his remaining teeth were sharp and crooked. His father had been a master falconer, but the modern hunt didn't call for birds anymore.

The dogs and the dog handlers went first, and the rest of the party entered the woods an hour later. Luke Honey accompanied the Texans and

Mr. Liam Welloc. They rode light, tough horses. Mr. McEvoy commented on the relative slightness of the horses, and Mr. Welloc explained that the animals were bred for endurance and agility.

The forest spread around them like a cavern. Well-beaten trails criss-crossed through impenetrable underbrush and into milky dimness. Water dripped from branches. After a couple of hours, they stopped and had tea and biscuits prepared by earnest young men in lodge livery.

"Try some chaw," Mr. Briggs said. He cut a plug of tobacco and handed it to Luke Honey. Luke Honey disliked tobacco. He put it in his mouth and chewed. The Brits stood nearby in a cluster talking to Dr. Landscomb and Mr. Liam Welloc. Mr. Briggs said, "You in the war? You look too young."

"I was fifteen when we joined the dance. Just missed all that fun."

"Bully for you, as the limeys would say. You can shoot, I bet. Every-body here either has money or can shoot. Or both. No offense, but I don't have you pegged for a man of means. Nah, you remind me of some of the boys in my crew. Hard-bitten. A hell-raiser."

"I've done well enough, in fact."

"He's the *real* great white hunter," Mr. Williams said. "One of those fellers who shoots lions and elephants on the Dark Continent. Fortunes to be won in the ivory trade. That right, Mr. Honey?"

"Yeah. I was over there for a while."

"Huh, I suppose you have that look about you," Mr. Briggs said. "You led safaris?"

"I worked for the Dutch."

"Leave it be," Mr. Williams said. "The man's not a natural braggart."

"Where did you learn to hunt?" Mr. McEvoy said.

"My cousins. They all lived in the hills in Utah. One of them was a sniper during the war." Luke Honey spat tobacco into the leaves. "When my mother died, I went to live with my uncle and his family, and those folks have lots of kin in South Africa. After college I got a case of wander-lust. One thing led to another."

"Damned peculiar upbringing. College even."

"What kid doesn't dream of stalking the savanna?" Mr. Briggs said. "You must have a hundred and one tales."

"Surely, after that kind of experience, this trip must be rather tame," Mr. McEvoy said.

"Hear, hear," Mr. Briggs said. "Give up the ivory trade for a not-so-likely chance to bag some old stag in dull-as-dirt U.S.A.?"

"Ten thousand sterling silver buys a lot of wine and song, amigos," Mr. Williams said. "Besides, who says the kid's quit anything?"

"Well, sir, I *am* shut of the business."

"Why is that?" Mr. Briggs said.

Luke Honey wiped his mouth. "One fine day I was standing on a plain with the hottest sun you can imagine beating down. Me and some other men had set up a cross fire and plugged maybe thirty elephants from this enormous herd. The skinners got to work with their machetes and axes. Meanwhile, I got roaring drunk with the rest of the men. A newspaper flew in a photographer on a biplane. The photographer posed us next to a pile of tusks. The tusks were stacked like cordwood and there was blood and flies everywhere. I threw up during one of the pictures. The heat and the whiskey, I thought. They put me in a tent for a couple of days while a fever fastened to me. I ranted and raved, and they had to lash me down. You see, I thought the devil was hiding under my cot, that he was waiting to claim my soul. I dreamt my dear dead mother came and stood at the entrance of the tent. She had soft, magnificent wings folded against her back. White light surrounded her. The light was brilliant. Her face was dark and her eyes were fiery. She spat on the ground and the tent flaps flew shut and I was left alone in utter darkness. The company got me to a village where there was a real doctor who gave me quinine and I didn't quite die."

"Are you saying you quit the safaris because your mother might disapprove from her cloud in heaven?" Mr. Briggs said.

"Nope. I'm more worried she might be disapproving from an ice floe in hell."

IN THE AFTERNOON, Lord Bullard shot a medium buck that was cornered by Scobie's mastiff pack. Luke Honey and Mr. Williams reined in at a remove from the action. The killing went swiftly. The buck had been severely mauled prior to their arrival. Mr. Wesley dismounted and cut the animal's throat while the dogs sniffed around and pissed on the bushes.

"Not quite as glorious as ye olden days, eh?" Mr. Williams said. He took a manly gulp of whiskey from his flask and passed it to Luke Honey.

Luke Honey drank, relishing the dark fire coursing over his bloody teeth. "German nobles still use spears to hunt boars."

"I wager more than one of those ol' boys gets his manhood torn off on occasion."

"It happens." Luke Honey slapped his right thigh. "When I was younger and stupider, I was gored. Hit the bone. Luckily the boar was heart shot—stone dead when it stuck me so I didn't get ripped in two."

"Damn," Mr. Williams said.

Mr. Briggs and Mr. McEvoy stared at Luke Honey with something akin to religious awe. "Spears?" Mr. Briggs said. "Did you bring one?"

"Nope. A couple of rifles, my .45, and some knives. I travel light."

"I'm shocked the limeys put up with the lack of foot servants," Mr. Briggs said.

"I doubt any of us are capable of understanding you, Mr. Honey," Mr. Williams said. "I'm beginning to think you may be one of those rare mysteries of the world."

AN HOUR BEFORE dusk, Scobie and a grimy boy in suspenders and no shirt approached the hunters while they paused to smoke cigarettes, drink brandy, and water the horses.

Scobie said, "Arlen here came across sign of a large stag yonder a bit. Fair knocked the bark from trees with its antlers, right, boy?" The boy nodded and scowled as Scobie tousled his hair. "The boy has a keen eye. How long were the tracks?" The boy gestured, and Lord Bullard whistled in astonishment.

Mr. Williams snorted and fanned a circle with his hat to disperse a cloud of mosquitoes. "We're talking about a deer, not a damned buffalo."

Scobie shrugged. "Blackwood's Baby is twice the size of any buck you've set eyes on, I'll reckon."

"Pshaw!" Mr. Williams cut himself a plug and stuffed it into his mouth. He nudged his roan sideways, disengaging from the conversation.

"I say, let's have at this stag," Mr. Wesley said, to which Lord Bullard nodded.

"Damned tooting. I'd like a crack at the critter," Mr. Briggs said.

"The dogs are tired and it's late," Scobie said. "I've marked the trail, so we can find it easy tomorrow."

"Bloody hell!" Lord Bullard said. "We've light yet. I've paid my wage to nab this beastie, so I say lead on!"

"Easy, now," Mr. Welloc said. "Night's on us soon and these woods get very, very dark. Crashing about is foolhardy, and if Master Scobie says the dogs need rest, then best to heed his word."

Lord Bullard rolled his eyes. "What do you suggest, then?"

Scobie said, "Camp is set around the corner. We've got hunting shacks scattered along these trails. I'll kennel the hounds at one and meet you for another go at daybreak."

"A sensible plan," Mr. McEvoy said. As the shadows deepened and men and horses became smoky ghosts in the dying light, he'd begun to cast apprehensive glances over his shoulder.

Luke Honey had to admit there was a certain eeriness to the surroundings, a sense of inimical awareness that emanated from the depths of the forest. He noted how the horses flared their nostrils and shifted skittishly. There were boars and bears in this preserve, although he doubted any lurked within a mile after all the gunfire and barking. He'd experienced a similar sense of menace in Africa near the hidden den of a terrible lion, a dreaded man-eater. He rubbed his horse's neck and kept a close watch on the bushes.

Mr. Landscomb clasped Scobie's elbow. "Once you've seen to the animals, do leave them to the lads. I'd enjoy your presence after supper."

Scobie looked unhappy. He nodded curtly and left with the boy.

Camp was a fire pit centered between two boulders the size of carriages. A dilapidated lean-to provided a dry area to spread sleeping bags and hang clothes. Stable boys materialized to unsaddle the horses and tether them behind the shed. Lodge workers had ignited a bonfire and laid out a hot meal sent from the chef. This meal included the roasted heart and liver from the buck Lord Bullard brought down earlier.

"Not sure I'd tuck into those vittles," Mr. Williams said, waving his fork at Lord Bullard and Mr. Wesley. "Should let that meat cool a day or two, else you'll get the screamin' trots."

Mr. McEvoy stopped shoveling beans into his mouth to laugh. "That's right. Scarf enough of that liver and you'll think you caught dysentery."

Lord Bullard spooned a jellified chunk of liver into his mouth. "Bollocks. Thirty years afield in the muck and the mud with boot leather and ditch water for breakfast. My intestines are made of iron. Aye, Wes?"

"You've got the right of it," Mr. Wesley said, although sans his typical enthusiasm. He'd set aside his plate but half finished and now nursed a bottle of Laphroaig.

Luke Honey shucked his soaked jacket and breeches and warmed his toes by the fire with a plate of steak, potatoes, and black coffee. He cut the meat into tiny pieces because chewing was difficult. It pleased him to see Mr. Wesley favoring his own ribs whenever he laughed. The Englishman, doughty as he was, seemed rather sickly after a day's exertion. Luke Honey faintly hoped he had one foot in the grave.

A dank mist crept through the trees, and the men instinctively clutched blankets around themselves and huddled closer to the blaze, and Luke Honey saw that everyone kept a rifle or pistol close to hand. A wolf howled not too far off, and all eyes turned toward the darkness that pressed against the edges of firelight. The horses nickered softly.

Dr. Landscomb said, "Hark, my cue. The wood we now occupy is called Wolfvale, and it stretches some fifty miles north to south. If we traveled another twelve miles due east, we'd be in the foothills of the mountains. Wolfvale is, some say, a cursed forest. Of course, that reputation does much to draw visitors." Dr. Landscomb lighted a cigarette. "What do you think, Master Scobie?"

"The settlers considered this an evil place," Scobie said, emerging from the bushes much to the consternation of Mr. Briggs, who yelped and half drew his revolver. "No one logs this forest. No one hunts here except for the lords and foolish, desperate townies. People know not to come here because of the dangerous animals that roam. These days, it's the wild beasts, but in the early days, it was mostly Bill."

"Was Bill some rustic lunatic?" Mr. Briggs said.

"We Texans know the type," Mr. Williams said with a grin.

"Oh, no, sirs. Black Bill, Splayfoot Bill, he's the devil. He's Satan, and those who carved the town from the hills, and before them the trappers and fishermen, they believed he ruled these dark woods."

"The Indians believed it too," Mr. Welloc said. "I've talked with several of the elders, as did my grandfather with the tribal wise men of his era. The legend of Bill, whom they referred to as the Horned Man, is most ancient. I confess, some of my ancestors were a rather scandalous lot, given to dabbling in the occult and all matters mystical. The town library's archives are stuffed with treatises composed by the more adventurous founders, and myriad accounts by landholders and commoners alike regarding the weird phenomena prevalent in Ransom Hollow."

Scobie said, "Aye. Many a village child vanished, an' grown men an' women, too. When I was wee, my father brought us in by dusk an' barred the door tight until morning. Everyone did. Some still do."

Luke Honey said, "A peculiar arrangement for such a healthy community."

"Aye, Olde Towne seems robust," Lord Bullard said.

Dr. Landscomb said, "Those Who Work are tied to the land. A volcano won't drive them away when there's fish and fur, crops and timber to be had."

"Yeah, and you can toss sacrificial wretches into the volcano, too," Mr. McEvoy said.

"This hunt of ours goes back many years, long before the lodge itself was established. Without exception, someone is gravely injured, killed, or lost on these expeditions."

"Lost? What does 'lost' mean, precisely?" Mr. Wesley said.

"There are swamps and cliffs, and so forth," Dr. Landscomb said. "On occasion, men have wandered into the wilds and run afoul of such dangers. But to the point. Ephraim Blackwood settled in Olde Towne at the time of its founding. A widower with two grown sons, he was a furrier by trade. The Blackwoods ran an extensive trapline throughout Ransom Hollow, and within ten years of their arrival, they'd become the premier fur trading company in the entire valley. People whispered. Christianity has never gained an overwhelming mandate here, but the Blackwoods' irreligiousness went a step beyond the pale in the eyes of the locals. Inevitably, loose talk led to muttered accusations of witchcraft. Some alleged the family consorted with Splayfoot Bill, that they'd made a pact. Material wealth for their immortal souls."

"What else?" Mr. Williams said to uneasy chuckles.

"Yes, what else indeed?" Dr. Landscomb's smile faded. "It is said that Splayfoot Bill, the Old Man of the Wood, required most unholy indulgences in return for his favors."

"Do tell," Lord Bullard said with an expression of sickly fascination.

"The devil takes many forms, and it is said he is a being devoted to pain and pleasure. A Catholic priest visiting from the city gave an impromptu sermon in the town square, accusing the elder Blackwood of lying with the Old Man of the Wood, who assumed the form of a doe, one night by the pallor of a sickle moon, and the issue was a monstrous stag. Some hayseed wit soon dubbed this mythical beast 'Blackwood's Git.' Other, less savory colloquialisms sprang forth, but most eventually faded into obscurity. Nowadays, those who speak of this legend call the stag 'Blackwood's Baby.' Inevitably, the brute we shall pursue in the morn is reputed to be the selfsame animal."

"Sounds like that Blackwood fella came from Oklahoma," Mr. Williams said.

"Devil spawn!" Luke Honey said, and laughed sarcastically.

"Bloody preposterous," Lord Bullard said without conviction.

"Hogwash," Mr. Briggs said. "You're scarin' the women and children, hoss."

"My apologies, good sir," Dr. Landscomb said. He didn't look sorry to Luke Honey.

"Oh, dear." Lord Bullard lurched to his feet and made for the woods, hands to his belly.

The Texans guffawed and hooted, although the mood sobered when the wolf howled again and was answered by two more of its pack.

Mr. Williams scowled, cocked his big revolver, and fired into the air. The report was queerly muffled, and its echo died immediately.

"That'll learn 'em," Mr. Briggs said, exaggerating his drawl.

"Time for shut-eye, boys," Mr. Williams said. Shortly after, the men began to yawn and turned in, grumbling and joshing as they spread their blankets on the floor of the lean-to.

Luke Honey made a pillow of the horse blanket. He jacked the bolt action and chambered a round in his Mauser Gewehr 98, a rifle he'd won from an Austrian diplomat in Nairobi. The gun was powerful enough to stop most things that went on four legs, and it gave him comfort. He slept.

The mist swirled heavy as soup and the fire had dwindled to coals when he woke. Branches crackled, and a black shape, the girth of a bison or a full-grown rhino, moved between shadows. It stopped and twisted an incomprehensibly configured head to survey the camp. The beast huffed and continued into the brush. Luke Honey remained motionless, breath caught in his throat. The huff had sounded like a chuckle. And for an instant, the lush, shrill wheedle of panpipes drifted through the wood. Far out amid the folds of the savanna, a lion coughed. A hyena barked its lunatic bark, and much closer.

Luke Honey started and his eyes popped open, and he couldn't tell the world from the dream.

LORD BULLARD SPENT much of the predawn hours hunkered in the bushes, but by daybreak he'd pulled himself together, albeit white-faced and shaken. Mr. Wesley's condition, on the other hand, appeared to have worsened. He didn't speak during breakfast and sat like a lump, chin on his chest.

"Poor bastard looks like hell warmed over," Mr. Williams said. He was dressed in long johns and a gun belt. He sipped coffee from a tin cup. A cigarette fumed in his left hand. "You might've done him in."

Luke Honey rolled a cigarette and lighted it. He nodded. "I saw a fight in a hostel in Cape Town between a Scottish dragoon and a big Spaniard. The dragoon carried a rifle and gave the Spaniard a butt stroke to the midsection. The Spaniard laughed, drew his gun, and shot the Scot right through his head. The Spaniard died four days later. Bust a rib and it punctures the insides. Starts a bleed."

"He probably should call it a day."

"Landscomb's a sawbones. He isn't blind. Guess I'll leave it to him."

"Been hankerin' to ask you, friend—how did you end up on the list? This is a mighty exclusive event. My pappy knew the Lubbock Wellocs before I was born. Took me sixteen years to get an invite here. And a bribe or two."

"Lubbock Wellocs?"

"Yep. Wellocs are everywhere. More of them than you can shake a stick at—Nevada, Indiana, Massachusetts. Buncha foreign states too. Their granddads threw a wide loop, as my pappy used to say."

"My parents lived east of here. Over the mountains. Dad had some cousins in Ransom Hollow. They visited occasionally. I was a kid and I only heard bits and pieces . . . the men all got liquored up and told tall tales. I heard about the stag, decided I'd drill it when I got older."

"Here you are, sure enough. Why? I know you don't give a whit about the rifle. Or the money."

"How do you figure?"

"The look in your eyes, boy. You're afraid. A man like you is afraid, I take stock."

"I've known some fearless men. Hunted lions with them. A few of those gents forgot that Mother Nature is more of a killer than we humans will ever be and wound up getting chomped. She wants our blood, our bones, our goddamned guts. Fear is healthy."

"Sure as hell is. Except, there's something in you besides fear. Ain't that right? I swear you got the weird look some guys get who play with fire. I knew this vaquero who loved to ride his pony along the canyon edge. By close, I mean rocks crumbling under its hooves and falling into nothingness. I ask myself, what's here in these woods for you? Maybe I don't want any part of it."

"I reckon we all heard the same story about Mr. Blackwood. Same one my daddy and his cousins chewed over the fire."

"Sweet Jesus, boy. You don't believe that cartload of manure Welloc and his crony been shovelin'? Okay then. I've got a whopper for you. These paths form a miles-wide pattern if you see 'em from a plane. World's biggest pentagram carved out of the countryside. Hear that one?"

Luke Honey smiled dryly and crushed the butt of his cigarette underfoot.

Mr. Williams poured out the dregs of his coffee. He hooked his thumbs in his belt. "My uncle Greg came here for the hunt in '16. They sent him home in a fancy box. The Black Ram Lodge is first class all the way."

"Stag get him?"

The rancher threw back his head and laughed. He grabbed Luke Honey's arm. There were tears in his eyes. "Oh, you are a card, kid. You really do buy into that mumbo-jumbo horse pucky. Greg spotted a huge buck moving through the woods and tried to plug it from the saddle. His horse threw him and he split his head on a rock. Damned fool."

"In other words, the stag got him."

Mr. Williams squeezed Luke Honey's shoulder. Then he slackened his grip and laughed again. "Yeah, maybe you're onto something. My pappy liked to say this family is cursed. We sure had our share of untimely deaths."

The party split again, Dr. Landscomb and the British following Scobie and the dogs; Mr. Welloc, Luke Honey, and the Texans proceeding along a parallel trail. Nobody was interested in the lesser game; all were intent upon tracking down Blackwood's Baby.

They entered the deepest, darkest part of the forest. The trees were huge and ribboned with moss and creepers and fungi. Scant light penetrated the canopy, yet brambles hemmed the path. The fog persisted.

Luke Honey had been an avid reader since childhood. Robert Louis Stevenson, M. R. James, and Ambrose Bierce had gotten him through many a miserable night in the tarpaper shack his father built. He thought of the fairy-tale books at his aunt's house. Musty books with wooden covers and woodblock illustrations that raised the hair on his head. The evil stepmother made to dance in red-hot iron shoes at Snow White's garden wedding while the dwarves hunched like fiends. Hansel and Gretel lost in a vast, endless wood, the eyes of a thousand demons glittering in the shadows. The forest in the book was not so different from the one he found himself riding through.

At noon, they stopped to take a cold lunch from their own saddlebags, as this was beyond the range of the lodge staff. Arlen trotted from the forest, dodgy and feral as a fox, to report Scobie had picked up the trail and was hoping to soon drive the stag itself from hiding. Dr. Landscomb and the British were in hot pursuit.

"Damn," Mr. Williams said.

"Aw, now that limey's going to do the honors," Mr. Briggs said. "I wanted that rifle."

"Everybody wants that rifle," Mr. McEvoy said.

Mr. Williams clapped his hands together. "Let's mount up, *hombres*. Maybe we'll get lucky and our friends will miss their opening."

"The quarry is elusive," Mr. Liam Welloc said. "Anything is possible."

The men kicked their ponies to a brisk trot and gave chase.

* * *

AN HOUR LATER, all hell broke loose.

The path crossed a plank bridge and continued upstream along the cut bank of a fast-moving stream. Dogs barked and howled, and the shouts of men echoed from the trees. A heavy rifle boomed twice. No sooner had Luke Honey and his companions entered a large clearing with a lagoon fed by a waterfall did he spy Lord Bullard and Mr. Wesley afoot, rifles aimed at the trees. Dr. Landscomb stood to one side, hands tight on the bridle of his pony. Dead and dying dogs were strewn everywhere. A pair of surviving mastiffs yapped and snarled, muzzles slathered in foam, as Scobie wrenched mightily at their leashes.

The Brits' rifles thundered in unison. Luke Honey caught a glimpse of what at first he took to be a stag. Yet something was amiss about the shape as it bolted through the trees and disappeared. It was far too massive, and it moved in a strange, top-heavy manner. Lord Bullard's horse whinnied and galloped blindly through the midst of the gawking Americans. It missed Luke Honey and Mr. Williams, collided with Mr. McEvoy and knocked his horse to the ground. The banker cursed and vaulted from the saddle, landing awkwardly. His horse staggered upright while Mr. Wesley's mount charged away into the mist in the opposite direction. Mr. Briggs yelled and pulled at the reins of his mount as it crow-hopped all over the clearing.

"What the hell was that?" Williams said, expertly controlling his horse as it half reared, eyes rolling to the whites. "Welloc?"

Mr. Liam Welloc had wisely halted at the entrance and was supremely unaffected by the debacle. "I warned you, gentlemen. Blackwood's Baby is no tender doe."

Mr. McEvoy had twisted an ankle. He sat on a rock while Dr. Landscomb tended him. Scobie calmed his mastiffs and handed their leashes to Mr. Liam Welloc. He took a pistol from his coat and walked among the dogs that lay scattered and broken along the bank of the lagoon and in the bushes. He fired the pistol three times.

No one spoke. They rubbed their horses' necks and stared at the blood smeared across the rocks and at the savaged corpses of the dogs. Scobie began dragging them into a pile. A couple of flasks of whiskey were passed around, and everyone drank in morbid silence.

Finally, Mr. Williams said, "Bullard, what happened here?" He repeated the question until the Englishman shuddered and looked up, blank-faced, from the carnage.

"It speared them on its horns. In all my years . . . it scooped two dogs and pranced about while they screamed and writhed on its antlers."

"Anybody get a clear shot?"

"I did," Mr. Wesley said. He leaned on his rifle like an old man. "Thought I nicked the bugger. Surely I did." He coughed and his shoulders convulsed. Dr. Landscomb left Mr. McEvoy and came over to examine him.

Mr. Liam Welloc took stock. "Two horses gone. Five dogs killed. Mr. McEvoy's ankle is swelling nicely, I see. Doctor, what of Mr. Wesley?"

Dr. Landscomb listened to Mr. Wesley's chest with a stethoscope. "This man requires further medical attention. We must get him to a hospital at once."

Scobie shouted. He ran back to the group, his eyes red, his mouth twisted in fear. "Arlen's gone. Arlen's gone."

"Easy, friend." Mr. Williams handed the older man the whiskey and waited for him to take a slug. "You mean that boy of yours?"

Scobie nodded. "He climbed a tree when the beast charged our midst. Now he's gone."

"He probably ran away," Mr. Briggs said. "Can't say as I blame him."

"No." Scobie brandished a soiled leather shoe. "This was lying near the tracks of the stag. They've gone deeper into the wood."

"Why the bloody hell would the little fool do that?" Lord Bullard said, slowly returning to himself.

"He's a brave lad," Scobie said and wrung the shoe in his grimy hands.

"Obviously we have to find the kid," Luke Honey said, although he was unhappy about the prospect. If anything, the fog had grown thicker. "We have four hours of light. Maybe less."

"It's never taken the dogs," Scobie said so quietly Luke Honey was certain no one else heard.

THERE WAS A brief discussion regarding logistics where it was decided that Dr. Landscomb would escort Mr. Wesley and Mr. McEvoy to the prior evening's campsite—it would be impossible to proceed much farther before dark. The search party would rendezvous with them and continue on to the lodge in the morning. Luke Honey volunteered his horse to carry Mr. Wesley, not from a sense of honor, but because he was likely the best tracker of the bunch and probably also the fleetest of foot.

They spread into a loose line, Mr. Liam Welloc and Mr. Briggs ranging along the flanks on horseback, while Luke Honey, Scobie, and Mr. Williams formed a picket. Mr. Williams led his horse. By turns, each of them shouted Arlen's name.

Initially, pursuit went forth with much enthusiasm, as Lord Bullard had evidently wounded the stag. Its blood splattered fern leaves and pooled in the spaces between its hoofprints and led them away from the beaten trails into brush so thick, Luke Honey unsheathed his Barlow knife and hacked at the undergrowth. Mosquitoes attacked in swarms. The light dimmed and the trail went cold. A breeze sighed, and the ubiquitous fog swirled around them, and tracking soon became a fruitless exercise. Mr. Liam Welloc announced an end to the search on account of encroaching darkness.

Mr. Williams and Luke Honey stopped to rest upon the exposed roots of a dying oak tree and take a slug from Mr. Williams's hip flask. The rancher smoked a cigarette. His face was red, and he fanned away the mosquitoes with his hat. "Greg said this is how it was."

"Your uncle? The one who died?"

"Yeah, on the second go-around. The first time he came home and talked about a disaster. Horse threw a feller from a rich family in Kansas and broke his neck."

"I reckon everybody knows what they're getting into coming to this place."

"I'm not sure of that at all. You think you know what evil is until you look it in the eye. That's when you really cotton to the consequences. Ain't no fancy shooting iron worth any of this."

"Too early for that kind of talk."

"The hell it is. I ain't fainthearted, but this is a bad fix. The boy is sure enough in mortal danger. Judging what happened to them dogs, *we* might be in trouble."

Luke Honey had no argument with that observation, preoccupied as he was with how the fog hung like a curtain around them, how the night abruptly surged upon them, how every hair of his body stood on end. He realized his companion wasn't at his side. He called Mr. Williams's name and the branches creaked overhead.

An unearthly stillness settled around him as he pressed his hand against the rough and slimy bark of a tree. He listened as the gazelles at the waterhole listened for the predators that deviled them. He saw a muted glow ahead: the manner of light that seeped from certain fog banks on the deep ocean and in the depths of caverns. He went forward, groping through coils of mist, rifle held aloft in his free hand. His racing heart threatened to unman him.

Luke Honey stepped into a small grove of twisted and shaggy trees. The weak phosphorescence rose from the earth and cast evil shadows upon the foliage and the wall of thorns that hemmed the grove on three sides. A statue canted leeward at the center of the grove—a tall, crumbling marble stack, ghastly white and stained black by moss and mold, a terrible horned man, or god. This was an idol to a dark and vile Other, and it radiated a palpable aura of wickedness.

The fog crept into Luke Honey's mouth, trickled into his nostrils, and his gorge rebelled. Something struck him across the shoulders. He lost balance, and all the strength in his legs drained and he collapsed and lay supine, squashed into the wet earth and leaves by an imponderable force. This force was the only thing keeping him from sliding off the skin of the earth into the void. He clawed the dirt. Worms threaded his fingers. "Get behind me, Devil," he said.

The statue blurred and expanded, shifting elastically. The statue was so very large, and its cruel shadow pinned him like an insect; the voices of its creators, primeval troglodytes who'd dwelt in mud huts and made love in the filth and offered their blood to long dead gods, whispered obscenities, and images unfolded in his mind. He thrashed and struggled to rise. A child screamed. The cry chopped off. A discordant vibration rippled over the ground and passed through Luke Honey's bones—a hideous clash of cymbals and shrieking reeds reverberated in his brain. His nose bled.

Fresh blood is best, the statue said, although it was Luke Honey's mouth that opened and made the words. *Baby blood, boy child blood. Rich red sweet rare boy blood. What, little man, what could you offer the lord of the dark? What, you feeble fly?* His jaw contorted, manipulated by invisible fingers. His tongue writhed at the bidding of the Other. A choir of corrupt angels sang from the darkness all around—a song sweet and repellent and old as Milton's pit and its inhabitants. Sulfurous red light illuminated the fog and impossible shapes danced and capered as if beamed from the lens of a magic lantern.

Luke Honey turned his head sideways in the dirt and saw his brother hoeing in the field. He saw himself as a boy of fourteen struggling with loading a single-shot .22 and the muzzle flash exactly as Michael leaned in to look at the barrel. Luke Honey's father sent him to live in Utah and his mother died shortly thereafter, a broken woman. The black disk of the moon occulted the sun. His massive .416 Rigby boomed and a bull elephant pitched forward and crumpled, its tusks ploughing the dirt. Mother stood in the entrance of the tent, wings charred, her brilliant nimbus dimmed to reddish flame. Arlen regarded him from the maze of thorns, his face slack with horror. "Take me instead," Luke Honey said through clenched teeth, "and be damned."

You're already mine, Lucas. The Other cackled in lunatic merriment. The music, the fire, the singing, all crashed and stopped.

Mr. Williams leaned over him, and Luke Honey almost skewered the man. Mr. Williams leaped back, staring at the Barlow knife in Luke Honey's fist. "Sorry, boy. You were having a fit. Laughing like a crazy man."

Luke Honey clambered to his feet and put away the knife. His scooped up his rifle and brushed leaves from his clothes. The glow had subsided, and the two men were alone except for the idol that hulked, a terrible lump in the darkness.

"Sweet baby Jesus," Mr. Williams said. "My uncle told me about these damned things too. Said rich townies—that weren't followers of Christ, to put it politely—had 'em shipped in and set up here and there across the estate. Gods from the Old World. There are stories about rituals in the hills. Animal sacrifices and unnatural relations. Stories like our hosts told us about the Blackwoods. To this day, folks with money and an interest in ungodly practices come to visit these shrines."

"Let's get away from this thing," Luke Honey said.

"Amen to that." Mr. Williams led the way and they might've wandered all night, but someone fired a gun to signal periodically, and the two men stumbled into the firelight of camp as Mr. Liam Welloc and Mr. McEvoy were serving a simple dinner of pork and beans. By unspoken agreement, neither Luke Honey nor Mr. Williams mentioned the vile statue. Luke Honey retreated to the edge of the camp, eyeing Mr. Liam Welloc and Dr. Landscomb. As lords of the estate there could be no doubt they knew something of the artifacts and their foul nature. Were the men merely curators, or did they partake of corrupt ceremonies by the dark of the moon? He shuddered and kept his weapons close.

Dr. Landscomb and Lord Bullard had wrapped Mr. Wesley in a cocoon of blankets. Mr. Wesley's face was drawn, his eyes heavy lidded. Lord Bullard held a brandy flask to his companion's lips and dabbed them with a handkerchief after each coughing jag.

"Lord Almighty," Mr. Williams said as he joined Luke Honey, a plate of beans in hand. "I reckon he's off to the happy hunting grounds any minute now."

Luke Honey ate his dinner and tried to ignore Mr. Wesley's groans and coughs, and poor Scobie mumbling and rocking on his heels, a posture that betrayed his rude lineage of savages who went forth in ochre paints and limed hair and wailed at the capriciousness of pagan gods.

There were no stories around the fire that evening, and later, it rained.

* * *

Mr. Wesley was dead in the morning. He lay stiff and blue upon the lean-to floor. Dr. Landscomb covered him with another blanket and said a few words. Lord Bullard wept inconsolably and cast hateful glances at Luke Honey.

"Lord Almighty," was all Mr. Williams could repeat. The big man stood near the corpse, hat in hand.

"The forest is particularly greedy this season," Mr. Liam Welloc said. "It has taken a good Christian fellow and an innocent child, alas."

"Hold your tongue, Mr. Welloc!" Scobie's face was no less contorted in grief and fury than Lord Bullard's. He pointed at Mr. Liam Welloc. "My grandson lives, an' I swear to uproot every stone an' every tree in this god-forsaken forest to find him."

Mr. Liam Welloc gave Scobie a pitying smile. "I'm sorry, my friend. You know as well as I that the odds of his surviving the night are slim. The damp and cold alone . . ."

"We must continue the search."

"Perhaps tomorrow. At the moment, we are duty bound to see our guests to safety and make arrangements for the disposition of poor Mr. Wesley's earthly remains."

"You mean to leave Arlen at the tender mercy of . . . Nay, I'll have none of it."

"I am sorry. Our duty is clear."

"Curse you, Mr. Welloc!"

"Master Scobie, I implore you not to pursue a reckless course—"

"Bah!" Scobie made a foul gesture and stomped into the predawn gloom.

Mr. McEvoy said, "The old man is right—we can't just quit on the kid."

"Damned straight," Mr. Briggs said. "What kind of skunks would we be to abandon a boy while there's still a chance?"

Dr. Landscomb said, "Well spoken, sirs. However, you can hardly be expected to grasp the, ah, gravity of the situation. I assure you, Arlen is lost. Master Scobie is on a quixotic mission. He won't find the lad anywhere in Wolfvale. In any event, Mr. McEvoy simply must be treated at a hospital lest his ankle grow worse. I dislike the color of the swelling."

"Surely, it does no harm to try," Mr. Briggs said.

"We tempt fate by spending another minute here," Mr. Liam Welloc said. "And to stay after sunset . . . This is impossible, I'm afraid." The incongruity of the man's genteel comportment juxtaposed with his apparent dread of the supernatural chilled Luke Honey in a way he wouldn't have deemed possible after his experiences abroad.

"Tempt fate?" Mr. Briggs said. "Not stay after sunset? What the hell is that supposed to mean, Welloc? Boys, can you make heads or tails of this foolishness?"

"He means we'd better get ourselves shut of this place," Mr. Williams said.

"Bloody right," Lord Bullard said. "This is a matter for the authorities."

Mr. Briggs appeared dumbfounded. "Well, don't this beat all. Luke, what do you say?"

Luke Honey lighted a cigarette. "I think we should get back to the lodge. A dirty shame, but that's how I see it."

"I don't believe this."

"Me neither," Mr. McEvoy said. His leg was elevated and his cheeks shone with sweat. His ankle was swaddled in bandages. "Wish I could walk, damn it."

"You saw what that stag did to the dogs," Lord Bullard said. "There's something unnatural at work and I've had quite enough, thank you." He wiped his eyes and looked at Luke Honey. "You'll answer for Wes. Don't think you won't."

"Easy there, partner," Mr. Williams said.

Luke Honey nodded. "Well, Mr. Bullard, I think you may be correct. I'll answer for your friend. That reckoning is a bit farther down the list, but it's on there."

"This is no time to bicker," said Mr. Liam Welloc. "Apparently we are in agreement—"

"Not all of us," Mr. Briggs said, glowering.

"—Since we are in agreement, let's commence packing. We'll sort everything out when we return to the house."

"What about Scobie?" Mr. Briggs said.

"Master Scobie can fend for himself," Mr. Liam Welloc said, his bland, conciliatory demeanor firmly in place. "As I said, upon our return we will alert the proper authorities. Sheriff Peckham has some experience in these matters."

Luke Honey didn't believe the sheriff, or anybody else, would be combing these woods for one raggedy kid anytime soon. The yearly sacrifice had been accomplished. This was the way of the world; this was its beating heart and panting maw. He'd seen such offerings made by tribes in the jungles, just as his own Gaelic kin had once poured wine in the sea and cut the throats of fatted lambs. If one looked back far enough, all men issued from the same wellspring, and every last one of them feared the dark as

Mr. Liam Welloc and Dr. Landscomb and their constituency in Ransom Hollow surely did. Despite the loathsome nature of their pact, there was nothing shocking about this arrangement. To propitiate the gods, to please one's lord and master was ever the way. That expert killers such as the English and the Texans and, of course, he himself, served as provender in this particular iteration of the eternal drama filled Luke Honey's heart with bitter amusement. This wry humor mixed with his increasing dread and rendered him giddy, almost drunken.

Mr. Wesley's body was laid across the saddle of Luke Honey's horse and the company began the long trudge homeward. The dreary fog persisted, although the rain had given out for the moment.

"I hope you don't think I'm a coward," Mr. Williams said. He rode beside Luke Honey, who was walking at the rear of the group.

Luke Honey didn't speak. He pulled his collar tight.

"My mama raised me as a God-fearin' boy. There's real evil, Mr. Honey. Not that existential crap, either. Last night, I felt somethin' I ain't felt before. Scared me spitless." When Luke Honey didn't answer, Mr. Williams leaned over and said in a low voice, "People got killed in that grove, not just animals. Couldn't you feel it coming off that idol like a draft in a slaughter yard? I ain't afraid of much, but Bullard's right. This ain't natural and that kid is a goner."

"Who are you trying to convince?" Luke Honey said, although the question was more than a little self-referential. "The hunt is over. Go back to Texas and dream away the winter. There's always next year."

"No, not for me. My uncle made that mistake. Next year, I'll go to British Columbia. Or Alaska. Damned if I know, but I know it won't be Ransom Hollow." Mr. Williams clicked his tongue and spurred his mount ahead to rejoin the group.

Later, the company halted for a brief time to rest the animals and allow the men to stretch their legs. The liquor was gone and tempers short. When they remounted, Luke Honey remained seated on a mossy boulder, smoking his last cigarette. His companions rode on, heads down and dispirited, and failed to notice his absence. They disappeared around a sharp bend.

Luke Honey finished his cigarette. The sun slowly ate through the clouds, and its pale light shone in the gaps of the foliage. He turned his back and walked deeper into the woods, into the darkness.

THE SHRIEKS OF the mastiffs came and went all day, and so too the phantom bellows of men, the muffled blasts of their weapons. Luke Honey resisted the urge to cover his ears, to break and flee. Occasionally, Scobie hollered from an indeterminate distance. Luke Honey thought the old man's cries sounded more substantial, more of the mortal realm, and he attempted to orient himself in their direction. He walked on, clutching his rifle.

Night came and he was lost in the endless forest.

A light glimmered to his left, sifting down through the black gallery to illuminate a figure who stood as if upon a stage. Mr. Wesley regarded him, hat clasped to his navel in both hands, hair slick and shining. His face was white. A black stain spread across the breast of his white shirt. He removed a pair of objects from inside his hat and with an insolent flourish tossed them into the bushes short of Luke Honey. Dr. Landscomb stepped into view and took Mr. Wesley by the elbow and drew him into the shadows. The ray of light blinked out of existence.

The objects were pale and glistening and as Luke Honey approached them, his heart beat faster. He leaned close to inspect them and recoiled, his courage finally buckling in the presence of such monstrous events.

Luke Honey blindly shoved his way through low hanging branches and spiky undergrowth. His clothes were torn, the flesh of his hands and face scratched and bleeding. A rifle fired several yards away. He staggered and belatedly shielded his eyes from the muzzle flash, and a large animal blundered past him, squealing and roaring. Then it was gone, and Scobie came tearing in pursuit and almost tripped over him. The old man swung a battered lantern. He gawked at Luke Honey in the flat yellow glare.

Scobie's expression was wild and caked in dirt. His face was nicked and bloody. He panted like a dog. He held his rifle in his left hand, its bore centered on Luke Honey's middle. In a gasping voice, he said, "I see you, Bill."

"It's me, Luke Honey."

"What's your business here?"

"I came to help you find the boy." He dared not speak of what he'd so recently discovered, an abomination that once revealed was certain to drive the huntsman into raving madness. At this range Scobie's ancient single-shot rifle would cut Luke Honey in twain.

"Arlen's gone. He's gone." Scobie lowered the weapon, his arm quivering in exhaustion.

"You don't believe that," Luke Honey said with a steadiness born of staring down savage predators, of waiting to pull the trigger that would drop them at his feet, of facing certain death with a coldness of mind inherent to the borderline mad. The terror remained, ready to sweep him away.

"I'm worn to the bone. There's nothing left in me." Scobie seemed to wither, to shrink into himself in despair.

"The stag is wounded," Luke Honey said. "I think you hit it again, judging from the racket."

"It don't matter. You can't kill a thing like that." Scobie's eyes glittered with tears. "This is the devil's preserve, Mr. Honey. Every acre. You should've gone with the masters, got yourself away. We stayed too long and we're done for. He only pretends to run. He'll end the game and come for us soon."

"I had a bad feeling about Landscomb and Welloc."

"Forget those idiots. They're as much at the mercy of hell as anyone else in Ransom Hollow."

"Got anything to drink?" Luke Honey said.

Scobie hung the lantern from a branch and handed Luke Honey a canteen made of cured animal skin. The canteen was full of sweet, bitter whiskey. The men took a couple of swigs and rested there by the flickering illumination of the sooty old lamp. Luke Honey built a fire. They ate jerky and warmed themselves as the dank night closed in ever more tightly.

Much later, Scobie said, "It used to be worse. My grandsire claimed some of the more devout folk would drag girls from their homes and cut out their innards on them stone tablets you'll find under a tree here or there." His wizened face crinkled into a horridly mournful smile. "An' my mother, she whispered that when she was a babe, Black Bill was known to creep through the yards of honest folk while they slept. She heard his nails tap-tapping on their cottage door one night."

Luke Honey closed his eyes. He thought again of Arlen's pitiful, small hands severed at the wrists and discarded in the brush, a pair of soft, dripping flowers. He heard his companion rise stealthily and creep away from camp. He slept and awakened to the old man kneeling at his side. Scobie's face was hidden in shadow. Luke Honey smelled the oily steel of a knife near his own neck. The man reeked of murderous intent. He wondered where Scobie had been, what he had done.

Scobie spoke softly, "I don't know what to do. I'm a man of God."

"Yet here we are. Look who you serve."

"No, Mr. Honey. The hunt goes on an' I don't matter none. Your presence ain't my doing. You bought your ticket. I come because somebody's got to stand up. Somebody's got to put a bullet in the demon."

"The price you've paid seems steep as hell, codger."

Scobie nodded. He remained quiet for a while. At last he said, "Come, boy. You must come with me now. He's waiting for us. He whispered to me from the dark, made a pact with me he'd take one of us in return for Arlen. I promised you to him, God help me. It's a vile oath and I'm ashamed."

"Oh, Scobie." Luke Honey's belly twisted and churned. "You know how these things turn out. You poor, damned fool."

"Please. Don't make me beg you, Mr. Honey. Don't make me. Do what's right for that innocent boy. I know the Lord's in your heart."

Luke Honey reached for Scobie's arm and patted it. "You're right about one thing. God help you."

They went. There was a clearing, its bed layered with muck and spoiled leaves. Unholy symbols were gouged into the trees, brands so old they'd fossilized. It was a killing ground of antiquity, and Scobie had prepared it well. He'd improvised several torches to light the shallow basin with a ghastly, reddish glare.

Scobie took several steps and uttered an inarticulate cry, a glottal exclamation held over from his ancestors. He half turned to beckon, and his face was transformed by shock when Luke Honey smashed the butt of his rifle into his hip and sent him stumbling into the middle of the clearing.

Luke Honey's eyes blurred with grief, and Michael's shade materialized there, his trusting smile disintegrating into bewilderment, then inertness. The cruelness of the memory drained Luke Honey of his fear. He said with dispassion, "My hell is to testify. Don't you understand? He doesn't want me. He took me years ago."

Brush snapped. The stag shambled forth from the outer darkness. It loomed above Scobie, its fur rank and steaming. Black blood oozed from gashes along its flanks. Beneath a great jagged crown of antlers, its eyes were black, its teeth yellow and broken. Scobie fell to his knees, palms raised in supplication. The stag nuzzled his matted hair and its long tongue lapped at the muddy tears and the streaks of drying blood upon the man's upturned face. Its muzzle unhinged. The teeth closed and there was a sound like a ripe cabbage cracking apart.

Luke Honey slumped against the bole of an oak, the rifle a dead, useless weight across his knees, and watched.

Afterword to "Blackwood's Baby"

Raised in a wilderness setting, I have an affinity for the natural horrors of Algernon Blackwood and Cormac McCarthy, both of whom were direct influences upon "Blackwood's Baby." Bram Stoker's seminal *Drac-*

ula, especially its adventure and gothic horror elements, served as further inspiration in addition to my enduring fascination with all things occult. "Blackwood's Baby" is loosely related to "Catch Hell," published in Ellen Datlow's *Lovecraft Unbound,* which also features the Black Ram Lodge and environs. Further stories and a novel will be set in Ransom Hollow.

—LAIRD BARRON

Paul Park

Paul Park has written ten novels and numerous short stories in a variety of genres. His most recent major work is the Roumania Quartet, made up of *A Princess of Roumania, The Tourmaline, The White Tyger,* and *The Hidden World;* upcoming is a revised book version of his novella *Ghosts Doing the Orange Dance,* with additional sections by John Crowley and Elizabeth Hand. Park lives in Berkshire County, Massachusetts, with his wife and two children.

PAUL PARK

Mysteries of the Old Quarter

(Newly excerpted and translated from the journals and
correspondence of Dr. Philippe Delorme, among other
sources)

1. "THE RAIN AGAINST THE CASEMENT . . ."

. . . I write this from my hotel room, which constitutes the majority of
what I have seen so far, here in what was once the greatest city of New
France. Outside, the narrow road is full of water, fog, and sodden filth. I
have heard rumors of another, more modern metropolis on the other side
of Canal Street, broad boulevards and large houses that contain actual
Americans in their natural surroundings, as well as poorer but more vibrant neighborhoods of Germans and Italians. Though I could walk to
that metropolis in half an hour, I gather that would be to break some sort
of secret code. The indigenous culture of the city has curled in upon itself
because it knows it is dying, even though it is in itself quite new, by European standards. But these sequences run quicker here, partly because of
a mania for destroying and rebuilding, and partly because the land itself,
a bend of miasmic and mephitic swamp between the river and the lake,
appears to me a sink of dissolution, which has accelerated all natural processes of corruption and decay.

So far I have kept this opinion to myself. At least I am attempting to
do so. But perhaps some of my prejudices have already leaked out. This

evening, for example, I addressed a local scientific society on the subject of an experiment into the nature of electricity, and in particular the electrical impulses in the brains of rats and monkeys. Afterwards I answered questions from the audience. It is an infuriating and pervasive characteristic of this tour that these questions by no means have confined themselves to the subject of my demonstrations. A few days ago, a gentleman in Chicago asked me my opinion of the weather in the coming week—I might have predicted it would rain forever! And tonight I answered several questions about the theories of Mr. Charles Darwin.

The religiousness of these people does not cease to astound. After my second attempt at reconciling what cannot, after all, be reconciled, I allowed myself a joke, although I did not smile. "Perhaps," I suggested, "it was our simian ancestors that inhabited the Garden of Eden, as none of the activities described as taking place there would have required a brain much larger than an ordinary potato. It was in the land of Canaan, surely, that we began our inexorable descent, guided by the process of natural selection." The most foolish beasts, I meant to imply, have the wit to copulate, and our development as a species, and as individual moral beings, could commence only at the moment we had turned our back on God.

I was speaking in response to an enquiry about "reverse evolution," an absurd and backward theory that has nevertheless found nourishment here in the superstitions of the inhabitants. During the ensuing silence I was tempted to mention your own observation that since God is reputed to have created man in his own image, then perhaps the early migration of Africans to Europe is evidence of man's fall. Contrasting your and my complexions, you once observed how Lucifer's supposed "brightness" might be more properly translated to emphasize the pallor of his skin, at least in comparison with God himself. But that would be a joke too painful to express in this crude nation. As you know, I am sometimes irritated by how the Continental newspapers can scarcely mention my work without including a line or phrase that concerns my "Moorish grandmother," a lady whom I never had the privilege to meet. In Paris, a small amount of African or even Hebrew blood is considered a mark of distinction, perhaps of genius, at least in intellectual or artistic circles. That is not so here. If my history were well-known, my lectures would attract a different audience entirely, such as might buy tickets to observe a chimpanzee solve quadratic equations in the zoo.

Ah, my love, the hour is late. The rain against the casement rattles like escaping steam. Soon I will close the humid curtains, climb onto the lumpy bed. If you were here in my exile, I would embrace you, and you would no

longer complain that I was diffident or shy. I would run my fingers down
the buttons of your back, and lower still. Doubtless we would converse,
if at all, in the language of the angels in paradise, at least if our current
scientific thinking is correct . . .

(Addressed to Mme. Solange Baziat, May 23, 1888—unsent)

2. LATER THAT NIGHT:
"I DO NOT DWELL UPON MY FAILURES . . ."

. . . Why do I persist in seeking some relief in these attempts at correspondence? Why do I expect to find comfort in the act of sharing my thoughts
and actions with my friends, with you, for instance? No, it is more per-
tinent to ask why I am so often disappointed, why at these moments of
attempted intimacy my loneliness attacks me with renewed ferociousness.
I know already the attempt at connection will be in vain. And yet it is
natural to try again and again. Surely this is the foundation of the sexual
urge. And surely this is part of the religious urge as well, the faith that at
one time we understood each other, and the hope that after death we will
again, once we have lost the illusion of our separateness.

My friend, I have already abandoned my first letter of the evening. It
was to a woman of our mutual acquaintance. Always with her I am obliged
to hide something of myself, in order to preserve her good opinion. In this
case there was a name I must not mention for the sake of her jealousy—I
understand that. But even so the details and events that I described—some
trivial, some essential—had split so sharply from reality by the end of the
first page, that I threw down my pen. And then no sooner did I lie down
in darkness than I found myself fumbling for the lamp, gasping for breath,
with an elevated heart rate. There is no sleep for me tonight.

Now I will try again. Perhaps what I am about to say, I can share with
none but you.

The purpose of my previous letter was to allow me to distract myself
with nocturnal fantasies so that I might forget my anxiousness. Perhaps
you will be relieved to hear I have given up hope of that. My current missive has a different cause, though I will begin with the same base of fact,
the root of every possible narrative—it has not stopped raining since my
arrival. I am staying at the house of a Creole gentleman, a narrow, three-
storey mansion in the Rue Dauphine. He is the sponsor of my lectures, a
tall, thin, dignified, and upright person who is also, as it happens, quite
insane. His name is Maubusson, and he owns an indigo plantation outside

of the city, an enterprise that he himself must know is doomed to fail, because of a recent artificial synthesis.

Despite the weather, this evening I was well disposed. My host was generous enough to buy me supper at a restaurant that might not have offended even you. I observed during the meal that he seemed distracted and glum, but he showed no obvious lunacy—my dear, he was just lying in wait! After coffee we proceeded to the ballroom of a nearby hotel. Three-quarters of an hour afterwards, I had finished my lecture and then rapidly disposed of several infuriating and irrelevant questions about the origin of species. My friend, I thought I could perceive the finish line, when I espied his outstretched hand. "Sir," he said, "I would like to ask you news of some earlier experiments, in which you corresponded with the spirits of the dead."

I grimaced, then cut him off. "I do not like to dwell upon my failures. You understand—"

Alas, he understood nothing. He was not satisfied, and so obliged me to persist: "You speak of a line of inquiry that is several years old, during the course of which I must admit that I allowed my personal desires to dominate my scientific objectivity. It is true that through the use of electrical stimulation, I was able to prolong consciousness in a small number of recently expired subjects. But the accounts of these experiments were distorted by a sensationalist press, and I am now convinced that I was wrong in my conclusions. The boundary between living and dying is not as firm, perhaps, as we imagine, or at least as I imagined at that time."

While I was speaking, still he had not lowered his hand. His smile was skull-like, and exposed his yellow teeth. Because he was my host and benefactor, I was compelled to let him speak. "But I recall a description of a scene at the bedside of a Parisian lady—I forget her name—when she was reconciled to her niece and nephews, and was even able to explain to them the terms of her estate . . ."

"I recall the exact words of Mlle. de Noailles," I said, as coldly as I could. (But inside I was burning, you must imagine.) "I'm afraid I cannot repeat them in a public place. If her sister's children could find reconciliation in anything that occurred that day, they are more imaginative than I, who witnessed the entire event. As for the will, I believe it is in litigation. Now, if you please . . ."

But he would not be silenced! "Perhaps at that moment she was speaking to other emanations in the room," he said. "Perhaps in the hours since her death, these souls were as real to her as you are to me. Perhaps at that moment, you yourself were insubstantial as a ghost."

These words, indeed, reminded me of long-dismissed hypotheses. But I felt I could not display any uncertainty, perhaps out of a sense of foreboding. "If she was speaking to these other emanations, it is clear she was not pleased with them," I concluded in a tone that ended the debate. And in fact the meeting broke up shortly afterwards. Imagine my displeasure, subsequently, walking home with my host and even sharing his umbrella, when I heard him explain how the entire reason for my presence in this city, the entire reason he had found the money to invite me to address his miserable society—all that was a blind, a trick. He had no interest in my recent work, but had fixed instead on the death of Sophie de Noailles, which in my own terrible grief I had allowed myself to desecrate with criminal absurdities and humiliations. In other words, he begged me to revisit the worst moments of my life, because he also (as I might have guessed!) had lost someone who was dear to him. His only daughter, a young lady not yet twenty years old, was recently deceased under painful and mysterious circumstances.

"If I could speak to her once more," said Monsieur Maubusson. "Only to ask her what occurred. If I could hear from her lips who was responsible, no matter how veiled and shrouded her speech—you see it is a matter of justice! And I think it was not true what you said in the hotel, even according to your own description. That woman you mentioned, was it possible she spoke in code? You imply the words themselves were meaningless. But I think it likely that these spirits would employ a code."

I considered this. But Maubusson was wrong to say there was no meaning in the words that Sophie de Noailles spoke on her deathbed. It is that the words themselves were barnyard epithets I could not believe she knew.

Could one imagine a code made up of three or four of the most obscene vulgarities, repeated over and over? The street was very dark, very wet. The water swirled around my boots. We were passing a line of wooden cottages with wide porches and long shuttered windows. Light gleamed between the slats.

I stopped, and made him return with his umbrella. For several moments I had known what he was asking. "No," I said. "I cannot do this. I refuse."

His face was close to mine. But he would not look me in the eyes. "Please," he said. "If I could just . . ."

But at that moment something new occurred to me. It had been more than a month since I'd received his invitation. "When did your daughter die?"

"Six weeks ago." When he saw my look of horror, he put up his hand. "You needn't worry. I have taken all precautions."

He would not look me in the eye. But as he spoke I could perceive, as if vaguely through the fog, the lineaments of his insanity. For six weeks he had packed the girl in ice, which he had transported in boxcars to a city where every courtyard and alleyway is lined with banana trees and bottlebrush palms.

"Monsieur, I'm begging you," he said. "And you must forgive me for not telling you what I intended. But I guessed that if I asked you in a letter, you would have refused."

In addition, he had bought or reconstructed what he imagined were the instruments from my laboratory, as he had seen them represented or described, powered by a coal-fired dynamo of his own invention. "I also am a man of science," he protested. "Nor am I ignorant of medicine. Before the war my father would attend to all our laborers, as was the custom at that time."

I shuddered and looked away from him. A negress floundered toward us down the middle of the street, carrying a lantern. Her old-fashioned dress and her wide hat were drenched. She stood behind my host so that he couldn't see her—I had heard this district of the city, or nearby, was notorious for prostitution, either in large palaces or else small, individual residences. She was a pretty girl, of a type that I admire, and I studied the silent movement of her lips. "*Vous cherchez quelque chose?*"

"Sir," I said, "you must abandon this."

By the light of the lantern flame, I could see my host was weeping. "I cannot. Monsieur, you are my final hope. If you won't help me . . ."

I made a signal with my hand. The woman turned away, and we came here. Perhaps now you can guess why I lie sleepless in my room. I am on the third floor, but elsewhere, somewhere, I can hear the steam-powered generator, throbbing faintly in the walls. Tomorrow I will ask for the first train to Jackson. In the meantime, the rain hisses like escaping steam . . .

(Addressed to M. Joachim Valdor, May 23rd—unsent)

3. EARLY MORNING: ". . . A GESTURE I RECOGNIZED . . ."

. . . I ask myself if I should finish or amend this second letter now, at a remove of many hours. But when I re-read it, I can see it is as misleading as the first, in mood, in fact, in everything. No doubt it is useful to descend through layers, saying adieu at every step, first to the man I ought or else imagine myself to be. Second, perhaps, I could take leave of all my thoughts, feelings, and intentions. Then finally I am reduced to describing what I have done, or I will do. I only hope I am bold enough to admit them to myself.

After midnight, then, I closed my letter to Joachim and lay down for the second time. I was mistaken to say I would not sleep, for how else to describe what happened? Perhaps I was experiencing the first effects of the fever that this morning has registered on my thermometer, and which is at the stage now that it sharpens my awareness, rather than diminishing it.

But I anticipate—I was asleep in bed. This is what I must conclude, even though according to my own perception I lay awake, braiding my heartbeat with the throbbing in the walls. There was some disturbance in the street, a man shouting. Someone spoke, a different kind of voice, well-remembered, close to my ear. I started up, and then I saw her in a corner of the wall beside the curtain, her hand on the tasseled cord. "Solange," I said, because Solange Baziat was in my mind. Dressed in black, she turned toward me, smiled, and touched her hair in a gesture I recognized. "Mon Dieu," I murmured, because my interest in Mme. Baziat has always been measured by how much, at any given moment, she resembles someone else, someone who now approached me dressed in the same black beaded dress that I remembered from the night I had attempted to take her in my arms, in her father's apartment in the Place Vendôme. Then I had been cruelly, even violently rebuffed, but this time I expected something different, I don't know why. "Sophie," I cried, reaching out my hand to hide her face, and she moved under it and laid her cheek against my breast. Then I felt her fingers on my lips, while at the same time her other hand grasped me lower down, to such effect that I felt myself let go, as in a dream. I bent to kiss her, and she seized my lip between her teeth, and at that moment I knew I'd been mistaken, fooled by my regrets—Sophie was dead. This woman in my arms was someone else, younger and smaller, someone I didn't know at all, an actual woman who had slipped into my room, perhaps the same one I had seen that evening in the street outside. *"Vous cherchez quelque chose?"*

No, it was impossible, absurd. How could she have gotten in? And by the time I was fully awake, she had disappeared, although the door remained closed. She left me to wipe myself with my nightshirt and attend to my bleeding lip. A smell lingered in the air, a mixture of perfume and decay.

Now convinced I'd been asleep, I tried immediately to remember. But as so often happens, my dream faded, and the woman in it also faded from my mind. As she did so, her complexion changed and lost its color, so that I was no longer sure I was remembering the negress of the Rue Dauphine. In fact I was convinced it was not she. And yet the doctors say it is impossible to invent a new face in a dream, the face of someone we have never met.

Then the generator stopped, and the silence in the house was enormous, baffling. Over the course of the night I'd become accustomed to the sound, until I felt rather than heard it. I stood over the basin washing my face, and now I raised my head to look into the dark mirror. In the sudden quiet, I thought I heard the sound of my host's surrender, of his submission to his grief, at the moment (I thought—irrationally) of his success. How else could I explain the experience I'd just had? Subsequently I discovered several ways, but at that moment I was convinced. At the same time I imagined a new sympathy with my host, because in my own thoughts I had merged my unhappiness with his. And though the emotions of a father might seem different from those of a lover (if I could aspire to calling myself that—I speak only of my feelings, not of her response), still I could understand his grief in the death of a beautiful woman in her prime.

I wiped my face, threw on my clothes. I needed to confirm that the person from my dream, the small, delicate, cat-like woman who had bit me on the lip, was indeed Mlle. Maubusson. In my febrile state, it was imperative for me to verify this fact, and at the same time I felt some vestige of my excitement when I first attacked the problem of re-animation in the year prior to Mlle. de Noailles's death, little knowing that before long I would have such a personal interest in my success.

I opened the door of my bedroom and followed the new silence down the stairs. As I descended step by step, my candle in my hand, I reconsidered momentarily the contempt with which I had rejected my host's theory of ghosts, or spirits, or "emanations," in the light of my own recent experience. Was it possible that we are haunted in dreams by our beloved dead, not just in metaphor but in actual fact? If so, was it impossible to imagine a plane or space where they might commune, or even share each other's bodies, as I had conceived in that transitional moment between sleep and wakefulness?

The wallpaper was heavily patterned, pink and cream. Yet there was a dirty stripe opposite the banister, where many hands had slid. It was not hard for me to find, on the second storey, the room I sought. I heard low voices beyond the door.

I knocked, then entered. How can I describe the scene? I stood in a lady's bedroom, furnished with the dark, mahogany, over-embellished chests and cabinets that are habitual in rich Creole households. There was a four-poster bed—unoccupied. The wallpaper was pink and green, handpainted with scenes along the river. The gas was lit, and by its spectral flame I saw my host, dressed in shirt-sleeves, the electrodes still in his hand. The dynamo was in the courtyard outside, and the wires snaked in the open window, together with a number of black rubber tubes, which led to a zinc bathtub in the middle of the room.

There was another man also, a young, curly-headed fellow, and when he spoke, I could tell by his accent that French was not his native language: "Who the devil are you?"

I scarcely heard him. In the bathtub, packed in ice, was the woman from my dream.

She was dressed in a pink night-gown, and her rich black hair was loose around her shoulders. She had high cheekbones, a small, sharp nose, and a soft line of hair along her upper lip. Her skin was pale, but whether because of the constant refrigeration or else from the effect of the electrical stimulation, it still retained a rosy glow. Astonished by this, immediately I perceived that one of the tubes that ran to her must have maintained the circulation of her blood, while another, perhaps, pumped air into her lungs—I could see the harness and the plugs for her nostrils, which her father had just now cleared away.

"How have you fed her?" I enquired.

My host came toward me. "By means of a tube right through to her stomach. And a protein solution, which I saw described in—"

"Who the devil are you, sir?" repeated the curly-headed gentleman. But I was studying the electrodes in Maubusson's hands, and didn't answer. Besides, I thought, it was up to my host to explain my presence, which he did. "Henry, this is Professor Delorme, from Paris. I spoke to you—"

"Did you now? Well, perhaps he would be good enough to wait outside, until we are finished here. Under the circumstances—"

I looked at him now, a young man with a mottled complexion and side-whiskers. "Monsieur," said my host, "may I present my daughter's fiancé, Mr. Henry Lockett?"

"Enchanté," I said. "But am I right in thinking it was to the young lady's temples that you attached the posts? I can see the marks—"

"It was unclear in your description," confessed Monsieur Maubusson. Then he paused. "Professor, I can tell from your face that I have blundered—please, if you could help us now. It's not been five minutes since—"

"No, it's enough," cried Mr. Lockett, in English. He moved to confront me, a menacing, muscular figure, though he was not my height. "It is finished. Make an end, sir. Make an end."

He was talking to Maubusson, but he was staring at me. As for my host, he continued without stopping. "I had thought I could duplicate your results by following your descriptions. Forgive me. If that had been possible, I never would have thought to involve you . . ."

I had turned away from Mr. Lockett and was examining instead the face of Mlle. Maubusson in her zinc bathtub. I examined her long eyelashes and dark lips. Already, though, there was a yellowish pallor to her cheeks, which suggested we had not much time. "The electrodes must be divided, and fastened to several places on the cranium," I said. "Other places also."

I only said this because she resembled so completely the woman in my dream. Mr. Lockett threw up his hands. "By God, that's enough," he said. "Maubusson, I can't tolerate this—I won't have this fellow touch her with his black hands. I will not stay here. If you persist, I will inform the authorities the first thing in the morning—no, by God, sir, stand aside."

It occurred to me that Henry Lockett might have heard some chance rumor of my dear grandmama. In short, he might not have been so ignorant of me and of my reputation as he had claimed. Wishing to confound him, as he was speaking I had reached for the young lady's wrist.

A wet gust of wind pushed into the room, disturbing the curtains by the open sash, where a braided cable of wires and rubber tubes ran down into the courtyard. Reflected there, I could see indirectly the evil red glow of the generator. Monsieur Maubusson crossed the room as if to shut the window. But he turned back before he reached it, revealing a pistol in his hand. "Stand away, sir," he cried. "No, you—Henry. Please, my boy, you must understand. There is no time to be lost."

"Sir, you must be drunk or else insane," began the outraged fiancé, a diagnosis that coincided with my own, although I saw no reason why the two possibilities had to exclude each other. In fact, I wondered if Lockett himself had been excessively fortified with liquor, as I could smell it on his breath and clothes the moment he'd approached me, where I stood by Mlle. Maubusson's tub, testing the rigidity of her arm and elbow—her skin was very cold. Her father made a sudden gesture, and Lockett backed away from me all the way to the door, where he stood impotently, his eyes wet, his face red.

Another gesture, and he was gone. My host followed him to the open door. "I'll see him out," he said, putting the pistol aside. "Besides, I must restart the engine."

I was happy they were gone. I wanted Mlle. Maubusson to myself. No sooner had her father left the room than I went to work. Along one wall, incongruous against the painted wallpaper, there was a wheeled metal bed of a type that is used in hospitals. I brought it over, and, neglecting my clothes, I lifted Mlle. Maubusson onto the enamel surface. During my dream I had had such a strong impression of her weight in my arms, I felt I must confirm it at the expense of my waistcoat.

As my host had said, there was no time to be lost. But I had another reason to hurry. The electrodes must be divided, and at least one placed under her clothes, between her labia minora. I had not wanted to perform this operation under her father's scrutiny, although without it, or the equivalent procedure on my male subjects, I had had no success in the past—so strong in the dead are these bestial urges.

And as I fumbled under the young lady's drenched night-gown, I could not but remember the horrifying moment when I had discovered, in the underclothes of Sophie de Noailles, the pearl and sapphire ring I had given her in a past moment of happiness. Anticipating everything I did, she had secreted it there before her death, to mock me and torment me. She knew I would do everything in my power to resuscitate her, if only so that I could beg for her forgiveness.

An enamel tray hung from the bed-rail, containing an assortment of medical implements. I had pulled apart the second skein of electrodes and was attaching them to Mlle. Maubusson's cranium when I heard the roar of the dynamo, outside in the courtyard. I felt the electric thrill in my fingertips, as I was able to manipulate a cage of stimulation over the cerebral hemispheres. This is what Maubusson had already attempted. But at the same time I affixed the posts so as to enclose and affect the hypothalamus and the medulla oblongata, the most primitive portions of the brain. The effect was instantaneous; I felt her body shudder and convulse. Her spine curved like a bow, and her eyes snapped open as I bent over her. Because of the electricity, her lips pulled away from her teeth, and her mottled tongue protruded next to my ear. And she started in at once, in a harsh, breathy whisper—"Oh, I have waited for this moment—do not touch me. You have forfeited the right."

"Forgive me," I murmured next to her ear.

"I cannot. Instead, I must remember that night when you revealed yourself to me. Monsieur, perhaps it is not possible to know another person, to trust that you have seen into the bottom of his soul. But then at certain moments we reveal ourselves. That night I saw an animal, a creature whose only impulse was violence and desire. What is it that separates men from beasts, can you answer that? And how is it that a woman is expected to continue, once she has finally understood a man she trusted, or might have trusted with her soul? What shall a woman do, once she has seen the truth? For shame, Monsieur. Must I remind you of that night, when you would have taken me by force in my father's house? And I felt I could say nothing, because of your friendship with him and the money that he owed. Can you blame me for my response, which was to discover an extract of conium—you know where I found it! Ah, how cold I was!"

Her voice had risen to a shriek. I tried to restrain her, press her down to the enamel surface, but she struggled against me. With one hand, from the enamel tray she grabbed up a pair of scissors, which I had been using to cut pieces of surgical tape. Fearing for my life, I let her go and stumbled away as she clambered off the bed and stood brandishing the scissors, her eyes wide and staring. But she was held from attacking me by the wires in her hair, connected to the electrical cable that was stretched to its entire length across the room, and which by its weight was pulling her head back, so that the sinews stood out from her neck. Furious, she jabbed at me with the scissors, and when she realized that she couldn't reach me, with her other hand she ripped the net of wires from her head, and immediately fell lifeless to the floor.

"Brute," said Monsieur Maubusson, standing by the door. I had not heard him come in.

"Animal," he repeated. "To think I welcomed him into my house. Now I see why he wanted to impede us. Why he ran from us. He was afraid we would discover—"

"No," I murmured.

"And this apothecary," he continued as he came into the room and collapsed over his daughter's corpse. "I will hunt him down. I will have him arrested. He must be in a shop near here."

"You will not find him," I murmured. "Besides," I pleaded, after a moment, "you must not trust the literal accuracy of these words. You say yourself they speak in code . . ."

"Does this sound like a code to you, Monsieur? She told us straight out what has happened. Ah God, ever since her death, this has been my fear. I could have predicted this. And yet I saw no trace of poison, no discarded vial."

"These women are devious," I said. "You cannot trust them. Conium maculatum leaves no trace."

No matter what we undertook, we could not rouse her again. Instead, after another hour, we shut down the dynamo for the last time, and then deposed Mlle. Maubusson upon the table. My host picked up the scissors from the floor. "She must have mistaken you for him," he said. "I can only apologize on her behalf."

"She was evidently blind," I concurred.

I write this at dawn. Perhaps I can claim a few hours' sleep before my train. As I climbed the stairs, I saw my host descend to the front hall, an umbrella in his hand. I hate to think what he intends.

(From the private diary of Philippe Delorme, May 24th)

4. ". . . A CONGENITAL DEFECT . . ."

Q: You understand what I am saying to you?

A: Yes, Monsieur. Although I cannot speak English to my satisfaction, I can understand perfectly well.

Q: Good. How long have you worked for Mr. Maubusson?

A: Seven years.

Q: Good. Will you explain in your own words what happened on the morning of the 24th of May—that is, on Tuesday of last week?

A: What happened?

Q: I'm talking about Dr. Delorme.

A: Well, I brought him coffee in the morning. There was a break in the weather, and my master had already gone out. This was perhaps at eight o'clock. Professor Delorme was agitated and complained of a small fever. He told me he must take a carriage to the station, and so then I must inform him that the tracks were somewhat underwater between here and Jackson. You remember that morning—there was no steamship also, because the river was so high. Beyond St. Claude Avenue, the streets were all in flood.

Q: Delorme was a white man? What did he say?

A: Well, he was agitated, as I tell you. He said he would verify this information as he could.

Q: And Mr. Maubusson?

A: He was already gone, as I have said. I had no idea, yet, of the tragedy. And I must tell you, it was unnecessary. Mlle. Maubusson, she had a heart defect, it was well known. There was no mystery—she had a congenital defect, like her mother. But my master couldn't accept it. He was so distracted in his grief. He could not see what was before his face. He must persuade himself of something different, or else make himself to be persuaded. It was Delorme that must have accomplished this, I don't know why. But I must blame him. Monsieur Lockett and my master, until that night they were together in all things.

Q: A heart defect. You're a doctor, are you?

A: No, sir.

Q: No medical training?

A: No.

Q: No. Where were you born? Santo Domingo, isn't it? Tell me what Delorme did then.

A: He left his luggage and went out. It is still upstairs. He inquired from me after a girl, whom he had seen in the street the night before. A local girl, whom I recognized from his description. But he did not understand. He thought she was a woman of the town. But this was not the place, so close to Saint Roch's church—it was not possible. I gave him the address. I told him, "Oh, so you will get your fortune read?" But he did not understand. He was a bad man, I think. He looked for another meaning, because he was desperate for this woman, even so early in the morning . . .

(From the police deposition of Prosper Charriere, May 30th)

5. "Vous cherchez quelque chose?"

LADIES AND GENTLEMEN, ARE YOU LOOKING FOR SOMETHING OR SOMEONE WHO IS LOST AND CANNOT BE FOUND? ARE YOU LOOKING FOR THE ANSWERS TO YOUR SECRET QUESTIONS? IS THERE A MAN OR WOMAN WHOSE HEART YOU MUST UNLOCK? PERHAPS THERE IS A MAN WHO LANGUISHES IN PRISON, FALSELY OR ELSE RIGHTFULLY ACCUSED. MADAME SEMIRAMIS WILL HELP, EMPLOYING ALL THE LATEST SCIENTIFIC INSTRUMENTS. FOLLOW THESE SIGNS TO HER ADDRESS . . .

(Posted in the Rue Royale, earlier that week)

6. Post-script

. . . And one more thing, my God. An hour's sleep without rest, buffeted by dreams. You stand before me in your same black beaded dress, bloodless and pale. When you touch me, I can measure in your body's temperature the effect of the conium, which you discovered in my laboratory. And when you kneel down to unbutton me, where I once might have joyfully supposed you had been taught by nature alone, now I can perceive the course of your instruction in a brothel of dead souls, and a malign efficiency which gives me no pleasure or relaxation, but rather the reverse. I left France to avoid these dreams, but they have followed me. Where can I go to find relief?

(From the private diary of Philippe Delorme, May 24th, 8 o'clock)

7. OF POSSIBLE SIGNIFICANCE: AN INTERVIEW WITH MARIE LOUISE GLASPION, IN THE INFIRMARY OF THE URSULINE CONVENT, CHARTERS STREET, AUGUST 10, 1936

. . . I understand why you have come. You want to ask me about Madame Semiramis, how I left her house. Isn't that right?

Even last year I would have told you nothing. But now you see me lying here too weak to raise my head, connected by this tube to this machine.

For some weeks now I have understood that I am dying. I have treated many others through this same infection of the lung, especially this summer, because of my work here with the sisters. But that is not the only reason.

Many years I have denied this, though by now I am too tired to continue: I still have the gift, which I inherited from my mother and have tried to turn to God's purposes. When it refers to that night, my gift is where it starts, because of those two men that I saw arguing in the Rue Dauphine, when I was late returning to my mother's house. The older one, he stood at the abyss. The snake was out upon his temple, as we used to say, and of course in the next days his name was in the papers, because he had been shot by some American.

Always one pauses, wondering to intervene, but how could I? What intervention could be made? I was only a girl, not yet fifteen years old. Besides, it was the younger man who stared at me with such hostility, because he thought I was a prostitute selling my body in an alleyway. In those days I was full of pride, not like now.

That was the night of a big storm. In the morning the streets were flooded in the Third District, not yet where I was, but toward the Rue Claibourne. So long ago! But I was soaked when I got home, and my mother scolded me. She was with some customers around the fire, although it was almost midnight. The rain fell through the roof into some pots. She had killed the cock.

What came to disgust me finally were the images of saints around the altar, Saint Roch and Saint John especially, together with the devil's images from Saint Domingue. But in those days I saw this as normal. Maman told me to dry myself beside the fire, and I hated that also, because of the eyes of the customers, even though I knew full well that this was part of why they came, part of the devil's net, part of that nonsense with Damboolah and Bamboolah and these things, my mother knew it too. It was she who stripped the wet scarf from my throat.

Will you give me some water, please? Thank you. You see I am too weak to pour a glass. Oh, you must not spill water on your microphone. Bring it close. I will speak to it as if it were a priest—I was astonished to see that same man the next morning, the one who had watched me in the Rue Dauphine, a gentleman of color, but light-skinned. Grey eyes. The rain had stopped for a moment. A humid wind chased the clouds over the rooftops, away toward the river. He came in drunk out of the street, stinking of tafia. I was sweeping with the wet broom, my sleeves rolled up. I thought my mother was still asleep behind the curtain. But this fellow scarcely spoke a greeting. He took me by surprise. He backed me up against the wall before I could resist. He was begging for pity. I'd heard that from a man before! I screamed, and then my mother was there, and he released me. She was a tall woman with a powerful eye, dressed in her robe, and with her long hair bound up. "Forgive me," he protested.

She saw from his fine clothes that he had money. "I am Semiramis, Queen of Babylon," she said, which was her usual nonsense in those days. I was breathless in a corner, and Monsieur was in tears. Maman could see immediately that he was ill, because she began to assemble from her shelf of jars one of her nostrums. I see now, after years of training in this infirmary, how harmful this was. I believe now that she might have poisoned many customers over the years, but in those days I thought it only foolishness, as I saw her prepare a sachet of goufre dust and pepper, because of the man's fever. His eyes shone. My mother lit the altar candles, and then closed the shutters and the door into the yard.

"Monsieur," she said, "someone is haunting you."

"Yes."

"And this person is a woman."

"Yes."

"And she disturbs your rest."

"Yes."

She said this to every man, and it was always so. She had placed him in an armchair and put a stool under his boots. Then she sat down beside him to take his pulse and put a damp cloth over his brow. Nor did he pull away from her, because he was desperate to be comforted, and in spite of my past fear I looked at him, a gentleman not yet thirty-five, with good teeth and hair.

"Shall we ask her what she wants? But, Monsieur, please tell me. Must we search for her among the living or the dead?"

His expression was desolate. Maman gave a signal, and I went to the altar to light a pyramid of incense and then wash my hands.

Will you hand me my rosary, there from the table? Thank you. It is not a serpent! It won't bite you! I can see you are a skeptical person, as I was in my naiveté. But this Voodoo conjuring was not a matter of an error or harmless tricks, or the waste that comes from believing something that is not so. It is an opposing force. Not to believe, it is a kind of innocence. Now I think my faith commenced that day, the faith that brings me to this white bed. Before I was unable to distinguish, because I loved my mother, who jumbled them together, good and bad, sin and love. But this is our work on earth, to separate these things.

Now it began raining again, first gently, and then making spots on the dirt floor. I heard the thunder in the direction of Saint Roch. Superstitious, I touched the crucifix around my neck while my mother began to croon her language, most of it entirely invented out of nonsense words. Though I had heard these things before, and though they could not fail to embarrass me, still I was impressed to see her in her blue, flowered robe tied with a crimson sash, her thick hair knotted up. She was a tall woman, taller than I. She stood with her hand on Monsieur's forehead, while he stared up at her. An educated man, doubtless he was not convinced by her mumbo-jumbo, and at the same time he might have realized he was in a dangerous position, closed up in a poor woman's cottage. I saw him glance toward the door. At the same time I was fumbling through my mother's wooden chest, and laying out on the altar her scientific implements, as she called them, her beakers and alembics for distilling her love potions, her hypodermic syringes, her fortune cards and tablets for automatic writing. If these things reassured Monsieur, he gave no sign. "She is very near," my mother said. "I feel her wanting to come in," words I had heard before.

Often on these occasions she would contort her face, and the voice of the spirit would slip between her clenched lips in a whisper, easy to misunderstand. That morning I was surprised all this had progressed so quickly. Usually my mother would sit to ask some questions, gaining confidences that she then would give back, though nothing that might shock someone, for her purpose was always to console or reassure. These phrases that she used were very bland. But now Monsieur had not yet been a quarter of an hour in the house. And it really was as if something was desperate to get in. I could hear the shutters rattle in the wind. My mother's transformation was so violent and abrupt I was astonished. I dropped the vial in my hand and watched it shatter on the hearth, between the enormous bags of charcoal that my father sometimes brought. She did not stop to scold me. Her eyes were turned back in her head. When she spoke, it was in a type of language different from the patois I had always heard from her, a woman who could not write her name. In a moment she had the accent of the Creoles sent to Paris for their education. "Oh, Monsieur, I felt I could say anything, show you my secret self. Perhaps it even gave me pleasure to think of you as a more natural man, less civilized than others I had met, because of your heritage. But civilization has its uses, of which self-restraint is the most prominent—too late I see that now. When I stumbled back and collapsed on the settee, at that moment you mistook my hesitation for surrender! I can never forgive you for misjudging me. And even if it took me less than a minute to recover my strength, so that I was able to strike you in that area, the source of all your urges, still it was enough. A second would have been enough! It is in our impulses that we betray each other and ourselves. Our actions are pale shadows, chasing afterward. Besides, did you think it was impossible for me to have found out that you had come that evening from Mme. Baziat's house? Did you think I would not smell her perfume on your breath, while you were kissing me?"

"I had had a . . . glass of wine," faltered Monsieur. His cravat had come undone. My mother stood over him with her hand on his forehead, pushing him back into his chair.

Even when she beat me, I had never seen her in a rage like this, a mixture of ice and flame. "Do you think I am interested in your excuses? You betrayed me."

"But I never—"

"Fool, do you think I am still speaking of that night? You were to visit me the next afternoon, at two o'clock. I specifically told you. Did you forget? One month before, when you gave my father and me a tour of your laboratory, you spoke of the death of Socrates, and the poison you were using for your experiments—I stole it. I wanted to provide my own experiment, perhaps with a kitten or a mouse. But then at one o'clock, because of my despair, I thought I'd use a larger animal. How would I know you would not come? Can you be so stupid as to think I wished to die? No, I wished to punish you as you deserved. I imagined you'd have all the time to make the antidote. I'd read the book. Socrates—the fellow talked for hours. But how could you think that I was serious when I said I never wished to see your face again?"

There was thunder over the river, and rain upon the roof of our little house. Monsieur was quiet. I think he must have guessed what was to happen. He had a fever, after all, and his skin was yellow, streaked with sweat. He could not look my mother in the face. Instead, he glanced at me. But in place of helping him, perhaps I gave him the last shock to his system, for at that moment I felt something beside my ear. When I looked up, I saw my mother's serpent, which she used sometimes in her ceremonies. It lived in a wicker basket underneath the altar, but was forever getting out, a harmless creature from the swamp. So it was reaching toward me from one of the shelves, a long, green creature that was like this tube that runs to the cylinder of compressed oxygen, right by my nose, like this.

I brushed it away. Because I have the gift, I was afraid. But at the same time I was thinking how terrible this woman was, so cruel and such a liar. Innocent as I was, even I could see that if you reject this man one day, and kick him in the place she mentioned, perhaps you can't expect for him to visit you the next day as if nothing had happened. Who would swallow deadly poison, unless she wanted to destroy herself? And these mice and these kittens—at fourteen, I could not bear to think about them. I'd had enough. I stepped toward him, and Monsieur followed me with his eyes. I don't know what I was going to do. But I was finished with something. My mother turned toward me also, and I could see it mixed together in her face, something that knew that I was going to challenge her, and reject her, and run away from her, not only that morning, but forever in the years to come. Her face twisted with rage. She had her fingers locked in Monsieur's hair, and she forced his head back and forth, and turned his neck one way and another. When I came toward her, she turned his head so that he watched me, twisting his neck with her right hand. She was a strong woman, but what she used was not her strength. It was the strength of the devil that was inside of her, a devil in league with many others, and many other names. But always it requires a human agency. Another drink of water, please. You see I offer a confession at long last, but not just for myself . . .

(Recorded and transcribed as part of the research into a book, Mysteries of the Old Quarter, *by Ernest Butler Smith [Grossett & Dunlap, 1938], an interview never quoted or otherwise mentioned in the published text)*

8. THREE YEARS PREVIOUS: " . . . THE MORNING HAS COME
AFTER THE STORM"

September 10, 1885

My dear Monsieur,

I thank you for the flowers you have sent. I will be so happy to see you when I have returned from the sanatorium, which Papa tells me we have you to thank for the arrangements, due to your friendship with the director, a kind gentleman, even though he is a Swiss with a long beard. It is hard to remember how I must have behaved to be so desperate in that place. But now the morning has come after the storm, because of your generosity. Oh, I am so ashamed. But now Papa tells me there is no reason to concern myself, that these attacks of nerves are quite common and can be easily forgotten. To be a woman is to have these moods. Oh, I am happy to think so! I am quite sure you will be proud of me, and of the progress I have made. I wish it were tomorrow. But what will come, will come quickly, after all.

Fondly,

S. N.

(From a letter discovered in the inside waistcoat pocket of a corpse, otherwise unidentified, found in a coal sack in a flooded alley off the Rue Dumaine, May 26, 1888)

Afterword to "Mysteries of the Old Quarter"

For a while I lived in New Orleans, where this story takes place. Like many stories set there, it is haunted by the ghost of the 2005 hurricane.

—PAUL PARK

Jeffrey Ford

Jeffrey Ford is the author of the stand-alone novels *The Portrait of Mrs. Charbuque, The Girl in the Glass,* and *The Shadow Year,* as well as the Well-Built City Trilogy, consisting of *The Physiognomy, Memoranda,* and *The Beyond.* His short stories have been collected into three books—*The Fantasy Writer's Assistant, The Empire of Ice Cream,* and *The Drowned Life.* He is the recipient of the World Fantasy Award, the Nebula, the Shirley Jackson Award, and the Edgar Allan Poe Award. Along with his wife and two sons, he lives in South Jersey and teaches writing and literature at Brookdale Community College.

JEFFREY FORD

The Summer Palace

FOR GENERATIONS, THE ruins of the Well-Built City lay like some fallen monster we were unsure had really expired and thought might only be playing dead, all the while scheming. Decades passed and then slowly, cautiously, a few brave souls invaded its crumbled opulence, bringing back reports of wonders as if they'd travelled far away to some exotic other continent. In fact, the ruins were a few mere miles from our village of Wenau, which, as history has it, was spawned by those fleeing the city's destruction.

Once the intrepid few began to bring back both strange and useful artifacts from the ruins, the citizenry of our village took notice. On the day that one of those explorers bought everyone at the inn a round of Rose Ear Sweet and paid for it with a gold coin he claimed to have discovered amidst the remarkable debris, the entire populace instantly became treasure hunters. We, who had once cowered at the thought of what savage phantoms trod its broken streets, now swarmed over the place like a community of rats picking clean a carcass. At first we wanted wealth, but then those of us whose curiosities exceeded the mundane became a kind of troop of archeologists. We dug for meaning, the ideas and philosophies, the history of the place, trying to piece together where and what we'd come from.

Everyone has their keepsakes from the Well-Built City, and to be sure, I have mine. I never discovered gold or one of the strange mechanical devices that are so highly prized. What I discovered, few of my neighbors would consider worth a feather. In one of the hundred caverns created by the destruction of what must have been a towering building (from a mosaic circle inlaid in the marble floor of the place's entrance, I learned it had once been known as the Ministry of Physiognomy), I salvaged a box of old papers. Time had seared the pages brown, rain had played havoc with the ink, and the box itself was mildewed, smelling like an open grave. Still, I carried the sodden load back to my home in Wenau. There, I removed the hundreds of damp pages from the box and set them out, twenty-five at a time, in the summer sun.

Once they were dry, I began to study them. They were all written by the hand of the same individual, a man by the name of Cley. He was a physiognomist, a sort of investigator, who read, in the physical features of men and women, their guilt or innocence, their immorality and their grace. Bonikem, who is writing a history of the Well-Built City based on all that has been discovered, has told me that this fellow, Cley, rose to a high position in the government under the rule of Drachton Below, becoming Physiognomist, First Class. "I've not been able to find certain connections I need to corroborate it," Bonikem told me, "but I'm sure Cley had a hand in the city's demise."

What I had in my pile of papers was the record of all of those cases he'd investigated from when he was a student at the Ministry, to when he achieved the superior rank of First Class, at which point he either stopped writing or there is another box buried in the city somewhere. The interesting thing about them, though, is that they must be his personal record, for, as a student, he often disparages his professors and later, when he has become a professional, his superiors. They are by no means succinct reports but windy conflations full of opinion, outbursts, fractured narrative, and flights of a bleak fancy.

Although many of the cases have been completely obliterated by rain, words turned to black stains, many complete cases remain intact or at least readable. On the last night of the week, our club of archeologists gets together at someone's home. We smoke a pipe, drink a glass of Rose Ear Sweet or that whiskey brought back from the city whose label names it Tears in the River. At some point in the evening I will read one of Physiognomist Cley's cases for everyone. We have a hoot and a hallo over them, and later, beneath the moon, on the way home along the riverbank, we think about their implications. Here's the one I'll be reading this week:

The Summer Palace

Chibbins—I see the dolt now, sitting across from me in the carriage, his face as futile a bowl of porridge as has ever been whipped up through the grim processes of intercourse. His father is none other than the Master's,

Drachton Below's, personal butler, known to the populace by the full title Chibbins, My Good Man. This pale bag of potatoes that sits before me in my memory, though, has succeeded through the academy and into the physiognomical service due only to his father's exalted position. Everyone knew the son was an idiot—a cursory reading of his visage tells the dim tale—but no professor dared fail him, no administrator in the service would do more than grin and bear his buffoonery. It's just this kind of nepotism that is blunting the scalpel edge of the sweet science. When, in the future, I finally achieve the rank of Physiognomist, First Class, evicting Physiognomist Scheffler, I'll put things to rights concerning the Ministry. I believe my first order of business will be to have the mincing Scheffler sent off to the salt mines of Doralice, not the least of which for sabotaging only my third professional case by saddling me with the gibbering Chibbins. "If I were you, Cley, I'd make sure the young man has a wonderful experience, if you catch my drift," he said. I nodded while in my eye's-mind my hands were wrapped firmly around his throat.

OFF TO BELOW'S Summer Palace in the dead of winter. The snow was calf-deep, and the carriage driver had to navigate a path around the drifts in the road that led out beyond the circular wall of the city. It was my duty to fill Chibbins in on what it was we were investigating at the heart of the Willow Forest. I had little patience that morning, cold and tired as I was, but I was determined to perform my duties.

He sat across from me, staring out the window, clasping and unclasping his hands, unconsciously blowing saliva bubbles. "I've never been beyond the circular wall," he said, his mouth a hole in dough, his face, a flabby ass with a nose. "I'm a little worried."

"Very well," I said. "We'll be looking into a murder. Barlow, the caretaker at the Palace, was found two days ago, stabbed through the back by an icicle, which impaled his heart before exiting his chest."

Chibbins asked, "How's the food there?"

I shook my head. "The only people remaining on the premises are his wife, Mrs. Barlow, their daughter, Ludiya, and a handyman named Rothac."

Chibbins turned to face me. "Rothac did it," he said and nodded.

"An ingenious conclusion," I said, "but there had also been notice from the Palace recently of break-ins, of some stranger wandering the premises at night. Perhaps a story concocted by the guilty party to mitigate suspicion or maybe a real intruder out to do in Barlow, although, having met him once, I have to question the effort."

Chibbins made a face that I suppose was meant to convey deep thought but came across as a jagged evacuation. He burst out with, "Mrs. Barlow killed him."

He looked ready to explain, but I quickly raised one finger and said, "Now, Chibbins, it's time to be silent." That defused him and sent him back to the window and the mindless clasping and unclasping of his hands.

I WRAPPED MY cape around me to block the fierce wind. The snow was coming down at an angle. I told Chibbins to fetch the bags and ascended, through a series of drifts, the marble steps to the Summer Palace's main entrance. A woman with a shawl draped over her head and shoulders opened the glass doors and greeted me.

"Mrs. Barlow," I said.

"Miss Barlow," she said and removed the shawl from around her face. It was not the tiresome washerwoman I'd expected, but instead quite a physiognomical specimen, exuding a certain ripeness of age. I took her offered hand, delighting in the prospect of getting my calipers on her features.

"Thank goodness you've come," she said. "We fear for our lives."

I had the inclination that her fingers purposefully lingered in my palm, but the moment, of course, was shattered by the entrance of my fellow investigator.

"Physiognomist Chibbins," I said and waved in his direction.

Ludiya Barlow offered Chibbins her hand but instead of politely clasping it once and releasing it, he guided it toward his lips and kissed the back of it like blowing a saliva bubble. The young lady was startled and immediately flushed red. It was everything I could do not to kick him.

She took us on a tour of the Palace, four stories of white stone crammed with paintings and curiosities. Enormous arched windows, looking out on the snow and the bare, brown whips of the surrounding acres of willows. The carpets, the chandeliers, the conservatory, the library were magnificent. We finally came face-to-face with Mrs. Barlow, sitting before the fireplace in a room on the second floor. She appeared distraught enough, but in my immediate gross examination of her features, I detected through her maze of wrinkles an eye distance measurement that denoted a dangerous degree of shrewdness. It appeared to me that her hair was in the process of falling out, so I refused her hand, though it was offered twice. I allowed Chibbins to stand in for me, and he kissed her on the knuckles. She drew her hand back quickly and wiped it on her dress.

*   *   *

WEARING A FUR coat and a pair of men's boots, the old woman showed us outside, behind the conservatory where she'd found her husband. Steam wrapped her words in white puffs. "There," she said, pointing near the building. The brown bloodstains were evident even beneath the fresh snow. "He must have been working on the basement window, there."

"Fascinating," said Chibbins and got down on his hands and knees near the window.

I, instead, looked up. There were icicles as long and thick as my leg hanging from the gutter, jutting out from the fourth floor. They looked sharp enough to impale a man from that height. I looked at Chibbins, who, in an attempt to reenact the crime was pretending to fix the window.

"Off your knees, Chibbins," I said. "Back away from the wall." He did exactly what I'd asked, and when he was standing next to me, whispered, "How was that?"

"Well done," I said. At that moment one of the icicles cracked and shot straight down, spearing the fallen snow and shattering.

My partner jumped and gave a shout. The old woman shot me a look as if I was responsible for his foolishness.

"I think it's obvious what happened to your husband," I said.

"Your daughter did it," said Chibbins.

"Shut up," I told him and tweaked his ear. I turned back to the Mrs. "An unlucky coalescing of events is what I see. Your husband was only murdered if one can ascribe criminal intent to a falling icicle."

"You don't know, Physiognomist. There's a most unnatural spirit that pervades the grounds of the Summer Palace. We've seen it, at night, stalking through the halls. It's everywhere."

"How very insubstantial," I said.

"It's a ghost," she said. "It wants to kill us all."

"I'm not about to chase some fart of your imagination through the Willow Forest in the dead of winter."

"Help us," she said, and tears formed in her eyes.

I turned away from her and saw Ludiya staring at us from the conservatory window. She looked to her mother and then to me. I spun around. "On second thought," I announced, "I've decided we'll stay and get to the bottom of things."

Mrs. Barlow let out a sigh of relief that somehow excited me. She drew close and put her arms around my arm. "Thank you. Thank you," she said.

I remembered her scalp condition and shrugged her off, pretending to look for Chibbins. He was back at the basement window on his hands and knees, finishing whatever job he'd started earlier.

"CHIBBINS IS COLD," said Chibbins as we walked a snowy path through the willows. We'd been told by Mrs. Barlow that we would find the handyman, Rothac, out in his quarters on the eastern side of the fountains. The forest was cold and the day dim, overcast and sliding into late afternoon.

"Chibbins is cold and tired," said Chibbins, and he began dragging his feet and groaning every few seconds. I'd had enough of it long before it started. Stopping, I turned around and confronted my partner.

"Are we going home?" he asked.

I made a fist with my right hand and punched him in the face. It was like hitting a pillow. He stood there blinking at me as the blood began to trickle from a split lip. "My bowel has produced turds with more intelligence than you, Chibbins," I said. "Unless you want me to cut your throat, I'm going to require that you at least, for the rest of this investigation, say nothing. There will also be no more of your witless antics, kissing the lady's hands, crawling around, playing make-believe."

"My father will be sad to hear of this," he said.

"It won't matter because the news of your demise will undoubtedly cheer him. Do you understand?"

Chibbins nodded, and we continued on our way. Two minutes later, he said, "When is dinner?"

My hand was in my pocket, wrapped around the scalpel. The only thing that saved the idiot's life is that Rothac's cottage came into view. The chimney of the place belched a strange violet smoke, and as we drew closer to its door, the air filled with a sweet aroma.

At the cottage door, Chibbins turned his back to it and then knocked with the heel of his shoe. "How's that?" he asked.

I couldn't let him know because the door opened then and an exceedingly short, balding man, wearing a fur vest and holding a large knife, came into view.

"Rothac?" I said.

He nodded.

"Physiognomists Cley and Chibbins," I said. "We've been sent by the Master to investigate Barlow's death."

"Come in," he said.

I had to duck to get through the door, and once inside, the ceiling was mere inches above me. Chibbins was taller than I, and he was forced to keep his head down. The handyman showed us to small chairs at a small table.

"Welcome to my home," said Rothac.

"A droll trolliary, to be sure," I said. He smiled while I studied his form. The bulging, naked forehead accentuated by a ring of hair was an obvious sign of intellect, but the rest of the runtish fellow seemed underdone as if Nature had taken him from the oven before the yeast had risen. My instruments, I was sure, would indicate a propensity for treachery and animal desire.

"What can you tell us of ghosts?" I asked.

Rothac looked behind him and then leaning forward whispered, "The Sanctity of Grace. She hears everything, sees everything, knows everything."

Chibbins leaned to the side in his chair and farted. "Do you think she heard that?" he asked.

"She heard it before you were born," said Rothac.

"Who is she?" I asked.

"She comes at night, out of the old cemetery, sometimes wailing, sometimes humming as if to a child at bedtime. She glows green in the dark and her face is cruel."

"And she killed Barlow?" I asked.

"If you believe in accidents, then Barlow's death was one," he said.

"Don't speak to me in riddles," I warned him. "Your stature and this tragedy of a home are enough as it is to make me think I've fallen into a tedious fairy tale. Out with it directly."

"Hear, hear," said Chibbins and banged the table with his fist.

"One can't be sure, but the Sanctity has the ghost magic to have made it happen."

"The Sanctity?" I said.

"Of Grace," said Rothac. "As the fairy tale would have it, she was one of the workers, let's say, 'impressed' into service by Master Below to build this forest retreat. No one knows her real name, but there were many stories from the workers in the camp about her acts of kindness. There was even a story in which she breathed life into a dead calf."

"To the point," I reminded.

"Well, when the Palace was finished, because it contained secret passageways and tunnels that the Master wanted revealed to no one, he called in his security force and on a summer afternoon, at gunpoint, the workers were ordered to dig their own graves. When they were finished, they were to signal to the gunmen, at which point they would be shot and fall to their final rest. For their service to the city, Below had four hundred headstones brought, each expertly carved with one of the dead worker's names."

"Generous," I said.

"Munificent," said Rothac with a touch of seditious irony.

I was about to point out to him that a stone could easily be carved for him as well when Chibbins inquired as to what was in the bubbling pot on the hearth. "Stew?" asked my partner. I have to admit, I was wondering, myself, as the aroma from it was most alluring, like some kind of hot liquid pastry.

Rothac said, "Come and see this." He hopped down from his little chair, and I lifted my aching hindquarters off mine. We all repaired to the adjoining room where there was a very large fireplace, its brickwork taking up one entire wall. The fire blazed and bubbles were bursting in the pot, which hissed and spit like a wildcat. As we drew closer to it, a faint violet mist could be seen rising away from the brew and up the chimney.

We stood for a few moments staring into the pot. Chibbins stuck his finger in, burnt himself, and cried out. Rothac looked up at me and, I must say, conveyed an expression of sympathy.

"This isn't stew," he said. "This is a recipe left for me by the Sanctity of Grace. She wrote it, over a series of nights, in the ash of the fireplace. I'd wake each morning with excitement and run to see what she'd written. I wrote it all down, and to entice her to return, I'd leave her sweetmeats. On the morning that she left the last of the recipe, she also left a dollop of vomit on the platter that had held her reward."

"What is it?" I asked.

"What is it?" said Chibbins.

Rothac scratched his armpit. I took a step back. "It's a drug," he said. "It makes the imagination reel and real. Drink a mug of it and you'll see. Ludiya calls it Sheer Beauty."

"Ludiya?" I said. "She's been to this pen?"

"No, Physiognomist Cley. Don't get the wrong idea. I take it to the Palace sometimes when I'm invited for dinner, and we sip it afterward, lounging in the plush thrones. Mrs. Barlow is quite a devotee of the Beauty."

"Something like this would be illegal in the city," I said. "The Master wants no escape for his electorate."

"Try it while you're here," said Rothac. "You'll see."

"I'd rather drink your bathwater," I said. "I want this mess disposed

of by tomorrow. If the Master were present, you'd already have been immolated."

The diminutive creature bowed.

AT DINNER WITH Mrs. Barlow and her daughter, Chibbins seemed
hypnotized by the food. He was blessedly quiet but for the sounds of his
chewing as he dispatched each dish with a methodical rapacity. The main
course was stuffed meat hole and peppered thistle roots. It wasn't for me.
A charred tube of pig meat as big as a log stuffed with cremat—shit in a pit
is what it should have been called—and a peppered pile of the gardener's
rakings. No thank you.

"Rothac told me about Sheer Beauty," I said to the ladies.

Ludiya glanced nervously at her mother. Mrs. Barlow, who had a drib-
ble of cremat on her chin, said, "And what of it?"

"It's illegal," I said.

"Cley," she said, "you don't understand. Every summer, all summer
long, I am in contact with the Master. He treats me like I'm his mother.
We sit out in the statue garden, surrounded by rosebushes, beneath an umbrella, and he tells me everything. So you'll do nothing about the Beauty.
You'll say nothing about it. Or this summer I will be a mosquito in the
Master's ear, suggesting you be sent to Doralice." She smiled and wiped
her chin.

The old witch had me. I calmly turned to Ludiya and said, "What is it
like to take the Sheer Beauty?"

She was sopping up a puddle of cremat with a slice of bread. The sight
of her bringing the brown stained mess to her lips initiated a wave of erotic
nausea that swept through me. "Strange things happen," she said. "Odd
things that leave you unsure if they are real or unreal. The more you believe them unreal, the realer they prove themselves to be; but then put faith
in them, and their illusory nature begins to reveal itself again."

"Can you give me an example?" I said, smiling, even though her explanation was something Chibbins might have come out with.

"You can speak directly to the Sanctity of Grace if you drink it. Without the Sheer Beauty, a living person can only feel the force of her power,
hear her wailing, but with the drug, she appears clearly before you, as the
woman she was, and not merely a green glowing mist floating through
the night. She says that she went to her grave a saint, but her decades in
the dirt have made her bitter. She's returned for revenge against Master
Below. 'I've etched his headstone,' she told me one night in the gazebo.

'And yours,' she added. Then the sky lit up pink with fireworks and a buck came out of the willows and entered the gazebo. He sang 'Last Carriage to the Moon' accompanied by music that seeped out of the shadows. When the sky had again gone black and the beast had finished his song, the Sanctity mounted him, grabbing his antlers with both hands, and they loped away amid the trees toward the old cemetery."

IN A NIGHTMARISH turn of events, I was forced to share a room with Chibbins for the night. I protested vehemently, saying, "You mean to tell me that in a palace of this size there isn't another room for my partner? The basement will do."

Mrs. Barlow shook her head. "There is one room; the others are closed up for the winter. It has a nice big bed for you gentlemen."

"It won't do," I said.

"Like a mosquito in his ear," she said and stared directly at me. In that instant, I saw one of her hairs, a long white one, drop off.

"Very well," I said.

I made Chibbins turn around while I undressed and slipped beneath the blankets. Then he undressed, dropping his clothes in a pile on the floor. He approached the bed stark naked, all lumpen and the color of milk. I lifted the scalpel I'd placed on the night table next to me. Looking away from him, I said, "You're sleeping on the floor." I expected him to protest, forgetting for a second that this was Chibbins, whose reason was twisted as a pig's tail. In silence, his pale pile drooped down to the floor. I lay back and entertained my thoughts about the case.

This was really the case that was no case. It was obvious. An investigation was wholly after the fact. What had happened, as I could see it, was that Rothac cooked up a pot of heady swill that had them all cockeyed. Barlow wasn't paying attention to what he was doing and took a falling icicle through the back. Unable to deal with the old man's passing and high on Sheer Beauty, they'd conspired to concoct some outlandish tale about a bitter saint in search of revenge. That was it. The only concern for me that remained was delving deeper into Ludiya's personality, searching for the key that might open her and give access to her most sacred physiognomical junctures.

I rested back on the pillow and realized that Chibbins had shimmied under the bed. He was down there moving around and scratching on the underside of the mattress. "Damn you, Chibbins," I yelled. "What are you doing?"

"Making a nest," he said.

"Stop it," I told him.

All was silent. I lay back on the pillow and closed my eyes. Five seconds later, from beneath the mattress there came an extemporaneous song, like a child might concoct, about a monkey who worked at an island inn. I got out of bed, fully intending to beat him to a pulp. "Come out, Chibbins," I called. His head suddenly popped out from beneath my side of the bed, and I gave a start.

"Ever at your service, Physiognomist Cley," he said, looking up at me.

I kicked him in the side of the head with my bare foot. My large toe smashed against his rock skull, and the pain was exquisite. I hopped on one foot to the middle of the room, cursing wildly. By the time the pain had subsided, Chibbins had crawled out into the open and stood there, like some bitter ghost, returned to murder Reason itself.

I took one step toward him, and that's when we heard the strange cry. It came from outside, the sound of a woman wailing. Even with the window closed, it drilled through the glass and lodged in my spine, making my ears twitch and my neck hair rise.

"Get dressed," I told Chibbins. "Hurry."

MINUTES LATER WE were out in the dark, crunching through the snow. Chibbins carried a small lantern that emitted a weak light, and I carried my scalpel. The moon was absent, but there were stars above. A cry came again from off in the direction of the fountains. It was freezing and there was a stiff breeze, the bare willow whips tapping together with each gust.

"Nabdoodle," said Chibbins and spun in a circle, the beam of the lantern dancing wildly against the dark.

"To the fountain, ass," I said and ran. I could hear my partner scuffing through the snow behind me. I was winded by the time we reached the iced-over pool, and I sat on the edge of it. Chibbins soon arrived and held the lantern up to light the curious statue at the center of the circular stone basin. Its copper figures had gone green, and although I could not make out the features in the poor light, I knew, from having seen it earlier in the day, that one was the Master himself, Drachton Below, naked, holding his member in his hand, his head tipped back slightly. The other form was that of a woman made of leaves. She held, in both hands, a goblet fashioned from a small pumpkin. When the fountain wasn't frozen, the water represented the wine of Nature, continually being consumed by the Master, and at the other end, dispelled in an arc, so that it rained down upon a facsimile of the Well-Built City, which lay in miniature at his feet. The significance of it evaded me, but, of course, that was beside the point.

I listened to the wind and gazed at the constellations reflected in the pool's glazed surface. "Chibbins," I whispered. "Do you hear anything?"

"A physiognomist whispering," he said.

Too weary to kill him, I got up, having decided we should go pay a surprise visit to the handyman. From a physiognomical standpoint, a technical examination of Rothac's features in an attempt to conclude his potential for treachery was unnecessary. You couldn't miss that fact that he was less of everything, ergo also less of morality and justice. Let's be clear, he was, to my mind, part beast, and when Chibbins had sung his song about the monkey, beyond the fact that I wanted to gouge out his very eyes, I imagined Rothac as the monkey serving drinks and entertaining on the piano.

We'd not gone ten yards toward the handyman's house when Chibbins leaped into the air and loosed a scream. I turned back to see him frantically dancing in place, his feet moving in a blur. Something was scuttling on the ground next to him. "It bit me," he cried.

I raised the scalpel and moved toward him. "Lower the lantern," I said, and I couldn't believe he did as I'd actually requested. There was something there. As I got closer it appeared a snake rearing up to strike, but I knew it couldn't be as there was still too much shadowed bulk beneath and behind it. Then I saw, the snake effect was caused by the long neck of a bird, whose feathers suddenly opened behind it. Even in the dim light I could apprehend its beauty. It let out a wail, exactly as we had heard, and I took a step back.

A voice came from behind me. "A peacock," it said, and I turned to see Rothac with a cudgel in one hand and a lantern in the other. "The birds of the Summer Palace, they make a haunting sound, especially in winter."

"I thought it was your ghost, the Sacrilege of Anonymity."

"The Sanctity of Grace? You may see her yet tonight," he said.

Chibbins had cornered the peacock and was petting its neck, purring like a cat.

"What, pray tell, brings you out at this time of night? I'm sure it wasn't the cry of the Palace buzzard here. It wouldn't have alarmed you."

"I couldn't sleep. Something's about to happen, and I feel it's not going to be good."

"That statement could accurately have been made at any hour since my arrival. A sinister tedium, with dashes of the grotesque, yourself included."

"Before this is over, Cley, you will need to imbibe the Beauty."

"Think again, manikin. I . . ." The interruption was caused by a fearful noise coming from off in the distance. This too was a wail, but wholly different from that made by the bird. The very air seemed to vibrate from it.

"Look," said Rothac and pointed.

I turned and saw it out amid the netted shadow of the willow branches. There was a green mist, floating above the ground, moving along at the pace of a funeral procession. It was headed toward us. Truthfully, I wanted to run but was stunned by the sight of it. The green fog, though continually disintegrating into nothing at its edges, appeared at times to be a thin sheet wound around a body so that certain features of physiognomy became momentarily clear beneath the insubstantial wrap.

It was on the path, twenty feet away from us. It wailed again, and I raised the scalpel. At the sound of the spirit, Chibbins sprang into action and dashed toward it. "Back, you idiot," I yelled. Dropping the lantern, and making an arrowhead with his clasped hands in front of him, he dove into the miasma, still on his feet, and began laughing and flapping his arms as if to disperse it.

"It'll kill him," said Rothac.

"Could I be so lucky?" I said.

The handyman and I watched as the ghost left Chibbins behind, turning in circles, wildly waving his arms. Now it bore down on us. I thrust my blade forward for protection, only realizing then how useless it would be. Only a few yards from us, it stopped advancing. There came a loud popping noise from it, like a bottle of Sparkling Vertigo hastily uncorked, and something large and glistening shot out from within the green folds of mist. Whatever it was passed me by at a furious speed, and then I heard Rothac grunt. I turned to see him fallen back, his lantern on the ground. A huge icicle had pinned him through the chest, its partially shattered point, jutting from his back, keeping him inches off the snowy earth. I looked back to the mist, expecting the same fate, but the phantom had dispersed into night. Instead, Chibbins was beside me, very much alive.

"Chibbins is tired," he said, and I beat him remorselessly.

THE NEXT MORNING at breakfast, I described to Mrs. Barlow the demise of Rothac. We sat in a parlor with a wall-size window, looking out at the snow and willows. Sunlight streamed in, and I was happy for its comfort. Ludiya was there, and in the telling of the harrowing incident, I tried to make myself seem courageous and coolheaded. At one juncture, where I described wrestling with the spirit in a battle of life and death, the young

Miss Barlow smiled and nodded. Luckily, Chibbins, now with a blackened left eye and a missing front tooth, was eating and could not surface to contradict me.

"So do you still doubt what I told you of my husband's death?" asked the old woman.

I couldn't verbally acknowledge my mistake. Instead I very subtly shook my head.

"Last night, after it killed Rothac, it came to my room," said Ludiya. "It slithered up under my covers. Did I mention that I wear no sleeping apparel? I woke to its ghostly tongue, lapping my flesh. The green mist licked me from head to foot, and then I heard the voice of the Sanctity of Grace in my mind. She told me, 'By tomorrow night, I will have consumed you all.' Then she vanished."

I must confess to a certain tightness in the trousers after hearing Ludiya's tale; an exquisite confusion stirred my thoughts.

"Physiognomist Cley, you and Physiognomist Chibbins must drink the Beauty and do battle with the phantom in a more substantial form. I know you can defeat her and save us," said Miss Barlow. She reached across the table and laid her hand on mine.

My trepidation toward drinking Rothac's sweet swill evaporated with Ludiya's touch. I looked momentarily at the young woman's mother, and that wrinkled visage was staring at our nearly clasped hands, smiling and nodding. I quickly drew my hand back.

"We'll see," I said.

Chibbins threw his spoon into the empty oatmeal bowl in front of him. "I summon the spirit," he announced and belched loudly.

Mrs. Barlow winced. "The Ministry of Physiognomy is turning out some real chaff these days," she said.

"My apologies for my partner," I said, "but as you can see, I had a *word* with him about it last night."

"I was referring to you, Cley," she said.

"What's that?" asked Ludiya, pointing to the center of the table.

I looked to see the green mist rising from the dried gourd centerpiece. In a flash, it coalesced into the rippling winding sheet form I'd witnessed on the path the previous night. Chibbins applauded, but I was not so happy to see the thing again. Ludiya screamed. Mrs. Barlow stood and shook her fist at the apparition. "Be gone," she shouted in a cracking voice.

When I heard the popping noise, I dove to the floor. Somebody gave a sudden gasp of pain. When I finally lifted my head above the tabletop, I noticed the Sanctity of Grace had, of an instant, disappeared, and I remembered Rothac saying, "She hears everything, sees everything, is every-where." The next thing I knew, Ludiya was crying hysterically. I turned my attention to her mother, now pinned to the back of her throne with a thick icicle through the mouth. Blood and shattered teeth were everywhere. Her death stare was pointed in my direction.

"If we're to be saved, you must take the Beauty, Cley," said Ludiya amid her blubbering. Chibbins was busy placing coffee cups and saucers beneath the spots where the frozen shaft leaked onto the tablecloth. He lifted his empty oatmeal bowl, turned it upside down, and put it on Mrs. Barlow's head, covering her eyes.

THAT AFTERNOON, CHIBBINS and I made our way out to Rothac's place and retrieved the cauldron of Beauty that still sat on the fireplace hearth. Of course, by then the fire was out and the stuff was cold, but Ludiya had told us it could be reheated. Chibbins carried the pot by its handle, twitch-ing as he walked and sloshing the violet liquid so that some drops fell out. Wherever it fell, the snow turned not violet but black.

Once we returned to the Palace, I ordered Chibbins to drag Mrs. Bar-low's and Rothac's remains to the carriage house where the cold would keep them somewhat fresher in death than life. When he returned from that task, I sent him out again, this time to count the willow trees. In the meantime, I found Ludiya and proffered my condolences. We sat on the divan in one of the hundred rooms, my arm tightly around her shoulders, like I was a favorite uncle. Her bosom pressed against me, and I lightly kissed her ear as she sobbed and said, "Poor Mother." *Poor Mother* was not the appellation I'd have used for the old hag, although *Poor* might have been part of it.

After dinner, we retired to the plush thrones of the piano room, and Ludiya served us each a piping hot mug of the Beauty. The bubbling violet gave off a paradisiacal scent, and I found myself unable to resist it. So sweet, like a sweetness from the center of the earth or wrung out of the blue sky like rain wrung from the blouse of a field worker caught in a storm. I tasted it, and for a moment, my mind went blank. I saw pure white as if the powerful taste were instead a bright light. Once I began drinking, feeling the warmth of the brew as it traveled through me, I didn't stop until the mug was empty. I took mine away from my lips as Ludiya did the same with hers. Chibbins had beat us both to the finish.

"Now," said Ludiya, "give it a minute and you'll begin to see what I was talking about."

"How long do the effects of the drug last?" asked Chibbins.

I did a double take, unable to believe that my partner was capable of asking an intelligent question. In fact it was the question I was about to ask.

"Three or four hours," she said.

"Must I stay in my chair?" asked Chibbins.

"No," she said. "You will feel the need to rise and move around."

For my part, I was staring at Chibbins. Something had happened. A great change had come over him. Not only had the Beauty conferred upon him a sort of relaxed, confident persona, leaning back in his chair with one leg suavely over the left arm, but he now had, without my witnessing it having grown, a thin dark mustache. He looked over at me and said, "Cley, old boy, do we have a plan?"

"Chibbins, what's happened to you?" I asked.

"Nothing yet," he said. "I propose we charge the Sanctity of Grace simultaneously, scalpels carving the air. We'll slice her stem from stern and leave what's left for the peacocks."

"Calm down," I said. "We'll wait to see what the meeting brings."

"There are birds in the fireplace," said Ludiya, and I noticed piano music, although no one sat at the bench.

"It's starting," I said.

"Cley, you have a halo," said Chibbins.

"Where did you get the cigarette?" I asked.

"I've no idea," he said and took a drag. "Right now, there are green jewels crawling across the ceiling." His head was back and he was laughing.

Ludiya stood and approached me. I reached out and took her hand. Bringing it to my lips, I kissed the back of it.

"That's the ticket," said Chibbins.

I puckered my lips to kiss the hand again, but in the moment I'd looked away it had become a bird talon. Ludiya had somehow become her mother, but her mother covered in feathers and sporting a sharp beak. I dropped the talon and reared back in my seat. I blinked and the avian Mrs. Barlow was gone. Ludiya stood in the middle of the room, pointing up at the mirror over the fireplace. Not merely reflected in it, but within the world of the mirror the green mist rose. This time it cohered into more than a mere floating cloud. It became a woman with short dark hair and spectacles, wearing a plain grey dress, like a servant's uniform. She bobbed behind the glass and glanced from one to the other of us.

"Grab your scalpel," I called to Chibbins, but there was no reply. I looked over to see him kissing Ludiya. He had her dipped back in his arms; her mouth was open, and so was his. I shuddered. "No," I said.

"Yes," said the Sanctity of Grace, and then the floorboards slid away, and I fell into the dark, like the builders of the Summer Palace, falling into their graves.

WHEN I WOKE, I was sitting upright, strapped to a chair so that my arms could not move. The Sanctity of Grace was before me, lightly tapping my cheek.

"Wake up, Cley," she said. I opened my eyes and looked around. We were in a kind of study, rows of books lining the walls and gas lamps at the four corners. There was a door off to my right, and the Sanctity had taken her seat behind a desk, facing me.

"My office, Cley. Do you like it?"

"No doubt one of the Master's secret chambers you died to keep secret," I said. "Release me or you'll come to feel the full weight of the Well-Built City's security force upon you."

"And what will they do? Kill me?"

"You must have been one bitter ghost to have generated the supernatural energy to perform your deeds," I said.

"Bitter," she said, "is too weak a word. For every ounce of saintliness I possessed in life, I now have a thousand volts of hatred in death. You see, I was with child. If it was only me, I'd have gone to my rest."

"With child?" I said. "Not completely saintly, I see."

"Only the ruling classes see sex as immoral," she said. "And then, only for the lower class."

"I'm to be a sacrifice to your unborn child?" I asked. "Perhaps I can barter Chibbins's life for mine?"

"No," she said, "you're not to die, yet. You're a tool in my plot." She then picked up a pen and busied herself with some paperwork, reading documents and making minor corrections.

"There's paperwork in death?" I asked.

"You don't know the half of it," she said.

She was the plainest-looking woman I'd ever seen. Of course, I'd already eyed her physiognomical features, but I'd yet to garner a reading. She was very nearly an exact medium in intelligence and yet, the indicators that divulged her moral worth, chin to hairline, left eye to right earlobe, rendered readings off the top end of the scale. I was baffled as to how the two measurements could coincide on the same face without grotesquely twisting her appearance. It was, literally, supernatural.

"And how long must I sit here?" I asked.

She didn't look up but said, "Your partner will be along shortly to rescue you, and then we'll be finished here."

More time passed, and I wondered if perhaps all I was witnessing was a result of the Sheer Beauty. I watched closely for her image to ripple, for the walls of books to subtly waver insubstantially. And then the door burst in, wood chips flying. It was Chibbins, and he'd expertly kicked it in. I looked back to the Sanctity of Grace, who was rising from her chair. She walked around the desk and stood there.

"Physiognomist Chibbins, I believe you've got something for me," she said, clasping her hands behind her back, like a schoolmarm awaiting an answer.

"Yes, madam ghoul, I've got the best thing for you," he said and leaped forward into a somersault. While his body rolled, his left arm, hand holding a scalpel, was drawing back, so that when he sprang up onto one knee, he was ready to throw. The blade turned as it sailed slowly through the air. We all watched in anticipation, not the least the Sanctity of Grace, whom I was surprised took no effort to duck. With the sound of an eggshell cracking, the thing punctured her skull and dug into her ghostly brain. Her eyes glazed, she coughed up some dirt and then went over like a sack of laundry. A moment later, she turned to a green mist that quickly began to dissipate.

Chibbins was immediately at my chair, making easy work of the knots and straps that bound me. "Come quickly," he said. "It took me forever to find you in the maze of secret passageways." The catacombs beneath the house were impossibly complex, but Chibbins led the way with confidence and eventually brought us up, through a hidden stairway, back into the piano room. I will admit here, for no one else to see, that I'd still be there, beneath the Summer Palace, if it weren't for my partner. We found Ludiya, on the couch, sleeping.

"Did you have your way with her?" I asked Chibbins.

"Heavens no," he said, "to have done so would have been monstrous. I was administering artificial resuscitation. She passed out and I caught her." He gave a smile, and I wasn't sure if Chibbins was actually trafficking in irony or genuinely pleased with the aid he'd given. As it was, it didn't matter. By morning, once the Beauty had worn off, blithering and buffooning without mercy or mustache, he was as inane as he'd been before its odd sea change.

Now that we had eradicated the threat to the Summer Palace by killing the ghost of the Sanctity of Grace, Ludiya pretended to want nothing to do with me. I tried to comfort her some more in the fashion I had the previous day, and she shrugged off my grasp and told me I'd outstayed my welcome. A woman of such a tender age, she did not have the vocabulary to express her affection for me, and so her words became twisted, expressing the opposite of her desires. I could tell. I pressed my lips against hers and forced my tongue into her mouth. She bit it. True love is a sharp pain, I tell you.

WITH THE TASTE of blood still on my lips, Chibbins and I rode back in our carriage to the Well-Built City. We had brought with us Rothac's notes, and the cauldron of the remaining Sheer Beauty sat on the seat next to my partner. Every now and then, he'd stick his pinky into the cold mixture and bring it to his mouth, and for a few seconds he'd go from gibbering fool to sophisticated conversationalist, calling me, "Cley, old boy." All together, this amazingly erratic performance irritated me more than usual. Amid the kaleidoscope of Chibbinses, I wondered what our time in the Willow Forest added up to. It didn't seem to make any sense at all.

Physiognomist Scheffler had me report to the Master himself about the case. I was sent to his tower office at the center of the city. I'd met Drachton Below before. One night he'd mysteriously come to my rooms when I was a student in the Ministry and took me to see a young woman he'd transformed into an automaton. I'd not yet had to face him in a professional setting and was worried that he'd have little patience with the story I had to tell about his summer retreat.

His office was circular, with windows all around, a 360-degree view. I entered a room below its floor and then climbed a stair that left me in the middle of its circle. Below stood at the window, looking down.

"Physiognomist Cley reporting, Master."

He turned, cocked his head back and raised one eyebrow. "Cley, you've been to the Summer Palace?"

"Physiognomist Chibbins and I."

"Yes, well, the Chibbins boy is a subtraction of zero from itself," he said. "I'm sure it was a pleasure working with him."

"A delight," I said.

"His father will be pleased to hear it. Now sit down and tell me of this ghost Scheffler said you'd encountered."

I launched into my absurd story, mentioning Ludiya, Mrs. Barlow, Rothac, and the Sanctity of Grace. When I got to the part where the old woman's head was pierced by an icicle, he said, "Thank goodness for small favors." He referred to Rothac as "a curious and dirty little satyr," and at the mention of Ludiya, he smiled sardonically. He only really became interested when I began to describe the Sheer Beauty and its effects. The rest of the story disappeared for him, and he wanted to know every little detail of the violet brew. When I told him I'd brought Rothac's notes back with me and a cauldron of the stuff, he came around the desk and patted my shoulder.

"Excellent work," he said. Soon after, he dismissed me, and I went back to the Ministry.

In the days that followed, I developed the most overwhelming urge to again sample the Sheer Beauty. I could easily say my wretched bodily and emotional state was akin to withdrawal from addiction. Profuse sweating, itching of the scalp, and the darkest dreams, things far worse than death scuttling in the shadows of sleep. At times, when I passed the bakery on my way to the Ministry, I mistook the smell of their crumb cake for that of the drug. I was in a bad way and growing weaker, more confused as the days wore on.

One night, after working late, completing a desk so full of paperwork the Sanctity of Grace might have pitied me, I went home and climbed into bed. I was shivering convulsively and the sweat poured down my face. The Beauty had a grip on me and was squeezing me like a sponge. Through my delirium, I heard a knock at the door to my apartment.

"Yes?" I called weakly.

"I've come to fetch you at the request of the Master, Drachton Below," said the voice.

I groaned. "Coming," I said. I rolled out of the bed and eventually managed to get off my knees. Buttoning my shirt and trousers was a chore, what with shaking hands. Out in the carriage, I met, of all people, Chibbins, and the moment I saw him, I feared this meeting with the Master must have something to do with our investigation of the Summer Palace. It soon became clear to me that Chibbins was suffering withdrawal from the Beauty as well. His hands trembled as did mine, and he belched and farted at a furious clip. "Chibbins is ill," he said.

The Master sat before us in his office at the top of the city. I'd truly thought we were to be done away with, but Below was ecstatic. We greeted each other, with me showing the appropriate deference to our leader and Chibbins mumbling that Chibbins was going to vomit.

"This purple mess you've brought back from the Summer Palace, my dear physiognomists, this Sheer Beauty, is a revelation," said the Master.

"I've had my scientists ferret out its constituent ingredients, and quite the pharmacopeia it is too—shrubs and buds, bulbs and petals and roots from the wilderness we call the Beyond. How this woman's ghost devised this elixir is a mystery, but the results of imbibing it are exquisite."

"It's addictive," I said to him. "Since taking it I crave it more every moment."

"No longer a problem, Cley," said Below. "I've decided to make it liberally available to everyone in the physiognomical and security services." Here, he opened a drawer in his desk and took out a hypodermic needle, the phial of which was filled with a violet liquid. "That mixture in the pot you brought back was mild slop compared to what my people have done with it. They've boiled it down to its active essentials, synthesized them, and suggested a method of delivery a hundred times more potent than sipping from a mug."

He rose, walked over to Chibbins, who upon the Master's approach put his two fingers on Below's stomach and walked them up toward his chin. The Master laughed and looked over at me, "If it was anyone else, I'd kill them right now," he said, nodding to Chibbins. "Instead, in return for his asininity, I give him Beauty." He lifted the hypodermic needle and plunged the tip into Chibbins's neck, emptying a third of the phial. Before he removed it, the dim physiognomist had gone quiet. Below then walked toward me. Sharing a needle, I knew, was not healthy, and taking that needle in the neck was not a welcome thought, but I willingly bared my neck in order to feel the exquisite madness flowing through me again.

Chibbins, now mustached and elegant in his way and wit, the Master, and I stood at the window, staring down on the lights of the city. Oh, the things I saw, real and unreal, transpire before my eyes. Chibbins was ingenious in his use of metaphor when confabulating, off the cuff, a prose poem about the physiognomical deficiencies of the populace. The light snow that fell across town appeared golden confetti. In the distance there was piano music like in the parlor back at the Summer Palace. Everything was both profound and hilarious.

"You've inspired me, Chibbins, my good man," said the Master. He went to his desk and leaned over a funnel next to it attached to a tube, through which he spoke commands to his people on the lower floors. "Send out the security forces with flamethrowers. Order them to incinerate anyone they see on the street."

We watched from our great height as some minutes later small fires could be seen erupting in the streets beneath us. The Master clapped and howled with each one. Chibbins put his arm around our leader's shoulders and laughed uproariously. I was dazed with the visions and the glow of the drug and wore a fixed smile. Somewhere amidst the merriment, the high spirits, and hallucinations, it struck me, like an icicle to the heart, that the Sheer Beauty itself was the agent of revenge that would eventually topple the city. Having envisioned the destruction it would bring, I embraced it like a favorite uncle, and ever since have lived for the sharp pain of the needle.

Afterword to "The Summer Palace"

It's been ten years since last I wrote about Physiognomist Cley, the protagonist of the Well-Built City trilogy—*The Physiognomy, Memoranda,* and *The Beyond.* I'm not sure what caused him to rear his bleak, thoroughly opinionated head again. It wasn't like I had to conjure him. His carriage rolled up, and he just strode into this ghost story like he owned it. And, when all was said and done, he did. Perhaps he is a voice fit for our current time, perhaps he just grew weary of being relegated to the shadowy edges of my imagination. In any event, he's returned. This tale deals with his investigations before achieving the exalted rank of Physiognomist, First Class, the time period described in the novels. It seems a great trove of Cley's personal papers, records of early cases of his in the physiognomical service, has been uncovered by a conscientious citizen of Wenau, digging around in the ruins of the Well-Built City. He's informed me that he may stay around a while now and that I should consider surgery for my face, as it's a mockery of nature.

—JEFFREY FORD

About the Editors

JACK DANN has written or edited over seventy-five books and is the editor (with Janeen Webb) of the groundbreaking anthology of Australian stories, *Dreaming Down-Under,* which won the World Fantasy Award in 1999. The sequel, *Dreaming Again,* was published to rave reviews. The influential *Australian Bookseller + Publisher* wrote, "If you read short fiction you'll want this collection. If you don't, this is a reason to start." The anthology *Gathering the Bones,* of which Dann was a coeditor, was short-listed for the International Horror Guild Award and included in *Library Journal*'s "Best Genre Fiction of 2003." His anthology *Wizards: Magical Tales from the Masters of Modern Fantasy* (coedited with Gardner Dozois) was short-listed for the Shirley Jackson Award and the World Fantasy Award. He is also a recipient of the Nebula Award, the Australian Aurealis Award (twice), the Ditmar Award (four times), the Peter McNamara Achievement Award, and the Peter McNamara Convenors' Award for Excellence. He has been honored by the Mark Twain Society (Esteemed Knight). His own fiction has been compared to the work of Jorge Luis Borges, Roald Dahl, Lewis Carroll, Carlos Castaneda, J. G. Ballard, Ray Bradbury, Philip K. Dick, and Mark Twain. His website is jackdann.com.

NICK GEVERS is senior editor at the major UK independent press PS Publishing (www.pspublishing.co.uk), under the banner of which he coedits, with Peter Crowther, the twice-yearly *Postscripts* genre fiction anthology, the latest volumes of which are *Edison's Frankenstein, The Company He Keeps, The New and Perfect Man,* and *Unfit for Eden.* His other SF and fantasy anthologies include *Infinity Plus* (with Keith Brooke), *Other Earths* (with Jay Lake), *Extraordinary Engines, The Book of Dreams,* and *Is Anybody Out There?* (with Marty Halpern). A past book reviewer and author interviewer for such publications as *Locus, Locus Online, SF Weekly, Interzone, Foundation, SF Site, Infinity Plus, Nova Express,* and *The Washington Post Book World,* Nick lives in Cape Town, South Africa.

Copyright Acknowledgments